CAROL GOODMAN

The Ghost Orchid

arrow books

Published by Arrow Books in 2007

3 5 7 9 10 8 6 4 2

Copyright © Carol Goodman, 2007

Carol Goodman has asserted her right under the Copyright, Designs
and Patents Act, 1988 to be identified as the author of this work

Arrow Books
Random House, 20 Vauxhall Bridge Road,
London, SW1V 2SA

www.randomhouse.co.uk

Addresses for companies within The Random House Group Limited
can be found at: www.randomhouse.co.uk/offices.htm

Random House Group Limited Reg. No. 954009

A CIP catalogue record for this book
is available from the British Library

ISBN 9780099468134

The Random House Group Limited makes every effort to ensure
that the papers used in its books are made from trees that have
been legally sourced from well-managed and credibly certified
forests. Our paper procurement policy can be found at:
www.randomhouse.co.uk/paper.htm

Typeset by SX Composing DTP, Rayleigh, Essex
Printed in the UK by CPI Bookmarque, Croydon, CR0 4TD

To my brothers—Larry and Bob

Acknowledgements

I am lucky to have friends and family members who are willing to read unwieldy piles of paper: Barbara Barak, Laurie Bower, Cathy Cole, Gary Feinberg, Marge Goodman, Lauren Lipton, Andrea Massar, Wendy Gold Rossi, Scott Silverman, Nora Slonimsky, and Sondra Browning Witt. Also, thanks to Beth Berney for help with Italian phrases, Deborah Goldberg for gardening tips, and Richard LaFleur for his help with classical references.

Thanks to my agent, Loretta Barrett, and to my editor, Linda Marrow, for their continued guidance and insight. Many thanks to Gina Centrello, Kim Hovey, and Gilly Hailparn at Ballantine for all their support.

All the poems attributed to Zalman Bronsky in this book were actually written by my husband, Lee Slonimsky, author of the forthcoming sonnet collection *Pythagoras in Love* (Ochises Press). Like Zalman, Lee has been known to write a sonnet or two on a scrap of paper from his back pocket.

PART ONE

The Grotto

Chapter One

I came to Bosco for the quiet.

That's what it's famous for.

The silence reigns each day between the hours of nine and five by order of a hundred-year-old decree made by a woman who lies dead beneath the rose-bushes—a silence guarded by four hundred acres of wind sifting through white pines with a sound like a mother saying *hush*. The silence stretches into the still, warm afternoon until it melts into the darkest part of the garden where spiders spin their tunnel-shaped webs in the box-hedge maze. Just before dusk the wind, released from the pines, blows into the dry pipes of the marble fountain, swirls into the grotto, and creeps up the hill, into the gaping mouths of the satyrs, caressing the breasts of the sphinxes, snaking up the central fountain allée, and onto the terrace, where it exhales its resin-and copper-tinged breath onto the glasses and crystal decanters laid out on the balustrade.

Even when we come down to drinks on the terrace there's always a moment, while the ice settles in the silver bowls and we brush the yellow pine needles off the rattan chairs, when it seems the silence will never be broken. When it seems that the silence might continue to accumulate—like the golden pine needles that pad the paths through the box-hedge maze and the crumbling marble steps and choke the mouths of the satyrs and fill the pipes of the fountain—and finally be too deep to disturb.

Then someone laughs and clinks his glass against another's, and says . . .

"Cheers. Here's to Aurora Latham and Bosco."

"Here, here," we all chime into the evening, sending the echoes of our voices rolling down the terraced lawn like brightly colored croquet balls from some long-ago lawn party.

"God, I've never gotten so much work done," Bethesda Graham says, as if testing the air's capacity to hold a longer sentence or two.

We all look at her with envy. Or maybe it's only me, not only because I didn't get any work done today, but because everything about Bethesda bespeaks confidence, from her slim elegant biographies and barbed critical reviews to her sleek cap of shiny black hair with bangs that just graze her perfectly arched eyebrows—which are arched now at Nat Loomis, as if the two of them were sharing some secret, unspoken joke—and set off her milk-white skin and delicate bone structure. Even Bethesda's size—she can't be more than four nine—is intimidating, as if everything superfluous had been refined down to its essential core. Or maybe it's just that at five nine I loom over her and *my* hair, unmanageable at the best of times, has been steadily swelling in the moist Bosco air and acquired red highlights from the copper pipes. I feel like an angry Valkyrie next to her.

"Magic," says Zalman Bronsky, the poet, sipping his Campari and soda. "A dream. Perfection." He releases his words as if they were birds he's been cupping in his hands throughout the day.

"I got shit-all done," complains Nat Loomis, the novelist. The *famous* novelist. I'd had to stop myself from gasping aloud when I recognized him on my first day at Bosco—and who wouldn't recognize that profile, the jawline only slightly weaker than his jacket photos suggest, the trademark square glasses, the hazel eyes that morph from blue to green depending (he once said in an interview) on his mood, the tousled hair and sardonic grin. Along with the rest of the world (or at least the world of MFA writing programs and bookish Manhattan), I had read his first novel ten years ago and fallen in love—with it, with its young, tough, but vulnerable protagonist, and with the author himself. And along with the rest of that little world I'd been immersed in these last ten years, I couldn't help wondering where his second novel was. Surely, though, the fact that he's here is a favorable sign that it's only a matter of time before the long-awaited second novel is born out of the incubator of silence that is Bosco.

"It's too quiet," Nat says, now taking a sip of the single-malt scotch that the director, Diana Tate, sets out each night in a cut-glass decanter.

David Fox, a landscape architect who I've heard is writing a report on the gardens for the Garden Conservancy, holds up a Waterford tumbler of the stuff, the gold liquor catching a last ray of light as the sun impales itself on the tips of the pines at the western edge of the estate, and proposes a toast, "To Aurora Latham's *Sacro Bosco*—a sacred wood indeed."

"Is that what the name means?" asks one of the painters who've just joined us on the terrace. "I thought it was a funny name for an artists' colony—isn't it some kind of chocolate milk housewives made in the fifties?"

The other artists, who are just now straggling in from their outlying studios and cabins like laborers returning from the fields, laugh at their cohort's joke and grouse that the writers, as usual, have taken all the good chairs, leaving them the cold stone balustrade. One can't help but notice that there's a class system here at Bosco. The writers, who stay in the mansion, play the role of landed gentry. Nat Loomis and Bethesda Graham somehow manage to make their identical outfits of black jeans and white T-shirts look like some kind of arcane English hunting wardrobe. Even unassuming Zalman Bronsky, in his rumpled linen trousers and yellowed, uncuffed, and untucked dress shirt, looks like the eccentric uncle in a Chekhov play.

"She named it after the Sacro Bosco garden in Bomarzo—near Rome," I say, my first spoken words of the day. I'm surprised my vocal cords still work, but, after all, my book—my first novel—is set here at Bosco, which is why I know that the estate isn't named for a bedtime beverage. I address my remarks to David Fox, though, because the other writers, especially Bethesda Graham and Nat Loomis, still scare me.

Just remember, the director told me on the first day, *never call Nat Nathaniel, or Bethesda Beth.* I smiled at that evidence of vanity on their parts, but then I remembered that I'd been quick enough to modify my own name to Ellis when I published my first story. After all, who would take seriously a writer called Ellie?

"She saw it on one of the trips she and Milo Latham took to Italy," I add, "and was inspired to create her own version of an Italian Renaissance garden here on the banks of the Hudson."

We all look south toward where the Hudson should be, but the towering pines obscure the view. Instead we are looking down on crumbling marble terraces and broken statuary—statues of the Muses, whose shoulders are mantled with the gold dust of decaying pine needles and whose faces (at least on the statues who still have their heads) are cloaked in shadow and green moss. The hedges and shrubbery—once clipped and ordered—have overgrown their neat geometry and now sprawl in an untidy thicket across the hill. The fountain allée, with its satyrs and sphinxes who once spouted water from their mouths and breasts, leads to a statue of a horse poised on the edge of the hill as if it were about to leap into the dark, overgrown boxwood maze—Aurora Latham's *giardino segreto*—at the bottom of the hill. Somewhere at the center of the maze is a fountain, but the hedges have grown too high to see it now.

"Actually, the garden's closer in design to the Villa d'Este at Tivoli," Bethesda Graham murmurs, sipping her mineral water. "The idea of all these fountains and the springs running down the hill into a grotto and then out to the main fountain and from there to the river and finally to the sea . . . Aurora wrote in her Italian journal that she wanted to create a garden that was the wellspring of a fountain like the sacred spring on Mount Parnassus." Bethesda pronounces Aurora's name as if she were a contemporary who'd only moments ago quit the terrace. Of course, I remember, she's writing a biography of Aurora Latham. Bethesda's the expert here.

"The whole hill is a fountain," David Fox says. "One might even say the entire estate. Pumps draw the water up from the spring at the bottom of the hill and then pipes funnel the water down the hill through a hundred channels. On a night like this we would have heard the water cascading down the terraces like a thousand voices."

Zalman Bronsky murmurs something. I lean forward to ask him to repeat himself, but then the words, half heard and still lingering in Bosco's perfect silence, sound clearly in my head.

" 'The eloquence of water fills this hill,' " I repeat. "How lovely. It's iambic pentameter, isn't it?"

The poet looks startled, but then he smiles and takes out of his jacket a piece of paper that has been folded in quarters and begins to write down the line. When he sees it's too dark to, he gets up to go inside.

The artists have already gone inside for dinner, their manual labors having given them keener appetites.

"What happened to the fountains?" I ask David Fox, but it's Bethesda who answers.

"The spring dried up," she says, taking another careful sip from her glass.

"Not a particularly good omen for those who've come to drink at the wellspring of the Muses," Nat says, downing the last of his scotch. "We might as well go inside for dinner." He looks into his empty glass as if its dryness stood for the dried-up pipes of the fountain. Bethesda takes the glass from him as he gets up and follows him through the French doors into the dining room.

David Fox and I are left alone on the terrace looking down on the overgrown garden.

"So when you finish researching the garden, will it be restored?" I ask.

"If we get funding from the Garden Conservancy," he says, draining the last drop of scotch from his glass. I get up and he reaches a hand out to take my wineglass. As his hand brushes mine, I feel a tremor—as if the pipes of the old fountain below us had come to life and were about to send forth jets of water, into the last lingering glow of the sunset. The garden wavers and quakes like a reflection in a pool of water, and I see a slim white figure swimming at its center. I force my eyes shut and, ignoring the sweet, spicy smell that has swept over the terrace, count to ten. When I open them, the garden has gone still and I can see that the slim white figure is only a statue standing below the western edge of the terrace and the scent of vanilla has faded from the air.

"You're right," I say, "it is prettier as a ruin."

He laughs. "I agree, but I never said anything of the kind. The Garden Conservancy would have me fired if I did."

At dinner I sit between Zalman Bronsky and Diana Tate. I'm glad I'm not next to David Fox, because I'm still embarrassed at what happened on the terrace. Of course he hadn't said that the garden was prettier in ruins. It was only my imagination. Sometimes after a day of writing, after listening to the voices of my characters in my head, I begin to imagine that I can actually hear their voices.

Sitting next to Diana Tate, though, makes me feel the way I had in college when a professor sat down next to me in the cafeteria. I'm afraid she'll ask for a page count of my novel thus far, or a detailed outline (which I don't have), or, most frightening of all, an explanation for why I'm writing the damn thing. I have no explanation, because it's not the book I'm supposed to be writing. For the last few years I've written short stories about twenty-somethings living in Manhattan— spare, wry stories that my workshop classmates and teachers have praised and that I'd begun to publish in small but respected literary magazines. Then last year I went home for Christmas vacation (or, as my mother puts it, "to honor the solstice") and the pamphlet on the Blackwell case fell into my lap. Literally. I'd been reading on the ragged old couch in the sunroom when one of the planks in the bookcase over my head succumbed to centuries of dry rot and collapsed, spilling my mother's collection of manuals on goddess worship and treatises on herbal remedies. Among them I noticed an ancient, yellowing pamphlet entitled *A True and Intimate Account of the Blackwell Affair*.

When I finished it, I stayed up the rest of the night writing at a fever pitch and by the morning I had completed a story that I called "Trance." From the beginning the story seemed to have a life of its own. Not that everyone liked it. Half my workshop said it was too sensational, half were repelled by the character of the medium, but it engendered more passionate debate than the class had ever witnessed and Richard Scully, my teacher, said it had an interesting ironic stance and that if I cut down on some of the more "overblown" imagery, I might submit it to a short story contest called Altered States. "Trance" not only won the contest, but one of the judges brought it to the attention of an agent, who contacted me and urged me to consider turning it into a novel.

"Didn't that medium spend a summer at the Bosco estate?" the agent asked. "Why don't you apply for a residency there? It would be the perfect place to write it."

When I told Richard Scully my news, he warned me

to beware of melodrama. Hadn't I better stick to something more realistic? he asked. But still, he agreed to write me a recommendation—without which I would never have been "invited" to the famously selective Bosco. I know that the board doesn't require the "guests" to adhere to any prearranged course of work, but I suspect it is the book "about the medium" that they expect to see sometime at the end of my stay at Bosco. And so I am dreading the moment when Diana Tate asks me about the novel.

Fortunately, Zalman Bronsky is only too happy to talk about his work. He tells me and Diana Tate that the series of sonnets he's writing about Bosco was inspired by a Renaissance book. I have to ask him to repeat the name three times, until he draws out a piece of paper, folded in quarters, from his pocket and writes down the title: *Hypnerotomachia Poliphili.*

"Its English title is 'The Strife of Love in a Dream,' " he says. "The hero, Poliphilo, journeys to the island of Cythera with his lover, and there they wander through an elaborate garden full of groves and grottoes, mazes and fountains, until they achieve the . . . er . . . culmination of their love."

"You mean they make it in the garden?" the young girl sitting across from Bronsky asks.

"Daria," Diana Tate says, closing her eyes for a brief moment as if to call upon a reserve of inner tranquility to deal with her niece. The director had explained to me on my first day that Daria had dropped out of college and would be filling in as Bosco's secretary until a replacement could be found. "What have we spoken about?"

"What? He's the one who brought up people shagging in the woods. It's not as if it's a new idea. When I was twelve I came across that famous painter screwing that Yugoslavian poet half his age in the grotto."

"You'll have to excuse my niece," Diana tells us. "Her idea of appropriate dinner conversation was formed growing up in my sister's loft in SoHo."

At the mention of her mother, Daria blushes. She drops her fork onto her plate and pushes her chair back from the table—making enough noise to draw the attention of everyone at the table—and exits through the long glass doors onto the terrace, where she lights a cigarette and lounges on the marble balustrade, one long jean-clad leg bent and resting on the marble ledge, her chest thrust forward, so that the moon falls full on her snug white T-shirt. I notice that most of the men in the room are now gazing in her direction, especially, it seems to me, Nat Loomis, who's sitting at the end of the table next to Bethesda Graham.

"Why don't we go into the library," I hear Bethesda ask in a cajoling voice with a southern accent I hadn't noticed before, "and find a place by the fire before the yahoos get there first."

I see Nat look around the table as if sussing out his other opportunities. The artists are organizing a trip to the Tumble Inn, a dive halfway between Bosco and town. One of them asks me if I want to go, but I notice that Nat and Bethesda are getting up and heading toward the library. Maybe this is part of the unwritten division between the artists and writers. I wouldn't want to end up on the wrong side of the divide, so I politely decline and accept, instead, Zalman Bronsky's chivalrous offer to accompany me into the library.

"It's a funny thing about that line you gave me," he says as we cross the main hallway.

"Gave you?" I ask. "But I was just repeating something you said."

Zalman pauses at the door to the library and looks up at me, blinking his kind brown eyes. "I don't think so," he tells me.

"But you must have," I say, trying to laugh it off. "I couldn't write a line of metered verse if my life depended on it." And then, before he can question me further, I enter the library.

Nat and Bethesda are already there, lounging in the best Morris chairs by the fire. David Fox is standing above Bethesda, resting one arm on the broad oak mantel, another glass of scotch by his elbow. Nat, I notice, is glaring at the architect. Maybe he's jealous, I think, or, I suddenly feel sure, he's angry at David for drinking up all the single-malt scotch.

"We were just talking about Aurora Latham," David says, pointing above the mantel at the painting of Bosco's former mistress leaning against a marble column, her bare shoulders and the marble the same shade of creamy white against the velvety black backdrop of a night garden in which pale statues glow dimly in the distance. She is standing on the terrace at the top of the fountain allée, one slim hand extended toward a spray of water erupting from beneath the hoof of Pegasus, as if she had just commanded the water to flow. The artist has depicted her as a Greco-Roman goddess guarding the sacred spring of the Muses.

"That's the portrait by Frank Campbell, isn't it?" I ask. "It wasn't finished because he died of a heart attack while he was working on it."

"You seem to know a lot about Aurora Latham," Bethesda says. "Are you writing about her?"

"I'm writing a novel based on certain events in Aurora Latham's life," I say.

"A historical romance?" Bethesda asks, smiling, but at Nat, not me. I can feel myself blushing and for a moment can't think of anything to say.

"Of course there's no lack of sensational elements in Aurora's life," Bethesda goes on. "I'm sure it's hard to resist exploiting them."

"I'm not—"

"Perhaps you two could share material," Nat says. "After all, Bethesda has the cooperation of the Board and the Latham heirs."

"Yes," Bethesda says, glaring at Nat before turning back to me. "Do you?"

"Well, they know I'm working on a novel that takes place here at Bosco in 1893," I say, swallowing hard. It's the first time I've discussed my work with Nat and Bethesda and they're already attacking me—or at least Bethesda is. I can't tell if Nat is defending her or egging

Bethesda on. "Isn't that what she was famous for—inspiring artists? What was it Frank Campbell called her?" I falter, trying to remember the phrase. I'd read it somewhere . . . or had I? Then it comes to me.

"Muse of Water. That's what he called her."

Bethesda turns deathly white at the words, as if I'd stolen something from her. "I suppose it's the Blackwell scandal you're interested in," she says angrily. "That's all anyone ever cares about. Not Aurora's artistic vision—this sanctuary she created for artistic expression . . ." Bethesda throws her arms open wide as if to indicate not just the library but the whole house, the crumbling gardens, the four hundred acres of pine forest surrounding them. "She's been defined by that one malicious act against her instead of by all the good she did."

"Well, not for me," David Fox says. "I just want to know if she planted her hedges according to Francesco Colonna or Donato Bramante." He's trying to divert Bethesda's attention to save me from her tirade. "What's all this about a black well, anyway?"

"Corinth Blackwell," I explain, gaining strength from David's attention. It doesn't quite make up for Bethesda's disdain, but at least it's something. "Milo Latham brought her to Bosco in the summer of 1893 at Aurora's request to contact the spirits of their three children who had died the year before in a diphtheria epidemic. She was a medium."

"Ah, a spiritualist," Bronsky says, "like Madame Blavatsky. You know Yeats attended her séances . . ."

"She was a charlatan," Bethesda says, "and a con artist. She and her partner, a man by the name of Tom Quinn who had gained access to the estate that summer by posing as the amanuensis of Violet Ramsdale, a writer of execrable nineteenth-century melodramas"—here Bethesda pauses and looks straight at me as if to make clear to what literary tradition *I* belong—"kidnapped Alice Latham, the only Latham child who survived the diphtheria epidemic."

"They never proved that Corinth Blackwell was responsible," I point out. "Both she and Quinn disappeared. Some people think that Quinn might have been the kidnapper and set up Corinth Blackwell."

"Ah, so that's your angle." Bethesda smiles at Nat, but he doesn't smile back. "The medium as heroine. Don't tell me—you're calling your novel *Entranced*."

I'm about to tell her that there's already a novel called *Entranced* by Nora Roberts, but then I'd be admitting to either reading Nora Roberts or having done an Internet search for the title, because I *had* thought of using it. But then Nat interrupts.

"Hey—*Muse of Water*—isn't that what you're calling your book, Bethesda?"

Although I wouldn't have thought she could grow any paler, Bethesda turns a face so drained of color toward Nat that for a moment she looks more like one of the stone-cold statues in the garden than a living girl. Then without another word she rises and leaves the room.

"What's wrong with her?" David asks. "Why was she

so hard on Ellis?" He's approaching the decanter of scotch, but Nat reaches it before him and empties the last inch into his own glass.

"It's because you nabbed her title," Nat says, pointing his glass in my direction—almost as if he's toasting me for the feat. "*Muse of Water*. She found the phrase here last summer in a letter Frank Campbell wrote to Aurora, and she's kept it to herself since then. Since he wrote the letter the day he died, Bethesda thought it was probably the only appearance of the phrase. Where in the world did you come upon it?"

"I don't know. I must have read it somewhere," I say, although the truth is I have no idea where I first encountered the phrase.

Later in my room I lie awake cursing myself for provoking Bethesda Graham's anger. She's a major reviewer, after all, famous for her scathing dissections of hopeful new novelists. I should have known that the phrase *Muse of Water* came from her. It's not, I realized after checking the pamphlet and my research notes, anything I'd read or heard before. No, I heard it for the first time tonight, in the library, spoken as if someone had whispered it into my ear. Just as I heard the first line of Zalman's poem and David Fox's secret wish to leave the garden in ruins. Just as I've heard voices all my life that issue forth from no human lips. Sure, other writers may talk about hearing their characters *speak* to them and finding their *voice*, but I'm beginning to suspect they don't hear the kind of voices I do.

As if in mockery of my unhappiness, a girl's laugh suddenly rises from the garden below my window. I get up, pulling my T-shirt down over my panties as I cross the cold floor to the half-opened window. For a moment the moonlight on all that white marble is blinding. All I can see is the terrace that wraps around the first story of the house. The paths that lead into the garden and down the hill, the crumbling fountain allée, the statues that stand on the ledges, all fade into the shadows of the cypresses, the dense ilex branches, the deep overgrown boxwood hedges, and, beyond the boxwood maze at the bottom of the hill, the deeper blackness of the pine forest. As I peer into the impenetrable gloom trying to find the source of the laughter, a light wind stirs the tops of the trees and carries with it, along with a scent of pine and copper, that same sweet odor of vanilla and cloves I'd caught on the terrace earlier. Something white sways just beyond the western edge of the terrace, and I realize it's just the statue I saw earlier today, only someone must have draped a scarf around its neck, because I can see the girl's drapery floating on the breeze. Thank goodness, I think, the last thing I need is to add visions to my voices. I'm about to turn from the window when I see a white hand reach out to grasp the fluttering drapery and draw it close around her. A coppery taste pools in my mouth like blood, and I hurry back to bed before I can see anything else.

I pull the covers over my head, but I can still hear

the wind as it sweeps down the hill, skirts the Muses' drapery, pushes into the open mouths of satyrs and sphinxes, swirls around the overgrown parterres of the rose garden, solves the puzzle of the boxwood-hedge maze, and finally settles into the grotto dug into the hillside where the stalactites still drip with the last drops of the last spring. There I can feel the wind go to ground, its voice muffled at last by the webs the tunnel spiders spin in the underground pipes of the old fountain.

Tomorrow, though, it will rise again, carrying voices with its coppery breath, and even Bosco's legendary silence won't be able to still the voices in my head.

Chapter Two

"It's a long walk to the top, miss. My instructions are to take you up to the front door."

"I want to see the fountain first," Corinth tells the driver. "It's what the house is famous for, isn't it?"

A sound emerges from the driver's throat, but whether a cough or a laugh, Corinth can't tell. His face, shielded by his broad-brimmed hat so that Corinth has been unable since he picked her up at the train station to see anything of his features, isn't giving anything away. "One of the things it's famous for," he says, cracking his whip against the sweat-soaked backs of the horses. Then he leaves Corinth there at the bottom of the hill, at the edge of the garden.

The fountain is behind a hedge wall. Corinth can hear it murmuring to her, beckoning her through the arched opening carved out of the boxwood. It was the sound that made her tell the driver to stop, her heart beating against her tightly laced stays because it was the sound she'd been hearing for weeks now—ever since she'd agreed to come—a voice, heard just below the voices in the parlors, the shops, even the shouts on the city streets, muttering insistently in her ear, warning her not to go.

But if she listened to all the voices she heard, she'd never get out of bed in the morning. Another voice—the one that was forever counting the change in her purse, adding the bills, weighing the tea and sugar in their sacks, and measuring the distance from her comfortable, well-heated hotel suite to the street—told her it was too much money to say no to. And when had she ever said *no* to any money at all?

She'd managed to ignore, then, the *murmurer*, as she dubbed this new voice, until she heard it again at the gates of Bosco. This time the voice was unmistakably outside of her own head.

"What is that?" she asked the driver.

He told her it was the fountain, which she then remembered was, according to Milo Latham, the estate's most famous attraction.

It's only water, she thought, the voice that's been whispering in my ear all these weeks and ruining my sleep. It's only water. She was so relieved that she decided to get out and have a look for herself.

Now, though, as she stands outside the hedge wall listening to the fountain, she finds that she's afraid. She! The famous Corinth Blackwell who has summoned spirits from the maw of hell for the entertainment and enlightenment of crowned heads of Europe and persons of quality and discernment everywhere! Afraid of a little water!

Well, not for long. Corinth steps through the arch and finds herself facing a ten-foot-tall wall of greenery. She's wandered into a maze.

My wife, Aurora, enjoys puzzles, Milo Latham told her when he made the proposal for her to come and spend the summer at Bosco. *I try to keep her entertained, but there's only so much that I can do. She's asked for you especially.*

So I'm to be an . . . entertainment?

Think of yourself, rather, as a diversion.

She closes her eyes, listens to the water, and turns left.

Last summer at the Prince's villa in Viterbo the guests devised an amusing test for her—a diversion for a summer evening. They blindfolded her and let her loose in the hedge maze. She could have pointed out that her abilities as a medium had very little to do with those used to navigate a maze, but then that wouldn't have been *sporting.* Instead, she had a little talk with the head gardener, during which several coins passed from the little pocket in her sleeve into his rough glove, and learned that most mazes follow a few simple rules.

Within five minutes she's solved this one and finds herself at the heart of the maze: a parterred rose garden, its crimson rosebushes in full odiferous bloom, with a circular fountain at its center.

So this is who's been whispering in my ear all these weeks. It's a bit of a disappointment, really. After all the fountains she's seen in Europe—Bernini's muscular river gods in the Piazza Navona, the Alley of the

Hundred Fountains at the Villa d'Este at Tivoli, the Fountain of the Deluge at the Villa Lante—she expected something grander. After all, Aurora Latham's been to all those places, too, and with the money to buy some of the real articles. She's even been known to "buy up" the sculptors and landscapers as well—one of whom, a master of fountain installation and water "effects," is staying here at Bosco even now.

Corinth expected more than this lone figure of a girl kneeling at the center of a circular pool, her hands cupped together to catch the spray from a single jet of water. The girl's face is hidden by her loose hair, so Corinth walks around to the front of the fountain and is startled when she meets the girl's gaze. From beneath a fringed headband, the girl looks up like a wild animal that's been caught. Her clothes, which at first glance appeared to be Grecian drapery, are animal skins, fringed and beaded, which cling to her body. She reminds Corinth of a statue she saw only last fall at the Metropolitan Museum of Art—certainly not of the real Indians that she used to see at the settlement on the Sacandaga Vly.

More imposing is the statue that stands in a boxwood niche behind the fountain, of a youth of regal bearing and somewhat feminine features, wearing a sort of fringed toga. Carved into his pedestal is the name Jacynta.

My wife makes up stories for the children, Milo Latham told her, *all about a mythical hero named Jacynta and a beautiful Indian maiden named Ne'Moss-i-Ne.*

Corinth scans the marble rim of the fountain to see if the girl's name is inscribed there, but it isn't. She notices, instead, the low, dark-leafed shrub that grows around the pool. She kneels and breaks off a leaf, sniffs it, and then digs in the loose soil until she's unearthed the roots and, still wearing her gloves—which are of such a fine, supple leather that her fingers are as agile in them as if they had been bare—slips a piece of the root into the sleeve of her dress. When she's done, she quickly scans the garden, but the only eyes on her are the blind marble eyes of the girl in the fountain, who, she notices now, is bound to the rustic plinth on which she kneels. The straps, cleverly carved to look like leather, seem to press into the girl's soft white breasts— an effect so realistic that Corinth feels a sympathetic constriction in her own chest. She turns away from the statue, reflecting that whoever ordered those restraints carved out of marble took more delight in their bondage than their release. Nor can she help but feel, as she leaves the rose garden, that she's stepping straight into a net fashioned of threads stronger than the leather thongs that bind poor little Ne'Moss-i-Ne.

In fact, as she steps through the arched opening in the hedge that leads out of the maze and toward the path that goes up the hill to the house, she feels something brush against her. These threads are thinner and lighter than the leather thongs binding the Indian maid, but no less resistant. Even through the thick serge of her high-necked dress she can feel them unspooling across her breast and down her left arm. Another thread brushes against her cheek, and one clings to her mouth with a touch faint and insistent as a baby's cry.

Like walking through a ghost.

Corinth freezes on the path and traces the thin gossamer thread to where the spider has spun a cone-shaped web deep in the branches of the boxwood. Then she checks to see if she can be seen yet from the house. Directly in front of her is a waterfall cascading in thick sheets into an oval pool. A winged horse stands above the cascade, one hoof poised to strike the ground, its wings spread for flight. On either side of the fountain two nude males recline, the sprawl of their thick limbs echoing the sweep of the marble staircases that circle up to the next terrace. Corinth can see the path beyond the spreading wings of the horse, but not the house, and so she assumes it's unlikely that anyone in the house can see her. The only figures on the path above the waterfall are pale white statues that guard the marble terraces.

Still Corinth feels watched. It may be the statues of the river gods, or the satyrs who line the terraces and spew water from their gaping mouths, or even the spider who burrows deeper into her silk tunnel as Corinth steps closer to the hedge, but she doesn't think so. It's a feeling she's had before.

She looks behind her once, as if checking to see that the crouching Indian maid hasn't escaped her bondage and sprung out of her pool, and then twirls a gloved finger into the middle of the web, like a child scooping icing from a cake. She tucks the spider silk into her sleeve and then, without turning again, mounts the stairs above the river gods and takes the path to the house.

It's a long, steep climb up three terraces, not counting the main one that circles the house. At first Corinth takes her time. She notices the horseshoe-shaped stones around the fountain of the flying horse and, recognizing them as *giochi d'acqua*, carefully steps around them. She doesn't have time for tricks and she doesn't want to show up at the house soaking wet. She examines the statuary. On each terrace there are three females in Greek drapery, who, Corinth soon guesses, are meant to represent the Muses. One carries a sextant, one wears a smiling mask above a weeping face. One is flanked by a peacock and a tortoise. Several hold musical instruments. In the center of the path runs a stream of water down a marble channel much like the cascade at the Farnese Palace, but instead of dolphins rimming its edge there are leaping trout—one of a number of native touches. Stone beavers and bear cubs frolic among the gape-mouthed satyrs and full-breasted sphinxes. A crouching panther peers out from behind a pine trunk. The wooded slope of the hill is populated with these sculpted figures, all murmuring with the same voice— the sound of water cascading down the hill in a hundred rivulets—an effect that Corinth begins to find tiring as she ascends the second terrace from the top. She turns down the arbored path, thinking to rest for a moment on the little marble bench in an ilex grove at the end of the path, but stops when she sees that someone's already sitting there. She's more annoyed than relieved when she realizes it's just another statue—another Muse she guesses from the box-shaped instrument in her lap. She goes back to the main path and pauses for a moment to look up at the house, which has now come into view.

Milo Latham told her that while he'd given his wife free rein in the planning of the gardens, he had maintained control over the architectural style of the house. The divergence of their tastes can be clearly seen in the contrast between the two. While Aurora loved Italy, Milo admired the Swiss and the English. And so the imposing mansion, looming over the gardens like the snow-covered Alps over northern Italy, is an eclectic mix of wood-framed Tudor and Swiss chalet, its rough-hewn spruce beams a testimony to Milo Latham's lumber dynasty. A stone balustrade at the edge of the terrace stands like a border between the two realms, with even a matronly sentinel posted as border guard. For a moment Corinth thinks this figure is a statue as well—she holds herself so stiffly and her gray hair is the color of stone—but then she unfolds her hands from above her waist and, as her gaze falls on Corinth, her eyes widen.

Corinth, too, is surprised, but before she can say anything, the woman turns or, rather, pivots like one of those clockwork automata Corinth has seen in town squares in Germany, and precedes Corinth through a pair of open glass doors.

It takes a moment for her eyes to adjust to the dim room after the bright glare of sunlight on the marble terrace. She can just make out, at the far end of the long, narrow room, a figure seated in a wood-framed chair by the fireplace. Corinth is surprised to see that the fire is lit on such a warm day, but as she steps forward she sees that she was mistaken: what she had taken for flames is the streaming hair of a little girl—perhaps seven or eight years old, Corinth thinks—who is sitting cross-legged on a rug before the unlit grate, her long hair obscuring her face as she leans over a drawing tablet. When Corinth takes another step, the girl looks up from beneath her curtain of hair and Corinth is startled by something familiar in the girl, but then she realizes it's only that the girl's pose is the same as that of the statue of the captive Indian maid. She even has the same slanted eyes and the same look of cunning.

"That will be all, Norris," the woman in the chair says. Corinth listens for the sound of retreating foot-steps, but hears nothing. The only way she knows the housekeeper has gone is by the absence of the fountain's gurgle when the glass doors have closed behind her.

"Come and sit by me," says the woman, indicating an ottoman at her feet, "so I can see you. I want to see if the descriptions I've heard of you are accurate."

Corinth comes forward—pulling her skirts close to her as she passes the seated child, who doesn't make any effort to get out of the way—and sits on the ottoman, lifting her eyes to meet the pale blue eyes of the mistress of the house. Aurora Latham takes her time observing her, and so, although she knows it might be politer to look away, Corinth has time to study her hostess. The first thing she notices is her eyes. They're a blue so pale they aren't so much the color of the sky as the color of sky reflected in water—not so much a color as the ghost of a color. Her hair is a lighter version of the child's auburn hair, her skin a pure milky white.

It is said in town that Aurora Latham is ill, that the deaths of her three children last year dealt the final blow to an already frail constitution. And yet, for all her pallor and thinness, she doesn't look ill. She looks, Corinth thinks, like a woman haunted.

"She's much prettier than the last one," the little girl says. "Can she make noises with her knees and toes like—"

"Hush, Alice. Go sit with Mrs. Ramsdale for a little while."

Corinth turns her head and sees, in a dimly lit recessed alcove, a woman in an amethyst silk dress sitting at a library table writing . . . or, rather, she is holding a pen poised above a sheet of paper, her head tilted to show her fine Grecian profile to advantage, her eyes demurely lowered, so that her thick black eyelashes cast a shadow on the white porcelain of her cheekbones. A pose meant to indicate a woman of high society engaged in literary pursuits, and yet, Corinth can tell that the woman is acutely aware of her presence, while Corinth, until this moment, didn't even know she was there. It's not like her to enter a room without taking note of *all* its occupants. It must be the effect of passing all those statues in the garden: it's made her lose her sense of what's real and what's not. She'll have to be more careful.

"But she *is* prettier," Alice says sulkily as she gathers up her pencils and her pad.

Aurora Latham looks up from her daughter to Corinth. "Yes," she says slowly, drawing out the word, "but I'd heard your hair described as chestnut and it's really more mahogany." Aurora narrows her eyes—crinkling the skin beneath them, which is bluer than the eyes themselves—as if she had ordered a set of dining room chairs only to find they'd been fashioned out of the wrong wood. "But then, perhaps the persons who described you hadn't seen you in a well-lit room."

Corinth smiles what she hopes is a cool, placid smile and says, "The harsh glare of light is not conducive to communicating with the spirit world. Electric light especially is thought to interfere with the currents upon which the spirits travel."

"So you will do a séance, then? And bring back James and Cynthia and Tam?" the girl asks.

"Alice, I thought I asked you to go to Mrs. Ramsdale."

"Can I just show her my picture first?"

"Very well," Aurora says to the child, and then, lifting those transparent eyes to Corinth: "She's made such progress under Mr. Campbell's tutelage. Will you indulge her?"

Corinth smiles without speaking, because the question is, of course, unanswerable. It's not her place to indulge her hostess's child nor deny her anything she might want. Alice rises and holds out the tablet.

The pencil drawing is actually quite good. A dashing young man in fringed buckskin is battling with some sort of great-winged beast while a frightened-looking girl tied to a tree looks on. Corinth recognizes the Indian maiden from the maze fountain—the same ripe figure straining against the same buckskin dress, one sleeve of which is torn to reveal a rounded shoulder and bare bosom. Corinth lifts her eyes from the picture to the little girl, reassessing her age. It's only her small stature, she sees now, that made her appear younger. She's closer to eight or nine than seven.

"Will the brave young warrior save the lady?" Corinth asks.

"She's not a lady; she's only a stinking savage—"

"That will be enough now, Alice. Leave me and Miss Blackwell alone. You'll have to excuse my daughter," Aurora Latham says as Alice, with an exaggerated sigh, drags herself into the darkened alcove and scrunches herself into a narrow ledge beneath one of the floor-to-ceiling bookcases. "Since her brothers and sister have gone, my husband has made a bit of a pet out of her and my husband spent a great deal of his early life in the north woods of New York State—a noble wilderness from which Mr. Latham wrested the origins of his fortune, but not, I'm afraid, an environment conducive to refinement and culture."

Aurora lifts a long pale hand and twirls it over her shoulder to indicate the land north of the house—the thousands of acres of woods and lakes of the Adirondacks that stretch from here to the Canadian border. The house sits with its back to the woods, the terraced gardens sloping down, southward to the Hudson River and, by implication, toward the city and civilization. One can feel, though, the deep shadow of all those woods encroaching on the sunlit terrace, and Corinth, even though she sits with her back to the glass doors, has a sudden unbidden vision of the garden over-grown—the statues destroyed, the marble terraces crumbling, the hedges in the maze breaking free of their orderly, clipped shapes and transforming into great shaggy beasts like the one in young Alice's picture.

She takes a deep breath and, willing the vision to vanish, remarks, "Yes, I understand that Mr. Latham is in the lumber business."

"It's where he made his fortune, in logging and in the glove factories west of here in Fulton County and in many other investments, which I cannot pretend to follow. His interests are . . . eclectic. He's compelled to spend more and more time attending to business in the city, but he still likes to attend the log drive in the spring and watch his logs come into the Big Boom at Glens Falls. He used to take the boys up to the camp on hunting trips . . ."

"So will he be joining the party here this summer?" Corinth asks, even though she knows she might be risking too much by asking such a direct question. But

Aurora's description of Latham's lumber interests has only intensified her vision of a devastated garden—only now she pictures a river choked with logs bursting over the rim of the northern ridge and laying waste to the smiling nymphs and gape-mouthed satyrs. "I ask because I like to know who will be present in the circle."

"I'm afraid my husband is not a believer, Miss Blackwell. He agreed to ask you here as an indulgence to me." Aurora closes her eyes briefly, as if modest of such an uxorious husband. "He has declared that he will not attend your séances, but he will join us tonight at dinner. I'm afraid he's been delayed in the city . . . ah . . ."

Aurora lifts her head just as Corinth hears the latch turn in the doors behind her. A breeze, smelling of pine and sawdust, touches the nape of her neck and chills the pockets of sweat still drying beneath the buttons down the back of her dress. She can feel the cool surface of the bone buttons like a set of fingers drumming into her spine and she cannot, for a moment, force herself to turn around. What if the vision inside her head—the ruined garden, the broken dam, the deluge of splintered wood—isn't just inside her head?

When she turns to follow her hostess's gaze, though, she sees that beyond the darkened figure silhouetted in the doorway the garden lies placid and calm beneath the receding light of a summer afternoon. Corinth prepares her face to meet her host, but as the man steps into the room she sees he's much too young and slim to be Milo Latham. It takes her only a moment longer to recognize who he is.

Chapter Three

"Corinth looked up, surprised to see her old friend Tom Quinn silhouetted in the French doors."

I say the line out loud for the third time, and then push back my chair, put my feet up on the desk, and stare out the window. This is where I've gotten stuck each draft. The problem is that I can't decide whether Corinth Blackwell would have been surprised to see Tom Quinn at Bosco or if she knew very well that he would be there.

The anonymous writer of the pamphlet I found at my mother's house reported (on the authority of "sundry guests who were present at the séances that summer") that Tom Quinn and Corinth Blackwell pretended not to know each other when they met at Bosco in 1893, but that there was reason to believe that they had once been "intimate." I can't tell what the pamphlet writer, who could be maddeningly opaque at times, meant by this word or upon what evidence the deduction was based, but I suspect that while Corinth didn't expect to meet Tom Quinn at Bosco, they had been lovers before that summer. Would the sight of him, then, have aroused her old feelings for him? It is a difficult moment to pull off and I am beginning to despair of ever doing it.

For not the first time I consider abandoning the book altogether. My old teacher Richard Scully was right. It's really too hard and too big for a first book. There's all the period detail—the minutiae of clothing and food and customs—and then there's the ever-present threat that the use of those details will sound phony and the book will come out like one of those overheated bodice rippers that Bethesda Graham so disparaged last night.

I thought that being at Bosco would inspire me to re-create the nineteenth-century scenes. After all, that is what Bosco is famous for: inspiration. From my window on the west corner of the house I can see one of the surviving Muse statues on the first terrace. Originally there were three Muses on each of the three terraces—a phalanx guarding the wellspring of inspiration that was supposed to flourish here at Bosco. Certainly Zalman Bronsky doesn't seem to be lacking in inspiration this morning. There he is now, looking, in his loose linen smock and floppy hat, very Monet-at-Giverny, heading down the old fountain allée, saluting one of the Muses as he passes by, a spring in his step. He announced over breakfast that he planned to take a "sonnet walk" this morning. And he thanked me again for that line about the eloquence of water.

As his green hat vanishes into the tangled over-growth below the second terrace, I wonder if I shouldn't try writing outside as well. It worked yesterday, at least for a while, when I sat in the grove at the western edge of the first terrace. Deep in the ilex grove I was able to imagine, for just a moment, what the hill must have looked like when the gardens were intact, the hedges clipped in neat geometrical shapes, all the statues standing, and the water flowing from terrace to terrace. I imagined Corinth Blackwell climbing that hill against the flow of all that water, approaching the house that would ruin her. I started to write, but then I was seized by the feeling that there was someone watching me, as if I had conjured up the ghost of Corinth Blackwell by the force of my imagination and she would, at any moment, appear before me. I closed my eyes then and banished the image from my mind. It was a foolish idea in the first place—Corinth Blackwell no doubt approached the house for the first time like everybody else, through the porte cochere off the main drive. After a few minutes my heartbeat slowed to normal; my fear was gone, but so was the little trickle of inspiration.

It was just as Nat Loomis said last night on the terrace about the springs that had dried up: *Not a particularly good omen for those who've come to drink at the wellspring of the Muses*. Or, as I imagine Bethesda might say to me, maybe the problem is that there is no Muse of historical romance present on the grounds. Apparently Nat's muse is with him this morning. I can hear the clatter of typewriter keys coming from his room next door. I'd read once in an interview he'd given that he used a manual typewriter to "make a physical connection to the words." All morning the sound of the typewriter has summoned in my mind an image of Nat, the sleeves of his flannel shirt rolled up above his forearms, the light from the garden catching the red highlights in his tousled brown hair. It's an image, I decide as I pack up my laptop, a bit too physical for me. Maybe that's what's keeping me from getting any work done.

As I pass Nat's room his door flies open and he sticks out his head, unbrushed hair standing on end. "Oh," he says, sounding disappointed, "I thought you were the lunch delivery."

"Sorry," I say, "I'm just going down to pick up mine and take it outdoors . . . Uh . . . do you want me to get yours?" Bosco tradition dictates that the tin lunch boxes are left sometime after breakfast in the dining room for the guests to pick up. I've noticed, though, that Nat has a different arrangement.

"No," he says, "Daria will deliver it when it's ready. Mine takes a little longer because I have some special dietary requirements . . ." He leans closer and whispers, "Actually, it's just that I couldn't stomach those school box lunches anymore, so I told Diana that my ayurvedic nutritionist said I had to have hot food." He winks at me and I nod admiringly at his connivance. Really, though, I love the lunches here—the diagonally cut tuna sandwiches, the scraped carrot sticks and homemade sugar cookies. The thermos of lemonade or hot cocoa. They're exactly the kind of lunches I always begged my mother to make instead of her lumpy misshapen sandwiches made from homemade bread and pasty tahini spread.

"Well . . ." I say, taking a step backward, "I don't want to keep you from your work." And, I think to myself, we're breaking the rules talking between nine and five.

Nat nods. "Yeah, yeah . . . I'm having a good morning . . ." He starts to close the door but before he can, I happen to look inside his room and notice that the paper sticking out of his typewriter is a piece of Bosco stationery. I can recognize the engraved insignia of a Grecian Muse pouring water from an amphora beneath a pine tree. Is he typing his novel on Bosco stationery, I wonder, or has all that earnest pounding on his typewriter been letter writing?

"Good luck," I say. He looks up before shutting the door and gives me a curious look. Who am I, after all, to be wishing Nat Loomis luck on his novel? But then he grins and thanks me, and I suddenly have a good idea what the letter's about. He's writing his publisher for an advance on his advance.

"I'll need it . . . Ah . . . at least now I'll have sustenance," he adds, looking over my shoulder. I turn and see Daria Tate approaching us, swinging Nat's tin lunchbox on her index finger.

"Yeah, *substanance,* you could call it that," she says as she passes by me. I hear Nat shush her, and then Daria giggles and the door to Nat's room closes on both of them. I turn to leave, but then stop, sniffing the air. There's something there, perhaps that ghostly vanilla scent from last night. Maybe it's a scent that Daria wears. But no, I realize, it's just the more earthy smell of marijuana seeping out from beneath Nat's door.

I try the arbor on the west side of the allée, where I sat yesterday, but Bethesda's gotten there first. Although it's silly, I can't help thinking that Bethesda took it because she knows it is my favorite spot. Why does a biographer need the inspiration of working out of doors, anyway? Shouldn't she be in the library reading letters from the archives? It seems, though, that everyone has decided to work in the gardens today. As I head down the hill—taking a narrow set of stone steps that winds down the west side of the hill rather than following the central fountain allée—I hear a whispering that at first I think is the wind, and then water, and then finally realize is Zalman Bronsky pacing up and down the middle terrace, repeating the same line over and over again.

"The eloquence of water fills this hill . . . The eloquence of water . . ."

Each time that he finishes the line, he pauses and looks up at whichever of the three statues he's closest to and waits, folded paper in hand, as if he expects one of them to give him the next line. Unfortunately, two of the Muses on this terrace have lost their heads and the third, the one closest to where I stand hidden in the bushes, holds a finger to her lips. If she knows what the next line should be, she's not telling.

I wait until Zalman paces back to the east end of the terrace before continuing down the hill. I have to keep my eyes on the ground because the steps here are broken in places and overgrown with vines that hide shards of urns and broken pieces of statuary. I'm just stepping over a fragment of a sandaled foot when it moves.

Rearing back, I fall into a thornbush, all the time keeping my eyes fixed to the shrubbery, which seems to have come alive. It shakes for a full minute before disgorging—not a white-robed statue or an incorporeal phantom—but a lanky man in loose-fitting green canvas pants and shirt, leaves and bits of vine clinging to his tousled hair and a long, curved scythe in his hand. It's David Fox, the landscape architect.

"I'm sorry I startled you," he says, offering me a hand up. "I was trying to uncover one of the Green Men."

"Green Men?" I ask, struggling to my feet and ignoring his proffered hand. He could be talking about himself. His canvas pants and shirt, which look as if they might once have been part of a uniform from a park or botanical garden, are of a green cloth so soft and faded they might be made of moss. The leaves sticking to his hair make a kind of wreath around his head. The scythe, though, gives him a distinctly threatening air.

"They're medieval figures . . . a sort of wild man . . ."

"I know what they are," I tell him. "My mother has them all over our house." I neglect to mention that on various pagan holidays, such as Beltane and Samhain, my mother and her circle don the foliate masks—but very little else—and take to the woods around the house. "But I didn't think there were any here. I thought the scheme of the garden was Italian Renaissance."

"Well, they're sort of a cross between a satyr and a Green Man. See for yourself." David holds back a thick curtain of vines from the underbrush where he'd been kneeling. I have to kneel myself to see into the tunnel of greenery he's cut back. At first all I see are leaves and branches—a tangle of arborvitae and ilex covered with some rapacious vine growing so thickly I can't imagine how someone as bulky as David managed to crawl in. Or how he could stand to. There's a smell, faint at first but quickly growing stronger as if we had unleashed some maleficent spirit, curling out from the green-tinged gloom—some unnamable brew of mud and rot and . . . yes, at first I think I'm imagining it, but it's unmistakable . . . the metallic tang of blood. The worst thing is that from the bottom of this dank tunnel something is looking back at me. A man's face, carved out of stone but so covered in green lichen that it blends into the surrounding greenery, and it's impossible to tell where the stone foliage that encircles his face leaves off and the actual underbrush begins.

"I think it was part of the fountain," David says, crouching next to me. "It's like the satyr faces that lined the terraces, and you can see where the water would have spilled from his mouth, but I can't find a channel that would have led back to the central fountain allée.

I'm trying to trace the course the water would have taken. Do you want to see?"

I hesitate. The hours between nine and five are supposed to be reserved for quiet work; the guests aren't supposed to mingle. But then, understanding how the fountain worked could provide valuable background for my book. I look up the hill to see if anyone can see us from the house.

"Don't worry," David says, "there's only Zalman, and he's so deeply involved in that poem I don't think he'd notice if the headless Muses came to life and started to dance. I just wish he'd get the second line already."

I laugh, covering my mouth to muffle the sound. "His muse does seem to be holding out on him. The only one with a head looks like she's shushing him."

"That's Polyhymnia, the Muse of sacred lyric and mime. He would have done better to pick one who could talk . . ." David gets up, sliding the scythe into the tunnel with the Green Man, where I notice that there's a recess lined with hooks for gardening implements, and once again offers me his hand. This time I take it, noticing how cool and dry his skin is, and how strong his grip. ". . . But then, maybe she's a fitting Muse for Bosco."

"Why's that?"

"Because she's dedicated to the art of silence."

We continue down the hill by the side path instead of the fountain allée. "To fully appreciate the iconographic program of the garden, you have to start at the bottom, in the rose garden at the center of the maze," David informs me.

"Are you sure we won't get lost in the maze? Isn't it kind of tricky?" I ask. I hate mazes, always have. My mother once tried to explain that labyrinths were sacred and that walking them was a meditation of sorts, but I so loathe the feeling of being boxed inside a pattern that I could barely play hopscotch as a child.

David grins. "Not if you know its secret—which I do. You shouldn't go in by yourself, though: it's so overgrown that you really could get lost in there. Even if you navigate the labyrinth, you might not recognize the way out. See, this was the west door, but it's almost entirely grown over."

David gestures to a narrow slit in the hedge wall. It looks barely big enough to allow me through, let alone David with his broad shoulders; but when he turns sideways, I see he's slim enough to slip through—in fact, he vanishes so quickly it's as though the hedge had swallowed him whole.

"Come on in," he calls from behind the thick boxwood, "the water's fine."

I close my eyes and take a deep breath—as if I really were jumping into water—and plunge through the narrow opening. When I open my eyes, I might as well be underwater, the air is so thick and green. It even seems to ripple slightly as I peer down the long, narrow pathway hemmed in between the giant walls of boxwood to where David Fox is just turning a corner—but that's probably just my nerves, I figure, as I run to keep up with David.

We turn, and turn again, going deeper into the winding maze. The paths seem to grow narrower as we go, and to slope ever so slightly downward.

"Are we going downhill?" I ask, trying not to sound as nervous as I am.

"That's the trick," David says. "As long as you're going downhill you're going right—of course, the ground is so overgrown now that it's not always easy to judge the gradient—"

"But you do know where we are?"

Instead of answering, David laughs and half turns toward me, smiling. His face, seen at a three-quarters angle and in the green-tinged gloom of the maze, looks more like the face of the Green Man than ever. I'm immediately sorry that I've thought of that face, because it makes me wonder if there are more like it hidden in the walls of the maze.

"Are there statues in here?"

"Just two at the center," David answers. "We're almost there."

I'm not sure if I'm glad of that or not. The idea of being in the center of all these tightly coiling paths is not at all comforting. I notice that the hedges are thick with spiderwebs—tunnel-shaped webs that burrow into the branches. Maybe it's the spiders that give me that feeling of being watched. As I follow David I have the impression of shapes hidden in the green bushes—dark limbs and flashes of red. When David pauses at an intersection of three paths, I see that one of these shapes extends all the way to the top of the hedge, where a crest of red foams over the top of the greenery like a wave of blood about to crash down and engulf us.

"The rosebushes have really gone wild," I say, looking back down.

There's no answer, because David is no longer standing at the intersection. I rush to the crossing and check the three paths. There's a flash of white at the end of one of the paths, so I head down that one. Only when I get to the next turn do I remember that David wasn't wearing white—he was all in green. At any rate, the flash of white has vanished; it was probably just a splash of sunlight. I turn to trace my steps back to the last intersection, figuring that I'm better off waiting for David there than going farther astray, when I catch another glimpse of the white shape. It's deep inside the hedge.

"Hello?" I call, crouching down and peering through the tangle of boxwood and rosebushes. Maybe it's a child of one of the housekeepers who knows she's not supposed to be playing in the gardens. "It's okay," I say. "I won't tell anyone. Are you lost?"

A sigh moves through the hedges. I can't tell if it's the wind or a child's cry, but I suddenly feel a tightness in my own chest as if I'm about to cry, and I can't believe that the wind would stir such an empathetic response. "I'm coming to get you," I tell the child, "just stay where you are."

There's a narrow gap in the hedge near the ground,

like a tunnel that's been burrowed through the box-wood, that I'm able to crawl through. It's probably how the child got in here in the first place, only the child might be small enough to evade the thorny rose branches that tear at my hair and clothes. I try to keep my gaze on the white shape in front of me—I can just make out the girl crouched in a hollow carved out of the hedge, her white dress pulled down over her bent knees, a pink ribbon hanging in her ash-colored hair—but I have to turn twice to free my shirtsleeve from a thorn and when I turn back the second time, the girl is gone. In her place is a white flowering shrub.

"Ellis?" I hear David's voice from somewhere behind me.

"I'm in here," I call. He must hear the quiver of tears in my voice, because he's at my side in a moment.

"Amazing," he says, his voice so hushed with awe that for a moment I think he must sense the girl's presence. "*Plantanthera dilatata.*" He whispers the Latin as if saying a prayer.

"Bog orchid," I say, touching the splayed lip of one of the flowers. Its scent, a mixture of vanilla and cloves, rises on the air, carrying with it some indefinable sadness.

"Yes, how did you know?"

I hesitate, thinking that once again I've acquired some unexplained knowledge, and then, to my relief, I identify the source. "My mother took me looking for it once in a bog near our house. She said the Native Americans used it for a love charm. She said they had another name for it . . ."

"Ghost orchid," David says, "because if you saw it through a misty bog it would look—"

"Like you'd seen a ghost," I finish for him.

The fountain at the center is a bit of a disappointment after the intricate prelude of the maze. It's hardly recognizable as a fountain at all. The boxwood and roses have grown in a tangle into a tight circle around the marble basin, which itself is covered in a thicket of ivy and some kind of dark-leafed shrub that spills over the fountain and covers the surrounding ground. The statue of the crouching girl is overgrown, her face peering through a curtain of ivy. David circles around behind her and, pushing aside a shaggy bush, uncovers the other statue. This one is of a young man.

"These don't look classical," I say. I feel marginally calmer in this small basin of open space at the center of the maze. "I thought this was the center of the iconographic program. They look kind of . . . I don't know . . . hokey."

"They are. Look at this one's name . . ." He brushes aside a film of dirt and lichen growing on the statue's pedestal. Carved in the marble is the name Jacynta.

"Jacynta?"

"Aurora Latham made it up. It's an amalgamation of the names of the three lost children."

"Before they lost Alice, you mean."

"Yes . . . there was James and Cynthia and . . ."

"And Tam . . . short for Thaddeus."

"You've done your homework, I see."

I smile, pleased to finally receive a compliment here at Bosco, even if it's from a landscape architect and not another writer. "But I couldn't tell you who this is supposed to be," I say, walking back to the statue of the crouching girl.

"Jacynta's beautiful Indian girlfriend, Ne'Moss-i-Ne," David says, coming to stand beside me.

"Ne'Moss-i-Ne? It sounds . . . well . . . it doesn't sound like a real Indian name, but like something a camp owner in the Catskills would make up."

David laughs. "You're close. There was a real Iroquois girl who led a band of French explorers to this spring. The local legend goes that she fell in love with a French missionary who later betrayed her village to an Abenaki raiding party. She was taken captive, but she managed to escape and run west to a cliff above the Sacandaga River, where she jumped to her death. Her name was probably something that sounded like Ne'Moss-i-Ne and that was as close as the early settlers could get. Until the Lathams bought this land, the locals called the spring Mossy Spring. But then Aurora heard the story and claimed that she heard the girl was called Ne'Moss-i-Ne. She might have made it up, because the name is really too close to be coincidental."

"Too close to what?"

"Its Greek equivalent. Think about it. It's not an uncommon practice in New York place names. Seneca was originally named *Otsinika,* which is Algonquin for

'Stone,' and then through transliteration and folk etymology it became the classical 'Seneca.' "

"So Ne'Moss-i-ne . . . Ne'Moss-i-ne . . ."

I repeat the name until it begins to sound vaguely familiar . . . a name tickling at the edges of memory . . . and then I recognize it . . . of course, memory itself.

"Mnemosyne, the goddess of Memory."

"And mother of the Muses. The statues of the Muses on the terraces are her children," David says, gesturing toward the hill and walking toward a path in that direction.

We come out of the maze into the sunshine at the foot of the hill and walk toward one of the ruined fountains. I feel better out in the open space and better since my apparition turned out to be a harmless plant and the only ghost on the premises has been categorized as the orchid kind, placed into its proper genus and species. I can tell, too, that David likes me, and I feel inclined to let myself like him back even though I swore that I wouldn't get involved with anyone until I finished the book.

"Who are these guys?" I ask, pointing at the two nude males who lounge on either side of an oval basin that must have once held water but now is overgrown with weeds and ivy.

"This is the Fountain of the Two Rivers. The one on the left represents the Sacandaga and the one on the right is the Hudson. This was Milo Latham getting a little of his own program into the iconography. The Latham lumber would have been carried down from the

Adirondacks on the Sacandaga River—before it was dammed and turned into a reservoir in the thirties—and then carried on the Hudson to his mill."

While the Hudson is depicted as a mature man, the Sacandaga is a muscular young Indian brave, his head shaved into a Mohawk, with an expression so fierce that even though his face is split by a crack that runs from the top of his skull to his feet, I can feel some hostile animus emanating from the statue.

"What about the horse?" I ask, turning away from the angry river god—maybe having his river turned into a reservoir is what has turned him sour—and walking up the stairs. "What does a horse have to do with the Muses?"

"It's Pegasus," David answers.

"But this horse doesn't have any wings."

"They were broken off . . . vandals, I suppose . . . It's shocking how the gardens have been allowed to deteriorate. Hopefully my report to the Garden Conservancy will generate interest in restoring them." I glance at him, looking for any suggestion of what I sensed last night on the terrace—that he'd prefer to leave the gardens in ruins—but he appears genuinely devoted to the garden's restoration. It must have been my imagination. "They were an engineering feat," he goes on. "Aurora not only hired Italian sculptors and gardeners, she brought the most renowned *fontanieri* in all of Europe to design the fountains."

"*Fontanieri?*"

"Hydraulic engineers skilled in creating not just fountains but elaborate water effects. Giacomo Lantini

—whose journal I've been reading—was a genius, especially in creating *giochi d'acqua*—water jokes. For instance, this fountain, the Pool of Pegasus, what does it remind you of? Remember that we started with the Fountain of Memory."

I look up at David, but the sun, nearly overhead now, blinds me. I feel suddenly nervous at how much time is getting away. Time I'm supposed to be using for writing, not answering mythology trivia questions. But then I realize what he's getting at. "The spring on Mount Helicon, home of the Muses—Pegasus strikes the ground with his hoof and the water gushes up. Poets were supposed to drink from the spring for inspiration."

"Exactly—the Hippocrene Spring, it was called, or the Horse Well. So of course it makes sense that Aurora, with her love of the arts, would commission a fountain that celebrated the wellspring of creativity. The water that feeds all these fountains is pumped up the hill from the Fountain of Memory. But she didn't stop there. Look at the stones that pave the path leading to the fountain . . . what do you notice?"

The stones are broken in places, grass and weeds growing between the cracks. There's a pattern, though, beneath the layers of moss and dirt. "Horseshoes, how clever . . ."

"That's not all. When the fountain was intact, all you had to do was step on one and a jet of water would shoot out, drenching you." David kneels down by one of the horseshoe shapes in the stone, takes a Swiss Army knife out of his pocket, and pries loose the horseshoe.

Beneath it is a round copper ring—a pipe leading down into the bowels of the fountain. I crouch down next to it and hear a sound like that of someone drawing breath, as if someone were buried deep in the tunnels beneath the hill, waiting for us to let in the air.

And then I hear a voice.

"The eloquence of water fills this hill."

I look up at David but he lifts a finger to his lips and mouths a name—*Zalman*—and I understand. The poet must be standing above one of the fountain pipes reciting the first line of his poem for something like the two hundredth time today, only now I hear him exhale —a sigh that seems to reverberate through the hill— and the poem rushes out of him as fluid as the jets of the old fountain.

> *"The eloquence of water fills this hill,*
> *its history as winding as a maze,*
> *and influential yet, from vanished days*
> *that echo in the present, lingers still*
> *like ripples in a river, work their will*
> *in suppleness of sculpture, stone eyes' gaze;*
> *the symphonies of water, sound's sweet haze*
> *seduce a genius time could never kill.*
> *And yet one hears, while strolling past, a sigh,*
> *as if lamenting sudden loss of love;*
> *how beautiful the stone, but lost the art*
> *when sculptor and his subject have to part.*
> *Perhaps the water speaks, or else above*
> *a spirit floats, a soul that will not die."*

With the sound of Zalman's voice still echoing through the hollow hill, I suddenly know how I'll write the first scene of my book. Corinth will visit the Fountain of Memory first—I can easily have her make the driver let her off at the bottom of the hill so that she can see the *famous fountain*—and then, when Tom Quinn comes through the door, she'll feel as if her past has finally caught up with her. She'll feel as though the crouching girl in the maze has sprung up to trap her.

Chapter Four

It's not the past, though, that Corinth senses coming through the glass doors with Tom Quinn, it's the future, smelling of rust and decaying vegetation, hanging over the sunlit garden like a veil of green gauze.

Corinth blinks her eyes and the veil lifts.

"Mr. Quinn, you'll be wanting Mrs. Ramsdale, no doubt."

The young man takes a few more steps forward and, without taking his eyes off Corinth, answers yes. Mrs. Ramsdale rises from the table in the alcove and brushes past Corinth, releasing from the folds of her dress a sweet odor.

"Are you ready for your dictàtion, Tom? I have the next chapter entire in my head." Mrs. Ramsdale turns toward Aurora, laying a hand across her copious bosom and fingering a strand of pearls that are the shape and color of slightly spoiled Concord grapes. Beneath the sweet scent is the darker hint of decay, surprising in a woman as young and attractive as Mrs. Ramsdale, who surely can't be much past her midthirties. "We'll work in the garden, Aurora, so as not to disturb your interview with Miss Blackwell."

Aurora leans back in her chair and closes her eyes for answer. Mrs. Ramsdale gathers the skirt of her dress in her hand and sweeps out of the room, leaving in her wake another long trail of the sweet heavy smell.

Laudanum, Corinth thinks, taken to relieve some inner pain that's eating away at her, which explains the aura of decay that emanates from her.

The young man—Tom Quinn—inclines his head slightly in Corinth's direction and follows his mistress.

"Mr. Quinn is Mrs. Ramsdale's amanuensis," Aurora says, her eyes still closed and then, opening them. "You've perhaps read her novels?"

Corinth shakes her head. An image appears in her mind of a man and a woman in a moonlit garden, night-blooming flowers opening to release their scent; only instead of perfume the flowers exude the stench of death. "No, I haven't had the privilege . . ."

"They're abominable," Aurora says tonelessly, as if informing her butler that the wine has turned, "but she's a very sympathetic presence. I think you'll find her a welcome addition to our circle. She's quite interested in the spirit world. She claims to have seen the spirit of my little girl Cynthia playing in the garden."

With a laudanum habit strong enough to imbue even her clothing with the scent, she probably sees plenty, Corinth thinks, and then, turning to Aurora, considers how best to approach the issue of the children. A moment she always dreads.

"I felt," she begins, allowing her genuine reluctance to creep into her voice, because to appear reluctant is always a good effect, "a number of presences as I walked through the garden"—she thinks of the figure she saw at the end of the ilex grove—"especially in the little ilex grove to the west of the fountain allée . . . There's a bench beneath a wisteria arbor . . ."

"The drawing master used to give Cynthia her lessons there."

"And in the maze," Corinth says, suddenly picturing the statue of the crouching Indian maid transforming into a child crouched beneath an overgrown hedge.

"Of course they loved to play there. They played hide-and-seek and I'm afraid that sometimes the boys were naughty enough to forget about Cynthia. She once spent a whole day hiding in the hedges before one of the gardeners found her. Sometimes I'm afraid that their poor little spirits are lost in the windings of those paths. It's what haunts me the most."

Corinth leans forward and lays her hand over Aurora's cool fingers. It's a risky gesture, she knows, considering how reserved this woman is, but she's learned to trust her instincts when it comes to grief.

"Sometimes a spirit does get lost on its way to the spirit world. It gets confused. But we may be able to help it find its way."

Aurora turns her hand over and grasps Corinth's hand, squeezing the bones hard. "Yes, yes, that's what I'm afraid of, that they're confused. Milo thinks that I want to contact the children for my own sake, but that's not it at all. It's because I can still feel them wandering the halls and the garden paths . . ." Aurora pauses, and her gaze moves from Corinth's face to the glass doors and the steeply terraced garden beyond. Yes, Corinth thinks, remembering how she became disoriented walking up the hill, a spirit could find itself trapped in that garden. How must it feel to have designed a garden so complicated that the spirits of one's own children couldn't find their way out of it?

". . . and I worry, too, about Alice . . . about how their presences must affect her."

Corinth looks over at the little girl, who has remained crouched in her niche below the bookcase. She has made herself so small and quiet that Corinth forgot that she was still there. Corinth realizes that in Aurora's accounts of the children's games Alice's name has been absent. Indeed, the child has the look of the one left out, the one who lingers on the edges of the game to watch and listen. Has she been listening now? The girl looks pale and undernourished, but of perhaps even more concern is that picture she drew and the influence it seems to imply.

"We'll help them find their way," Corinth says, trying to make her voice sound reassuring. She's rewarded by a small wan smile and the release of her hand. As Aurora rings for the housekeeper, Mrs. Norris, to show Corinth to her room, Corinth looks down at her hand and sees that Aurora's fingernails have left four little half-moons in the dark blue leather of her glove.

Dinner has been delayed to give Milo Latham time to return from the city. The doors to the terrace are left open to let in a breeze and, as Aurora announces, so that the guests can enjoy the "music of the fountains" and the scent of the roses, which are at the height of their bloom. Tonight, though, the voice of the water is drowned by the sound of the wind and the roses can't compete with the sulfurous exhalations of the springs that feed the fountains.

Mrs. Ramsdale rearranges the limbs of the tiny quail on her plate, unable to eat a mouthful. It's not the reek of the fountains, though, that's taken her appetite away. That smell she'd grown accustomed to while taking the water cures in Europe and here in America. It's watching Tom Quinn watching the little medium that's awakened a fresh bloom of pain in her stomach. He's pretending to be drawing out Signore Lantini on points of garden design, but she can see that his attention is drawn to the new arrival. Of course, he can't help but include her in the conversation, since she is sitting between him and the little Italian (while Mrs. Ramsdale has been seated next to the tiresome portraitist, Frank Campbell), but still . . . she can see the way his eyes come back to her while the gardener drones on about Bramante and axial planning and the importance of alternating sunny spaces with shaded and the proportion between terrace and green, between the height of a wall and the width of a path . . . Well, who could blame dear Tom for allowing his eyes to rest on the one thing of beauty in this room while the beauty of the garden is parsed and dissected like some mathematical formula?

And she is beautiful. Even more beautiful than when Mrs. Ramsdale saw her two years ago at Baden-Baden. The fine dark hair, touched with sparks of red, lifting from her clear brow like the wing of a bird . . . yes, that's how she'd put it in one of her novels . . . her waist slim as a reed . . . Mrs. Ramsdale feels her own waist, which has been thickening this summer even though she lives on practically nothing but tea and toast and consommé, pressing against her stays. While dressing for dinner tonight, she'd had to let the dress out and pin it up with dressmaker's pins until she could get back to her dressmaker in the city to have it altered. And yet, Corinth Blackwell, who has eaten everything on her plate and is even now buttering a second roll, is slim. She eats, Mrs. Ramsdale, observes, like someone who has known hunger.

"What do you think of our new arrival?" Latham asks, leaning over to whisper softly in Mrs. Ramsdale's ear.

"She seems to be entertaining Aurora," Mrs. Ramsdale says, grateful for her host's attention if not for his choice of subject matter. Milo Latham hasn't been able to take his eyes off Miss Blackwell any more than Tom has, but then, she reasons, he's gone to considerable expense to have her brought here at his wife's request. And even the rich, as Mrs. Ramsdale has learned, want to be sure they've gotten their money's worth. Often enough that's how they've acquired their money in the first place.

"I wasn't in favor, you know, of satisfying this whim of Aurora's," he says, "but you know how determined she can be."

"She has a strong will," Mrs. Ramsdale says. "She never would have survived these last few years if she didn't. Of course, you've had to suffer as much . . ."

"Yes, but I have my work. There's nothing like a river full of logs to keep a man's mind busy, and then the gentlemen in the legislature have contrived to keep me lively . . ."

"You mean the new bill to protect the forests?" Mrs. Ramsdale asks, glad she's kept up with the news. "Will that affect your lumber business?"

Latham shrugs. "Not seriously. And that's if it passes at all. There's plenty of opposition."

Giacomo Lantini, overhearing this last remark, tears his eyes away from Corinth Blackwell and addresses his host in his faltering English. "But isn't it true that the cutting down of the trees is—how do you say?—making the springs to run dry? And if the springs and the streams that feed your great American rivers and canals dry up, then how will the ships carry their goods across such a huge country? From where will come the water to feed your great cities? Our ancestors, the Romans, understood the power of water."

"Signore Lantini is descended from a long line of fountain makers," Aurora says, bestowing a proud look in the little man's direction. "*Fontanieri*. He has designed our marvelous fountains for us and routed the springs to feed them. Only this summer the pressure has been so low that he's had to build a new pump to draw water from the springs at the bottom of the hill up to the top. There's barely enough water to keep the fountains going."

"Leave it to my wife to place her gardening plans above the demands of commerce and urban hygiene," Milo Latham says, smiling indulgently at Aurora at the other end of the long table.

"We should be grateful," Frank Campbell, the portraitist, says, speaking up for the first time this evening, "for Mrs. Latham's devotion to art and beauty. I know I am." He lifts his glass to his hostess, and the other guests follow suit. "Here's to our Muse of Water!"

"Easy for him to say," Milo Latham murmurs in a low whisper into Mrs. Ramsdale's ear as she touches her lips to the brim of her glass without drinking. "He doesn't pay the bill for Aurora's devotion."

Corinth, on the other side of the table, overhears the remark. She has long ceased paying attention to Signore Lantini's lecture on gardening. She has found it difficult to concentrate on anything with Tom sitting next to her, but the exact nature of the Lathams' marriage is of moment to her, as her success here depends on pleasing them both. She wishes Tom were as concerned with his employer's feelings. Mrs. Ramsdale is clearly jealous of her amanuensis's attention to her. She wishes Tom would look away, but since he won't, she turns to him.

"You seem quite knowledgeable on the subject of classical gardens," she says. "Where were you educated?"

She knows full well that Tom Quinn was educated at a Catholic orphanage for boys in Brooklyn, New York, but she's hoping that if he remembers how much damage she can do to whatever history he's presented to his employer, he'll stop staring at her.

"I was home tutored by my mother, who was headmistress at a finishing school for young ladies in Gloversville. Perhaps you've heard of it? The Lyceum?" His face dimples as he mentions the name of the music hall where he and Corinth first met ten years ago. She understands Quinn's message: he can do at least as much damage to her as she can to him.

"I lived with the Van Dykes of Gloversville for a summer while painting their three daughters," Campbell says. "I don't remember a school called the Lyceum, but there was a rather disreputable theater . . ."

"Don't you own one of the glove factories in Gloversville, Milo?" Mrs. Ramsdale asks Milo Latham.

"Yes, Latham Gloves." He answers Mrs. Ramsdale's question, but his gaze is fastened on Tom Quinn now.

"*Veramente!*" Lantini exclaims. "Gloves and lumber! I didn't know your business ventures were so . . . how do you say? . . . *diverso.*"

"Leather and lumber both come from the same

source," Latham answers, regarding the Italian with unconcealed contempt. "Our great northern woods. My land holdings in the Adirondacks afforded such a quantity of deer pelts that it made sense to go into the leather-processing business."

"When I think of all the poor slain deer . . ." Aurora says, fanning herself with a black lace fan of Italian design that Corinth recognizes as a type made by the nuns of a certain order in Rome.

"And yet, my wife is one of our very best customers!" Latham says, lifting his glass to Aurora. "A dozen pairs of gloves are delivered to her each month, in all the latest colors and styles."

"I notice that Miss Blackwell is also a devotee," Aurora says, nodding at Corinth's gloved hands.

"I apologize for wearing gloves at the table," Corinth says. "I'm afraid that my hands are so sensitive to . . . certain sense impressions that I find it unbearable to touch anything with my bare hands. I'm not sure where these gloves were made, though . . ."

"Why, I believe I can see the manufacturer's label here," Tom Quinn says, touching the hem of her glove and turning it over to reveal the label. His fingers merely graze the underside of her wrist, but Corinth feels a wave of heat course up her arm and across her chest.

"Bravo, Mrs. Latham. You have indeed recognized your husband's handiwork," Tom Quinn says, taking his hand away from her wrist.

When Corinth looks up, she sees Mrs. Ramsdale watching her and her pain is so apparent in her eyes that

Corinth feels it herself—a twinge deep in her womb, just where life first quickens, but this sensation has nothing to do with life.

As soon as she gets back to her room Corinth strips off her leather gloves and lets them fall to the floor in a crumpled heap. She leans back against the door, closing her eyes and willing her heartbeat to slow. She'd known that she might have a problem with the mistress of the house, but she hadn't anticipated having to deal with Tom Quinn or his jealous employer. When she opens her eyes, she is calmer, but still warm. She steps toward the window, but then, noticing the delicate pale green gloves on the floor, and remembering how much they cost, she picks them up. A slip of paper, folded into quarters, falls out of one.

Corinth unfolds it and reads the message written in the familiar handwriting. *Meet me in the Grotto . . .*

She stretches the gloves over the wooden forms she's set up on the dressing table, smoothing out their wrinkles, and then leans across the glass perfume bottles and leather cases to open the window above the table, craning her neck to let the cool, moist air touch her face. It's not enough. She needs to feel the air on her throat, her breasts . . . she feels trapped in her clothes. Sitting down at the table, she takes out a buttonhook from one of the leather cases and starts undoing the buttons down the back of her dress. Aurora had offered her the use of her maid, but she declined, explaining that she required a great deal of solitude to nurture the trance state. She peels the dress down to her waist and lets the breeze from the garden bathe her overheated skin.

When she feels cooler, she opens her toiletry case and checks to see if the root she dug up in the garden is carefully hidden. Then she pulls out of the case the wad of spider silk she took from the hedge. She stretches it between her fingertips and holds it up to the window to watch the fine silken threads move in the breeze. She lets it brush against the underside of her wrist, but instead of the crawling sensation she experienced when she stepped through the web in the garden, she remembers the feel of Tom's fingers on her wrist.

Yes, she says to herself, pushing away the thought, this will do nicely for ectoplasm. She has only to let a thread of it loose at an opportune moment during the séance. Of course it would be easier with a partner.

She stuffs the spider silk into a corner of the Florentine leather case and snaps the lid shut, closing, too, the image of Tom Quinn's face that briefly appeared in her mind. No, he can't be trusted. That was only too clear from what happened in Gloversville.

Besides, she was perfectly capable of operating on her own. For reassurance she slips one of the flexible wires out of her corset and fits it into the long narrow slots sewn into her dress cuffs and, wrestling her arms back into the narrow sleeves, practices levitation. She has to make several small adjustments to the bend in the wires, but on her third try the little dressing table rises from the floor to a height level with the windowsill, its burden of cut-glass perfume bottles and silver-backed brushes gleaming in the moonlight, the gloves on their wooden forms hovering like disembodied hands. She keeps it there a moment to see how steady she can hold the table, but when she lifts her gaze to the window and sees the woman standing below in the garden looking up at her, the table drops with a loud crash.

Mrs. Ramsdale, in the room next to Corinth's, hears the thump. A certain amount of disruption is to be expected, she thinks, having a medium next door. Perhaps she should ask Aurora to change her room, but then, it's one of the very nicest suites in the house, with a large bedroom facing the garden and its own sitting room at the eastern corner of the house, from which she can see the drive and all the arriving guests. She's often wondered why Aurora doesn't take it for herself, but Milo prefers one of the rooms facing the forest to the north and Aurora's room must, of course, adjoin his. No, if anyone should move, it ought to be the little spiritualist.

Wincing at the pain in her side as she shifts in her bed, Mrs. Ramsdale tries to go back to the scene she'd been making in her head, but instead of picturing her heroine, Emmaline Harley, she thinks of the *thump* and pictures the twined columns of the Queen Anne bed in the room next door hitting the wall between the two rooms. She pictures that fire-flecked dark hair spread out on the white sheets, a slim hand (she noticed, at dinner, the medium's unusually long fingers, a sign, she has always believed, of a rapacious nature and a tendency to thievery) grasping the bedpost, then covered by a larger, masculine (but still beautifully molded) hand. Tom Quinn's hand, which she has watched for so many hours as he turns her spoken words, things of air, into written ones, the ones that last.

A fresh pain blooms in her side and she reaches for the little green bottle on the night table. It's only her imagination, she thinks, taking a sip straight from the bottle, her overactive imagination, which is both the novelist's curse and blessing. Even though a blind person could have told they'd met before (she's never bought that story about the impoverished schoolmistress-mother from Gloversville), that doesn't mean there's anything between them. She takes another sip and now when she closes her eyes, she sees only swirls of color: turquoise and jade and violet, the colors of the sea below the cliffs of the Villa Syrene, where her heroine has been imprisoned by the mysterious Prince Pavone. As she falls asleep, she imagines herself drifting above the cliffs, high over the water, free of pain at last.

Even after Corinth has gone down into the garden and stood in front of the statue whose gaze had so startled her before in her room, she still doesn't feel easy. She is not the nervous sort. She has sat through séances while ropes of ectoplasm disgorged from the mouth of a twelve-year-old girl and hideous apparitions floated overhead. She's had chairs and other articles of furniture pitched at her by putative ghosts and not-so-putative landladies. Once, at a revival on the outskirts of Buffalo, a snake handler tripped over her leg and spilled from his burlap sack into Corinth's lap a six-foot-long boa constrictor. She had stayed perfectly still, staring straight into the snake's yellow eyes, while the handler coaxed his charge back into its sack, and she hadn't felt anything like the dread she'd felt ten minutes ago meeting the gaze of this inanimate piece of marble.

There's certainly nothing threatening about the statue, which stands just below the main terrace to the west of the fountain allée. A young girl, draped in Grecian robes, one arm folded in front of her breasts, her empty marble eyes cast upward as if listening to the fluttering wings of a descending god. She's probably one of those silly girls who are seduced by a god in disguise. Corinth has seen dozens like them in the gardens of Italy and France. In fact, the statue's antiquity suggests that the Lathams looted it from some impoverished European noble—making it the foolish girl's second abduction. No doubt it was the girl's upward-tilting eyes and a chance moonbeam that gave Corinth the impression that she was staring at her window. She follows the statue's gaze back to the house and is startled to notice a girl in a short white chemise standing at one of the windows.

Corinth draws her dark cloak around her and steps behind the statue into the shadows of the ilex trees. When the girl's gaze doesn't follow her, Corinth assumes she hasn't been seen. Still, she chides herself for not being more careful. Instead of taking the central path by the fountain allée she slips into the densely planted grove and, keeping her cloak tightly wrapped around her, makes her way down the hill.

She finds the secret entrance to the grotto just where he wrote it would be, behind the left knee of the reclining river god—the one representing the Sacandaga. She follows the narrow passage, trying to keep her cloak from brushing the damp rock walls, and emerges onto a shallow ledge behind the waterfall. She expected it to be dark, but instead she is dazzled by the light that at first she thinks is coming from the water. A hundred phosphorescent fish seem to be swimming in the underground cave, but then she realizes that the light comes from candles set in niches recessed into the grotto walls, their light reflected in the water and cast back up onto the domed ceiling, which is glazed in ceramic tile and encrusted with jeweled sea creatures: spiny lobsters and hook-tailed sea horses, urchins and long-tentacled octopi. Reclining on a shallow bench that is carved into the rock wall is a robed figure, who might be another river god, only Corinth is in no danger of mistaking Milo Latham for a god of any sort.

"Did anyone see you come?" he asks, already pushing away her cloak and pulling her down into his lap.

She thinks about the girl in the white chemise but tells him no, because it's what he wants to hear. He's holding her breast with one hand and with the other parting her legs. Corinth straddles him and lowers herself down, letting out a gasp that Milo takes for pleasure but which is really the pain of her knees scraping against the rough stone bench. She braces her hands against the wall to lift herself up and feels herself soaring above him—she is the winged god swooping down to take whatever she needs—but when she closes her eyes, she sees the girl in the white chemise standing at the window. No, no reason to tell him about her. The window she was standing at was Corinth's own. Corinth stretches her arms high above herself on the wall, finds a crack in the stone, and digs her fingers into it until she can feel the stone scraping away her skin.

Chapter Five

"The third line is the prisoner of the rhyme," Zalman announces at breakfast.

"Why is that?" I ask.

"I should think it would be obvious," Bethesda says, lifting the silver serrated spoon (part of the original silver-ware Aurora designed for Bosco when, at the end of her life, she was planning the estate's conversion to an artists' colony) from the edge of her grapefruit and pointing it in my direction. "It's the first line that has to conform to one of the other lines. It has to rhyme with the first line if you're writing an Elizabethan sonnet—"

"And with the second if it's going to be a Petrarchan sonnet," Zalman finishes for her, beaming across the table at Bethesda. "You're a fan of the sonnet, then, Miss Graham?"

Bethesda saws a sliver of grapefruit onto her spoon and chews it thoughtfully before answering. I realize I'm holding my breath, afraid that Bethesda will unleash one of her critical storms on poor Zalman, who looks so innocent, from his gleaming bald pate to the sprig of rosemary in the buttonhole of his pale blue Mexican wedding shirt.

"When it's done well," Bethesda answers, when she has swallowed her mouthful of grapefruit.

"I don't see the point of it," Nat says. "Why write in an antiquated form? Isn't it a bit of an affectation?"

"My teacher, Richard Scully, always said that there was a discipline to working within a form," I say, anxious to defend Zalman.

"*Dick* Scully?" Nat asks, taking a sip of his black coffee. "Is he the one who encouraged you to write a gothic romance?"

"I'm not—" I begin, not sure what to be more hurt by—the disparaging way he's referred to my mentor or his calling my novel a *romance*.

"Isn't everything a form of some sort?" David Fox puts in. I give him a small smile, sure that he's trying to defend me, but wishing he'd leave it. It's foolhardy, really, considering he's the only nonwriter at the table. In the first week of October all the artists and composers in the outlying cottages left; only the four of us writers and David Fox have remained in the main house for the winter residency. "The thriller, the gothic romance, the novel of manners," David continues, "the angry-young-man bildungsroman? Isn't that your genre, Nathaniel?"

A deathly silence falls over the table that only Zalman, humming to himself as he butters his toast, seems oblivious of. Has David really just called Nat

Loomis a genre writer? Although I know he's only trying to speak up for me, I'm afraid he's gone too far.

Finally, after taking another sip of coffee and assembling his features into the patient mask of someone dealing with a very young and not very bright child, Nat answers. "Some writers are slaves to the form. They're called genre writers. And some endeavor to explode the form. They're called artists."

"I see," David says, "and so what exactly in your novel *Saratoga*—"

"*Sacandaga*," Nat corrects, his hand trembling slightly as he puts down his coffee cup.

"Yes, *Sacandaga*. What in *Sacandaga* explodes the form? If I recall, it's about a boy staying at his grandfather's cottage for the summer—"

"You've read it?" Nat asks with barely disguised surprise. His voice is calm, but his hand, still touching the rim of his coffee cup, is trembling. I can hear the faint ring of china rattling against china and the wings of the bluebirds painted on the cup are fluttering. "I didn't realize your reading extended beyond Burpee's seed catalog."

"Boys," Bethesda says reprovingly, but Nat and David both smile at her as if they each had no idea what her problem might be. They're engaged in a friendly discussion, their faces say, but only a fool—or someone as innocent of envy and malice as Zalman Bronsky—wouldn't feel the tension in the room. I can't help but feel partly responsible, since David started this to protect me, and, oddly, I feel sorry for Nat. When he gets angry or scared, I've noticed, his ears quiver and you can imagine what he looked like as a kid. I can picture him as that boy in his first novel, hiding in the woods behind his grandfather's cottage, scared of the old man and trying to get a moment to himself to read instead of having to go out again on those dreaded fishing trips. I can almost hear his grandfather's stern voice calling him, *Nathaniel*—

"Oh, I like a novel now and again," David drawls. He's from Texas, I've learned, but only sounds that way when it suits him. "And I liked yours fine. Especially the fishing parts. Only I don't really see what makes it any different from any other boy-growing-up story, say *The Catcher in the Rye,* or Hemingway's Nick Adams stories—"

"I'd be happy to include myself in that company," Nat says, his ears twitching. I get another clear picture of him as a boy, leaning against a tree, reading—

"Of course," I say, "those are classic influences. It's not as if Nat modeled his book on the Hardy Boys—"

A crashing sound cuts short my ill-conceived intervention. Nat's coffee cup lies in its saucer, in a mess of blue and white splinters and black coffee. Nat himself is already out the door, Bethesda following close behind him. Zalman looks up surprised and then begins mopping up the black coffee with his napkin. David looks at me and laughs.

"What's so funny?" I say.

"Don't you see?" he says. "Nat's just exploded his form!"

I head outside after breakfast. I feel that I need a breath of fresh air after the altercation between Nat and David, but it's colder than I expected. Indian summer, which had lingered through the first weeks of October, has come to an abrupt end. The ilex trees are still green, but much of the surrounding foliage has turned color and fallen. Having grown up in northwest New York, the abruptness of autumn shouldn't surprise me and yet, when I first saw the gardens in all their overgrown greenery, I imagined them staying like that throughout the winter. Now, though, there are denuded spots in the hillside where statues that lay hidden through the summer peer out, their lichen-stained faces and broken limbs appearing trapped in the tangle of bare branches. I remember the demonic face of the Green Man that David showed me weeks ago and wonder what else lies beneath the underbrush waiting to be uncovered.

Although it's definitely too cold to work outside in the garden today, I can't bear the thought of going back to my room. It's a perfectly nice room—certainly the most luxurious one I've ever slept in—but I've been feeling increasingly uneasy in it, especially in the mornings, when the sound of Nat's manual typewriter beats a maddening rhythm in my skull and the image of him at his desk seems to invade my room. I especially don't want to listen to it today after what happened in the breakfast room. Nat must hate me now, I think, heading down the path on the west side of the hill. What on earth possessed me to mention the Hardy Boys?

But then I know what it was. The picture of young Nat I conjured up, hiding in the woods. He'd been reading one of the Hardy Boys stories. Surely it was a detail I just plucked from the air—maybe it was even in Nat's novel—but no, I remember now that along with the vision I had I heard Nat's grandfather calling him. He called him Nathaniel, not the name of the narrator in the novel. And when I heard the voice, what I felt was that I understood why Nat hates to be called Nathaniel, because *he* called him that. Maybe if I could explain to Nat . . . what? That I heard voices? That I *felt his pain*. I could just imagine how he'd react to that.

"I swear I didn't tell her."

The voice comes from around the next bend in the path. I freeze and wait, willing the voice to go away. I've heard enough voices this morning. But it continues, "Why on earth would I even talk to her? She's a hack! And a plagiarist! She stole my title."

No, this isn't a voice in my own head. It's Bethesda Graham. And although I'd certainly guessed what she thought of me, I'm stung by her words. *Hack, plagiarist.* I turn around and walk quickly back up the hill, but the words pursue me. I know I've put too much distance between us, but it's as if I can still hear their condemnation. *Phony, fake.* In my eagerness to get away from them, I head off the path. The sound I make crashing through the dry underbrush is deafening, but I can still hear the insults, only they're no longer in Bethesda's voice. I can't recognize these voices, there are so many, a throng of them, as if in a crowded auditorium, jeering at me. *Charlatan, fraud, witch.* Thorns drag at my clothes like hands plucking at me, trying to drag me down.

When I break free from the brush, I'm scratched and breathless. I struggle up onto the terrace and head for the French doors that lead into the library. A gust of wind snakes in at my heels as if it had been coiled in the shrubbery, only waiting for an opportunity to gain entrance to the house. When I finally close the doors, I lean my back against them and breathe in the silence. The two Morris chairs by the fire are empty, the cushions on the side divans still fresh and undented from the morning housekeeping rounds. Standing on the threshold, I have a sense of relief that seems to go well beyond the good luck of getting the library to myself. It's as if real pursuers had chased me up the hill and I have come here seeking refuge from danger, instead of just a quiet place to get some work done. Then I hear a rustling from the alcove and realize I'm not alone after all.

Coming farther into the room, I see David Fox, ensconced at the library table in the alcove, drawings and blueprints spread out on it and every available nearby surface.

"Oh, I guess I'd better find someplace else—" I begin, but before I can finish my sentence, David has sprung up from his seat, scattering sheets of paper to the floor.

"No, don't go," he says. "There's something I've

been wanting to show you." He pulls me to the desk and begins riffling through a thick pile of blueprints. There must be a dozen of them, each as large as a full *New York Times* page, stretched out on the mission library table and held down by an assortment of smooth white stones. When he moves the stones back from the edge of one, it springs into a roll, like a pill bug curling into itself, only the paper, which is old and dry, snaps like a small firecracker. I look over my shoulder nervously, sure that at any moment we will be rebuked for breaking the sacred silence of Bosco.

"It's in here someplace," David says, apparently unconcerned about the "no talking" rule. "I thought it would help you in following the movements of your characters."

"That's okay," I tell him. "I have a floor plan of the house that I'm working with and I've made a rough sketch of the garden. I should really be getting back to work—" I take a step backward, but David still has a hold of my hand.

"You're still mad at me for what happened this morning. Honestly, Ellis, I didn't realize Nat couldn't take a little ribbing. And I was tired of hearing him and Beth ragging on you."

"I don't need your protection," I say, a little more coldly than I'd meant to . . . I can see the hurt in his eyes. "But I appreciate what you were trying to do."

"Nah, you're still mad . . . but I'm going to make it up to you. You don't have any floor plan like this," he says, grinning. "And as for the garden—"

He stops midsentence and lifts a finger to his lips. I hear it, too—the rusty latch of the French doors opening. Although I'm embarrassed to be caught "conversing" during writing hours, I'm startled by the violence of David's reaction, which is to gather up an armful of blueprints and shove me into the narrow gap between the bookcase and the alcove wall. I can see Bethesda come in, take a book down from a shelf, and sit down in one of the Morris chairs by the fireplace. She doesn't, however, open the book. Instead she stares into space, her eyes unnaturally wide, as if she's holding back tears.

I turn to David, who's so close that his face is practically touching mine, and turn my palms up. *What are we supposed to do now?* I hope to convey by the gesture, *There's no other way out of the library.*

But David is grinning, his face at this close range disturbingly like the stone satyrs in the garden. He reaches around the back of the bookcase, as if feeling for a light switch, and suddenly the bookcase swings open silently on well-oiled hinges.

I can feel my mouth open, gaping like one of the fountain satyrs, but luckily David has already disappeared into the dark passage and can't see how ridiculous I look.

"How did you find this?" I whisper when we've pulled the bookcase partially closed behind us.

"I found it on one of the old plans for the house," he says. "Here, hold these for a minute."

He passes over the heavy roll of blueprints and digs in the pocket of his corduroy blazer until he finds a flashlight. I can see all this in the faint light that seeps in through the cracks around the bookcase, but once he's got the flashlight in his hand, he pulls the bookcase more firmly closed and the seams of light vanish. I picture the lid of a stone sarcophagus closing, the light rimming the narrow rectangular slab, and my throat constricts in panic. When David switches on the flashlight, though, I see that we're surrounded by ample space, on a landing at the foot of a flight of stairs, which, while narrow, suggests there's a way out.

"Claustrophobic?" David asks, studying me closely.

"Not really," I lie. "Just afraid of the dark."

"And you're writing a book about a medium?"

I smile, considering whether I should tell him that it's worse than that, that not only am I writing a book about a medium but I'm the *daughter* of one as well, and that I'd disappointed my mother early on by being unable to sit through her circles. But David is already pointing the flashlight up the stairs.

"We'd better get you out of here, then," he says. "You go first and I'll hold the light."

I would rather hold the flashlight myself, but I start up the stairs, happy just to be moving, especially since I can see a door now at the top of the flight of stairs. When I put my hand on it, though, David lays his hand over mine and pulls it away from the door.

"That opens into the central suite on the second floor," he says, "Nat's room. Listen. I think he's gotten over our little morning spat."

I lean closer to the door and hear the clatter of typewriter keys. "He's probably turning me into a nasty character already," David says. "That is what you writers do, isn't it?"

"Sometimes," I answer. I notice that there's another door across from it and wonder if it goes into my room.

"Does anyone else know about this passage?" I ask, nervously imagining midnight intruders—or daytime intruders checking my laptop for signs of progress on my novel.

"I don't think so. There's only one plan that included them, and you'd have to be an architect to even recognize them on the drawing."

" 'Them'?" I ask as we reach the door at the top of the second flight of stairs. I put my hand on it and try to push it open. Claustrophobic or not, I've had enough of this narrow space. The door doesn't budge. David reaches over my head and releases a small metal catch that springs the door open into a room that, despite its northern exposure, looks positively incandescent to my light-starved eyes.

"Oh, yes, there's a whole network of secret passages," he says, "and not just in the house."

"What do you mean, not just *in* the house?" I ask.

Instead of answering, David takes the blueprints from me and begins to unroll them across his unmade bed. I look around, nervously wondering what I'm doing here in David's room. The last thing I need is to have it whispered that I spent my time at Bosco sleeping around—and I know how quickly rumors fly in the writing community. To make things worse, the furnishings exude masculinity, the drapes and rug a deep red, the bed so massive and rustic it looks as if some arboreal giant had uprooted the living trees from the forest to furnish his lair. The bedposts are rough, unpeeled birch logs topped with crudely carved bear heads. An enormous eagle spreads its wings across the top of the headboard. When he's found the blueprint he was looking for, David pats a corner of the bed for me to sit down. I lower myself gingerly onto the very edge of the mattress, which creaks under my weight and releases a smell so woodsy and musky it's as if the somber wooden bears guarding the four corners of the bed have awoken from their long hibernation and exhaled their stale winter breaths.

"Look, this is a plan that Lantini drew up in the summer of 1892. The springs had already started failing and Aurora had commissioned him to create a new system of pumps to draw water up the hill to feed the fountains."

I lean over the unrolled paper to make out the faded drawing. I'm expecting a technical outline—a blueprint—but I'm pleasantly surprised to find a pen-and-ink drawing, washed over with pale watercolor and touched with white, black, and red chalk. It looks like a scene from Italy, complete with little figures dressed in nineteenth-century costumes strolling along the paths. Water cascades down the central fountain allée under the benign gaze of the Muses, gushing out of the mouths of satyrs and from the full breasts of sphinxes, finally falling in a great cataract beneath the hooves of the winged Pegasus.

"Wow, did the gardens really look like this?"

David laughs. "Well, they did to Lantini. I believe he may have been embellishing a bit. This was his *idea* of what the gardens would look like when he completed them."

"Completed them? You mean they weren't finished by 1892?"

David shakes his head. "No, they were never finished. Aurora was always adding another statue or commanding Lantini to design more *giochi d'acqua*, and then, after Milo Latham's death and the decline of the lumber business, her money began to dry up."

"Like the springs."

David smiles. "You find it hard to resist a simile, don't you?"

I smile back and settle myself more securely on the bed. "Yeah, my writing workshop was always telling me to pare down on the figurative language, but to me it's the really fun part of writing—the way something becomes something else. It's like . . ."

"Magic?" David asks.

I blush, more embarrassed at what I've given away about myself than at sitting on the rumpled bed of this strange man. "I don't mean to sound all mystical. More often than not, the end result doesn't live up to my original vision."

"No, it never does. I think that was Aurora Latham's problem," David says, turning back to the drawing. "The vision she had of the garden far exceeded what Lantini could create for her out of marble and water and shrubbery. Look at the plantings in this picture: the trees and underbrush are practically tropical, and the cascading water looks as if Niagara had been let loose on the hillside."

I look more closely at the drawing. David is right. There's something disturbing beneath the calm facade of this garden. The trees and bushes, lush and over-grown, seem to be encroaching on the marble terraces and graveled paths, looming over the heads of the couples strolling through the garden. The statues peer out of the dense underbrush like hunters lying in ambush, and the water rushes down the hill with so much force it appears as if the whole scene will be swept away at any moment.

"It looks," I say to David, "as if the garden were about to self-destruct."

"Yes, exactly! And it practically did. When the springs started to dry up, Aurora ordered Lantini to tunnel into the hill to tap deeper springs and build stronger pumps to draw more water up the hill. She practically excavated the whole hill! Look at this—" David unrolls a fragile piece of tracing paper from the pile of blueprints. "When I first found this, I wasn't sure what it was because it had been separated from the drawing it was supposed to go with." He holds up the paper so that I can see it. The paper is divided diagonally into halves; the upper triangle is empty, the bottom half is filled with a pattern of lines that look like the kind of maze you'd find on a diner place mat to entertain bored children. There's even a circular pit of some sort at the bottom of the left-hand corner that could be the lair of the Minotaur.

"Is it the plan to the maze?" I ask, remembering how David had led me through the winding paths so confidently.

"No, it's the wrong shape. I thought at first that it might be a plan for a maze that Aurora and Lantini never got around to executing, but then I realized what the shape reminded me of." He lays the transparent paper down over the drawing of the garden and the lines fit perfectly into the slope of the hillside. I can't, at first, understand what they're supposed to represent. It looks like a nest of snakes slithering beneath the surface of the gay fountains and luxuriant foliage. Then I notice that each "snake" is attached to a jet or cascade of water.

"Is it a plan for the pipes?" I ask, proud to have figured it out. I was never very good at those place-mat puzzles, having often been forced to leave Theseus lost midway in the labyrinth when my grilled cheese and chocolate milk arrived.

David smiles. "Almost," he says. "It's a plan for the tunnels."

Chapter Six

"I'll need something that belonged to each of the children," Corinth tells Aurora at breakfast.

Her hostess takes a sip of tea and lifts her pale blue eyes to meet Corinth's gaze. In the silence before she answers, Corinth has time to notice that her eyes look, if possible, even paler this morning, their color less like the blue in the teacup that she raises to her lips than the spaces where the blue has bled onto the white background. *Flow blue*, as an English countess once told Corinth that kind of china was called, *a mistake*, she added, *in the firing process which you Americans have grown so fond of that our manufacturers now purposely produce it to send to your shores.*

If only all mistakes looked so lovely, Corinth thought at the time, admiring the softly blurred pattern, like a landscape in a fine rain. Looking now at her hostess's eyes, she imagines that the grief of losing three children has leached her eyes of their color and she regrets asking for her children's belongings so abruptly.

"Do you mean to practice psychometry?" Mrs.

Ramsdale asks. Aside from Mr. Campbell, who is up early to catch the morning light, she and Corinth are the only guests at breakfast. Milo Latham left the house before dawn to travel upriver to his lumber mill, and Signore Lantini, according to Aurora, is already at work in the garden effecting some adjustments to the fountains. No one has mentioned the whereabouts of Tom Quinn.

"Psychometry?" Frank Campbell asks, pronouncing the word as if it were some kind of unmentionable disease. "What's that?"

"The belief that inanimate objects retain latent memories," Mrs. Ramsdale answers. "I once saw a medium evoke a dinosaur from a lump of coal. Perhaps Miss Blackwell could conjure the Chinaman who painted this teacup," she suggests, holding up the flow blue cup, her long, elegant fingers curled around the delicate china, "or the ox whose bones were crushed to make the china?"

"Does it matter what objects?" Aurora asks, pushing away her teacup abruptly, as if it were tainted with blood.

"Something special to the child . . . a favorite toy or piece of clothing . . ."

"Really!" Mrs. Ramsdale exclaims. "Is it necessary to torture a grieving mother in this fashion?"

Aurora lays her hand over the novelist's hand. "Violet, remember that Miss Blackwell is here at my request."

"Is she? If I remember correctly, Mr. Latham was

the first to mention Miss Blackwell's name," Mrs. Ramsdale says, looking in Corinth's direction with a meaningful gaze. But meaning what? Corinth wonders. What does she know? She doesn't believe that Tom would have told his employer about her history with Milo Latham, but Mrs. Ramsdale has keen powers of observation and she had been at Baden-Baden when Corinth and the Lathams were also in residence. She and Milo had been discreet, but the novelist may have picked up some whiff of scandal. In her experience, artists and writers often share something of the psychic gift.

"I'm sure that when Mr. Latham mentioned the popularity of Miss Blackwell's circles in the city," Frank Campbell, buttering his toast, interjects, "he had no intention of suggesting that she be brought here. In fact, if I remember correctly, he was against the idea."

Campbell seems oblivious of not only the veiled glances exchanged between Aurora and Mrs. Ramsdale but of Corinth's presence altogether. In fact, Corinth has the sudden impression that she herself is no longer in the room. As Mrs. Ramsdale and Mr. Campbell debate the point of whose idea it was to invite "the medium" to Bosco, she can feel herself growing cold, her toes and fingertips and the top of her scalp tingling, as if her body were being drained of blood, but instead of flowing downward, she can feel something—some vital essence—rising upward, quitting her body and then hovering a few feet above the breakfast table, where she regards her own body as a thing of no more substance or import than the china teacup it holds in its hand. She can feel her personality merging with the surrounding air, seeping into the atmosphere in the same way that the cobalt glaze on the teacup flows over the bounds of its pattern . . .

And then she's back in her body, spirit smacking into flesh so violently that she drops the teacup in her hand and it shatters in an explosion of blue and white shards, like sparks from a fire.

"What a shame," Mrs. Ramsdale says, rising from the table and shaking a few pieces of china from her lap. "Aren't those the cups you had ordered especially from England for the children?"

Aurora nods, and Corinth notices that in the china cabinet behind Aurora's chair there's a row of the flow blue cups, each settled into its matching saucer like a bird brooding on its nest.

Mrs. Norris, who came silently into the room during Corinth's trance, kneels with a broom and dustpan to collect the fragments.

Frank Campbell rises from the table and follows Mrs. Ramsdale out of the breakfast room. Only Aurora and Corinth remain seated.

"You'd better come with me to the children's nursery," Aurora says, lifting a shard of china impaled in the soft white flesh of her boiled egg, "to select the objects yourself."

After quitting the breakfast room, Mrs. Ramsdale follows Frank Campbell out onto the terrace and, leaning against the balustrade, watches him set up his easel and mix his paints. This gives her an excellent view, as well, of the main paths through the garden, just in case Tom Quinn has decided to take an early morning walk. It's not like him to sleep so late, unless something kept him up late last night. The only person she sees in the garden, though, is the little Italian, who is crouched in front of one of the satyr fountains on the west side of the second terrace, his right arm buried up to its elbow in the satyr's mouth. He pulls his arm out and produces a long curved knife—a scythe—and uses it to cut back a vine that's grown into the satyr's mouth. Even from here Mrs. Ramsdale can hear Lantini lavishing elaborate Italian curses on the foliage that threatens to choke up his plumbing. Behind him, in the ilex grove, another marble face peers out of the underbrush as if overseeing the engineer's progress with his brethren.

"I'm surprised that Aurora has time to pose for you today," she says, snapping open her parasol and angling it to protect her complexion from the morning sun and shield her face from anyone who might be looking from the house, "what with all the excitement of tonight's entertainment."

"I have the background to work on," he replies. "I'm nearly done with the figure of Mrs. Latham, anyway. Today I'll be working on *her*." He points to one of the Muses just below the edge of the terrace.

"Ah, a model who knows how to remain still," Mrs.

Ramsdale observes. "You must be glad of the change."

"Mrs. Latham is a most cooperative model," Campbell says in that prissy tone that Mrs. Ramsdale has come to recognize as the one he uses when he wishes to distinguish his position from hers. *I am an artist,* the tone implies, *while you are of that damned mob of scribbling women writing trash for filthy lucre.* As if he weren't just as much a slave to his wealthy patrons as she is to her readers.

"Yes," Mrs. Ramsdale says, giving her parasol a twirl. "If there's one thing Aurora is good at, it's staying still. Like a cat stalking a mouse."

"I don't think that's a very apt analogy at all," Campbell says, stroking his brush along the curve of the Muse's breast. "Mrs. Latham possesses the stillness of eternity, not the cunning of a wild beast."

"Oh, yes, I know, she's your *Muse of Water.*"

Campbell waves his brush, splashing white paint on the balustrade. "You can mock if you like, Mrs. Ramsdale, but if you were a true artist, you would appreciate what she has created here. Her vision of Bosco as a haven for artists embraces the future, which is why I am so opposed to tonight's 'entertainment,' as you call it."

"You disapprove of contacting the spirit world?" Mrs. Ramsdale asks, and then, not waiting for an answer: "Or perhaps you are afraid."

Campbell's narrow shoulders stiffen underneath his linen smock. "Afraid? Of knocks and rattling tables and disembodied voices? I've been to my share of séances, madam, and I can assure you that if I didn't find the motive behind them so reprehensible, I would be amused."

"The motive?"

"To exploit the grief and vulnerability of the bereaved. But then, I suppose you adore such sensational spectacles. It's like something out of a novel."

"You're confusing me with Mrs. Braddon, I think. I abhor the use of the supernatural in fiction," Mrs. Ramsdale says, placing her hand over Mr. Campbell's and lowering her voice to a whisper. "And I abhor the exploitation of a mother's grief just as much as you do. I would much rather see the medium leave Bosco, but then, I suppose that will depend on the outcome of tonight's séance."

"What do you mean?"

"Well, if the Blackwell woman is able to trick our hostess into believing she can contact the children, there will be no end to her stay here . . ."

Mrs. Ramsdale allows her voice to trail off. She has just realized that what she took for a marble face in the underbrush is really a man's face. It's Tom Quinn, crouched in the ilex grove just behind where Lantini is fiddling with the satyr fountain—or where Lantini was a minute ago. He's disappeared so suddenly that Mrs. Ramsdale has the impression that he's been swallowed up by the satyr's mouth.

"But what can either of us possibly do about that?" Campbell asks impatiently.

"If Corinth Blackwell is unmasked as a fraud, then

Milo Latham will ask her to leave immediately," Mrs. Ramsdale says, moving her eyes away from Tom Quinn for only a moment.

"Then that is what must be done," Campbell says. "How do you propose to do it?"

Mrs. Ramsdale looks back toward the ilex grove and sees that Tom Quinn has also disappeared. It's as if the garden has suddenly swallowed up the two men. "I can do nothing, Mr. Campbell," she says, "but you can."

"But why me?"

"I attended one of Miss Blackwell's séances in Baden-Baden and spoke to several other of her *clientele*. She always insists that gentlemen alternate with ladies within her circle. She claims that the complementary energy of male and female produces a *charged* atmosphere. Milo Latham has already said that he won't be back tonight in time to participate, and I believe I can make sure that my amanuensis sits on the opposite side of the table, so that leaves you and Signore Lantini on either side of the medium."

"And what do you propose I do?"

"At the séance I attended, the chief effect of the evening was the appearance of disembodied hands floating above the table. It's her signature. The hands stray about the table, fondling the sitters in a most lascivious manner because, Miss Blackwell claims, her spirit guide is a blind Indian maiden who must touch the faces of the sitters in order to trust them. After this undignified groping, the Indian spirit guide breaks out into the most uncivilized whoops—" She stops, having noticed that Mr. Campbell has gone as white as the paint on his brush. "It's all a sham, of course, you mustn't be taken in. Miss Blackwell is very talented, I will admit, but her talents consist of ventriloquism and legerdemain. In other words, she has the fingers of a pickpocket and the stage talents of a music hall performer—which is where she appeared in her younger days."

Mr. Campbell's look of fear is replaced with a censorious expression. "A music hall performer! Here at Bosco!" His eyes scan the hillside as if he expected to see the Muse statues lift their skirts and break into a spirited cancan. What Mrs. Ramsdale notices, doing her own survey of the garden, is that the Italian has reappeared on the east side of the Pegasus fountain. How, she wonders, did he get to the other side of the garden without crossing the fountain allée? And where has Tom gotten to? "But why not just tell Mrs. Latham of her history?" Campbell demands of her, drawing her attention back to himself. "Surely she would never have allowed her here if she knew she'd appeared on the stage."

"You underestimate the power of a mother's grief, and"—Mrs. Ramsdale takes a step closer and, though she has already been speaking in hushed tones, lowers her voice even more to demonstrate that she is taking Mr. Campbell to a new level of confidence—"as much as I love Aurora and revere her dedication to the arts, there are times when I fear that she is willing to forgive too much in the name of art. Now, if Miss Blackwell were an artist"—here she allows her gaze to drift admiringly over Campbell's portrait, suggesting the gulf that exists between genuine art and the kind of rude theatrics practiced by entertainers such as Corinth Blackwell—"I'd be the first to forgive the eccentricities and the irregularities of her upbringing. I've heard it said, by the way, that the reason she is able to so convincingly reproduce an Indian guide is that she herself is a half-caste."

"No!"

Mrs. Ramsdale shrugs. "I think it's quite possible, but that's not what's really important. We both want to protect our patron, but more than that, I think there's something larger at stake here." Mrs. Ramsdale lifts her eyes to the garden spread out below them—to the water cascading down the central fountain allée, the white marble statues glistening in the sun—and then finishes by resting her eyes on the painted moonlit garden in the background of Campbell's portrait. "If Aurora's vision of Bosco as a haven for true artists is to be fulfilled, we can't allow it to become a circus of freaks and mountebanks." She picks up a tube of white paint from Campbell's paint box and slips it into the painter's pocket. "I believe that the spirit guide's hands belong to Miss Blackwell. That during the séance she somehow manages to slip her hands free of the circle to roam among the guests. Perhaps she does it with a false set of gloves. So, if you were able to smear a bit of white paint on Miss Blackwell's hands . . ."

"Won't she notice the feel of paint on my hands?"

"You can say you've just used some hand cream to ease your chapped skin. In fact I'll make a show of loaning you some. At the worst, she'd be afraid of using her hands and then the séance will be 'a blank' and Aurora will think she's unable to contact the children. But if she does use her hands, the evidence of her touch will be all over the room. When we turn on the lights, we'll unmask her duplicity and Aurora will ask her to leave in the morning. What do you say, Mr. Campbell? Shall we do it for the sake of Aurora and Bosco?"

Corinth follows Aurora up the west stairs, trying to regain her equilibrium. It's been years since she had a spell like the one she just had in the breakfast room. As a child she had them quite frequently. In fact, it was her spells that led her to her life as a medium.

The first time it happened she was six years old, sitting at the kitchen table while her mother and two other women from the Vly, Mary Two Tree and Wanda White Cloud, played cards and smoked their pipes, which meant it was a night her father was out, because he objected to the sight of women smoking. A dirty Indian habit, he called it. Corinth loved the smell of the women's pipes, though, an altogether different smell from what the men smoked. The women used an herb that her mother gathered from the edges of the cranberry bogs when they traveled in the summer to visit her people at Barktown, the settlement on the Big

Vly, the marshy lands west of the Sacandaga River. The smell reminded her of the way the grass smelled when the men from Barktown burnt the fields for autumn hunting, the smoke mingling with the fogs that rose over the marshes and bogs.

Her mother had been the daughter of an Iroquois chief. She left Barktown to marry the white logger named Mike Blackwell. They came to this mill town just before Corinth was born, after Mike had broken his leg on a log drive on the Sacandaga. A curse, some of the other rivermen said, for marrying an Indian. But in the stories the Barktown women told, it was the Indian women who were cursed for the lovers they chose.

Mary Two Tree told a story about the daughter of a chief who was planning to marry a white man. When the chief found out, he poled himself and his daughter out into the bogs on a spruce log raft and then, after binding himself to his daughter with leather thongs, toppled them both into the bog. People said that when you heard a loon calling across Cranberry Bog on a foggy night, it was really the voice of the drowned girl.

"At least she died with her father and so her spirit was not alone on its journey to the Sky World," Wanda White Cloud said. "Better than the girl who lay with a French missionary. When he learned she was pregnant, he ran away. She was so ashamed she ran to Indian Point and threw herself over the cliff. My cousin, Sam Pine, said he was hunting for deer in the woods by Indian Point two winters ago when a fog suddenly arose out of the ground and out of nowhere stepped the prettiest and saddest-looking girl he'd ever seen. He called to her, but she walked away. He followed her right up to the edge of the cliff and nearly fell over. They say she prowls the woods looking for young men to lead to their deaths and that if you ever see a fog rising by the Point, you'd best head the other way."

There seemed to be a fog in the kitchen, so heavy was the smoke from the women's pipes. The smoke and the talk of spirits made Corinth light-headed, so that the edges of things began to blur. She watched as the blue of her mother's gingham dress began to bleed out onto her white apron, like blueberries staining white milk, and then Corinth was suddenly rising up, looking down on her own body and the bodies of the three women sitting around the table, her spirit carried upward on a plume of the sweet smoke. The smoke from up there was like a light frost lying on top of everything—clear enough for her to see through but making everything seem separate and faraway and close all at the same time. She could see the bald spot on the top of Mary Two Tree's scalp, where a hank of hair had gotten pulled out by a threader at the glove factory where she worked before coming to the lumber mill. She could see the cards in Wanda White Cloud's hands—a two and a six of spades, an eight and a three of clubs, and a jack of hearts—and she watched while Wanda raised the bid and Mary folded her cards down on the table.

Just like Wanda White Cloud to bluff, Corinth thought. Her mother always said that Wanda White Cloud would tell a lie when the truth would do. *I've got to tell Mama,* she thought, and the thought, as if it were a lead sinker, dragged her right back down into her bones—so fast and hard she gasped as if the wind had been knocked right out of her.

"Have you been into the molasses again, Cory, and choked yourself?" her mother asked.

She shook her head and then, climbing into the warmth of her mother's lap because her whole body felt cold, like a coal stove that's been left unlit all summer long, whispered into her mother's ear, "Wanda doesn't have any cards that match, Mama, you can beat her easy."

She felt her mother stiffen and was afraid she'd made her angry, but when she looked up, she saw her mother studying her the way she did when she thought she was sick. She touched a hand to Corinth's brow and Corinth leaned into it, hungry for its warmth.

"You feel cold, child. Go sit by the fire."

And then her mother met Wanda's bet and raised her two bits. When she put down her cards, Wanda turned around in her chair and looked at Corinth long and hard with her black eyes, and Corinth, even though she was crouched right next to the fire, felt a cold breeze blow right through her . . . as if she were still outside her body and Wanda White Cloud had sent a wind to scatter her spirit to the four corners of the earth.

Later when she was in bed her mother came into her room and, sitting on the edge of Corinth's mattress, asked her how she'd known what Wanda's hand was. Had she sneaked under the table and peeked? Corinth explained how she'd risen above the table with the smoke. She didn't think her mother would believe her, but she did.

"Women of our people have been able to do this before," she said, smoothing the woolen blankets across Corinth's chest. "I had an aunt once who the people called Find-Anything because whenever anyone lost something, she could rise up out of her body and go find it. At first, she used her gift for important things like finding where the deer were grazing in the hunting season or where the best berries were growing in the spring, but then people would ask her to find a lost sewing needle or a child's toy and then there were those who wanted her to spy on a straying husband or a wife when she went to the village to trade. Her spirit left its body so often that one day it couldn't find its way back to her body. Find-Anything became Can't-Find-Her-Way-Home. She was like an old tree that's rotted inside—and smelled bad, too." Her mother wrinkled her nose. Then she lowered her head so that Corinth could hear her whisper. "And that's not the worst thing that can happen. Sometimes, when your spirit is outside of your body, another spirit may try to enter your body and steal it from you. That's why I named you after the place on the earth where you were born. So your spirit would always know where to come back to. Still, you must use this gift for important things—not for games or tricking people."

"But how can I stop it?" Corinth asked, terrified at the thought of ending up like Find-Anything, a piece of rotting wood or, worse, losing her body to an evil spirit.

Her mother took out a soft leather pouch stitched with blue beads in the shape of a turtle from her pocket and opened it to show Corinth the sharp-smelling herbs inside and the bone needle punched through the leather flap.

"When you start to see the edges of things blurring, prick your finger with this needle and rub some of this rosemary under your nose. It will keep your spirit tied to your body"—she tapped the beaded turtle on the pouch's flap—"just as the mud stuck to Turtle's back to make the land."

The needle and the rosemary had worked—at least most of the time—until her father had found out about her "gift" and thought of ways he could make money with it.

Now, as Corinth climbs the last flight of stairs to the attic nursery, she draws from her pocket a shard of blue china from the broken teacup. The color of the china where the blue has bled into the white is the color of ghosts. At least it's the color of that poor wisp of a thing haunting Indian Point, whom she saw later, many years after hearing Wanda White Cloud's story. She slips the shard into her glove until its sharp point presses into the palm of her hand. The last thing she wants at the séance tonight is to encounter any real spirits.

Chapter Seven

"I can show them to you, if you want." He pushes aside the pile of blueprints that lie between us and moves closer to me.

"Show what to me?" I ask, rising from the bed. The springs make a sound like a small animal's cry when I get up. I rest my hand on one of the bedposts to steady myself and notice what look like claw marks in the soft birch wood.

"The tunnels. The passage goes straight down from this room into the basement and from there into the entrance to the underground tunnels." He's already moving toward the bookcase and feeling along the side for the hidden hinge.

"I don't know," I say. "I'm not much for tunnels and mazes, and I can't imagine they'd be very safe after all these years."

"I've already been down in them," David says, swinging the bookcase open into the dark passage, "and I can give you my word as an architect that they're structurally sound."

I wonder if a *landscape* architect is really qualified to make that kind of judgment. Isn't it a bit like having a PhD in literature give you a medical checkup? I'm thinking of a polite but firm way of saying no when David Fox dangles the final enticement.

"Think of how important this could be for your book. It's the key to the mystery of what happened that summer, I'm sure of it. And no one else knows about it—not even Beth Graham."

The basement at Bosco, more like a cave than part of a house, is hewn out of the living rock. The walls gleam damply where David points his flashlight.

"I thought the springs were all dried up," I say. "Are you sure these tunnels won't flood while we're in them?"

"Here," David says, ignoring my question, "hold the flashlight for a minute. I think this is the entrance."

"I thought you said you'd gone down in them already?"

"I did. It's just that Aurora went out of her way to keep the tunnels a secret." David is running his fingers up and down the surface of the dark, slimy rock. I can't imagine how he can bear touching it, but then, he must be used to getting his hands dirty. His fingers pause on a ridge in the rock, dig into a shallow crevice, and a piece of the wall suddenly swings open. The flashlight reveals a narrow passage behind it.

"Okay," David says, "this time you hold the

flashlight to light the way and I'll walk ahead—just in case."

"Just in case what?"

"The tunnels pitch forward sometimes, and if you aren't careful, you can slip." He turns to me and smiles, trying, no doubt, to look reassuring. The flashlight shining up onto his face creates a very different effect; he looks more like a demon about to descend into the maw of Hades. He must guess from my expression how he looks, because as I follow him into the tunnel, I hear him intoning in Italian, *"Lasciate ogni speranza, voi ch'entrate."*

"Very funny," I say, recognizing the warning on the gates of Dante's hell: Abandon all hope, ye who enter.

The tunnels aren't so bad, though. They're wider than I would have thought and neatly lined on both sides with slate. Copper pipes run above our heads. David tells me at several junctures what part of the fountain he thinks a specific pipe is attached to. Only when we have made half a dozen turns does it occur to me to worry about getting lost.

"It's the same as the box-hedge maze," he tells me. "All roads lead to Rome. As long as you keep going downhill, you'll get out."

"You mean there's an exit," I say, relieved that we won't have to go back up through the tunnels.

"I thought you would have figured that out by now. Here—" he says, pointing up at a hole in the ceiling through which I can see a tiny chink of light, "this is the pipe we uncovered that day I met you in the garden. One of the *giochi d'acqua*."

"So that means we're right near—right below—the Pegasus fountain."

"Exactly. This large pipe here must be right under its foot. It would have sent up a jet that reached twenty feet into the air."

I look up, imagining the enormous marble statue directly above our heads, the winged horse's heavy hoof stamping the ground, and feel suddenly dizzy. I can hear the rush of my own blood in my ears and then a voice.

"The ghostly spring still murmurs; water moves," I hear, "with atom-knowledge old as heat and light."

"It's Zalman," I whisper, feeling a little better when I identify the poet's voice. "He must be working on a new sonnet." David and I stand in silence listening to the poem. It feels as if we're standing in church listening to a service.

> *The ghostly spring still murmurs; water moves*
> *with atom-knowledge old as heat and light*
> *along the grotto's ancient limestone grooves,*
> *its soft caress of stone concealed from sight*
> *but rapturous as any human love,*
> *a soothing blood for ancient bones of Earth*
> *that never ceases flowing. Listen, now:*
> *a sudden bubbling whirl, as if the birth*
> *of yet another passageway in stone,*
> *quick-spins and spills directly overhead,*
> *arousing dread as timbers whine and moan.*

Yet somehow reassuring; time has wed
this water, rock, and dark moist soil of Earth
in silver-tumbling merge, ceaseless rebirth."

Although the poem is lovely, the idea of an ancient spring eroding the rock above us is hardly reassuring. I shine the flashlight ahead, looking for a way out, but the beam hits a solid wall that curves into an apse. It looks exactly like the bulbous dead ends I remember from those diner place-mat mazes.

"I thought you said there was a way out down here."

"There is—but first I want to show you something." He climbs up on a narrow ledge that is carved into the wall and waves for me to join him. There's a small window—way too small for us to get through—covered by a metal grate. David presses his eye to it and then moves so I can look. "It would be better if there were more light in there, but you can still make it out."

I press my face up to the grate. At first I can't see anything, but as my eyes adjust I can just make out a dark circular space beyond the grate illuminated by tiny spots of light. Then a breeze blows through the grotto and the lights waver and swell, sparkling on the enamel tiles that cover the walls and ceiling of the dome-shaped room. The light of a dozen candles are reflected in a pool of water.

"It's the grotto," David says. "Aurora had Lantini add this little window so she could see inside. Doesn't it make you wonder what went on in there that she wanted to see so badly?"

I nod, speechless at the glowing spectacle. It's like looking into one of those sugar Easter eggs (the kind my mother would never let me get because white sugar was "poison"). The more I stare, the brighter the scene grows, the lights dancing off the water and sending ripples onto the walls, so that the room seems to be moving, the enameled sea creatures and mermaids on the walls writhing as if alive, the whole room pulsing, keeping beat with the lapping of the water against the stone. It feels as if something is trapped inside, some creature trying to escape. I can hear it, something scraping at the stone just below the grate as if it is crawling up the wall, its fingers prying deep into the rock—

I pull away from the grate, stepping into air. David catches me before I can fall to the ground. "There's something . . . someone in there," I say. "I saw a hand . . ."

"Really? I don't know how you can see anything in the dark. Let me see."

He looks through the grate and then looks back at me. "I don't see anything. It must have been a shadow."

"No," I say. "I saw it in the candlelight."

"Candlelight?" David asks, his face blank. "What candles?" He looks through the grate and then pulls me toward it so I can look, too. I hold back, but he moves me as firmly and gently as if I were a tree he was replanting. When I look this time, all I see is a bare stone room, dim and dry and still.

"What did you see?" David asks.

"Nothing," I tell him. "It was just a trick of the light.

I thought for a moment there were candles—" And water, and enamel sea creatures, and a hand grasping the stone ledge below the grate. "Can we get out of here now?" I feel, suddenly, as though if I don't get into the air, I might start scratching at the stone walls.

"It's a bit of a scramble. The tunnel is partly collapsed."

"Another tunnel? Aren't we already in a tunnel?" I try to keep my voice from shaking, but the word *collapsed* has completely unnerved me.

"I guess you can say it's a tunnel within a tunnel. Someone went to a lot of trouble to conceal it; I wouldn't have found it at all if I didn't have Lantini's plan." David steps off the ledge and kneels on the stone floor, shining his flashlight along the bottom edge of the wall. When he rests the flashlight on the ledge and starts pulling out bricks, I kneel beside him and help pile the bricks to one side. If necessary, I will dig my way out of here.

"Did you put all these back after you went through before?" I ask when we've dislodged a few dozen bricks. The bottom ones, I notice, are damp.

"Uh, I haven't exactly been through. I wanted to recheck Lantini's plans first, and it's quite clear that the underground passage was intended to reach the grotto."

"Intended? But you said before that Lantini left a lot of the garden unfinished. What if he never completed the tunnel?"

"Don't worry; I'll go first," David says. "If I get

through, you'll know it's wide enough for you. You're awfully slim for a tall girl."

I can feel David's eyes traveling along the length of my body as if his gaze were a warm current. The sensation is distracting enough that I fail to object fast enough to David's plan to stop him. He's down on the ground, wriggling through the narrow opening below the ledge before I can point out the flaw. What if he gets trapped in the tunnel? I'll never find my way back to the house through the winding maze to get help. I'll be alone underground . . . alone but for whatever *thing* was trying to scratch its way out of the grotto.

I take a deep breath, willing myself to forget that image. Like the candles, it was only a mirage, I tell myself. I pick up the flashlight and aim it under the ledge just in time to see the soles of David's feet disappear into the black hole. "David?" I call. "Are you through?" When there's no answer, I call again, my voice echoing shrilly in the tight space, the light from the flashlight trembling along the dirt walls like a firefly trapped in a jar. And then David's face appears at the end of the passage, graven as stone in the flashlight's beam.

"It's a bit of a squeeze, but I'll help you through," he says. "Hand me the flashlight first."

I do what he says and then, closing my eyes, flatten myself on the ground and crawl through the tunnel, willing myself not to think about the weight of stone and dirt above my head. The ground is damp and covered with some kind of slime. With my ear practically pressed to the ground I imagine I can hear beneath me the sound of running water. The ghost of the old spring Zalman wrote about in his poem whispering with its last breath in a voice so seductive that for a moment I pause to listen. But then I feel something crawling down the back of my neck and push forward as fast as I can, not waiting for David's hands to pull me out or pausing when something sharp digs into my thigh.

"Okay, okay, easy now," David says, half lifting me onto the stone bench. "You're through."

I know he means *through the tunnel,* but for a moment I understand him to mean, *You're finished, you're done,* and I realize that the panic I felt in the tunnel came less from the touch of the spider than from the sudden conviction that the hand scrabbling on the stone wall and the voice speaking to me from beneath the ground belonged to someone who'd been buried alive.

"You really *are* afraid of the dark," David says. "I guess I shouldn't have brought you down here."

"No," I say, "it's okay. I wanted to see it." I look around the grotto. It's not really all that dark. A wedge of light comes in from a narrow opening to the right of the bench. I can see traces of enamel on the ceiling and patches of white that might be paint or salt deposits. The basin that once held water from the fountain is covered in soft green moss. "And I'm trying to get over being afraid of the dark."

"Did something happen?" he asks.

"It's because of the séance," I tell him.

"Séance?"

"You see, my mother was—still is, I guess—a medium."

"Really? You mean, like, for a living?"

"Well, she claims not to charge for 'spiritual services,' but 'contributions are always welcome' and she lets it be understood that the spirits are always more willing in an atmosphere of open-mindedness and generosity. She also makes some money selling herbal salves and lotions and honey from the bees she keeps."

"You're kidding."

"Do I look like I'm kidding?" I ask, allowing myself to look as miserable as I feel. I've always dreaded this moment with any new friend, but especially with men. I remember that when I told Richard Scully what my mother did, he was fascinated at first. *Good material*, he called it. But after my story won the contest and the agent asked me to write a novel about a medium, he said that I was in danger of losing control of my objectivity. *People will think you believe in all that crap.* I decided after that not to tell anyone about Mira's "profession" or the peculiar way I grew up. Today, it seems, I've gone far underground to avoid admitting to this particular man why I dread the dark and yet it hasn't been far enough. When he doesn't answer, I take a deep breath and, staring up at the rounded dome ceiling, tell him the story.

"You see, I grew up in a town where everyone's a spiritualist of some sort. It's called Lily Dale, and my family has lived there for over a hundred years, although by 'family' you have to understand I mean the matriarchy. Somehow, men never seem to linger long with the Brooks women; I never knew my father or my grandfather or any of my uncles, and my mother and my grandmother acted as if conception were a matter of mixing the right herbs and roots in their Crock-Pots, which, for all I know, is how I was conceived—in a witch's cauldron from eye of newt and a shot of wheat-grass juice. Anyway, when I was twelve, my mother said I could start attending the 'spirit circles' to see if I had 'the gift,' as they call it. I only made it through one . . . apparently I fainted. For months after that I wouldn't sleep in the dark or stay alone in the house, which, in a town like Lily Dale, was considered eccentric behavior."

"Do you remember why you fainted?"

I take another deep breath, wishing there were more air in the grotto. Is this what Richard Scully meant by "mining my deepest pain"? What I had wanted to ask him was, how would I know if I dug too far? Even miners took canaries with them to test the viability of the air down in the deepest shafts. I look at David and wonder if he would be able to categorize what I saw at that séance the way he'd named the ghost orchid in the maze.

"No," I say, deciding not to confide everything all at once, because there is no reassuring Latin term for the thing I saw at my mother's spirit circle, no scientific explanation, either, for the voices I hear or the hand I saw from behind the grate. "I couldn't remember any-thing. My mother wanted to put me into a 'spirit trance' so I could recover what happened, but I've never let her."

"I don't blame you. It's bad enough that she let you attend that séance in the first place. No offense to your mother, but it seems irresponsible." He slips his arm around my shoulder and, after a moment's hesitation, I lean into him, feeling how solid he is, how . . . of this world. Not a very good canary, really, because he'd be breathing long after I succumbed to poisonous vapors, but he'd be good at pulling a girl out of a collapsing mine. I like how his fingernails are rimmed with soil and how he smells, faintly, of shaving lotion, a clean, citrusy smell with none of the cloying sweetness that I still smell when I think of that séance.

"No offense taken; I agree entirely. I couldn't wait to get out of Lily Dale. I would never raise a child there."

"So you don't believe in any of that stuff?"

I turn to answer and realize how close his face is to mine, his dark unshaven cheek just inches away. I can feel my heart pounding, a sound like beating wings, like something caged trying to get out. David's arm tightens around my shoulders and as he pulls me toward him over the rough stone bench I feel something sharp pierce my thigh and I cry out.

"What?" he asks, pulling away, the moment broken.

I reach down and pull something out of the cloth of my jeans. Turning it over in my hand, I see that it's a broken piece of blue-and-white china, the edges of its pattern blurred, as if the china pattern had faded with time.

"It must have gotten caught in my jeans at breakfast," I say, "from when Nat's cup broke."

At the mention of Nat's name David stiffens and stands up. "I guess we should get going," he says. "I don't want to keep you from your writing."

"No," I say, getting up, not sure if I'm sorry that the kiss was interrupted. Although I am drawn to David, the last thing I need is to get involved with someone here. "I guess I should get back, but thank you for showing me this . . . It's . . ." I turn around in a circle, looking for a word to describe the grotto. My gaze falls on a chink in the stone above the bench. "Is that the grate?" I ask. "You really can't see it from this side."

"I guess that was the point," David says, already heading out the side passage. Instead of following him, I step up onto the bench and run my hands along the stone wall until I've found the opening in the rock. I press my face up against it, but the tunnel on the other side is too dark to see anything. As I move away I notice something embedded in the stone, a chip of paint or fragment of shell. I lift it up and see that it's neither of those things: it's the thin white crescent of a fingernail.

Chapter Eight

"As you can see, the nursery is rather lonely for poor Alice. She does little but draw all day long."

The girl is seated on a wide window seat beneath the steeply sloping attic roof, her drawing pad balanced on her knees. She doesn't bother to raise her head when her mother and her guest (the woman whose long dark hair and slanted eyes remind her of the captive Indian maidens in her own pictures) come into the room.

The room, though low-ceilinged, is huge, stretching almost the length and breadth of the house; only a small portion of the west side has been sectioned off into a separate room. Along the north wall four narrow beds are lined up like cots in a dormitory. Corinth shivers, remembering the year she spent working in the glove factory in Gloversville, sharing an unheated attic dormitory with a dozen other factory girls. She walks to the south-facing windows to warm herself in the sun and catches a glimpse of Frank Campbell, standing with his easel set up on the far edge of the terrace, talking to Mrs. Ramsdale. The novelist's mauve peau de soie dress

soaks up the early morning light like a deep, unlit pool—
an image of stagnant water that rises in Corinth's mind
and threatens to seep over the sunlit garden.

Turning from the window, she sees that Aurora has
also been observing the two figures on the terrace.

"Here are all the children's toys," she says, indicating the shelves below the windows. "As you can see,
there's plenty to choose from, although much of their
playthings are sadly worn. Heaven knows, I tried my
best to impress upon them the importance of taking care
of their possessions, but they were always leaving their
things scattered abroad willy-nilly."

Corinth looks down at the now neatly arrayed
shelves and sees that indeed many of the book spines are
tattered and broken and the dress-up clothes folded in
their baskets are stained and frayed. One basket is full
of broken toys, a tin gun missing its trigger, a hatchet
without a handle, and an adult-sized bow with a
quiverful of featherless arrows. It's not the hard use
that seems sad to Corinth, though, it's the present
neatness, the way the well-used toys have been so
lifelessly corralled onto their shelves and into baskets.
Even the rocking horse—so often ridden that its brown
fur is worn down to its wooden frame—looks like an old
dray horse waiting to be taken away and made into glue.
Corinth touches the horse's head, which is festooned
with feathers and pink ribbons, just to set it into motion.

"That's Belle," Alice says, looking up from her drawing pad at the sound of the horse's runners creaking on
the wide-planked floors. "She was Cynthia's favorite."

Corinth crouches down so that she's at eye level with the horse. She can see herself in its glass eye. "Are these Cynthia's ribbons on her bridle?" Corinth asks.

"Well, they certainly didn't belong to James or Tam," Alice says.

"Don't be rude, Alice," Aurora says. "Answer Miss Blackwell's questions civilly."

"Yes, Miss Blackwell," Alice recites in a singsong rhythm, "the ribbons belonged to my sister Cynthia. Pink was her favorite color. She was buried with a pink ribbon in her hair, but I imagine that ribbon isn't such a pretty color now."

"That's enough, Alice. If you're going to speak like that, I'll send you to the storage room." She points toward the door at the west end of the attic.

Corinth sees the girl's look of defiance instantly melt into fear.

"Please, Mrs. Latham," Corinth says, "I'm sure Alice can be of help to me in identifying each child's favorite plaything. I think I'll take one of these ribbons for Cynthia—"

"Take the one with the green stripe down the middle; that was her favorite," Alice says, swinging her legs down from the window ledge and hopping to the floor. "I can tell you what the boys liked best, too."

Perhaps it is gratitude for being spared the punishment of the storage room that turns Alice into a suddenly pliable child. The look she gives Corinth is the first she's seen free of spite. She almost forgives her the "stinking savage" remark she made yesterday. After all, what kind of life is this for a child, living in this cavernous attic surrounded by the relics of her dead siblings?

It's these relics, though, that seem to bring out the child's best side as she confides to Corinth each one's provenance.

"James made these arrows himself," she says, drawing a sharp-tipped arrow—the only one with its feathers intact—from its birch-bark quiver. "He even found the feathers on a hunting trip with Papa up at the camp. They're quail feathers . . . Tam carved this bear out of wood and gave it to James as an 'animal totem' to help him on hunting trips. Tam loved Indian things . . . see, he made this beaded headband for me."

Throughout Alice's recitation Aurora stands at the window, her arms clasped behind her back, looking out at the gardens. She doesn't offer any anecdotes of her own or suggest any objects that she remembers as precious to her dead children. Her face is pale and impassive in the clear morning light, but Corinth can see a tightening in her jaw and the knuckles of her clasped hands are white. Perhaps, Corinth thinks, seeing her dead children's playthings disturbed is too painful for her.

"I'll take the ribbon for Cynthia," Corinth says, coming to stand beside Aurora at the window, "and the arrow for James. But for Tam . . . well, all of the things Alice has shown me are things he made for someone else. Since they're things he gave away, they might not have any *attraction* for his spirit."

Aurora turns from the window with a look so nakedly full of pain in her blue eyes—*flow blue eyes*, as Corinth has begun to think of them—that Corinth has to look away. She looks down at the terrace, where Mrs. Ramsdale is slipping a tube of paint into Mr. Campbell's pocket. When she looks back up, Aurora is removing something from her own pocket: a length of soft leather that unwinds as she holds it up. It makes Corinth think of the leather straps that bind the statue of the Indian maiden in the garden, but then she sees that it's a necklace. The leather is wrapped around an ancient arrowhead carved from bone.

"Tam found this in the garden," Aurora says, holding the necklace up until Corinth puts her hand under the dangling arrowhead. "He wore it every day of his life. Will it do?"

When Corinth nods, Aurora lets the leather strap coil into the palm of her hand. The moment she closes her hand over the carved bone, a red veil washes over her eyes and her ears are filled with the sound of her own blood rushing in her veins. She squeezes the sharp bone in her palm to keep from losing consciousness, watching Aurora's lips moving without hearing a word.

"What?" Corinth says over the roaring in her ears. "I'm sorry, I didn't hear what you said."

"I was saying that Signore Lantini is making some adjustments to the water pressure in the fountains. I wanted them to be at their best tonight when we have the séance, but something has been blocking the flow from the main spring. I asked him to have more water pumped up from another spring, but I'm afraid he's overdone it a bit."

Corinth looks out the window and sees that water is coursing down the fountain allée like a mountain stream after the snow melts; it is spurting up from beneath Pegasus's foot like a geyser. The gentle lapping and gurgling of the fountains has been replaced with a torrent of floodwater, and for a moment Corinth could swear she feels the house trembling on its foundation, as if it were about to be swept away. Then the force of the water in the fountains subsides altogether and the rushing in her ears becomes a dull hum.

Aurora sighs. "Oh, dear, I'm afraid one of the pumps must have broken. Let's hope he gets it fixed by tonight's séance in the grotto."

"The grotto?" Corinth asks, surprised. It's the first she's heard of this plan. "Why there?"

"Because I think that's where the children have gone. They liked to hide there from their nurse when it was time to come in to dinner. Maybe they're hiding there now. Surely you felt their presence—" Aurora pauses until Corinth looks at her. "Oh, I forgot, you haven't been to the grotto yet."

After dinner the servants carry a folding table and chairs and candles down to the grotto. Candles have been lit all along the fountain allée to illuminate the path down the hill, and each guest has been given a candle to hold.

Aurora, who has asked Corinth to walk with her a little ahead of the other guests, carries a candelabra made from the spreading antlers of a moose. When they reach the bottom of the hill, Aurora stops and steps into a small niche carved out of ilex and motions for Corinth to follow her. Before she does, though, Corinth looks up the hill to see the candlelit procession—like a swarm of fireflies descending from a castle. She imagines the statue of Jacynta, hidden in the boxwood maze, his sword drawn and ready to do battle with the regiment of lights. Then she follows Aurora.

"Have you seen my Egeria?" Aurora asks, holding the candelabra aloft to light the little niche.

Corinth thinks for a moment that she must be referring to an errant housemaid, but then she notices the small statue nestled in the ilex: a slim girl drooping over a marble basin filled with water.

"She was a nymph who married Numa, the second king of Rome. When he died she wept so inconsolably that the gods took pity on her and turned her into a spring. I found her this winter, after the children died, in an old villa in Tivoli, serving as a feeding trough for the family's chickens. When I saw her I thought, yes, that's what almost happened to me, my grief nearly melted me to water. But seeing something so lovely— that spoke so eloquently to my grief, I felt an easing of my pain, as if my spirit had been lifted out of my body and freed of its pain. Do you know what I mean?"

Corinth nods, startled by a description so like what she experienced only today. It's not what she expected from Aurora Latham, and she feels a swelling of compassion for the woman that's not entirely welcome. "Yes, yes, I think I do," she says.

"I determined then that my home here at Bosco would be more than just a tribute to the children. It would be a tribute to the power of art to console grief. I want to do more than collect some statues; I want to bring artists together to be inspired by this place so that they, too, can produce works that will comfort others in their grief. Mr. Campbell called me his Muse of Water last night," she says, pulling a folded sheet of pale gray paper out of her pocket. "See, he gave me a letter today in which he addresses me as such"—Aurora holds up the sheet so Corinth can see the salutation, but it is folded so she can see nothing else—"and implores me not to conduct this séance. But he doesn't understand the necessity. Look, look around you! Can't you see them?"

For a moment Corinth thinks that she means the other guests, who are walking down the hill, but then she sees from the way that Aurora's eyes are darting all over the garden, into the recessed niches and dark groves and the candlelit paths, that she has something else in mind.

"The artists who will come here! The writers and painters and musicians! The very air is thick with them! They've come to drink of the spring, but the spring must be cleansed for them first."

Aurora's voice is so urgent, so filled with conviction, that Corinth half expects to see a crowd of ghostly supplicants kneeling at Egeria's basin, lapping up springwater, but the little nymph is alone, her head bowed so deeply over her basin that she looks as if she'll drop into the water at any moment. Corinth feels a sudden unreasoning pity for the lifeless marble girl, wrested from her home in Italy and transplanted in this foreign soil.

"So you mean to collect artists as well as statues," Corinth says, before she can consider the way her words might be construed.

She can sense the other woman stiffen, her limbs in the moonlight becoming as immobile as those of the marble statue. "I suppose you could put it like that," Aurora says, her voice cold. She holds the candelabra up to light the way out of the niche, but as Corinth is passing her, Aurora turns back to look at the statue of the nymph and says, "Another interesting thing about Egeria. Her spring was sacred to the vestal virgins. If one of them broke their vows of chastity, they were condemned to death. Do you know how they were killed?"

"No," Corinth says. "How?"

"They were walled up in a tomb," Aurora says, "and left to die. They were buried alive."

When they come out of the niche, Mrs. Norris is standing in front of the statue of the river god, holding up a lantern to light her mistress's way into the grotto.

The light etches deep grooves into the housekeeper's face, making it look as fiercely weathered as the face of the Indian brave representing the Sacandaga.

"Will you be attending the séance, Mrs. Norris?" Corinth asks, addressing the housekeeper directly for the first time since she's arrived at Bosco.

"She'll be standing outside," says a voice from behind Corinth. Turning, she sees that it's Mrs. Ramsdale, leaning on Tom Quinn's arm as she comes down the steps. "So that we'll be certain that the séance is uncorrupted. I suggested as much to Mrs. Latham."

Corinth bows her head to Mrs. Ramsdale. "An excellent idea," she says. "We wouldn't want the circle corrupted." She gestures for the novelist to precede her into the grotto, but Mrs. Ramsdale suddenly realizes she's dropped her vial of smelling salts and enlists Tom Quinn to look for it. As she crouches on the ground Corinth catches once again Mrs. Ramsdale's peculiar scent—a combination of Aqua di Parma, laudanum, and something else that Corinth recognizes as the reek of death—a corruption that springs from the woman's womb and spreads outward in a miasma so thick Corinth is overwhelmed by it and feels herself growing faint. Frank Campbell puts out a hand and steadies her as she precedes him and Signore Lantini into the grotto.

A table has been set up so that the stone bench serves as one of the six seats. Corinth sits there, directly across from Aurora Latham, and the men take the chairs on either side of her. When Frank Campbell is seated, he crosses his hands on top of the table and it immediately begins to rock.

"Ah, already the spirits make themselves known!" Lantini exclaims.

"I'm afraid it's a waste of your engineering talents, signore," Aurora says, "but perhaps you can find some way to steady the table."

"*Certo!*" Lantini flashes a quick smile and disappears beneath the table.

Corinth turns to Frank Campbell. "I hope you don't mind being seated next to me, Mr. Campbell. Sometimes the vibrations of the spirits are felt strongest by the sitter closest to the medium. There was a gentleman in Naples—a prince, in fact, of an old Neapolitan house—who complained that his hand was numb for a week after our séance. I wouldn't want to interfere with the progress of your marvelous portrait of Mrs. Latham."

Campbell's eyes cut across the table to where Mrs. Ramsdale is being helped into her chair by Tom Quinn, but she doesn't meet his look. Quinn does, though, with a curl of his upper lip as if he were amused at the medium's brazen attempt to frighten Campbell.

"Nonsense," Campbell says, his voice echoing in the domed space. "I am only afraid that my hands will be rough to you. The solvents I use to clean them are not very gentle . . ."

"Here, Mr. Campbell," Mrs. Ramsdale calls from across the table. "I promised you a bit of my hand cream when we spoke earlier." She passes a small jar to

Lantini, who passes it to Campbell. When he opens it, the grotto is instantly filled with the odor of roses. Instead of using the hand cream, though, he reaches into his pocket and squeezes a dab of white paint on his hand. When he looks up, he catches Aurora staring at him. It was foolish to write the letter, he realizes. Aurora is a proud woman and doesn't like her plans put into question. He only hopes that after the medium is unmasked, she will see that he was right.

"Mrs. Norris will stand guard at the entrance to the grotto so we won't be disturbed, Miss Blackwell," Aurora Latham announces. "Are we ready to begin?"

Before answering, Corinth lays on the table the pink and green ribbon, the bone arrowhead, and James's quail-feathered arrow. "Now, if everyone would please extinguish their candles—except for yours, Mrs. Latham. We can leave that one at the center of the table."

Aurora places the antlered candelabra at the center of the table—now steady, thanks to Lantini's adjustment to its legs—extinguishing all but one of its candles, which spreads a circle of light that just reaches the fingertips of the twelve hands spread out on the table. The rest of the grotto—the domed enameled ceiling, the rock walls, and the faces of the men and women seated around the table—recedes into the shadows.

"We'll join hands now," Corinth says, her disembodied voice seeming to float on the still air. "Remember, whatever happens, do not break the circle."

For a long time the only sound is the sound of water falling from the fountain above and around the grotto and lapping into the small pool inside the grotto. It's a sound, though, that contains a multitude of sounds within it. One could imagine voices, footsteps, or even music in the melodic gurgle and rush of the water . . . or a drumbeat, which the sitters, one by one, begin to hear above the sound of the water . . . a sound that seems to arise out of their own heartbeats, hardly noticeable at first but then drowning out every other sound. Then the beats grow louder and are joined by a high keening cry— like that of an animal or a woman in pain.

It is joined by another voice, coming from the place where Corinth sits, but unlike the medium's natural voice. "We are looking for the spirits of the three children. James, Cynthia, and Tam. They may have lost their way home. Their mother is waiting for them here; she wants them to know they can come home now."

"I won't be angry that you were hiding from me," Aurora says. "It's all right to come out now."

The sound of drums fades, and a wind rises in the *giardino segreto* outside the grotto, a high wind that whistles through the hedge maze and sounds, at one moment, like laughter, and the next, like weeping. Beneath that sound: a halting beat, not drums this time, but footsteps . . . only they're faltering, like the footsteps of someone whose feet have been bound.

The sound strikes such terror into Corinth's heart that she feels her spirit beating up against the walls of her body, like a firefly trapped in a jar, looking for a way out. She squeezes Tom's hand until the china shard embedded in her glove digs into her palm, but she doesn't even feel its point. She is rising above the table, passing through the domed ceiling of the grotto and moving through water, like a trout swimming upstream, fighting the current of the fountain . . . and then she's free, rising above the garden. Looking down, she can see the fountain allée and the terraces, the marble statues of the Muses glowing in the moonlight . . . but something is different. The clipped yews have burst out of their trimmed shapes, the ilex has grown wild and covers the hill in a thorny mass. The statues lie broken and what she thought were statues are actually ghostly shapes walking along the paths—the shades of Bosco's future artists that Aurora's little speech in Egeria's niche has summoned forth. She can see a pair of figures, pale and insubstantial as fog, walking through the maze, only the maze has turned into a thicket; the roses have gone wild and twined themselves into the shaggy boxwood hedges, twisting themselves into the shapes of women struggling to free themselves of their bonds . . . and she sees that they're all the same figure: the bound Indian girl who's limping along the overgrown paths, trying to find her way out.

"Ne'Moss-i-Ne," Corinth whispers, pulled back into her body by something brushing against her lips, something light and feathery as a kiss.

A strange giggle bubbles out of Aurora Latham. "It can't be. I made her up." But then something brushes against Aurora's face and her laugh turns into a scream.

Whether made up or real, dead or alive, something is moving through the hedge maze and getting closer. A gust of wind rushes into the grotto and blows out the candle. Like a trapped creature the wind scours the walls, shrieking into the niches set into the rock and scraping the tiles down onto the table.

A dampness spreads on the back of Mrs. Ramsdale's neck and slithers down her dress.

Something pulls Signore Lantini's mustache.

Frank Campbell feels hands all over him, tugging at his pockets. Once, when he was a student at the Academy in Rome, a band of child pickpockets assaulted him as he strolled through the Pincian Gardens, swarming over him just like this—like rats! Later he was ashamed to tell the carabinieri that he'd been robbed by children and instead made up a story about a gang of street thugs, knowing full well that the police officers knew he was lying. He feels that same shame now as the insidious fingers work their way down his waistcoat. He tries to fend them off, but his left arm has gone entirely numb. One of the little hands slides between his legs and, first gently, and then not, squeezes his testicles.

He opens his mouth to cry out, but the sound dies in his throat as a searing pain pierces through his chest.

All the while, Aurora Latham calls out, "James, Cynthia, Tam," repeating the names of her dead children like a prayer.

Then something flashes in the darkness. A match is struck, a candle lit, and a pool of light spreads out from the candelabra, which Tom Quinn is holding over Corinth. At first her eyes seem unfocused in the glare of the candlelight, but then, slowly, she comes back to herself and recognizes him.

The look she gives him makes his throat go dry.

He turns away, moving in a slow circle to shine the candlelight onto the grotto walls, but nothing is there. No one is in the grotto but the six sitters, all of whom, except Frank Campbell, who is leaning forward with his hands covering his face, stare back at him with glassy, frightened eyes.

"My God, look at the ceiling!" cries Signore Lantini.

They all look up at the domed ceiling above their heads. It's covered with white marks.

"They look like handprints," Tom Quinn says, climbing up onto the chair that he vacated and holding the candelabra as close as he can to the ceiling. Then he climbs down and moves to the back wall, where a trail of handprints snakes down to the stone bench.

"Look at her hand!" Mrs. Ramsdale cries, getting up from her seat and coming around the table on unsteady legs. She grabs Corinth's hand and holds it up so that everyone can see the smear of white paint on Corinth's glove. Tom reaches across Mrs. Ramsdale and takes Corinth's hand from her, pulling Corinth toward the wall and placing her hand next to one of the painted hands. He can feel her hand trembling under his and he can smell the rose water she uses to rinse her hair as she leans against him for support.

"The prints are much too small to be made by Miss

Blackwell," Signore Lantini says. "They appear to be children's hands."

"*My* children's hands!" Aurora says.

"I don't know about that," Tom says, "but I think I do know where the paint came from." Tom turns and holds the candelabra over Campbell's head. "It's no good, Mr. Campbell, I saw you dabbing your hand with paint when you were pretending to put on hand lotion."

Campbell remains motionless in his chair.

"The poor man's fainted," Mrs. Ramsdale says, her voice trembling now, not because of the fright the séance gave her but because she can see that Tom Quinn is still holding Corinth Blackwell's hand. And because she saw the look that passed between them before.

Lantini steps forward and grabs the painter's shoulders, giving them a firm shake, while Mrs. Ramsdale leans forward with her little vial of smelling salts. Campbell's head falls back limply, and Mrs. Ramsdale, dropping the vial to the floor, screams.

A tuft of feathers protrudes from the lapel of Mr. Campbell's evening jacket. It looks oddly decorative until Lantini moves the jacket's lapel aside to reveal the blood-soaked waistcoat underneath. The homemade arrow—James's arrow—has been driven clean through his chest.

PART TWO

Giochi d'Acqua

Chapter Nine

With November the skies over Bosco grow heavy and gray and the gardens draw in on themselves. In the overgrown hedges, seed pods, like small bells, rattle in the cold wind that sweeps down out of the north woods. The dried brush, instead of seeming sparser, feels thicker—a thicket of thorns woven by a malicious fairy to insulate us from the outside world. There are no phones in the main house, only in the office in the old gatehouse, and so our only contact with the outside world depends on the phone messages taken by Daria Tate.

The pink slips that haphazardly find their way into our lunch boxes, though, might as well be written in Sanskrit. I receive a message from my mother that reads, "The keys are in the alarm," which makes no sense because my mother owns neither an alarm system nor a car and there aren't even locks on the doors to her house. David gets a message about a job opening at the New York Botanical Garden a week after the job has been filled. Bethesda learns that her cat has been taken to the vet for "his yearly dairy injection," and Nat gets a pink note with a smiley face informing him that Oprah has picked his book for her book club. When he calls the number on the message, though, he reaches his agent, who tells him that her aunt's book club in Boca is reading his book and would he answer a few questions for them on the speakerphone?

The strangest message, though, is the one that comes for Zalman from his Russian grandmother. The message, translated from the Russian (a language, Daria explains, she picked up from a Russian muralist her mother once dated), is that she has fallen and broken her leg; the problem is that Zalman's grandmother has been dead for thirty years.

"Which means I was on the phone with a dead woman," Daria tells me when I come into the office to pick up my mail.

"I'm sure you just got the name wrong," Nat, who's come up behind me and is helping himself to a ream of Bosco stationery, says. "Like you thought my agent was Oprah." He rolls his eyes at me. "Sheesh, like I'd even consider going on *Oprah*." But he would have. I have a sudden image of the suit he'd planned to wear. A Hugo Boss he'd gotten on sale at Barneys last year. I can even see in my vision how handsome he looks in it.

"Yeah, well, actually it wasn't as weird as the callers I get who want to tell their stories to the writers," Daria tells us.

"You're kidding," I say.

"No, I get a couple a day." Daria holds up her right

hand, thumb and pinky extended to mimic a phone receiver. " 'Hello, is this the place that has all the writers? Well, go get one, 'cause I've got a story to tell they'll pay good money for.' "

Nat laughs, but I'm thinking of how lonely those people must be. "Amazing," he says. "If they think that's all it takes, why don't they write it themselves?"

Daria shrugs. "Too much trouble, I guess. Easier to tell it to someone over the phone like a psychic hotline. Diana tells me to hang up on those calls, but they just keep calling back, so now I have them tell their story to me and I pretend to be writing it all down."

"Really?" I ask. "But why do you bother?"

"I don't know; it's something to pass the time. There isn't much else to do—I've already read all your files."

We both stare at Daria openmouthed. "Our files? You're allowed to read our files?" Nat asks.

"Yeah, but—no offense—I'm really more interested in the older stuff. Like this letter I came upon today." Daria lifts up a delicate sheet of onionskin paper, its surface embossed with the impressions of an old manual typewriter. It's been so long since I've seen anything manually typed that the page looks as antiquated as an illuminated manuscript. "This is from a historian researching Bosco. He says that there's a local story, supposedly passed down by the Lathams' servants, that the artist Frank Campbell was shot through the heart during a séance here."

"I thought he died of a heart attack," I say.

"That's the *official* story," Daria says, her voice lowering to a theatrical whisper and her eyes widening with delight. I see now why she loves listening to the crank callers. I'll bet she also loves conspiracy theories, urban legends, and telling ghost stories around a camp bonfire. "The local lore is that the ghost of an Indian shot an arrow through his heart to avenge the massacre of his tribe *on this very spot.*" She punctuates the last four words by stabbing the air with her index finger.

I glance over at Nat to see how he's reacting to this ghost story and am surprised to see how ashen he looks. But it's not the specter of slaughtered Indians that has him rattled.

"You're allowed to read our files?" He repeats his earlier question, but before Daria can answer, Diana Tate's voice bursts out of the intercom demanding Daria's presence in her office.

"Gotta go," Daria says, grabbing a steno pad and a bottle of water.

"I can't believe that adolescent is reading our files," Nat says as we walk back to the mansion together. "That means she's read our letters of reference."

I wonder why that upsets Nat so much and then I remember that his mentor was Spencer Leland, the director of the famous MFA program Nat had attended. Leland had written a groundbreaking experimental novel in his twenties and then nothing but a slim collection of short stories and an even slimmer memoir in the next forty years. He was famous, though, for mentoring young writers. When he died, seven years ago, of lung cancer, Nat wrote an essay about him in the *Atlantic Monthly* that had brought me to tears. I picture the old teacher, in the donnish English tweeds he always wore, and his trademark shock of white hair, writing a letter, and I *know* what Nat is worried about. He's always been afraid that Leland's original letter of recommendation contains some hint of an inner failing in Nat's writing. Some inner failing that explains why he hasn't been able to write his second novel. The reason I'm so sure this is what Nat's afraid of is it's the same thing I'm afraid of—that the recommendation letter Richard Scully wrote has some similar caveat about my own character and talent.

"I'm sure she'll keep whatever she reads to herself—" I begin.

"Are you? The girl's a pothead. She'll probably post our letters on the Internet."

"Talk about the pot calling the kettle black," I say before considering my words. I'm not sure what I'm more appalled at, insulting Nat or using such an obvious cliché combined with an unintended pun. Nat looks genuinely abashed, and I realize he has no idea that we all know he's been getting high with Daria.

"Nat," I say, "I'm in the room right next to you. It smells like a Nirvana concert in there."

"Really? Shit . . . Do you think anyone else has noticed . . . ?" He looks so worried I'm genuinely sorry for him.

"I wouldn't worry. I mean, it's not like they're going to kick you out—"

Nat stops in the middle of the path and looks so pale I'm afraid he's going to pass out.

"Here," I say, leading him to a bench on the side of the terrace. "Sit down. I didn't mean to upset you. You're Bosco's most famous writer. They wouldn't dare kick you out."

Nat drops his head into his hands and moans. "A writer who hasn't produced a book in nine years," he says. "You don't think they're all looking over my shoulder every minute of the day waiting for me to fuck up?" He lifts his head and looks down the hill. More than ever the tangle of brush looks like a wall closing in on us—as if the tangled shrubs were growing, encroaching on the house. "God, sometimes I can't stand this place." He gets to his feet and starts heading back inside, but then he stops a few feet away and looks back at me. Cocking his head to one side, he manages a weak smile. "Hey," he says, "do you want to get high?"

If I was nervous about being in David's room—in the back on the third floor—I have all the more reason to refuse Nat's offer to share a joint with him in the central suite. Although I told Nat that I didn't think Diana Tate would have him evicted for smoking pot, I'm not so sure about what she might do with me—an unpublished author, breaking the rules of nine-to-five quiet, and engaging in illegal activities. But that's exactly what I find myself doing. Maybe because Nat had looked so hopeful when he asked me; maybe because anything is better than going back to my room and facing the blank screen of my computer.

We don't meet anyone on the stairs going up, or in the hallway. After placing a rolled-up towel against the bottom of the door and opening a window, Nat assures me that Bethesda—whose room is on the opposite side of the suite from mine—has no sense of smell and is so absorbed in her work that she would never notice anything. "And she wouldn't say anything if she did," Nat says, lighting the joint. "She's my pal."

I suspect that if Bethesda knew I was in here with Nat, sitting cozily across from him on the cushioned window seat, our feet almost touching, she'd be less than congenial. I wonder if Nat simply has no idea how she feels about him or just chooses to ignore it.

"You've known her for a long time?" I ask, taking the joint from him and inhaling. It's been ages since I've smoked pot and I'm afraid that I won't be able to keep from coughing, but the sweet smoke coils down into my lungs and stays there like an animal curling into its lair.

"Since college," he says. "We were in writing classes together. If she hadn't decided to write criticism instead of fiction, I'd probably hate her by now."

I laugh and exhale at the same time. It's the first time since I've met Nat that I feel he's being totally honest. What I wonder is if Bethesda's decision to write biographies instead of novels had something to do with knowing that Nat wouldn't have been able to put up with competition from her.

"Well, she certainly doesn't like me very much. I honestly had no idea *Muse of Water* was her title. I had no intention of poaching on her territory."

"Yeah, she can be a little crazy that way. That's the thing about writing biographies: you have to worry no one else is working on your subject at the same time. Bethesda's been researching Aurora Latham for years now—she's *invested*."

"Well, she doesn't have anything to worry about from me—I'm not writing a biography, and if things go on the way they have been, I probably won't even finish the novel."

"Not going well?" Nat asks. I glance at him and see that he's arranged his features into a look of polite concern, but he can't disguise the hidden pleasure in his voice. Nothing makes him happier, I realize, than to hear that someone else is having trouble writing. I look toward his desk and see the ream of blank stationery neatly stacked by the side of his ancient Olivetti typewriter, the black Moleskine notebooks arrayed like soldiers next to a green glass bottle that seems to gather all the sunlight in the room into its dark, musty interior.

"I'm a little stuck," I say. "I've gotten to the first séance, the one where the artist Frank Campbell dies, but I can't figure out what happened. It was supposed to be a heart attack, but he was a young man." I'm still staring at the green bottle. There's a smell coming from it, something sweet and decaying, emanating from the bottle like a small black cloud.

"So you think someone killed him?"

I drag my eyes away from the green bottle and see that Nat has leaned forward to pass me the tiny nub of the joint. His face is only inches from mine, so close I can see the shadows his long, dark eyelashes make on his cheekbones and smell the scent of pine needles on his skin. I close my eyes after drawing in the smoke, and the spark of the joint becomes a candle flame burning in the dark. My whole body is prickling, as if hands were moving over my skin, pulling me deeper into the blackness. And then I feel something brush against my lips, a light, feathery touch that could be the sweep of a bird's wing or a kiss.

I open my eyes and find myself looking into Nat's eyes, which have turned the same green as the old medicine bottle on his desk, and I can't for the life of me tell if he's just kissed me or I imagined the whole thing.

"I've got to go," I say, swinging my legs down from the window seat, too embarrassed to know what else to do. "I've just thought of something."

"When inspiration strikes . . ." Nat says, looking away from me out toward the ruined garden.

"Yeah, thanks . . ." I say, involuntarily touching a finger to my lips and feeling again that sweet, fleeting pressure against my lips. Whether it was a kiss or not, I know that it tugged at something inside of me, pulling me out of the darkness.

"Sure, anytime," he says, keeping his face toward the window. It's only from his reflection that I can see the look of disappointment on his face.

I close Nat's door as quietly as I can, but it's not quietly enough. Before I can turn to walk back to my room, I hear a door open at the end of the hallway and look up to see Bethesda standing there. She looks as severe in her black cardigan and jeans as a nineteenth-century governess who's caught her charge playing hooky. Without a word she holds up an imperious finger and points toward her room. I consider ignoring the enigmatic hand signal because I'm dying to get back to my room to write down what I've just thought of. On the other hand, it occurs to me, Bethesda might be able to verify a hunch I have.

I follow her into her room, where she sits down at her desk and offers me a chair before speaking. I have a feeling that she can't stand to be away from her desk for more than a few minutes. In contrast to the barren sterility of Nat's workspace, Bethesda's is a monument to productivity. Books are stacked so high that they would block out the light from the window even if the drapes were open. Clearly, though, the curtains have not been opened in some time, as Bethesda has taken to using their thick muslin as a bulletin board. Small squares of notepaper, in a rainbow of colors, are affixed to the fabric with long pearl-tipped pins. The handwriting is so tiny that I have trouble making out what's written on the notes without seeming to pry, but from the dates on top of each note I guess that she's trying to assemble some kind of time line for her book. I notice that she has several of the pearl-tipped pins stuck into the sleeve of her black cardigan. When a draft steals in under the windowsill, fluttering the notes like a crazy patchwork quilt, I have a sudden image of Bethesda as a beleaguered fairy-tale princess locked in a tower to complete some impossible task, like spinning gold from straw or weaving silk from feathers.

Bethesda waits for me to look away from the window to speak. "Are you encouraging Nat in his pot smoking?" she asks.

I almost laugh, but when I see how serious she looks, I don't. "He asked me to join him," I answer. "I only went because he looked so . . . lonely."

"He doesn't need new friends," Bethesda tells me, sliding one of the pearl-tipped pins in and out of her sweater sleeve. "He needs to work and he'll never do that if he keeps smoking pot."

Thinking of the strange miasma I'd seen curling out of the green bottle on Nat's desk, I'm inclined to agree with her, but I'm too annoyed at her condescending tone to admit it. "I don't know," I say, "I got rather a good idea when Nat and I were talking. In fact, I was just going back to my room to write—" I start to get up, but my eye is caught by one of the slips of paper pinned to the curtain. It's a letter on pale gray stationery with an engraved artist's palette and the name Frank Campbell beneath it. The opening salutation reads: *To My Muse of Water!* Bethesda notices what I'm looking at and stands up, blocking my view.

"In fact, I wanted to check this out with you," I say.

"Daria Tate says there's a local legend that Frank Campbell was shot through the heart by an arrow during the first séance."

Bethesda laughs and sits down on the edge of her desk. "By an angry Native American ghost," she says. "Yes, I've heard the legend. Don't tell me *that's* what you're putting in your book. I didn't realize it was horror as well as romance."

"It's neither, really," I say, smiling. "I just wondered if you'd come across anything that validated the actual cause of Frank Campbell's death."

"Yes, of course." She turns from me and leans over her desk, one hand resting on the small of her back, the other rustling the slips of paper with her fingertips. She unpins a slip of paper, sliding the long pin into her sleeve so carelessly I'm surprised she doesn't stick herself, and hands it to me. "This is Campbell's death certificate. Heart attack. See."

"Of course," I say, noticing that one of the witnesses was Corinth Blackwell. "I just thought I'd check—"

"There's no substitute for careful research," Bethesda says, waving a stern finger at me, and then, leaning over the desk, she spears the death certificate to the muslin curtain with the pearl-tipped pin, where it flutters for a moment like an impaled moth.

I rush back to my room as quickly as if I am cupping a handful of water that I have to carry to a dying person before it spills out between my fingers. I've been stuck at the first séance for weeks now, trying to imagine the moment when Frank Campbell died. My desk is littered with aborted versions of the scene, each thin pile of paper weighted to the wooden surface by a smooth white rock. Spread out, its pages held open by another one of the rocks, is the pamphlet *A True and Intimate Account of the Blackwell Affair.* I read, for the sixth or seventh time, the account of Frank Campbell's death during the first séance.

> Mr. Campbell was known to have a sensitive nature, as many artists do, and it is well known that such natures are often accompanied by an organic weakness of the body. In Mr. Campbell's case, this weakness resided in his heart. He had confided in a letter written to Aurora Latham the very day of the séance that he had experienced a sense of "oppression" all day in anticipation of the séance. No doubt, it was this strain on his heart combined with the effects produced in the séance—wind blowing and footsteps approaching, drums and Indian war whoops, the voices of children and their little hands everywhere (whose ghostly handprints we afterwards saw on the ceiling of the grotto), even a frog dropped down the back of one of the ladies' dresses—that hastened him to his untimely demise.

The voices of children and their little hands everywhere. For a moment the words summon the prickling sensation I'd felt before in Nat's room, but I dismiss it as an aftereffect of the pot and concentrate on the reference to the letter. Frank Campbell wrote a letter to Aurora on the day of the séance—that was the letter pinned to Bethesda's curtain, from which she had gotten her title *Muse of Water.* I'd managed, while she unpinned the death certificate, to read the rest of it. Now I copy it down before I forget it.

> *To My Muse of Water!*
>
> *All day long my heart has been oppressed by a sense of dread at what will come tonight. It is not that I fear the supernatural, but that I fear for your reason and goodness. I know what you are trying to do, dear Aurora, and I know that it will never work. No one could blame you, but still I implore you to abandon your plans. If you don't I may be forced to take actions that I would sincerely regret but that my conscience, nevertheless, compels me to perform.*
>
> *Ever your faithful servant,*
> *Frank Campbell.*

What could Aurora have been planning that Frank Campbell wanted to stop? Did he simply wish her to abandon what must have seemed a fruitless effort to contact her lost children? Or was there a more sinister plan he'd learned of? Whatever he was alluding to, it seems suddenly clear to me that Aurora could have easily read the letter as a threat. Was it a coincidence that he died the same day he sent her that letter?

I look up from the page and out the window toward the garden. After a minute I realize that I'm scanning the garden—but for whom? Nat? No, I can hear the sound of his typewriter coming from his room and, besides, I think, pressing my fingers against my lips, it's not as if he really kissed me. David, though . . . ever since we almost kissed in the grotto I've had disturbingly erotic dreams. That's the real reason I haven't gotten any writing done, I think, looking with despair at the notes I've scrawled across the sheets of paper that lie sprawled on my desk amidst the white stones he gave me. While Nat's desk had been barren and Bethesda's a beehive of activity, mine strikes me now, with its litter of white stones, as a graveyard. Half the time I'm sitting here my body is present but my spirit is drifting up the secret passageway to David's room, into his rough-hewn bed with its quartet of bears standing guard and the eagle taking flight over the headboard. At night I'm making love in that bed, the wings of the eagle, come to life, beating above me, my hands wrapped around a rough bedpost. When I wake in the morning, I find myself holding on to a post of my own bed, splinters embedded under my fingernails. What scares me the most about the dreams is that I'm never able to see the face of the man I'm making love to.

I look down at my hands now and see that I've picked up the shard of china I found in the grotto and pressed its sharp point into my palm as if the physical pain could bring me back into my body. I drop it when a bead of blood rises to the skin and look up, out the window, and catch a glimpse of something white shimmering in the garden. For a second I think it's snow, but then I realize I'm thinking of the beginning of "Snow White" where the queen pricks her finger and, looking from the drop of blood to the snow, wishes for a child with lips as red as blood and skin as white as snow. There's no snow in the garden. But there is a woman dressed in a long, flowing white robe standing on the lowest terrace staring directly at me.

Chapter Ten

"You can't really mean to leave him here all night? He'll be eaten by wild animals!" Mrs. Ramsdale is teetering so close to the grotto's pool that Tom Quinn is obliged to leave Corinth to draw his employer back from the edge. The moment he is by her side, she leans heavily on his arm and begs for her smelling salts.

"Norris will stay with him," Aurora reassures her houseguest. "She will keep the animals at bay."

The housekeeper has already posted herself at the head of the body, which Lantini and Quinn have stretched out on the stone bench. She looks as solid and impassable as the stone statues that ancient Egyptians placed at the doorways to their tombs. Corinth, for one, can't imagine any animal getting past her. Mrs. Ramsdale, though, is still not satisfied.

"But why not take him back to the house?"

"I would rather wait until Milo returns," Aurora answers. "He will know how best to handle the situation. You must realize, Violet, that Mr. Campbell is beyond our help, but his legacy and the legacy of Bosco is not. If Bosco is to be a haven for artists, we can't have it said that the very first artist invited here died under mysterious circumstances."

"But how did he die?" Tom Quinn asks. "That arrow didn't fly into his chest by itself."

The remaining five members of the séance turn to the body stretched out on its stone bier. For a moment the only sound in the grotto is the sound of water falling from the fountain, and then a tentative voice breaks the silence.

"*I bambini.*" Signore Lantini, his eyes wide and gleaming, translates for the sake of his American audience. "It was the children."

As they walk back up the hill, it is impossible for Tom to get a word alone with Corinth. He practically has to carry Mrs. Ramsdale up the steep steps along the fountain allée and then, even at the house, she is unwilling to let him go.

"I would feel better," she tells him at the foot of the main staircase, "if you would have a look in my room to make sure it is quite safe. I don't want to wake up and find a murderer hiding in the armoire."

"So you don't believe Mr. Campbell was murdered by the ghosts of the Latham children?" Tom asks, allowing his lips to curl into a faint smile.

"Please, Tom," she says, returning the smile, "this is real life we're talking about, not one of my novels."

Squaring her shoulders, she precedes him up the stairs, no longer relying on his support. He's seen her rally herself like this after treatments at the spas and clinics that would melt a strong man's resolve. He's seen her gird herself in her finery and sit up half the night at dinner parties and balls even though, he knew, she was in pain. "Material," she would tell him when he suggested she turn down some of the invitations. "I must take every opportunity to study the aristocracy, Tom, or my readers will be disappointed." And in the morning she would be up at the crack of dawn with another whole chapter in her head to recite to him. This is what's made the years of his employment with her bearable—well, that and the generous salary she pays—that beneath the pretty face and soft flesh and silly novels there's a core of strength that he can't help but admire.

As she opens her door he hears the door to the next room open. He lingers behind long enough to see Corinth looking out into the corridor.

Meet me in the library. He mouths the words, knowing how good she is at reading lips. It was part of the act she had worked out with her father. For a second, though, he thinks she might not have understood him—she seems to be looking right through him—but then she nods and retreats into her room.

"Well, unless you want me to save *you* from the brigands who might be hiding under my bed . . ." Mrs. Ramsdale's voice summons him into her bedroom. She's seated at her dressing table taking down her hair. When he turns around he hears a chiming sound and knows that she's dropping those pearl-tipped pins, one by one, into a china cup on the dressing table. He's not supposed to notice that she's had to let out her dress and pin it up, so he takes his time checking under the bed and examining the insides of the tall oak armoire with its carved panel depicting an Indian maiden paddling a canoe on a pine-fringed lake. He even inspects Mrs. Ramsdale's Saratoga trunk, although only a midget intruder could be hiding in there. When he turns around to tell her that all is safe, he sees that the china cup is full of the pearl-tipped pins and she's lowered the bodice of her dress to her waist. Her bare shoulders gleam white in the moonlight, the hollow between her finely carved shoulder blades—a space just wide enough for a man's hand—glowing with a thin sheen of dampness. He meets her eyes in the reflection in the mirror.

"All the same," she says, "I would feel safer if you stayed with me . . . a little while longer."

In the library Corinth has fallen asleep on the divan while waiting for Tom. She's dreaming of the Indian girl, Ne'Moss-i-Ne, who's escaped her bondage and is running toward the cliff above the Sacandaga River to throw herself over it. Corinth can see her running through the dense underbrush, her legs and arms scratched by the thorns, her bare feet shredded by the rough forest floor. A fog is rising past the cliff face, obscuring the valley beyond. When she reaches the edge of the cliff, she turns and Corinth is looking at herself; she's the one falling into the fog . . .

She startles awake on the divan to catch herself from falling and falls instead into Tom Quinn's arms.

"I'm sorry," he says, "I didn't mean to scare you."

She leans into his arms, but then she catches the smell of something sweet on his skin. Laudanum. She straightens herself and moves away.

"I was having a bad dream," she says. "The Indian girl in the garden, Ne'Moss-i-Ne . . ."

"Don't tell me you're beginning to believe your own creations! You told me once that was the most dangerous mistake a professional medium could make."

"I'm beginning to think there are worse mistakes," she says, "like coming to Bosco."

"I'm glad you see it that way—that's what I wanted to talk to you about. You must leave Bosco."

"*I* must leave? Since when do you tell me where to go, Tom Quinn? If I remember correctly, the last time you told me to stay in a place and wait for you—"

"I came back, Cory, but you had already left. They told me you'd gone to work at Latham's factory. What was I to think?"

That I must have been truly desperate to go to Milo Latham, Corinth thinks, but she says nothing. *It's too late.* Instead she stands up to leave, but he catches her hand. He pushes back the hem of her gloves and turns her hand over, tracing the scars that circle her wrists.

"Whatever happened back then is over and done

with, Cory. What I care about is right now. A man was killed tonight, and I, for one, do not believe the murderer was a ghost."

"You think I had something to do with it? That I rigged the séance?"

"No"—his lips curl into a faint smile—"at least not all of it. You couldn't have created all those effects working alone."

"Ah, so all I lack is an accomplice to have committed murder?" Corinth tries to pull her hand away, but Tom closes his fingers around her wrist, his thumb and forefinger describing a loop that exactly matches the mark that circles her wrist. The minute he sees the expression in her eyes he releases her.

"I don't believe you're capable of murder," he says, "but clearly someone here at Bosco is. Promise me you'll at least think about leaving. I'll do anything I can to help you go. I'll go with you if you'll let me."

She holds her hand to her chest, rubbing the wrist to ease the ache that's never wholly gone from there. Even now she can feel the bands tightening, closing in on her . . . Maybe Tom is right. Whatever happened ten years ago matters less than getting out of here. *Maybe it's not too late.*

"I'll think about it," she tells him. And then, before he can say anything else, she turns and leaves the library.

Corinth has little choice, she reflects when she's back in her room, but to think about Tom's offer. She's certainly not going to sleep after the dream she had in the library. Although Tom is certain that Campbell was killed by a living person, Corinth is less sure. She knows, of course, how to fake a séance, but she didn't fake this one. She can imagine, though, how most of the effects were produced in the grotto: a wooden form on a telescoping stick to print the hand marks on the ceiling, an accomplice outside—Corinth sees the stony face of Mrs. Norris—to create the sound effects, someone armed with a bow to shoot the arrow into Campbell's chest while everyone was preoccupied with the sounds. But there's one detail that troubles her. When she came back to herself in the grotto, someone—or something— had its fingers around her wrist, just as Tom had a moment ago in the library, only these fingers were unable to complete the circle because they were too small. It was a child's hand. Corinth is sure of that much.

She looks down at her wrists and sees that the marks there have nearly faded. If you didn't know they were there . . . but Tom did know, because he was at the show where she got them.

It was her last night performing at the Lyceum in Gloversville. By then it was just her and her father on the road. Her mother had died a few years before, shortly after giving birth to her younger sister, and her father had left the baby with a childless couple (the man had a good job at the glass factory in Corning, New

York), promising that they would come back to get her once they had enough money.

"We can't have an infant with us on the road," he'd told Corinth. "You'll be of more use to her making money than trying to take care of her yourself. Besides, what do you know about keeping house?"

It was true. Corinth knew precious little about any of the ordinary domestic skills. Once her father had learned of her talents—Wanda White Cloud had told him after she lost at poker one time too many—he'd taken her to a revival meeting in Buffalo for her "debut." At first her act consisted of telling people what they had in their pockets or what card they were holding, but once Mike had seen a few other spiritualists perform, he started adding to her repertoire. She learned to produce rapping noises by cracking the knuckles of her toes, and she learned how to "throw her voice" so that she seemed to be speaking to inanimate spirits. She learned the trick "one ahead" in which she would read written messages from the audience by holding up a piece of folded paper to her forehead and reciting a prearranged message that was confirmed by someone Mike had hired. Then, when she opened that message, she knew what the "next" message would be. After a while they had acquired enough tricks that Corinth no longer had to bother going into a trance state. In fact, an actual trance state interfered with the performance.

As her act gained in popularity, though, she drew as many doubters as believers, hecklers who would cry fraud and charlatan and worse from the back rows.

Mike's approach was to meet any skepticism head-on. At the beginning of each night's show he invited any authenticating tests that the audience could dream up. The burliest men were invited to hold on to Corinth's ankles and hands. It wasn't long before ropes were suggested to bind her hands and ankles to the chair on which she sat.

At first the sensation of being bound drove her wild. She had to be carried off a stage in Utica kicking and screaming. After that her father made her wear loops around her wrists and ankles to get used to the sensation—but she never did get used to it. Instead she learned to leave her body at the first touch of the rope on her skin. It wasn't a full trance—she kept her spirit tethered to her flesh, hovering just a few inches above, her body so relaxed that she was able to slip her hands and feet out of their bonds and so perform the tricks of her act. In time she learned to manipulate the knots without feeling the touch of the ropes on her skin.

It worked until that night in Gloversville. The night before, a man had approached them after the act. He'd lost a son in the war, he explained to Mike. Instantly Mike made up a fictitious sibling for Corinth also slain at Antietam. Real tears stood in Mike's eyes while he talked about "Charlie's" last letter home and Corinth half wondered if he wasn't thinking about the baby abandoned in Corning, New York. The man wasn't softened by Mike's story, though.

"There's something I must know," he said, turning away from Mike and addressing Corinth directly, "but I won't be made a fool of." Corinth saw the color rising to the man's face and felt her own chest muscles constrict, but with empathy not for the man's grief but for his fear of being shamed. Something about his son's death shamed him and it was this—shame, not grief—that he was trying to expunge. Corinth turned away and the man addressed Mike again.

"I'll pay handsomely, but I must have certain conditions met." And he whispered a sum into her father's ear that Corinth knew instantly was enough for Mike to sell her body and soul.

The conditions were that the man would himself tie the ropes around Corinth's arms and legs.

"You won't even feel it," Mike said when the man had gone and Corinth objected to the conditions. "You're not even there, are you?" Corinth looked at her father and saw that the look of hard avarice that usually resided in his eyes had slipped. What Corinth saw instead was fear—fear of her and what she did. She realized then that she could use this fear against him— that she could leave him. But go where? He was the only family she had except for the baby sister who was already part of someone else's family—a *normal* family. She thought, then, of the mill owner in Corinth, Milo Latham, who had once told her that she could always come to him . . . but then, she thought, that would be exchanging one sort of servitude for another.

That night Mr. Oswald (Corinth never learned his first name) came up onto the stage with a length of thick, rough hemp rope. He looped the rope first around her chest and then he bound her wrists behind her back and pulled down on the rope so that her shoulder blades were drawn together—the way a chicken is trussed—and then threaded the rope in between the rungs of the chair and tied her ankles to the chair legs. Some of the audience hissed while he was tying her, but this only made him pull the rope tighter. She could hear laughter in her head—and then she realized that the laughter was in Mr. Oswald's head. It was a young woman laughing, but it was a joyless sound.

"She needs something of your son's to hold," Mike said when the ropes were tied.

Mr. Oswald withdrew something from his pocket, but before she could see what it was he crouched behind her and slipped it between her bound hands. A slim disc made of metal, Corinth thought, on a chain.

Corinth closed her eyes and tried to rise out of herself, but the ropes were too tight. It was as if her spirit were trapped by the ropes as well as her body and for the first time she imagined what it would be like to be trapped in her flesh for all eternity even after that flesh began to decay. To be buried alive in the prison of her own body.

She could feel sweat dripping down her arms and legs, soaking the rope. She tried to move her wrists to loosen her bonds, but that only made the ropes around her chest constrict so tightly she could barely breathe. They'd been tied in such a way that struggling pulled them tighter. *He'd learned it out west in the Indian Wars . . .*

And then Corinth wasn't on the stage anymore. She

was in a cabin and it was cold . . . the cabin smelled of rancid fat and unwashed men, the way the loggers' cabins smelled after a long winter. She smelled something else, something burning, and realized it was her own hair. Through the smoke she could see, with her eyes still closed, a small boy hiding behind a chair watching his father light the woman's hair on fire. The woman, inexplicably, was laughing. Around the boy's neck was a chain with a saint's medal . . .

"Saint Thomas," she said aloud, but in a whisper only she and the two men on the stage could hear, "because that was his name, Thomas. He saw what you did to his mother and got away from you as soon as he could. Ran away to join the army at thirteen . . ."

Mr. Oswald bowed his head but not, as Corinth thought at first, in shame but to reach the end of the rope and yank it. All the air was pressed out of her lungs and her hands felt as if they were encircled in fire, but she didn't call out because *she* hadn't . . .

"You told her if she screamed, you'd kill the boy and so she laughed instead," Corinth whispered, her voice so constricted by the ropes that she knew no one but Mr. Oswald could hear her.

He pulled the rope tighter, and this time her last breath was pushed out of her lungs in a long silent scream. She could see her father, as if through a fog, trying to pull Mr. Oswald away from her, but more clearly she saw the man who was scrambling over the seats in the theater, not caring whom he stepped on to reach her, his black coat spread out behind him like the wings of a giant bird. She recognized him as one of the magicians who had performed earlier in the evening. He vaulted to the stage and, heaving Mr. Oswald up by the hair, drove his fist into his face.

By then a crowd had stormed the stage and begun to drag Mr. Oswald off. Corinth wasn't sure to where. She could feel her spirit, like a bird trapped in a cage rattling against the ruined frame of her body, trying to get out, but then the man who'd come to her rescue bent over her and she fastened her gaze onto his eyes. They were such a vivid, clear blue-green that they seemed to hold her there while he used his knife to cut the ropes, which were sunk deep into her skin, from her wrists. When he'd picked the hemp fibers from her wounds, he pried her hands open. There, embedded in the flesh of her palm, was the saint's medal, St. Thomas's face seared into her skin. Then her spirit found its way out at last and she lost consciousness.

Corinth opens her hands now and looks at the oval indentation in her palm. The image printed on her skin has faded faster than her memory of Tom Quinn. She had realized that tonight when she came to in the grotto with him leaning over her. Once again he'd come to rescue her.

Only he hadn't. Not when she'd needed him most.

Corinth looks out the window and sees that shapes are emerging in the garden, the white statues gleaming in the early morning mist. A man in a dark coat comes out onto the terrace and lights a cigar, and then he walks down the fountain allée, the mist seeming to part before him. Yes, Tom had gotten her to quit the act and sever her ties with her father. He'd promised to quit the stage himself, only there was one more engagement in New York City he had to do and then there'd be money enough for them to buy a house, maybe start a business. He'd found her a place in one of the better glove shops—a family-run business with a proper boarding-house for the glove makers to stay in. She'd be safe there until he came back. Only he hadn't come back—or at least not until it was too late.

Corinth draws on her gloves and wraps a shawl over her head and shoulders. She wears her lightest slippers and steals downstairs and out onto the terrace without making a sound. As she makes her way down the allée, the mist seems to close up behind her, but at least one resident of Bosco watches her progress. At the foot of the stairs she finds Milo Latham leaning against the statue of Sacandaga, still smoking his cigar.

"Did Aurora tell you what happened?" she asks.

Milo takes a long puff of his cigar and exhales smoke into the fog. "At least I won't have to pay his fee now for that abominable portrait of my wife," he says. "Muse of Water, my ass!"

"What are you going to do?"

Milo shrugs. "I've called in a couple of favors from town. It turns out that Mr. Frank Campbell had a bad heart—all that loose living artists do these days." Milo clicks his tongue against the roof of his mouth and puts his arm around Corinth, pulling her toward him. "I hear you put on quite a show, my dear. I didn't expect such fanfare—it's far more than we agreed upon. You certainly didn't need to kill the portraitist to convince my wife of your authenticity."

"You know I had nothing to do with that," Corinth says, stiffening under his arm.

"*I* know that, but I'm afraid the authorities might have a different opinion. But don't worry, our story about the heart attack will work perfectly well. In fact, I think it would be a nice touch if you were to witness the death certificate when Dr. Murdoch is done." He points toward the grotto.

"All the same," Corinth says, "I think I should leave."

Milo rolls back his head, resting it on Sacandaga's shoulder, and laughs. "Leave? After last night's performance? Why, Aurora was positively electrified! She's convinced you've contacted the children. She wants to have another séance tonight."

"It doesn't bother her that a man is dead?"

"Oh, my dear, it will take more than one death to sway my wife's fancy once she's set her mind on a thing. And believe me, she's set her mind on *you*."

Chapter Eleven

The woman in white stands on the terrace as still as any of the statues. *Like an apparition,* I think, feeling suddenly cold. And then, moving back from the window, I chide myself that it must be a sightseer come to gawk at the artists. Although the estate is private, some find their way onto the grounds every year and have to be escorted off by the local police. I should probably go tell Diana Tate about this interloper. The woman's stare, although not malevolent, is intense enough to be unnerving; it's as if she's directing all her energy at the house, willing one of its occupants out into the garden. And then, suddenly, I'm struck with the horror of recognition. The robed figure on the terrace is my mother.

When I get down to the first terrace, my mother is nowhere to be found. I think for a moment that I must have imagined seeing her. I had, after all, thought she was an apparition at first. Maybe that's what she was. It's a testimony to how horrified I am at the thought of my mother's presence here at Bosco that the idea that I've seen a ghost instead is comforting.

I head down the steps, picking up the faint aroma of marijuana on the air. For a second I imagine the worst— that Mira is getting high in the garden—but then I remember that Daria often sneaks into the garden at lunchtime to smoke pot in the brambles. Then I hear a hissing noise from the bushes across the path from the cracked and crumbling river god. I call softly into a patch of dense ilex, "Mira? Are you in there?"

For an answer a many-braceleted hand snakes out of the bush and pulls me through a narrow opening into a small round glade. I'm so struck by the perfect circle carved out of green brush that for a moment I hardly look at my mother. Instead I look at the little statue at the center of the niche: a diminutive nymph drooping over a marble basin beside a marble bench.

"She's pretty, isn't she?" my mother says, looking at the statue, but stroking my hair back from my brow. "She's the only statue here I get a good vibe from. That's why I waited with her." The statue *is* pretty—at least from what I can see that is left of it. The elements have so worn down the marble that the features of her face are nearly gone, as if she were melting into the water caught in the basin she holds.

"But how—?" I'm going to ask how she knew the little statue was in here, but, looking up at my mother and taking in her flowing white caftan, the ropes of crystals slung around her neck, and her long gray hair that hangs loose over her shoulders, I despair of questioning such particulars. My mother will no doubt tell me that the little nymph called to her or some such nonsense. I might as well get to the real question.

"What are you doing here, Mira? I thought I explained to you that Bosco doesn't allow outside visitors."

"Yes, but when you didn't respond to my message, I knew something was wrong."

"Your message? It was something about a key and an alarm. I don't understand what I was supposed to respond to."

"I told that girl that 'the bees had started to swarm.' "

"Oh," I say, taking a seat on the bench beside the water nymph, "that's different. If I'd known it was a bee emergency . . ."

"Don't mock, darling. You know how important the bees are to me. And to you. When you were a baby sleeping in your hammock, a bee walked over your lips without stinging you. You know what that means."

"It means that I'm destined to become a great storyteller," I say, dutifully reciting the words like a lesson learned by rote. This time, though, I don't need to be reminded not to mock. I've always liked this piece of folk wisdom, especially since I learned that it originated with the ancient Greeks, who called bees, because of this, the birds of the Muses. "It is unusual for them to swarm this late in the year, isn't it?"

Mira takes a seat on the bench and lays her hand over mine. The feel of my mother's skin, softened by years of working with beeswax, melts something in me. I'd like to rest my head on her shoulder and inhale her aroma of honey and patchouli, but I've grown taller than Mira and would have to slump to reach her shoulder.

"An out-of-season swarm foretells a death," Mira says. "That's why I called you. I felt immediately that it had something to do with you."

"Unless someone stabs himself with his pen or slips on a manuscript page, no one is going to die here."

"But someone has died here, and died badly. I can feel it." Mira's eyes rake the walls of the ilex niche as if looking for intruders hidden in the greenery. In spite of myself, I feel the same chill I felt when I first saw my mother standing on the terrace. That feeling of something shimmering just on the edge of vision.

"Of course people have died here, Mira; the estate is over a hundred years old. Poor Mrs. Latham lost three of her children to diphtheria . . ."

"It wasn't diphtheria."

I'm taken aback by how certain Mira sounds. "I'm pretty sure that it was—"

"And it's not the children I'm talking about. There are others . . ." I follow Mira's gaze through the opening in the hedge toward the entrance to the grotto. "I felt something when I went by that fountain out there."

"I think what you felt was a contact high from Daria Tate's pot. I smelled it when I came down here . . ." I stop, taken with a sudden idea. As much as I've tried over the years to dismiss my mother's *intuitions*, I can't deny that Mira has an uncanny instinct. It might be just the thing to get me "unstuck" in the séance scene.

"Something did happen in that grotto," I tell Mira. "It's where the medium Corinth Blackwell held her first séance at Bosco. A man died of a heart attack. I've been trying to work out what happened. Maybe if we went inside . . ."

Mira's eyes widen for a moment—a look of fear that I've rarely seen in my mother's face—but then she asks, "It's important for you to find out what happened?"

"Well, I'm kind of stuck at that part."

Mira nods once and gets up off the bench. She lets go of my hand to briefly touch the head of the statue, and then she squares her shoulders and strides through the hedge, hips swaying, like some Amazon warrior ready to do battle. I follow in her wake, trying not to feel guilty about enlisting Mira's aid to do something she obviously feels frightened of. I'm planning to tell her it's not necessary to go inside the grotto if she really doesn't want to, but when I come out of the bushes, Mira has already passed behind the limbs of the river god, having found the hidden entrance without any help from me.

Following my mother into the grotto, I can't help remembering my almost kiss with David here, but then, when Mira turns to me in the domed room, any lingering erotic memories are banished. My mother's eyes are glassy with fright; the hand she holds out to me is trembling. "Tell me everything you know about what happened here," she commands with a voice that echoes in the domed room like an oracle.

I tell her everything I've read about the séance. About the wind and the children's voices and the footsteps. When I tell her about the children's hand-prints on the ceiling, Mira looks up and immediately finds the paint marks that I had seen before.

"Then Frank Campbell screamed and Tom Quinn—the novelist's assistant—lit a candle and found that Campbell had had a heart attack."

Mira shakes her head. "No, it wasn't a heart attack . . ." Mira places her hand over her own heart. "A blow to the heart, yes, but not a heart attack."

"You're saying Frank Campbell was murdered by a ghost?"

Mira laughs. The sound, echoing off the grotto's walls, takes me totally by surprise. "No, dear, ghosts don't kill like that. I think it must have been one of the circle. I have a feeling the whole séance was a sham. Handprints on the ceiling . . ." Mira kneels and reaches under the stone bench. After a minute of groping around she pulls out what looks like a bundle of sticks but, when unfolded, turns out to be a telescoping rod with a carved wooden hand at its end. ". . . oldest trick in the book."

"How . . . ?" I'm going to ask Mira how she knew the rod would be there, but then I realize that, like the question of how she found the nymph statue, the answer is unlikely to be satisfying. "So you think Corinth Blackwell was a fake?" I ask instead.

"I didn't say that, dear. Authentic mediums have been reduced to using inauthentic means. Sometimes it's easier than exposing oneself to genuine spirits. There are things better left unseen," she says, and I know she's thinking of the one séance I attended when I was twelve. I wonder for not the first time if she saw what I saw. Or did she only guess at its horror from my reaction? "I imagine your medium didn't want to conjure up a real spirit—but she did anyway. When you have the gift, you can't hide from it. Sooner or later it will come looking for you."

Suddenly Mira looks very tired. She places her hand on the ground to steady herself and then pulls it away as if she's touched something hot. "I think I've exhausted what I can tell you here," she says, getting slowly to her feet. "I'm sorry I haven't been more of a help, but I think I'd better . . ."

Before she can finish her sentence, Mira is already leaving the grotto. When I join her outside, I'm alarmed by how washed-out and weak my mother looks.

"Come on up to the house, Mom," I say. "You need to rest."

"No, it's against the rules and I don't want to get you in trouble." Mira puts her arm around me and draws me to her, hugging me tightly. "I know how important it is for you to be here. This is your journey; I can't take it for you."

When she lets me go, she holds my gaze for a moment and then turns away. I'm surprised. I had thought she was going to try to get me to leave, warn me off Bosco, beg me to come home . . . but instead she's already walking away toward the hedge that surrounds the *giardino segreto*. She turns at an opening in the hedge and raises an arm in farewell. I wave back, stifling an urge to call her back. When she disappears into the hedge, I have the uncomfortable feeling that the opening in the hedge has closed up behind her. I feel not so much that my mother has been swallowed up, as that I have been sealed in.

My mother's visit was so brief that I begin, in the next few days, to wonder if it happened at all. The image of my mother standing at the bottom of the garden, white-robed and loose-haired, merges with half a dozen other images that haunt my dreams: various girls in flowing white drapery who wander the gardens of Bosco as if lost. The dreams always end the same way, with me following one of these figures through a grove of ilex so dense that all I can see of the fleeing girl are wisps of her white dress that catch on the branches and leave diaphanous shreds on the thorns. The thorns tear at my own skin, but I know that if I let the girl out of my sight, I'll lose my way and be trapped in the thicket forever. I follow her down a path sloping toward the center of the maze, a green tunnel that grows darker and narrower until I realize that it's not leading into the center of the maze, but into the center of the earth. I catch up with the girl just as she begins her descent into the underworld, and she turns, there on the brink between light and dark, her face pale and smooth and featureless as a river stone. Only it's not time and water and wind that have wiped her face clean, but thorns that have flayed her flesh as she ran through the groves. The white-blazed trail I've been following is a trail of flesh.

Any doubt, though, that my mother's visit was imaginary is put to rest when, after three nights of these dreams, Diana Tate calls me to her office in the gatehouse. I walk over after breakfast, clutching my thin cardigan across my chest in the cold wind, fearing the worst. The Board has realized they made a terrible mistake letting me in; my professors have retracted their recommendations; I've been unmasked as a fraud. The Tudor gatehouse, at the end of a long, winding path through tall pine trees, looms in their shadows like the witch's house in "Hansel and Gretel." I have to struggle against the wind to get the door open, and when I do the wind follows me in, stirring the pamphlets about Bosco on the shelves in the reception alcove. Each one is decorated with a drawing of a Greek goddess pouring an amphora into a spring beneath a pine tree, and each of these girls seems to look up at me as if challenging me to defend my right to stay here at Bosco. The only live girl in the alcove, Daria, is behind the reception desk, slumped in her chair with her eyes closed and legs sprawled on her desk, listening to a voice that drones from the speakerphone.

"And what I ask you is, if it wasn't a real spaceship, then why did I begin to have dreams about Nefertiti afterwards . . . ? Do you want me to spell Nefertiti?"

"No," Daria says, "I've got it." She cracks open her eyes as I walk by and twirls her finger in a circle by her ear and mouths the word *kooks*.

I roll my eyes in agreement even though Mira once spent an entire summer channeling the fourteenth-century-BC Egyptian queen's memoirs. I suddenly have the queasy feeling that the forces of New Age mysticism have followed me to Bosco—a feeling that's confirmed when I enter Diana Tate's elegantly appointed office and spy on the quartersawn oak surface of the director's vintage Stickley writing desk one of Mira's crystal necklaces coiled between the base of a Tiffany lamp and a white stone paperweight.

"Please have a seat, Ellis," Diana says, gesturing toward a Morris chair in front of the desk.

The cracked leather upholstery lets out a sigh as I sink into it, as if the chair had absorbed every demeaning experience it had ever witnessed: every servant dismissed by the head housekeeper (whose office this was until the early twenties) and every secretary admonished for lateness, sloppiness, typographical errors, bad spelling, misfiling, and petty thievery by the administrative director.

As I sit back in the chair I remind myself that I'm a guest here, not an employee.

"Thank you for taking time out from quiet hours to see me," Diana begins, touching a manicured hand to her pearls. She's dressed in slacks, a silk pullover, and a pale green tweed jacket—casual office clothes that make me acutely aware of my jeans and moth-eaten cardigan and SUNY Binghamton T-shirt, but then, as Diana has just said, these are *quiet hours,* working hours. I'm not meant to be dressed for an interview.

"Not at all," I murmur, trying to sound, if not offended, then at least slightly put out that my work's been interrupted.

"I'll get to the point because I know you're anxious to get back to your book. How's it going, by the way?"

"The book? Oh, very well, thank you . . . I mean it's hard . . . trying to get the period details down and establish the characters, but it's really beginning to flow . . ." I stop myself on the word *flow,* realizing that if I'm not careful, I'll lapse into "Mira-talk." It won't be long until I'm blathering on about unblocking energy chakras.

"Good," Diana says curtly. "I know the atmosphere at Bosco isn't always salutary for first-timers. The freedom from work and family responsibilities can lead to an unhealthy lassitude instead of the flourishing of creativity that Aurora Latham envisioned for Bosco. And the presence of well-known novelists can be . . . distracting. Especially to impressionable young women such as yourself."

Great. She's heard I've been smoking pot with Nat and she thinks I'm sleeping with him. She thinks I'm an author groupie trading sexual favors for letters of reference and agents' phone numbers . . . but then Diana leans forward in her chair and picks up the crystal beads and interrupts my paranoid fantasies. "We found this in the garden and footprints leading from the *giardino segreto* to the back gate, which has been chained closed for over a century. This was found on one of the gateposts"—Diana unfolds a piece of white cloth and hands it to me; the feel of the gauzy fabric instantly reminds me of my dream, the fabric turned to flesh—"and one of the guests saw you from her window talking to a woman dressed in white at the bottom of the garden," Diana concludes, sitting back in her chair.

"Yes," I admit, "it was my mother. She came because she was worried about me."

"Had you given her any reason to be worried?" Diana asks, arranging her features into a look of concern. "In your letters, perhaps?"

As if I were a homesick camper writing hysterical letters home to Mommy.

"No, not at all. She had a bad dream."

Diana lifts one eyebrow, but says nothing.

"My mother puts a lot of stock in her dreams," I say. "She's . . . well, she's sort of a psychic."

"Ah, so that explains your interest in Corinth Blackwell. I didn't realize that your Blackwell novel was autobiographical."

I'm not sure what to be more offended by: the idea that I'm using my mother as source material for the book or the accusation of autobiography. It had been, in Richard Scully's classes, the fatal flaw in all juvenilia— the taint of the personal. It was understood that every writer must write a poorly disguised autobiographical *Bildungsroman*, but that was the book meant to be discarded and moved past.

"I'd hardly call a novel about a nineteenth-century spiritualist *autobiographical*. And it's not as if I believed in all that—"

"Well, of course not. If the Board had believed you were writing a supernatural thriller, you would never have been invited here. You're not, are you? Writing a supernatural thriller?"

"No, of course not. I mean, there are scenes in which it might look like supernatural occurrences are taking place, but they're meant to be ambiguous—like in *The Turn of the Screw*."

"Oh. Not my favorite Henry James. But how you're handling your material is your own business. My concern is that the rules of Bosco, which were set in place to assure the optimum working conditions for all the guests, are respected. The guest who saw your mother in the garden was quite distracted. She said she thought she'd seen a ghost!"

Diana finishes with a dry little laugh. I know that the note of levity is supposed to signal that I'll be forgiven if I apologize properly, but the description of my mother as a ghost brings to mind the image from my dreams of the white-dressed girl fleeing through the ilex grove and her stone-smooth face turning on the brink of the path's descent into the underworld. Although the girl's features have been washed clean as the paperweight on Diana Tate's desk, I imagine there's a faint smile and the shadow of a taunt in the girl's eyes: *Follow me,* the look says. It's the same look that I see in Diana Tate's eyes right now, daring me to notice what she's let slip. *She said she thought she'd seen a ghost.* The feminine pronoun repeated three times as if it were a charm. The only other female guest at Bosco is Bethesda Graham.

I deliver my little speech of apology. It'll never happen again. I'll make sure my mother understands. No, there's no one else in my family likely to pay a surprise visit. It's always been just me and my mother. And I'll apologize to my fellow guest for scaring her.

Diana Tate looks satisfied—at the sparseness of my family unit *and* that I've caught on to the fact that it was Bethesda Graham who informed on me.

❧

"It sounds like Bethesda's jealous of you," David tells me.

I'd been too upset after my interview with Diana Tate to go back to work. I couldn't go to Nat to complain about Bethesda, of course, even if I weren't still smarting from Diana's comment about *impressionable young women such as yourself.* So I'd made my way up to the room I've come to think of as the animal den because of its carvings of bears and eagle. Sitting on the edge of David's bed, I feel that I have indeed found my way to an animal's lair, one padded and lined with blueprints and maps instead of fur and feathers. The clutter on the bed has grown to such thickness that I can't imagine where David finds a place to sleep. Not that he looks as if he's been getting much sleep. The healthy outdoors look he had when he came to Bosco has been replaced with pale skin and dark shadows under his eyes. His black hair hangs lankly over his forehead. He's been skipping breakfast and dinner, so I haven't seen him in several days.

"Why in the world would Bethesda Graham be jealous of me?" I ask.

David shrugs and looks away from me. "Maybe because you've been smoking pot in Nat Loomis's room."

Ah, I think, so that's why he's been avoiding me. "David," I say, moving a few inches closer to him on the bed. "I was only hanging out with Nat because he seemed so lonely that day . . ."

"You don't owe me an explanation," he says, his voice cold.

"But, I do . . . I mean, I don't want you to think there's anything going on between me and Nat . . ." As I say the words, I realize how false they sound. *Is* there something going on between Nat and me? I wonder, remembering that ghostly kiss I'd felt in his room.

He looks up, his dark hair falling in front of his eyes, and moves toward me, the old mattress creaking under his weight and sinking into a trough that pulls me toward him, almost as if the bed itself were delivering me to him. But when his hand touches my face, I hear a sound like beating wings and I can't help looking toward the headboard to see if the carved eagle has come to life as it does in my dreams. When he feels me tense, he shifts away from me and stands up.

"You should get back to work," he says, his back to

me, and then, as if regretting the preemptory dismissal: "Here, I found this in an old trunk up in the attic. I thought you might find it interesting." David riffles through the stacks of paper on his desk and extracts a yellowed and dog-eared poster for the Lyceum Theater, Gloversville, New York, advertising the program for July 9, 1882. The headliner is a woman called Queen Eusapia, "The Clever Lady of Mystery." Below Queen Eusapia, "Retained for one week longer owing to her enormous success," is Corinth Blackwell, "The girl who talks to ghosts."

"Wow, this is great," I say, wincing at the false brightness in my voice. "I knew that Corinth appeared on the stage before she did private séances, but I never pictured her performing alongside juggling acts and burlesque dancers."

"Look at the bottom of the bill," David says, turning and sitting on the edge of his desk.

I look at David first, searching his face for a sign that he's forgiven me for taking up with Nat, but it's as if a film has settled over his eyes, as if a part of him isn't really here. I look down at the poster and see the last act on the bill: *The Great Quintini, Master of Disappearances.*

Chapter Twelve

Tom watches Corinth enter the grotto with Milo Latham's arm around her waist. He was a fool to think she'd leave with him now when she wouldn't wait for him ten years ago. He moves back into the niche and sits on the bench by the small statue and rinses his hands in the water trickling from her upturned vase into the basin below. Violet had shown him the statue when they first arrived at Bosco and told him the story behind it. It was the kind of story she enjoyed: a nymph who'd been so grief-stricken by her husband's death that she'd melted into water. Mrs. Ramsdale's heroines were always wasting away, but in Tom's experience women very rarely melted away from grief. Such transformations, he believed, were illusions, and illusions were something he knew about. They were all about misdirection, leading the audience's attention away from the real trick, which, in a way, was the trick Corinth had practiced on him.

In those first few weeks with Corinth, all he saw was a girl who'd been badly hurt. It wasn't just the rope burns on her wrists and ankles, although those were so bad that she was unable to stand or lift so much as a spoon to her mouth, or her cracked ribs, which had to be taped because that brute Oswald had pulled the ropes around her chest so tight. Something inside her had been squeezed out by those ropes, as if her spirit had been forced out of her body. She lay on the bed in the boardinghouse where he took her from the Lyceum, staring up at the ceiling, her eyes open but unseeing.

Corinth's father came and looked at his daughter lying still on the bed and said, "This is what her mother was like before she died. It won't be long." And then he'd left. Tom found out later from the manager at the Lyceum that he'd collected Corinth's wages and said he planned to try his luck out west.

The doctor came and examined Corinth. He said it was shock and would pass, but Mrs. McGreevey, who ran the boardinghouse, said she'd seen this happen before to Indians from the settlement up at Barktown who'd come to live in the town and lost their way. "Like a light gone out in them," she said, not unkindly, but letting Tom know what he might be up against.

"Indians? But she's not . . . ?"

For an answer Mrs. McGreevey had slipped her fingers under the neck of Corinth's nightgown and pulled out a blue beaded leather pouch hanging from a leather thong around her neck. She drew out from the bag some dried green leaves and crumbled them between her fingers, releasing a sweet aroma.

"Sweetgrass," Mrs. McGreevey told him. "I've seen

the Indian medicine men burn it to bring back those lost souls." She held a pinch of the dried grass under the girl's nose and she stirred faintly. "Mind you, I wouldn't like my neighbors to know that pagan ceremonies were going on up here," she said, placing the leaves in Tom's palm. "I've got my four girls to think about and their reputations. I'd smoke a pipe, if I were you, to cover the smell."

And so for four days Tom had burned the sweet-grass in a copper saucer beside Corinth's bed while he sat on the window ledge and puffed pipe smoke into Mrs. McGreevey's backyard. The four McGreevey girls sat outside in the shade of a white viburnum tree and sewed gloves. They did piecework for one of the local glove shops—nearly all the women in Gloversville did. "Respectable work," Mrs. McGreevey said. "A man could do worse than marry a woman who can contribute to the family with such respectable work done in her own home."

The leather pieces, already cut, were dropped off in the morning by one of the factory cutters, and the finished gloves were picked up by another man in the evening. The cutters all wore gleaming white long-sleeved shirts and ties and striped waistcoats. Watching them reminded Tom of his brief stint as a watchmaker's apprentice. He'd been good with his hands, but he'd found the regular hours dull. Then he'd found other uses for his nimble fingers and gone on the stage. He'd been touring for seven years—since he was fourteen—and had thought it a decent life up until now.

On the fourth day he'd heard a rustle from the bed and saw that the girl had turned her head and was looking at him. When Mrs. McGreevey came up with the lunch tray, she helped him get her into a chair so she could look out the window "and get some air on that white face of hers."

A few days later the girl spoke for the first time. "What are they making?" she asked Tom, tilting her chin toward the circle of girls under the viburnum.

"They're sewing gloves," he told her. "We're in Gloversville. That's what people do here."

She'd looked down at her own bandaged hands, which lay like slaughtered doves in her lap, and smiled. "I like that. A town named for what people do in it."

When the bandages came off, Tom asked one of the McGreevey girls (they were named Nora, Jane, Elizabeth, and Sue, but he could never quite tell them apart) for some of the leather and thread and asked if she would show Corinth how to sew gloves. "To help her get the use of her hands back," he said.

She agreed and the next morning—it turned out to be Nora, the second-to-oldest sister—came upstairs with a packet of white kid leather and white thread. She drew a chair up close to Corinth's and patiently showed her how to sew the delicate leather, their heads bending together—Corinth's dark, red-flecked hair and Nora's pale yellow curls—in the sunshine.

Corinth learned fast. The nimble fingers that could pick apart knots now learned to make tiny, almost invisible stitches in the leather. In a few more days she was well enough to sit with the other girls in the yard and, soon after that, to take walks with Tom in the meadows that sloped down from the McGreevey house to the edge of the millpond. She told him about the town she grew up in—a lumber town with the same name as hers. She mentioned the name of the man who owned the lumber mill, and he said he recognized it from one of the bigger glove factories in town. A shadow had passed over her dark eyes then, but Tom hadn't asked her to explain. He remembered it, though, later.

He told her about the orphanage in Brooklyn, the apprenticeship, and then his exploits on the stage. He did simple tricks for her: producing a bouquet of wildflowers from behind her ear and walking coins across his knuckles. He asked her to show him how she slipped her wrists and ankles out of the ropes during her séances.

"How did you know about that?" she asked.

"You can't trick a fellow magician," he told her. She showed him the knots she knew and how to release them, even though, he knew, she hated touching the ropes.

They found a stone icehouse on the other side of the pond, its wide-planked floor covered with the sawdust used to store the ice in winter, which was cool even on the hottest days and held in its old stones the smell of snowmelt and the mountains. Lying side by side on the sawdust-cushioned floor, she told him the names of the rivers and streams that flowed out of the mountains. Saranac, Raquette, Moose, and Chateaugay. Shroon and Black, Beaver and Salmon. All the tributaries and rivers that carried spruce logs from the heart of the mountains down to the Big Boom at Glens Falls. The Saint Regis and the Oswegatchie, Mill and Trout Brooks, Otter Creek, and the Sacandaga, which flooded the marshes of the Big Vly, where her mother's people came from. While she named the rivers, Tom traced the lines the sun made, shining through the slats of the roof, on her skin. Turning to him, her dark hair falling over her bare shoulders, the light rippling over her breasts and hips, she was like a river herself. Making love to her was like being pulled into a strong current.

When the grass in the meadow began turning purple, he asked her if she wanted to travel with him. They'd make a great act together. But she said no, she didn't want to ever go onstage again after what had happened with Oswald. More than anything, she wanted to stay in one place so that if her soul ever left her body again, it would know where to come back to.

It had been her idea to stay in Gloversville.

He reminds himself of that now, coming out of his memories to find himself staring at the blank and featureless face of the little nymph. The plan was to save enough money to start their own glove shop—only he'd seen a way to do it quicker. He had an engagement in New York City that fall. He'd keep it and make enough money to get them started. He'd be back by Christmas.

He left her safe in the bosom of the McGreevey family—in that circle of white-dressed girls sewing beneath the viburnum tree, the blossoms of which had turned tea-colored and rattled in the wind like dry paper when he kissed her good-bye. It was true that he hadn't made it back by Christmas—the engagement in New York had lasted longer than he'd expected and then he'd gotten sick—but he had written to explain. It was March before he made it back to Gloversville, and by then she had left the McGreeveys and gone to work at Milo Latham's factory. He'd gone to look for her at the dormitory where she'd lived since late December, but one of the girls said she'd left the week before—taken in one of Mr. Latham's carriages.

Tom pats the little statue on the head and gets up. He stands at the hedge for just a moment, listening for voices, but the servants have come and gone, carrying the body of Frank Campbell up to the house on a stretcher. Milo and Corinth have gone back to the house as well.

He slips behind the statue of the river god into the grotto and finds it empty. There's a dark stain on the stone bench and splotches of white where the paint from the hand marks on the ceiling has flaked off. A damp footprint near the dark stain. Latham must have stood there and inspected the marks. He was a thorough man, one who liked to make sure personally that any job he commissioned was done to his satisfaction. He paid well enough to see that it was. In the end, Tom can't really blame Corinth for tossing in her lot with him. He kneels down by the stone bench—like a man come to this pagan shrine to do homage to the resident god of the place—and reaches under the bench, where he finds a telescoping rod and a bow. He pushes both implements farther under the bench and then, flattening himself against the cold stone floor, crawls into the tunnel.

Corinth walks up the fountain allée two steps behind Milo Latham and the doctor, who have ceased discussing Frank Campbell's cause of death and gone on to more interesting topics: the effect of the current drought on the logging business, the legislature in Albany's creation of the Adirondack Park and that bill's effect on logging, and the threat that further legislation might curtail logging on state-owned land. In short, the body borne before them on a canvas stretcher (an implement generally used in the Latham household to transport firewood) might as well be made of wood as far as the two men who precede Corinth onto the terrace are concerned.

They are greeted by the lady of the house, in a subdued fawn-colored robe, her red hair hanging in two long braids over her shoulders. The *déshabillé,* to Corinth's eye, is carefully calculated. *A man has died in my house,* it says, *and I won't stand on ceremony.* The dark circles under her eyes also speak of the effect the painter's death has had on her, but beneath the pallor of her skin, Corinth senses a tremor running through her hostess's thin frame that is closer to excitement than nerves.

"Thank you for coming so quickly, Dr. Murdoch. We are grateful for your assistance in these dreadful circumstances."

"Not at all, Mrs. Latham. It must have been quite a shock to you."

"I only wish I could have prevented . . ."

"You mustn't blame yourself. It is clear from Mr. Campbell's color and physique that he suffered from a congenital weakness of the heart."

"So it wasn't the arrow—"

The doctor purses his lips together and pushes out a puff of air. "A mere child's toy that barely pricked the gentleman's shoulder. It was the shock of the thing that killed him. Of course, in the excitement of the moment and in the poor lighting of the grotto, some of your guests might have thought they saw an arrow protruding from the dead man's chest, but that would have been a delusion, as I'm sure they will all see in the calm light of morning. And I hope," the doctor continues, his voice acquiring the patronizing tone he uses with recalcitrant patients, "they will also see the folly of such experiments."

Aurora inclines her head and lowers her eyes demurely, an attitude of humility Corinth has never seen her hostess adopt before. Her deference to the doctor's words gives Corinth some hope. If Aurora chooses not to pursue the séances, Latham might be forced to let her go, after all.

"Would you mind," Aurora asks, lifting up her head, "seeing to one of my guests? Mrs. Ramsdale, whom I believe you met when she stayed here last year, was quite undone by the incident. Her health is not the best to begin with . . ."

"Of course," Dr. Murdoch replies. "I'm an admirer of Mrs. Ramsdale's work. I'll be happy to look in on her."

Milo escorts the doctor into the front hall and up the stairs to the second floor, their conversation as they go progressing from logging to hunting and a promise from Latham that he'll take the doctor up to his camp on the Sacandaga in the fall. The servants, at Aurora's instruction, carry Campbell's body to the east parlor, where he will await the arrival of the undertaker. Corinth would like to slip into the house and up to her room, but Aurora catches her at the doors to the library and pulls her back out onto the terrace.

"I'd like a word with you, Miss Blackwell," she says. "Will you walk with me in the garden so our voices don't disturb the other guests? I'm afraid that the tragedy has taken a particularly heavy toll on Mrs. Ramsdale."

Corinth bows her head at her hostess's suggestion, taking a cue from her hostess's humble bearing before the doctor, and they walk together down the steps to the second terrace and from there along the shaded arbor bordered by a marble trough into which water trickles from the wide-open mouths of satyrs.

"I usually find the sound of water soothing," Aurora says when they have walked for several minutes in silence, "but this morning even Bosco's fountains fail to calm me. I feel . . . I feel . . ."

"It was a horrible thing," Corinth interrupts. "Of course you'll want to discontinue the séances—"

"Discontinue the séances!" Aurora wheels around to face Corinth, her glossy red braids whipping around like snakes. Her face—white and openmouthed—looks exactly like that of a statue of Medusa that Corinth remembers from a gallery in Florence. "When we made such progress last night? I heard my dear, sweet children's voices. I felt their little hands on my face—" Aurora lifts her own hands and places them on either side of Corinth's face. Her fingers are ice-cold, but when she pats Corinth's face it feels, for just a moment, the way a child's hand—*no, an infant's*—strokes its mother's face. Corinth has to bite her lip to keep from striking the woman's hands away from her.

"—I can feel them now, all around us." The two women have come to the end of the arbor, to the semicircular bench in the ilex grove, where Corinth remembers seeing on her first day—was it really only the day before yesterday?—a seated statue. There's no statue now. Aurora sits on the bench and draws Corinth down beside her. "I believe you have awoken them. I must speak to them—there's something I must explain. You see, I'm afraid I wasn't always the best mother. I was sometimes impatient with them when they would play their games and hide from me in the garden or refuse to take their medicine when they were sick. James, especially, was very, very willful. Like his father. When my husband sets his mind on a thing . . . At times I had to be quite strict with him—James, of course, not

Milo—for his own good. But then he would convince Tam and Cynthia to join him in his little rebellions." She lowers her voice and leans closer to Corinth, her lips only inches from Corinth's face. "He's doing it even now," she says in a whisper that Corinth feels on her skin, "using the other two to do his little tricks. I believe he's keeping them from their salvation. So you see how vital it is we contact Cynthia and Tam *alone,* without him. Can you do that?"

Corinth stares at her hostess, unable at first to grasp what she means. Then she does.

"You're asking me to separate the children?"

"I knew you would understand," Aurora says, rising from the bench with the satisfied air of a mistress whose orders have been comprehended by a not particularly bright servant. "I told my husband I must have the best medium because I knew that he always gets what he goes after. There's no time to waste. We'll have to have another séance tonight." She stands for a moment, waiting, no doubt, for Corinth to rise, too, but when she doesn't, Aurora smiles. "Of course, you want to commune with their spirits here to prepare yourself for tonight. I can feel them, too." Her eyes dart around the encircling trees with a hectic glance, and then, before Corinth can stop her, she flees down the arbor like a deer that's heard the huntsman's horn.

After she goes, Corinth sits in the grove, as rooted to the bench as that statue she imagined seeing here. She's had peculiar requests in her day: a countess in Marienbad who wanted to contact her dead spaniel; a doctor's wife who came to her circles at the hotel in New York for three weeks in a row to contact her daughter, who, Corinth learned when the doctor finally paid her a call, was alive and well and living in Paterson, New Jersey; and of course there was Mr. Oswald, who wanted forgiveness from his dead son for torturing the boy's mother. Most of the people who come to her to contact a lost loved one do so because they have unfinished business with the dead. But this . . . reaching into the darkness to sever the children's ties to one another . . . Even if she didn't find the idea sickening, she can't imagine how she could perform such a delicate operation. She doubts that anyone—even the *best medium*—could.

She smiles in spite of herself. *The best medium.* Yes, Milo Latham certainly gets whatever he goes after. He got her—but then, she wasn't all that difficult a quarry. The first time she resisted, that time he found her alone in the mill, sweeping sawdust off the floors. He came up behind her and touched her hair. "Indian hair," he said, moving his hand from her hair to her breast and pulling her by the hips toward him, "but with sparks of fire." She'd wheeled around so quickly that the broom handle hit him in the stomach, and while he bent over in pain, she ran out of the mill and all the way home, where she found Wanda White Cloud helping her mother bake bread in the kitchen. When she told what happened, Wanda White Cloud said it was only a matter of time. He'd *spoilt* near a dozen girls in the town. What could anyone do? He owned the town.

"You should let Mike take her to that revival show like he's been wanting to," Wanda said. "At least she'd be out of harm's way."

Six years they'd been on the road before Gloversville. Who would think a man like Latham would even remember who she was. But he had.

It was three weeks after Tom Quinn had left Gloversville to go to New York and two weeks after she'd realized she was pregnant. She'd woken up every morning for the last week in Mrs. McGreevey's boardinghouse sick to her stomach and scared, until finally, on this morning, she'd gotten up before dawn and written Tom a letter. He'd have to come back for her sooner than Christmas, she explained in her letter. She couldn't expect Mrs. McGreevey to keep her. For all her kindness, all she ever talked about was the respectability of her establishment and the marriageability of her four daughters. She couldn't do that to them. She had to know if Tom would marry her or . . . or she'd have to make some other arrangements.

She wondered, while walking the three miles into town, what those "other arrangements" could possibly be. She walked across the fields where she and Tom had lain that summer, the long purple grasses brushing against her skirts with a dry papery sound like women whispering. She thought of the McGreevey sisters sitting in their white dresses beneath the viburnum tree and it was like a childhood memory she'd left behind a long time ago. She thought of her mother in a grave in a strange place and her baby sister growing up with strangers. What had it mattered, she wondered, that she'd gotten away from Milo Latham six years ago if she'd ended up coming to the same thing? She was still wondering as she walked up the steps to the post office and heard the voice behind her. "Indian hair," it said—a voice that made her scalp prickle, "but with sparks of fire."

She turned around slowly this time, and when she saw Milo Latham standing below her on the steps of the Gloversville Post Office, she wondered if she were dreaming. The edges of his black coat were blurring in the morning sunlight, the rustle of dried grasses was deafening. She remembered that her mother always said that a ringing in the ears was bad luck. Then she was watching herself from above, a stupid girl fainting on the post office steps.

She came to on a green velvet couch in a room with purple drapes. Milo Latham was sitting in a chair across from her, smoking a pipe.

"You really must take better care of yourself, Miss Blackwell. A life on the stage has not been kind to you."

"I've left the stage," Corinth said. "I make gloves now."

"Even worse," he said, "for a woman of your talents. You should allow me to take care of you." He got up and joined her on the couch. Ran his hand through her hair, which someone had loosened from its pins. She knew she had to get up off the couch—and part of her did. She watched the man touching the girl, unbuttoning her dress, pushing her skirts up, and thought, if the other one doesn't come back, she can tell this one the baby's his.

In the ilex grove Corinth pushes the heels of her hands into her eye sockets and wills the memory away. She would like to think that she succumbed to Milo Latham in a moment of weakness, not a moment of cold-blooded calculation, but why then hadn't she mailed the letter to Tom, after all? Hadn't she decided even then that being a rich man's mistress might be easier than being a poor man's wife? Who is she, after *that*, to judge Aurora Latham? To judge anyone? She made her plans and, as it turned out, she'd been wise. When Tom didn't come back at Christmas, she went to Latham's factory, and because he was away for the holiday, she'd taken a job there and waited for him. Even after Latham returned she waited to see if Tom might still show up, but when she couldn't wait any longer she went to Latham and told him she was pregnant with his child, and he was true to his word. He took care of her.

She opens her eyes and spots of color swim across her vision: blooms of orange and red that waver like flames in the glossy green foliage and then, dying out, spark the thicket like fireflies. When her vision clears, she is staring into the face of a little girl standing on the edge of the grove. She's wearing a white dress with a pink ribbon in her hair and she's holding a smooth white stone in one hand. The girl turns and melts into the bushes, looking once over her shoulder to see if Corinth is following her.

Chapter Thirteen

I take the poster back to my room and tack it to the window frame above my desk. At first it's hard to get back to work. I'm unsettled by the fact that both Diana Tate and David—and Bethesda, if David's right—think something's going on between me and Nat. I'd sworn to myself that I'd never let this happen to me again when rumors started circulating last year that I was having an affair with Richard Scully. I'd promised myself that I'd be more careful in my choices, but apparently I have a knack for being drawn to exactly the wrong kind of man. Damn—Nat Loomis wasn't even *nice* to me (then, neither, in the end, was Richard Scully). The worst thing is that if Nat heard the rumor, he might think I'd actually encouraged it!

I stare at the theatrical poster and try to think about Tom Quinn instead of Nat Loomis. I picture a dashing dark-haired man performing amazing feats of magic on the stage. Then I start to write. I rewrite the séance scene, hinting that it's Tom—*Master of Disappearances*—who shoots the arrow through Frank Campbell's heart.

I'm so engrossed in my writing that when I look up from my laptop and out the window, I see that the last light is fading in the western sky. The clock on my screen reads 4:00—only another hour of quiet hours. Up until now the phrase has sounded like an admonishment from the ghost of some mad librarian, but today those hours have stolen past me so stealthily that I imagine them personified as Greek goddesses—like the Muses or the Graces: The Quiet Hours, barefoot girls in white dresses dancing around me in a sacred circle. I can almost hear them padding softly by my door . . .

I close my laptop and listen, then move to the door. Someone *is* walking by. I swing open the door and surprise Bethesda Graham walking barefoot down the hall in pajamas, cradling a blue-and-white teacup, which slips from her hands at the sound of my door opening.

"Shit," Bethesda says, moving back from the splash of hot water and stepping on a piece of broken china with a sickening crunch.

"Your foot! God, I'm so sorry. I didn't mean to startle you."

"You could have fooled me. You swung that door open like the cuckolded husband in a bad French farce."

"Can I get you a Band-Aid?"

"I've got some in my room." Bethesda hops forward and nearly falls, but I grab hold of her arm and steady her.

"Let me at least help you to your room."

Although she's light, I have a hard time getting

Bethesda down the hall because of the disparity in our heights and because she's such an unwilling cripple. Instead of leaning on my arm, she alternately pulls on it and lurches away from it. By the time I lower her onto her unmade bed, my back aches and I feel as if I've pulled a muscle in my shoulder.

"The Band-Aids are in the desk drawer—do you mind?" Bethesda says, propping her foot on the opposite knee and leaning over to examine her wound.

Going to look for the Band-Aid, I can't help but notice the change in Bethesda's desk since I was last here. If my muses are a circle of barefoot girls, Bethesda's muse must be the goddess Kali dancing her dance of destruction. The stacks of books and papers have careened into one another like a stack of cards that's been shuffled, forming a mound several feet high and covering the entire surface of the desk. The chaos, like an overfertilized houseplant, has sent runners up the muslin curtains, where the number of notes and documents has doubled in the last three days. Turning to Bethesda, I see that she's taken one of the pearl-tipped pins off the sleeve of her shirt (not a pajama top, as I first thought, but an oversized man's dress shirt worn over thermal gray leggings) and is using it to pry a splinter of china out of her heel.

"Can I help?" I ask, bringing the package of Band-Aids to Bethesda.

She shakes her head and continues digging into her flesh, impassive as a surgeon. I can't help thinking of the cutting reviews that Bethesda is famous for and the dissection of lives that she practices in her biographies. I look from the slight figure with pale skin and shadowed eyes back to the monument to research she's erected on her desk. It's bigger than she is.

"Can I ask you a question?"

Bethesda looks up. "Okay, but if you're going to interrogate me, you might as well be holding the implement of torture." She hands me the pin. "My eyesight is shot."

I pull the desk chair over to the edge of the bed and bend over Bethesda's foot. A half-inch-long blue splinter is wedged into the heel, the skin of which is surprisingly soft and uncalloused. I press my fingernail into the skin just below the point of the splinter and slip the pin under the skin. This is something I'm actually quite good at—something Mira taught me.

"Did you tell Diana Tate that you saw me in the garden with a woman in white?" I ask as I scoop the pin under the splinter.

"I don't know what you're talking about. A woman in white? Are we in a Wilkie Collins novel now— Hey, you got it!"

I hold up the sliver and hand it to Bethesda along with the pin. "My mother is sort of like a character from Wilkie Collins," I say. "That's who it was. She paid me a surprise visit. Diana Tate said a guest—a female guest— saw us from her window."

Bethesda laughs. "That's one of Diana's tricks. When she has a complaint, she always pretends that it originated with another guest."

I'm tempted not to believe her, but then I take another glance at her desk and realize that it couldn't have been Bethesda who saw me—at least not from her room. "I'm sorry," I say, looking toward her desk. "Of course it wasn't you. You can't have opened those drapes for weeks."

Bethesda follows my gaze to the pinned drapes and turns pink. "I suppose that looks like the work of a madwoman."

"Then I guess we're all mad. I've been sticking notes up all over, too. I just tacked an old theater poster to my window frame—"

"A theater poster?"

"I found one that lists Tom Quinn on it as a magician. It made me think he might have been the one behind the effects in the first séance."

"You think he was Corinth's accomplice?"

"Well, maybe," I say, oddly uncomfortable with the notion of Tom as accomplice—it somehow doesn't feel right—but then something else occurs to me. "Maybe he was working for Milo Latham."

"Hm," Bethesda says, with a look of grudging admiration, "you might have something there. After all, Milo *was* having an affair with Corinth—" Bethesda stops when she sees the surprise in my face and smiles — glad, I think—that I haven't figured out everything, after all. "You didn't know?"

I shake my head. "Did Aurora know?"

"Oh, yes, she mentions it in her journal. Let me see, I've got the reference here somewhere . . ." Bethesda goes to her desk and rummages through a stack of papers, some slipping loose from the piles and drifting to the floor. "Here it is. She wrote, 'Today the medium arrived at Bosco. She is pretty in a common way, but I don't quite see what Milo sees in her.' "

"But I thought Aurora herself invited Corinth Blackwell to Bosco."

"Yes, she did. That's what makes it so poignant. Aurora was so desperate—foolishly desperate—to contact her lost children that she was willing to undergo the humiliation of entertaining her husband's mistress under her own roof." Bethesda sighs and shakes her head. "Here, I want to show you something." She gets up and goes to her closet. I'm expecting her to produce some document proving her point, but instead she comes back with socks and a pair of green rubber boots, which she proceeds to put on over her leggings.

"Come on, you can wear one of my sweaters," she says, pulling on a white fisherman's knit sweater and handing an almost identical one to me. "It's cold outside."

"But where are we going?" I ask.

"To the children's cemetery."

We go out the side door on the western end of the house and down a narrow path that leads directly to the ilex grove on the second terrace. No wonder she always beat me to it after breakfast; she had a shortcut.

Bethesda pauses in the center of the clearing as if listening for something. At first all I hear is the wind sifting through the underbrush, rattling bare branches and sweeping dried pine needles along the marble terraces, but then I hear a voice so faint I'm not sure whether it's real until I recognize it as Zalman Bronsky's.

"When water's heart is silver, it will beat," he recites, "so silently it can't be found through sound." The two lines, repeated, grow fainter until the words can't be made out but the cadence remains, like the garden's pulse.

"Where is he?" I ask.

Bethesda shrugs. "He's probably on one of the hidden paths that Aurora had carved out of the hedges. The whole hillside is really a maze. I was sitting here a few weeks ago reading one of Aurora's journals, and I came across a reference to 'the white-blazed path to the children's cemetery' and I happened to look down and notice this—" Bethesda kneels at the edge of the circle directly across from the marble bench and pushes away a vine to reveal a round white stone nestled in a bed of dried pine needles like an egg in a bird's nest.

"These are all over the house," I say, kneeling beside Bethesda, "in the library and on Diana Tate's desk—I even found a few in my room." I don't mention that David Fox has a dozen of them in his room, because I don't want Bethesda to know I've been there.

"The children collected them on hiking trips up at the Lathams' summer camp. They're from a river gorge in the mountains where they were rounded and smoothed by the water." Bethesda picks up the stone and holds it, one hand over the other like a child trapping a firefly, and then passes it to me. It fits perfectly in the palm of my hand and feels cool. Holding it is like cupping water. I pass the stone back to Bethesda, who replaces it on its nest of pine needles as carefully as if it really were an egg. "She used them because the children were so fond of them." She gets up, brushing gold pine needles from her legs, and sweeps aside a curtain of vines that hangs over an opening between two ilex trees. "Come on."

I follow her onto the narrow path, but when I try to straighten up as Bethesda has done, my head hits the branches of the ilex trees, which have twisted into a low canopy above the path. Even when I crouch, the prickly ilex leaves catch at my hair. It's all I can do to keep Bethesda in sight as we wind our way down the steep hill passing from the ilex grove into the maze of overgrown box hedges. Fortunately, Bethesda's white sweater stands out against the dark green hedges even as the light fades in the sky above us and the path grows dark. I can also see the white stones that mark the path whenever another path crosses over it—at least most of the time. Some of the crossroads are unmarked, their stone markers either sunken into the brush or picked up as souvenirs by previous houseguests. Bethesda, though, appears to know exactly where she's going, and she also seems to be in a rush to get there, not sparing a look back to see if I'm keeping up. In fact, I can't help wondering if this isn't some nasty trick Bethesda has cooked up to get back at me for that afternoon in Nat's room. Maybe she plans to lead me into the dense underbrush of Bosco and abandon me.

The idea makes my skin prickle with shame. It's like high school all over again, when my classmates would draw pentagrams on my locker. It was after I'd transferred from the local Lily Dale school (where half the children had parents who were psychics) to a magnet school with a gifted program. No matter how hard I had tried to blend in—ditching Mira's organic lunches and saving my babysitting money to buy clothes at the mall to replace Mira's hand-sewn tunics and peasant dresses—I had been a pariah. It wasn't until college and writing classes, where an eccentric background was deemed an asset, that I began to make friends. Now I feel I'm back where I started: the butt of a practical joke.

The path levels off and I guess that we've passed the *giardino segreto* and are behind the rose garden. Thick thorny rose branches reach up through the hedges, the dead roses and rose hips rustling in the wind with a dry papery whisper that sounds like the whisper of *witch* I'd hear as I walked to my table in the school cafeteria. I swipe angrily at my face, and my hands come away sticky. I've walked through a spiderweb and a strand of the sticky silk has gotten in my mouth. I stop and spit and rub at my face with the rough sleeve of my sweater. When I lift my head up, the hedges ahead have closed around me; there's no sign of Bethesda or the path.

"Okay," I say out loud, "I'll just go back, then." But when I turn, I see that the path behind me is barely discernible in the gloom and that it divides in two not far from where I stand. There is, though, something white snagged on a rose thorn in the hedges on one of the paths—a scrap of wool maybe from either my sweater or Bethesda's—which would tell me which path we came on. As I reach my hand into the hedge, I'm suddenly visited by an image from my dream—the white-blazed trail of flesh—and as I touch the scrap of white, I know immediately that it's not wool or cloth but some kind of skin. As much as I want to draw back my hand in horror, I don't. I extract the scrap from its nest of thorns and watch as it uncrumples into the shape of a hand.

A glove. Made of the palest green leather and lined with spotted yellow silk. I turn back the hem and read the label—*Latham's Gloves*—and then look more closely at the lining. What I thought was a pattern in the silk is really a stain of some sort—red wine, maybe, or blood. A shallow pocket has been sewn between the silk and the leather.

"There you are! I thought I'd lost you." It's Bethesda, right behind me on the path. "I passed the entrance to the cemetery, but I see that you found it." She brushes past and, pushing back a curving branch of dried roses that clatter like hanging beads, steps into a round clearing encircled by tall cypresses and filled with the white round stones—or at least so I think until I step into the circle myself (carefully folding the glove and tucking it into the back pocket of my jeans) and look down at one of the stones to see that it's actually a grave marker inscribed with a name and a date. James

Latham, March 3, 1879. The single date of birth and death telling his whole story: a stillborn child. Spinning in a slow circle, I see that the sunken gravestones spiral out from the center, a tightly coiled snake burrowed in a nest of the same black-leafed shrub that grows in the rose garden, and that there are nearly a dozen of them.

Bethesda leads me on a tour of Aurora's lost children, walking between the stones and pointing down at each one as though she were naming flowers in an exotic nursery. "This was the first Cynthia," she says, pointing to a stone that's sunk so deep into the black ground cover that it's like looking down into a miniature well. "She only lived a week. And here are James number one and James number two, both dead before their first birthdays."

"My God, I had no idea. I knew she lost the three children and then Alice—"

"Those were the only children who lived past infancy. She had four stillbirths and three children who died of 'crib death,' as they called it in those days. After she lost the third child, she wrote in her journal"— Bethesda stops and, tilting her head, squints up toward the sky as if listening for the approach of a winged messenger—" 'I have begged my husband to release me from this torture chamber of procreation.' Then Milo would go off to the city and his women and leave her alone for a while, but as soon as he came back . . ."

Bethesda's voice trails off and she holds both hands out at her sides, palms up. Standing in the middle of the cypress-ringed circle in her long, white voluminous sweater, she looks like a figure from a Greek tragedy, standing alone on the stage after five acts of unspeakable carnage. "Imagine what it was like to lose this many children! Can you blame her for doing anything—even suffering the humiliation of harboring her husband's mistress under her own roof—to contact their spirits?"

I can't think of an answer. Instead, I scan the circle of cypresses and notice a broken marble column lying beneath one. "What's that?" I ask, walking toward the column.

"I don't know," Bethesda says, joining me at the edge of the circle. "I hadn't noticed it before." I pull back a cypress branch, uncovering a hollow in the greenery, like a cave that's been carved out of the trees. The trunks of these trees, though, are dappled white and green, almost like the bark of a sycamore, although they're much too slim and low to be sycamore. Moving closer, I can see that they're actually marble columns that have been covered in vines and lichen, holding up a low triangular pediment.

"Maybe it's a crypt," Bethesda says, kneeling between the two columns. "Look, there are stairs going underground. In her journals Aurora refers to 'the well of sorrows that lies beneath the garden and inside the pit of my soul.' I'm going to see what's down there," she says, getting to her feet and starting down the marble steps.

"Be careful," I call after her. I hope Bethesda doesn't think I'm going down there. On the last step that the light reaches, though, she turns around to see if I'm following and I start to tell her that I'll wait up here, but no sound comes out of my mouth. A form is emerging out of the darkness, just below where Bethesda is standing.

When I call out to warn Bethesda, she wheels around and loses her balance on the slippery marble, falling to the bottom of the stairwell along with whoever, or whatever, had been coming up out of the crypt, both figures disappearing into the darkness at the bottom of the stairs.

I take one look behind me, hoping that someone working in the garden may have heard my scream, but there's nothing in the circle but the silent white gravestones. Then I plunge down the stairs. It takes a moment for my eyes to adjust to the light, and then I make out a raised circular well in the middle of the floor and beneath it two figures lying on the floor, one whose legs are skewed at such an unnatural angle that my stomach clenches. But then I realize that one of the figures on the floor is a broken statue, the other is Zalman Bronsky, one leg bent at an angle that's almost as painful looking as the statue's. Bethesda is crouched by his side, her ear pressed to his chest. "Is he—?"

"He's breathing," Bethesda says, "but he's unconscious. I think he's broken his leg *and* hit his head. We'll never get him up the hill on our own. You've got to go get Nat and David."

"But I don't know the way."

"Just follow the white stones," she says. I'm about to ask why doesn't she go, but Bethesda snaps, "Well, don't just stand there! The man could die while you dawdle." Her voice is so coldly dictatorial it propels me right out of the crypt. I cross the circle of white stones and duck under the arch of dead rose vines onto the narrow path. I turn toward the house and see again that there are two paths, both going uphill, and no white stone to tell me which way to go. I know that if I keep going uphill I'll eventually find my way to the house, but I also know that every minute I waste might prove fatal to Zalman.

I'm about to go back to Bethesda to tell her I can't do it when someone steps out of the brush onto the right-hand path about ten feet ahead of me. It's a small girl—about eleven or twelve—in an old-fashioned white dress, and she's carrying a white stone. When she turns her head away, I see the pink ribbon in her hair and realize she's the same girl I saw crying in the hedge maze the day I went there with David, and I wonder how I could have believed she was only an orchid—even though that's what I smell now, the spicy scent of vanilla flooding the darkening evening air.

She starts up the path, looking once over her shoulder to see if I'm following—and of course I am. What choice do I have?

She leads me—skipping ahead of me so quickly that I can barely keep up (and at first I'm terrified of over-taking her)—on an entirely different path up the hill. She could be leading me anywhere, I think, but I stifle the thought, and we emerge on the first terrace within minutes. She's shown me a shortcut. I look for her on the terrace, but she's gone. Only a single white stone sits on the marble balustrade that I could swear wasn't there earlier today.

I can see lights on in the library and head there, hoping that at least Nat has come down early for drinks. When I open the doors, I smell the peaty aroma of Nat's scotch, but it's David I see. He's standing in front of the bookcase in the alcove putting a bottle back into a false-fronted cabinet.

"So that's how you're getting the stuff." I startle at the voice and turn to see Nat. "Diana thought I was into the private stock."

David looks up and sees me and Nat and a shadow crosses his face. He holds up his glass to both of us, and for a second I see the same curl of black smoke that had snaked out of the green medicine bottle in Nat's room wafting out of the golden liquid in David's glass. "Here's to Bosco," he says, "and finding inspiration where you can get it. It seems like you two have been into your own private stock." He sniffs, and I can smell, along with the smell of peat and decay coming from the scotch, the marijuana on Nat's clothes. I don't have time, though, to explain to David that I haven't spent the afternoon smoking with Nat.

"Zalman's been hurt," I say. "We have to get him to the hospital."

I lead them down the hill on the path the girl showed me.

"How did you find this path?" David asks.

I don't answer. I don't even know how I remember the twists and turns and manage to avoid the false crossings, but I do. It's as if the route has been imprinted on the insides of my eyelids. If I'm not sure which way to go, I close my eyes and I see the girl pointing the way. She's inside me now, I think, and the thought fills me with dread.

By the time we reach the children's cemetery, the sky is completely dark, but a full moon is rising in the eastern sky and its light makes the gravestones glow.

"What the hell is this?" David asks. "It's not on any of my maps."

" 'There are more things in heaven and earth, Horatio, than are dreamt of in your philosophy,' " Nat quotes.

"Fuck off, Loomis."

"Guys," I say, wheeling on the two of them, "we don't have time for this." And then, looking down into the dark crypt: "We should have taken a flashlight. I can't even see the steps."

David removes a small Maglite from his jacket pocket.

"Boy Scout," Nat mutters under his breath as we follow David down the steps.

"Bethesda," I call, "are you there?"

There's no answer at first, but then David's flashlight beam finds the two figures (three if you count the broken statue), and Bethesda looks up, her eyes reflecting back the light like a cat's.

"Beth—" Nat says, approaching her. "Are you okay?" She nods but still doesn't speak. Instead it's Zalman who says something in slurred speech that sounds like "We have visitors."

"Sure, Zal," David says, placing two fingers on Zalman's neck and then running his hands down the poet's leg. "This is a busy place. What brought you here, anyway?"

"I was looking for the source," Zalman says, pointing behind him with his chin, "But I found more than I bargained for, I'm afraid, and gave myself quite a scare."

I look past Zalman into the crypt. A hole in the ceiling lets in a circle of moonlight directly above a round cistern. It's shaped like a well, but is more an idealized reproduction of a well than a real one. A broken hand rests on the edge, as if the marble figure on the floor had once stood there, looking down into the well. A large stone has been fitted over the opening—or partially over the opening. Someone—Zalman, as it turns out—has pushed the stone half off.

"I thought it might be the source of the spring," Zalman says, his voice weak. "So I poked my nose in where I shouldn't have."

David gets up, and Nat and I follow him. He shines his flashlight into the well, and I look over the edge of the marble basin. The well is half-filled with the same rounded white stones that marked the path down to the cemetery, but lying on top of the stones, and bleached as white, are bones. The arrangement of the leg and arm bones suggests someone who died huddled in a tight ball. Someone who was buried alive.

Chapter Fourteen

Corinth hesitates only a moment after the girl turns, but still when she steps between the ilex trees onto the path, the girl in the white dress is nowhere to be seen. All Corinth sees is the green pollen floating down from the pines that tower above the ilexes, turning gold in the ribbons of sunlight that unfurl from the treetops, and then emerald as it settles onto the forest floor, where it lies thick and smooth and untrodden.

Then something white flashes in a patch of sunlight a few yards ahead, and Corinth starts down the path toward it, the carpet of pollen swallowing the sound of her footsteps. It's only a stone, though, a white round stone like the one the girl had held in her hand. Corinth kneels and picks it up and blows the coating of pollen off it; clearly no one has picked it up in some time. The stone is perfectly round, veined gray, and familiar to Corinth, but it's not a memory she wishes to relive at the moment. She rises to her feet and, brushing the dust from her hands, sets off down the path.

At the bottom of the hill the path continues through

the box hedges surrounding the *giardino segreto*. Corinth can smell roses and hear the water from the fountains and, at one point, a voice, which may belong to Giacomo Lantini, saying something about the source of the spring, and then she sees a flash of pink in one of the hedges, which she guesses is an errant rose strayed from the rose garden. When she gets closer, though, she sees that beneath a spray of roses there's a ribbon caught on a thorn—a pink ribbon, just like the ones tied to the bridle of the rocking horse in the children's nursery. Cynthia's favorite color. *She was buried with a pink ribbon in her hair*, Alice said.

Corinth reaches into the hedge to retrieve the ribbon, but when she touches it, the ribbon slithers through the branches and falls deep into a thorny thicket.

"Very well," Corinth says out loud, as if she were a governess cajoling a willful charge, "keep your ribbon, Cynthia." When she tries to pull her hand back, though, a thorn pierces the thin leather of her glove, digging deep into the skin on the underside of her wrist.

Corinth draws back her hand, unpeeling it from the glove, and instantly the pink ribbon falls out of the hedge at her feet.

Corinth laughs. "A trade, then," she says, bending to pick up the ribbon and consigning her glove to the hedge. A breeze moves through the hedge then, shaking loose a cascade of crimson petals from the spray of roses, which, Corinth notices now, forms an arch over a narrow gap in the hedge. She steps through into a circle of cypress trees, the loose petals settling onto her hair like a crown.

She kneels at the first stone and reads the child's name and the dates of its short life and then walks to the next and kneels again and again . . . After the fourth stone she crawls on her hands and knees from stone to stone, not because she is tired of standing and kneeling, but because she is too dizzy to stand. Milo had told her that his wife had lost "several" babies at birth, but she hadn't imagined there were so many. It is unimaginable.

Although the day is warm, the grass in the shaded circle is damp and the skirt of her dress is soon soaked through and tainted with the smell of rot. The chill travels from her knees up her thighs until it settles between her legs and deep in her womb. To have borne this many children into the hands of death . . . ! Corinth had barely survived the one.

She sits back on her heels so abruptly that the cypresses start to spin around her like a ring of children clasping hands in a circle. In fact she can almost hear them.

> Ring-a-ring o' roses,
> A pocket full of posies,
> Ashes, ashes,
> We all fall down!

Corinth squeezes her eyes shut and presses her hands—one gloved, one bare—over her ears. She knows that if she opens her eyes, she will see them. Aurora's lost children, all of them, not just James and Cynthia and Tam, but the ones who lived for months and even, God forbid, the ones who never breathed at all. And what she is most afraid of is that among those bereft spirits—water spirits, her mother called them, children who never lived to breathe outside their mothers' watery wombs—she will see her own child, dead before the sun set on her first day on earth.

When she told Milo Latham that she was pregnant, he told her that his wife was also with child. "She is very anxious," he told her, "because she has already lost several children at birth or soon after."

Corinth bowed her head, gauging that the only appropriate response to the misfortune of her lover's wife. They were in his office at the glove factory. A large gilt-edged glass window overlooked the sewing room. To the women looking up from their sewing it must have looked as if Corinth was being fired. *Let them think what they will.* Her work had been falling off these last weeks. Her fingers felt cold and numb all the time, as if the baby were drawing to it all the blood in her extremities, which made it difficult to work the needle. At night, in the women's dormitory beside the factory, when the other girls whispered and gossiped to one another, Corinth drew into herself, wrapping herself into a tight ball on the narrow cot. She couldn't seem to get warm. The snow piled up outside in drifts that covered the ground-floor windows of the factory. Sometimes she wondered if Tom wanted to come back but couldn't. She dreamed that he was trying to come up the Hudson, but that his ship had gotten stuck in the frozen river. Sometimes she even dreamed that he was caught beneath the ice, and that she was swimming beneath the ice looking for him. In the mornings her fingers were as blue as if she had indeed spent the night swimming through cold water, but she knew that was foolish. He had abandoned her. He preferred a life on the stage to a life with her. He had vanished as deftly as the handkerchiefs and bouquets he made disappear in his act.

When the other girls began to rest their eyes on her stomach under the layers of her dress, she went to Milo Latham. She had been right after all to have him in reserve. He, at least, didn't abandon her.

"You will be taken care of," he told her, "but of course you must leave here. I have a place that is secluded where you can go—accompanied by a trustworthy and competent servant who's attended my own wife through her travails. Be ready at first light tomorrow. The carriage will be waiting by the factory gate."

Corinth dared only then to raise her eyes. She had to see if he was telling the truth—whether she could trust him or not. The look that she saw in his face was more than she could have expected; his eyes were resting on Corinth's swollen waist, and when he lifted his eyes to hers, they were actually wet with tears.

The carriage he sent was his private brougham, the seats upholstered in rich red velvet and draped with thick fur rugs. She could have wished, though, for a less conspicuous conveyance, knowing that the girls in the dormitory would be looking out and that they couldn't help but recognize the owner's carriage. If Tom Quinn ever did come back . . . but it was too late to worry about that. The driver was already urging on the horses, who leapt at the touch of the reins as if anxious to be gone. Corinth settled back into the soft upholstery, drew the furs up around her, closed her eyes, and willed herself into oblivion.

When she awoke, the carriage had stopped. She wasn't sure how long she had been asleep, but she expected that she had slept through most of the day. When she raised the window shade, it was impossible to tell what time of day it was, though, because they were surrounded by a deep fog. Corinth tapped the roof of the carriage and the driver, only his eyes showing between hat and scarf, slid open a little window.

"Why are we stopped?" Corinth asked.

"We're picking up another passenger here, miss; only I'm afraid that they might miss us in this fog. My orders are to wait until dusk."

The driver slid the window shut before Corinth could ask any further questions. She tried to settle back in her seat, but the motion made the weight of the child shift over her bladder. She hadn't relieved herself since early morning. She peered out the window again and saw the looming shapes of shaggy hemlocks dimly through the fog. The only sound was the shuffling of the horses' feet and the drip of water from the trees. Of course Milo would have chosen a secluded spot for them to meet the "trustworthy servant." She listened to the slow drip of water from the hemlock branches until the pressure on her bladder became unbearable, and then she opened the carriage door and stepped out into the muddy road. The driver, muffled in a hooded black cloak, barely turned to look at her.

"I'm going to walk a bit to stretch my legs," she said.

The driver turned back without any comment, but as Corinth started toward the woods, she heard his voice behind her. "Watch you don't fall into the river. We're not far from the cliff."

When she entered the woods, her boots sinking into the deep snow, she heard a rushing sound that must have been the river, swollen with the winter's heavy snows. It sounded faraway, but that may have been because the fog muted the sound or because it was so far below the edge of the cliff—which might actually be quite near. She took careful steps forward, resting her gloved hands on the trunks of the pine trees and peering into the fog-shrouded woods. The fog was deeper in between the trees, rising from the snow and mingling with the dripping hemlock branches. When she had gone far enough, she squatted behind a tree broad enough to block the view from the road and, pressing one hand on the trunk to steady her awkward weight, relieved herself. When she was done, she stood up too quickly and for a second the fog seemed to go darker and then, as she recovered, become brighter—as if some light were trying to pierce the gloom.

Perhaps the driver had lit a lantern to help her find her way back. But no, it was in the wrong direction. The light was coming from the opposite direction from the road . . . unless she'd gotten turned around. It must be the driver's lantern, or the servant's carriage had arrived. Corinth took a step toward the light and the light receded. When she stopped, the light stopped. Then it seemed to stretch and grow in the fog, a candle flame reaching toward a draft, pulsing in a rhythm that matched the quickened beats of Corinth's heart. She took another step forward, and the light flickered, almost went out, and then throbbed back, rising with the fog from the snow and gathering itself into the shape of a slim girl in a pale leather dress, her bare feet delicately poised on the crust of a snowdrift.

The girl smiled and held out her lovely bare arms to Corinth. Two torn leather straps dangled from her wrists, and Corinth could see that, like hers, the girls' wrists were scarred from the marks of her bonds. Then the girl rested one of her hands over her swollen belly. Yes, Corinth thought, she understands everything that I have suffered. As soon as Corinth stepped forward the girl turned, leading Corinth through the deep snow away from the road, away from Milo Latham's blood-padded carriage and *that* imprisonment. At the edge of the cliff the girl turned again and held out her hand for Corinth to take. She would not be alone. But as Corinth reached her hand out, she felt an angry thump—so strong that at first she thought it was a blow from outside, but then she realized it was the baby flipping inside her like a trout leaping against the current of a fast-moving stream. She drew back her hand, and the girl's mouth opened wide, the black hole of her mouth melting into the two black holes of her eyes until her face dissolved into long, sinewy ropes of fog. All around Corinth the fog was shredding, lifting off the ground like decaying flesh falls off the bone, and the air was full of the sound of beating wings. She could see clearly the river below the cliff, the fast-moving water and the hard, rocky beach where the river bent sharply. She could see, in impossibly crisp detail, the round white stones that lay at the bottom of the sheer, bone-shattering drop.

Inside the circle of cypresses Corinth opens her eyes and sees one of the round white stones resting on one of the gravestones. The stones could so easily have marked her own grave. She has often, over the past ten years, wished herself buried beneath them, her bones washed clean by the river, bleached to the same color as those stones. The baby who asserted its life so forcibly there on the edge of the cliff didn't have the tenacity to last till the first night of its life. Why, Corinth has wondered every day of the last ten years, did it hold her back if it hadn't meant to stay?

She lifts her eyes up off the ground, and something,

a flicker of light between the cypresses, draws her attention to the far side of the circle.

"Ashes, ashes . . ."

"Alice?" she calls, walking between two tall cypresses. "Is that you?" The song stops and she notices, half hidden in the shade, a low white building. A mausoleum, perhaps? There couldn't possibly be more dead children, could there?

The building is little more than two columns and a porch covering a flight of stairs leading down into the ground. The iron gate above the stairs stands open. Pausing at the threshold, Corinth listens for any movement from below, but all she hears is the faint gurgle of water, which becomes louder as she walks down the stairs. The sound is coming from a round marble cistern, which is open to the light that pours through an oculus in the ceiling. A statue of a hooded woman leans against the basin, one hand on the cistern's edge, the other resting over her belly. *The Grieving Mother*. That's what it would be called, Corinth thinks, approaching the statue to get a better look at its face, which is cloaked by deep folds of marble drapery. Her expression is unexpected. If there's grief, there's no drama. In fact, the face looks curiously washed clean of emotion, as worn as the stone from which it's carved, its eyes sunken and pitted where the sculptor has drilled the pupils. Corinth takes another step closer and then stops, frozen. Within the carved rim of one eye a drop of water gathers, wells, and, as Corinth watches, spills down the smooth marble face. The statue is weeping.

"Very lifelike, eh?"

For a second Corinth thinks the voice is coming from inside the marble basin, but then Signore Lantini rises from behind the well where he had been kneeling.

"Yes," Corinth says, taking a breath to calm herself, "very lifelike, indeed. *Bravissimo!* Your work, I assume?"

The little man places one hand on the lapel of his shiny, threadbare waistcoat and sweeps the other out behind him as he takes a low, dramatic bow. For a moment he is every inch the impresario receiving applause for the show he has produced. For the show that is Bosco.

"*Naturalemente.* Signora Latham asks that Egeria weep, and *ecco!* She weeps."

"Egeria again. But why? She wept for her dead husband, not her children."

Lantini shrugs. "I am a *fontaniere,* signora. I make the water flow, I don't ask why. I come down here today to check the spring because she's not flowing so good today, and look what I find."

Signore Lantini leans over the edge of the well so far that Corinth has to suppress an urge to catch him by the seat of his pants and haul him back in. She looks over the marble wall and for a moment she is back on the edge of the cliff looking down at the fast-flowing Sacandaga. The bottom of the well is covered with the same white stones.

"Somebody has been throwing stones into the well," he says, "and they have blocked the pipe that feeds the fountains."

"Who would do that?" Corinth asks.

Lantini doesn't answer at first. Instead, he springs back down behind the well and rises with a coil of rope, which he hands to Corinth.

"Can you tie a good knot?" he asks.

Corinth knows all about tying knots—and how to get out of them—but she doesn't want to touch the rope, so she shakes her head. Lantini shrugs and then kneels at the feet of the statue and ties one end of the rope around the pedestal on which the statue stands—the pedestal being affixed solidly to the floor—and the other end around his own waist.

"Last year it was the children," he says as he swings his legs over the edge of the well and, holding on to the rope and bracing his feet—which, Corinth notices for the first time, are bare—against the curved marble wall, begins to lower himself down. "They liked to throw rocks into the well to hear the sound they made. Plonk, plonk, plonk." Lantini's voice echoes off the walls of the well, making him sound like a larger man than he is. Corinth leans over and watches his progress anxiously. When he gets to the bottom he splashes knee-deep into the water and then, unfolding a burlap sack from the waistband of his pants, bends to pick up the stones and load them into the sack. "So I had made a cover for the well to protect the spring, but still the little devils would take it off and throw more stones in."

Corinth notices that there's a white circle of marble resting against the wall of the crypt that must be the cover Lantini is talking about. She walks over to it and gives it an experimental push. It doesn't budge. Perhaps three children together could move it, but it seems unlikely.

"Mrs. Latham told them that if they kept it up, someday one of them would fall inside and get trapped. . . . Signora, if you would do me a great favor . . . please to pull up the rope very slowly. I've tied the bag of stones to it."

Corinth goes back to the well and begins hauling up the bag of rocks, wincing each time the rope touches her bare right hand. When she's gotten the bag over the edge and untied it from the rope, she stands at the rim of the well and holds the rope up. The Italian's mobile face, seen at this angle, with his mustache and high cheekbones, looks like the mask of a devil in a comic opera. His hands on the small of his back, he leans back and laughs. "It is very good we are friends, eh, Signora Blackwell? Or else you'd have me at quite the disadvantage."

Corinth tries to return the laugh, but finds she can't. As she lowers the rope back to Lantini, she can't help but wonder, if the children were the ones who threw the stones into the well *last* year, who is doing it *this* year?

Chapter Fifteen

We take Zalman to the emergency room in David's Oldsmobile, which has a backseat large enough for Zalman to put his leg up and still leave enough room for Bethesda to sit next to him.

"Man, this thing's a boat," Nat says with grudging admiration. "What's it got under the hood?"

"A 307-inch V-8 engine," David says, swinging the car out the front gates onto the main road. "It was my dad's. He was a clothing salesman—east Texas and Oklahoma territory—and liked a big trunk for samples."

"And liked a good cigar, as well, I might venture," Zalman says from the back, his eyes closed.

"That's right. Havana Montecristos, when he could get 'em. How's that leg feeling, Zalman?"

"Delightful, just delightful."

Before we left, Nat had run upstairs to his room and emptied his supply of Percocets (left over from a back injury last year, he told us) into his pockets and fed two to Zalman with a bottle of Saratoga Spring Water he'd grabbed from the kitchen. The pills seemed to have an almost instantaneous effect on the poet. "Would anyone like to hear the poem I composed today?" he asks, waving the cobalt-blue water bottle in the air.

I'm scrunched in between David and Nat on the long bench seat up front, but I turn and try to catch Bethesda's eye. She hasn't said a word since I left her with Zalman in the crypt and her silence is beginning to get on my nerves. "I think we overheard part of it," I say to her. "Do you remember, Bethesda?" She tilts her head and assumes the same upward-glancing pose that she assumed in the children's cemetery when quoting from Aurora Latham's journal. She even moves her lips as if mouthing something she's listening to, and then finally she breaks her silence to recite: " 'When water's heart is silver, it will beat / so silently it can't be found through sound.' "

Zalman presses the blue bottle to his heart and then extends it toward Bethesda as if offering her a toast. "I am honored to be remembered," he says, and then begins to nod off. I exchange a worried glance with Nat (Bethesda's eyes are still trained on the roof of the Oldsmobile), and he raises his voice loud enough to pierce Zalman's Percocet fog.

"I, for one, would like to hear the rest of that poem, Zalman." I murmur my assent and nudge David to do the same. Zalman opens his eyes and, fixing them on the blue bottle in his hand as if it were the source of his inspiration, recites from the beginning.

"When water's heart is silver it will beat
so silently it can't be found through sound,
nor echo nor, since hidden underground,
by sight of stone-veined pulse; it can defeat
all those who seek its dripping, chill retreat.
Yet water must still rise and seek the ground
in tiny tributaries, circling round,
until their throbbing pattern's made complete.
Such mysteries the earth secretes away
below the streams that merge and run to seas,
in honor of Egeria's sad day
and destiny of tears that never cease.
If only one could glimpse a silver heart!—
that pulsing pool where tearstained rivers start."

The poem seems to jar Bethesda out of her fog. She looks around the car as if wondering where she is. "Egeria was the wife of Numa, wasn't she?" she asks in a hoarse voice. "She grieved so deeply she melted into a pool of her own tears."

Nat and I both turn around and stare at Bethesda to see that her own face is wet with tears. Nat seems as shocked as I am to see her crying. "Did *she* hit her head?" Nat asks me in a whisper.

"I'm not sure," I whisper back.

Only David thinks to answer Bethesda's question. "I believe you're right there, Miss Graham," he says. "There's a spring dedicated to Egeria just outside of Rome. I bet you that broken statue we saw down by the well was supposed to represent her, because that's the source of Bosco's springs." He pulls into the entrance to the hospital and steers the wide-bodied car to the door of the emergency room. When he's put the car in park, he turns around toward the backseat. "But what I'm wondering is how Zalman found the source of the spring. I've been looking for it for months."

Zalman half opens his eyes, his face dreamy. "I found it by following my heart," he says.

The examining room is too small for the five of us. Since David, as the physically strongest, has helped Zalman into the emergency room, he's one obvious choice to stay. I'd like to volunteer to stay with him, but instead I suggest that Bethesda should. Then, before leaving, I whisper to one of the attendings that someone should have a look at Bethesda to see if she's okay. "She had a fall as well," I tell the young intern, "and she's been acting funny ever since."

Nat and I find ourselves unlikely companions in the hospital cafeteria. I buy a tuna fish sandwich, while Nat opts for the turkey tetrazzini after a long consultation with the hairnetted server that—to my surprise—leaves the woman blushing and giggling. This flirtatious, bantering side of Nat is not one I've seen at Bosco. In fact, I can't help but notice that despite the cafeteria's fluorescent lighting Nat looks not only happier but even healthier outside of Bosco. As if a weight has been lifted off him. Even the feverish green glow his eyes have acquired in the last few weeks seems tempered in this light, and I can see hints of a calmer-looking blue, as if a storm were clearing somewhere behind them and a blue sky was beginning to peak out.

"Poor Zalman," I say when we sit down. "I guess he won't be able to go on any more sonnet walks. I wonder if he'll stay for the rest of the winter."

Nat looks up from his plate of steaming noodles and frowns. "Oh, I don't think he'd leave. The board really hates it if you cut short your stay. There was an Israeli composer who left early one summer because the pine pollen gave him asthma attacks, and he was never invited back."

"But if Zalman left because of his leg—"

"It's not his arm," Nat interrupts. "He can still write."

"Still, he might want to go. And once Diana Tate learns about the bones in the well, there will probably be a police investigation, which is bound to change the atmosphere at Bosco."

"Oh, no, I don't think Diana will call the police. For one thing, they're bound to want to park under the porte cochere."

I laugh so hard I nearly choke on my tuna fish. Plastered all over the sitting room of Bosco are ancient mimeographed rules, the first of which is "Guests must NEVER, under ANY circumstance, park under the porte cochere." It was practically the first thing Diana said to guests upon their arrival: "You haven't parked under the porte cochere, have you?" And the last thing when they were leaving: "Make sure you tell the taxi not to pull up under the porte cochere."

"You know what I think?" I say when I've successfully swallowed my tuna fish.

"No, what?"

"That Diana only made the rule so she can go around saying *porte ko-SHARE*." I draw out the last syllable, exaggerating the French pronunciation. "Because it makes her feel important that she works someplace with a fancy French name for the carport."

Nat rewards me with a smile that rivals the one he gave the hairnetted cafeteria worker, and I feel lightheaded to be caught in the high beams of his attention—and glad that I've perhaps found an ally at Bosco.

On the drive back, though, I begin to suspect that David and Bethesda have also used their time together to form a bond. Neither thinks that Diana should be told about the bones in the well.

"I'll never be allowed to work on the garden," David says. "Even if the bones are a hundred years old, which I'm sure they are, they'll call in forensic anthropologists and cordon off the site."

"Imagine all the people tromping through the garden, disturbing the quiet," Bethesda says. She's sitting up front between David and Nat, so I can't see her face. I'm wedged into the backseat with Zalman, who is snoring loudly, his cast-encased leg propped up on the seat between us. It began to snow while we were inside the hospital, and there's already a good two inches on the road. The Olds, without snow tires or front-wheel drive, fishtails on the curves and struggles up the slick hills, but when I lean forward to watch the road in front of us, I seem to be the only one worried about making it safely back to Bosco.

"Don't you want to know whose bones they are, Bethesda?" Nat asks. "Isn't that important to your research?"

"I'm more interested in Aurora's accomplishments than in the lurid details of the Blackwell affair," Bethesda answers, her voice imperious. When I asked the intern if he'd had a look at her, he said she'd adamantly refused to be examined. Certainly she sounds like her old self now, although I can't help feeling that there's still something *distant* in her manner. But then, she's always been a little cold. "I can imagine well enough whose bones they are," she continues. "Corinth Blackwell and Tom Quinn obviously conspired to kidnap Alice Latham, but one of them—Quinn, I would imagine—decided to work alone, so he killed Corinth and left her in the well. And I certainly don't care about *her* bones."

"But why is the well filled with rocks?" I ask. "That was done before the body was put in there."

"Maybe she filled the well with stones out of spite," David answers, "to destroy the fountains of Bosco."

"Yes, that makes sense," Bethesda says. "People have always been jealous of Bosco."

"But when the fountains ran dry," I ask, "why didn't Aurora look at the source of the spring to see what was the matter?"

"Because," Bethesda answers, her voice growing impatient, "she thought the fountains running dry was a judgment against her for trying to contact her lost children, as was Alice's abduction. The poor woman spent her life trying to atone for her mistakes by making Bosco a haven for artists. The least we can do is make good use of it. Don't you agree, Nathaniel?"

Nat hesitates, glancing guiltily back at me, and I sense I'm losing his allegiance. "What worries me," he says, "is that if we don't tell Diana and then she finds out, we might be asked to leave," he says.

"If we stick together in this, no one will get in trouble," Bethesda says. "No one is going to ask *me* to leave!"

"And in the meantime, we can be working out what happened on our own," David adds.

From the backseat I can see David's and Bethesda's profiles as they turn toward each other. The look they exchange suggests that they discussed this point while they were together in the examining room with Zalman. I feel a pang of jealousy, remembering how I'd pulled away from David earlier today. Has he decided to give up on me and pursue Bethesda instead? David turns back toward the road, but Bethesda's face, tilted up toward the car roof, reminds me uncomfortably of the smooth white face of the statue in my dream. But it's only the moonlight. The snow has stopped and the moon has come out from behind the clouds. As we turn to pass through the gates of Bosco, I see that the grounds have been swathed in white, the overgrown hedges lumpy under their mantles of snow, the statues draped in voluminous drapery. The garden looks like a stage set that's been covered between acts and is waiting for the stagehands to come back and whisk away the dustcovers to reveal the next scene.

David parks the Olds under the porte cochere. Bethesda and I get the rented wheelchair out of the trunk and unfold it by the door, while Nat and David maneuver the heavily medicated poet out of the backseat and into the chair. When we've gotten him into the front hall, David pauses on the threshold.

"If you guys can manage from here, I'd better move the car. Diana's going to be riled enough when she hears about Zalman's leg without me breaking the port coach-her rule."

As soon as David says the words *porte cochere*, Nat smiles at me. "No, we wouldn't want to break the porte ko-SHARE rule," he says, using the same exaggerated pronunciation that I had used when we were in the cafeteria.

He's trying to make up for going back on our agreement, I think, returning his smile.

"Well, however you pronounce it," David says from the doorway, scraping a chunk of ice from the bottoms of his work boots. I have just enough time to make out the scowl on his face before he turns around and leaves.

"Damn," I say, realizing that he must have thought Nat and I were making fun of him. I follow him outside, but he's already in the car. The passenger door handle is locked and the window is fogged over, so I knock on the glass, but the roar of the eight-cylinder engine drowns out the sound. The car pulls out, leaving me in a cloud of exhaust fumes.

I watch the car accelerate past the office and down the hill, going way too fast for the road conditions. Instead of turning into the guest parking lot, though, it skids to a stop at the bottom of the hill.

He's seen me through the rearview mirror, I think. He's waiting for me. I set out down the hill, trying to hurry to make up for the unintended insult, but the light coat of snow has made the road slippery and the cloud of exhaust fumes from the Olds, condensing in the cold air, obscures my footing. I concentrate on the Olds's red taillights as I frame words of apology in my head. *We weren't making fun of your Texas accent?* No, that just sounded condescending. *Nat and I had been laughing about the whole porte cochere thing . . .* but that made it sound as if we've gotten really chummy. And so what? What did I have to apologize for when obviously David and Bethesda had been plotting how to handle the "bones" question on their own?

I stop dead in the middle of the road. What if David's not waiting for me at all? What if he just stopped the car to . . . what? It's an odd place to stop, unless . . .

Something draws my attention away from the car at the bottom of the hill and into the woods just beyond where the car has stopped. I've been staring so long at the red taillights that they've burned an afterimage into my retinas—a hazy reddish blob that hovers under the old ilex trees. I see there's a gap in the trees here—a path like the one Bethesda led me on earlier today. Of course, Bethesda knows all the secret paths around the garden, and so does David. What if they'd agreed to meet here?

The reddish blob swells as my eyes fill with tears. What an idiot I've been! Here I thought David was interested in me when all the time it was Bethesda.

I blink and the reddish blob wavers and thins, turning into a girlish shape that darts between the tangled branches of the ilexes. For a moment I think of the spectral girl who'd led me up the hill today, and it's a testimony to my jealousy that I find myself hoping that the girl in the trees is a ghost. But no, although my vision is still blurred from the tears that fill my eyes, and staring at the taillights, I can see it's Bethesda moving stealthily through the woods. Of course it's Bethesda he's waiting for, not me. I turn away and creep back up the hill, staying in the shadows so that no one will see my humiliation.

The snow does not stop David from his plans to excavate the well the next morning. At breakfast, once Diana

Tate leaves to order a hospital bed for Zalman and Daria is sent back to the office to answer the phones, David announces his plans to remove the bones first and asks for a volunteer to help him. I see him look in my direction, but I keep my eyes down, studying the way the brown sugar I've just spooned into my oatmeal is melting into the milk. After a moment of silence, Bethesda offers to help.

"Thanks," David says. "I'll need a burlap sack to put the bones in. There should be one in the pantry."

We all look toward the kitchen, where we can hear the sounds of the cook making our lunches. "I'll distract Mrs. Hervey," Nat says.

"I guess that leaves me to get the sack," I say. "Shall I bring it down to the crypt?"

"Oh, we won't need it until after lunch," Bethesda says. "Why don't you watch Zalman this morning?"

I look toward David. If he really wants me there, he could say he needs the sack sooner, but he says nothing. Which must mean he wants the morning alone with Bethesda. When I look away from David, I see that Bethesda has been watching me. I never noticed how pale her eyes are, the same color as the milky blue in the teacup she lowers from her lips now in order to smile at me.

⁂

While I'm unloading potatoes from a sack in the pantry, I can hear Nat talking to the cook. I notice that Nat remembers not only the names of Mrs. Hervey's three children but the ages and names of *their* children—one of whom, Danielle Nicole, is working as a housemaid this winter at Bosco.

"That'll make six generations of Herveys that's worked here at Bosco," the cook tells Nat, "which'll have us beating out the Tates."

"Really? I didn't know that Diana's family worked here. Was she related to Evelyn White, the first director?"

Mrs. Hervey sniffs. "No, Diana was Miss White's assistant, but Diana's grandfather was a gardener and his mother was housekeeper for Mrs. Latham . . ."

Sneaking out of the pantry behind Mrs. Hervey's back, I give Nat a wave so he can make his escape, but I hear him accepting Mrs. Hervey's offer of tea and fresh-baked brownies and what Mrs. Hervey refers to as "a nice long chat."

From Zalman's room on the first floor, I watch David and Bethesda leave from the side door and enter the path that leads down to the children's cemetery. "I think it's wrong to move those bones without contacting the police first," I say, plumping up Zalman's pillows so he can sit up and drink the tea I've brought for him. I give the last pillow a hard punch, remembering how Bethesda had pretended to be reluctant to help David and then volunteered anyway.

Zalman nods sympathetically, but after he's taken a sip of tea, he asks me a question on an entirely different subject. "Do you find that you have particularly vivid dreams here at Bosco?"

I can feel the color leave my face. It had taken me a long time to get to sleep after climbing back up the hill, but when I did, I'd had the dream about the statues again, only this time when the girl in the maze turned, her stone face was so worn down that I could see that there were bones beneath the marble.

"Yes, yes, I have."

"Last night I could have sworn there was a white dog on my bed, lying over my broken leg." Zalman points to the lumpy mass beneath his bedspread.

"Did you have a white dog when you were growing up?" I ask, thinking that Zalman's dream seems comfortingly benign compared to my nightmares.

"No, we lived in an apartment building in Riverdale that didn't allow dogs." And then, leaning forward in bed, he confides in a whisper, "I think it was Madame Blavatsky's dog who came to visit me last night."

"Madame Blavatsky's dog?"

"She was a famous medium—"

"Yes, I know who she was. My mother is a big fan of hers. She even belongs to the Theosophical Society, which Madame Blavatsky founded. You see, my mother thinks she's a medium—"

"Of course she is," Zalman says to my bewilderment. I check the vial of painkillers that Zalman brought home from the hospital to see how many are still there.

"I'm sure she's heard of the white dog. I learned about it when I was an undergraduate at Penn. I was writing my thesis on Yeats's forays into spiritualism, and I wandered into a little cafe on Sansom Street one day, and imagine my surprise when I read on the menu that the cafe—the White Dog Cafe—was the former home of Madame Blavatsky! A serendipitous coincidence, wouldn't you say?"

I look up from counting Percocets (Zalman appears to have taken only one since last night) and nod in agreement. Zalman's eyes are glittering and his hair is standing up in wispy fluffs from his pink scalp. I lay a hand on his forehead to see if he's got a fever, but his brow is cool.

"The story on the menu explained that Madame Blavatsky had injured her leg and that her doctors wanted to amputate. 'Imagine my leg going to the spirit world without me,' she retorted. And then within days her leg was miraculously healed. She said a white 'pup' from the spirit world came to her each night and lay on her leg to heal it. Now it's come to heal my leg. What do you think of that?"

"I think I'll bring my laptop down here today," I say, patting Zalman's quilt, "in case you need anything." *And in case you lapse into delirium.* "If that's okay with you."

"Of course, *shayna maidela,* but you can't fool me." Zalman wags a reproving finger at me. "I know the real reason is so you can see the white dog for yourself."

When I go back to my room to retrieve my laptop, I notice that the theatrical poster listing Tom Quinn and Corinth Blackwell has fallen from the window frame and slipped under my desk. I pick it up and see that on the back of it there's a message written in pale, faded ink. *"Cory,"* it reads, *"I'm leaving Bosco tonight. If you want to go with me, meet me in the Rose Garden at midnight.—Q"* Below the florid *Q* is another line: *"We'll follow the rivers north."* So the poster must have been in Corinth's possession at some time, but why would she leave it behind? David said he found it in the attic in an old trunk. Is it Corinth's trunk? And if her trunk is still here, might that prove she never left Bosco at all? That the bones in the well are hers?

Although I'm nervous about leaving Zalman unattended, I decide to take a quick trip up to the attic. Hurrying up the stairs, I admit to myself that I'm hoping that I won't find Corinth's trunk. Since we found the bones yesterday, I've been fighting the idea that they could be Corinth's. I can picture the stone lid closing over her, picture it as though from inside the well. I can feel the last breath of air slip out between the cracks and hear the muttering of the spring boiling up to claim her bones. The image is so real to me that when I reach the attic, I'm gasping for breath as if I myself were trapped in the well. The four narrow beds that line the north wall like shrouded mummies cast a funereal gloom over the room. I quickly cross to the south side, threading my way between discarded furniture and books and toys that lie in disordered heaps, nearly tripping over an ancient rocking horse whose baleful eye looks up at me through a tangle of decaying pink ribbons, and wrench open a window. I rest my arms on the windowsill and draw in breath after chill breath, trying to dispel the awful claustrophobia of my vision.

"I'm leaving Bosco tonight," Tom Quinn had written. *"If you want to go with me, meet me in the Rose Garden at midnight."* Had she ignored his message or had she gone and been betrayed by Tom and left in the well to die? To have never left here, to have been trapped here at Bosco for all time. It's not the end I want to envision for Corinth Blackwell . . .

Even though it's beautiful here. From this height I can see the entire garden spread out below me, the newly fallen snow masking the signs of age and decay. I can see all the way down into the *giardino segreto,* where the statue of the Indian maiden crouches in a shimmering pool of snow that glitters like water as it catches the sunlight. The wind whips the snow up into plumes like sprays of water, and suddenly I can see Bosco as it must have looked when the fountains were on—the flash of water everywhere. But still, as beautiful as it might have been, what I want to picture is a coach waiting at the drive at the bottom of the gardens and Corinth Blackwell getting into it. Leaving Bosco forever. Following the rivers north, as Tom Quinn had promised. I almost do see it, a black shape coalescing out of the shadows at the bottom of the hill; but then instead I see myself, standing in the road last night, breathing in exhaust fumes while David waited in the commodious Olds for Bethesda.

I turn away from the window and see the open trunk just next to the toppled rocking horse. I kneel down beside it and lift up a dark blue dress. Two letters are stitched inside the collar: *CB*.

I go through the rest of the trunk and find a leather satchel that holds a curious assortment of wires and picks. I saw one like it in Lily Dale, at the home of a medium who my mother said was a fraud. "This is how she tilts tables," my mother said sadly—lies of any kind saddened my mother so much that I had early on given up telling even the smallest ones, since my mother could detect them immediately.

I look inside the cuffs of the dress sleeves and find the sewn-in pockets that would have held the wires Corinth used to perform her levitating acts. When I'm done, I fold all the clothes away and, taking only the satchel with me, close the trunk. As I head back downstairs, I wonder why the contents of the trunk sadden me so. After all, the evidence that Corinth was a fake supports the way I'm writing my book—it's what I've always believed, that even mediums like my mother, who don't practice intentional fraud, are merely responding to subconscious messages from their clients. So what if Corinth has turned out to be a more egregious fraud. It's just as ridiculous to feel that Corinth has betrayed me as it is to feel that David has. But that's exactly how I do feel.

I stop on the first-floor landing and look out the window. Although the sun has transformed the garden into a glittering mirage of its former glory, I can imagine that before long the garden will disappear beneath the snow, the paths will be impassable, even the roads out difficult to navigate. I've heard that guests are sometimes snowbound at Bosco for days . . . weeks, even. As I knock on Zalman's door, I try to shake off the gloom that has descended on me—if only for Zalman's sake—but as I turn the knob (Zalman must be asleep, as he doesn't answer my knock), I can't help feeling that before long the snow will seal us all inside Bosco just as the stone lid sealed Corinth into the marble well.

When I push open Zalman's door, a gust of cold air hits me so forcibly I take a step backward. The wind snakes by me as though it were escaping from the poet's room. I step inside and cross right away to the open window. A drift of crystalline snow has mounded on the sill, and as I struggle to get the window closed, it blows up in my face in a malicious little whirlwind that stings my cheeks and hangs in the air a moment before dispersing into the garden.

"Who in the world left this open?" I ask, turning to face Zalman's bed.

Zalman is sitting straight up in bed, a red paisley shawl draped over his shoulders, his eyes bright and his cheeks an alarming shade of pink. I hurry over to him and lay my hand on his forehead, which is, to my surprise, cool. Looking closer at him, I see that the pink in his cheeks is makeup: two stripes of rouge applied like Indian war paint.

"The children came to pay me a visit," he says. "I'm afraid I've been a victim of their little tricks."

And suddenly I realize what it was Zalman said last night when I came back to the crypt with Nat and David. It wasn't "We have visitors"; it was "We had visitors." No wonder Bethesda looked so dazed.

"Zalman," I say as I scrub the paint off his cheeks with a damp wash towel, "did the children visit you and Bethesda yesterday in the crypt?"

"Oh, no," Zalman says. "It was their mother."

"Their mother? You mean Aurora Latham? Is Aurora Latham here now?" I look around as if the founder of Bosco were to be found lurking in the corners of Zalman's room. Somehow the idea of seeing the ghost of Aurora Latham is far more frightening to me than seeing the children.

"Oh, no," Zalman says, patting my hand reassuringly, "she's not here. She's with Miss Graham."

Chapter Sixteen

On her way back up to the house Corinth is drenched again and again by sprays of water that spring out of the fountain allée and arc across her path. The water pressure, now that Lantini has removed the stones from the well, has clearly been restored, but still the fountains are behaving erratically. The smooth cascade thrashes against the carved marble borders as if live trout were struggling upstream against the current. The jets that leap out of the fountain slap her with the weight and muscle of live fish. When she gets to the second terrace, she tries to turn down into the ilex grove, but a geyser erupts from between two paving stones and fans out in front of her, each drop of water refracting the bright sunlight into a rainbow that shimmers in the air, like a peacock displaying its tail. She can even see, as the water hangs suspended for a fraction of a second longer than seems possible, the eyes of the peacock's tail, and then, as the mirage vanishes, she feels the eyes following her. The children's eyes.

No, that's one thing she can't bear. She continues

up the main path, her head bowed to the ground against the onslaught of water. *Giochi d'acqua.* Water tricks, indeed! She remembers what Aurora told her this morning—that James was the ringleader, enticing Tam and Cynthia into his *little rebellions,* to do his *little tricks.* Were these geysers some of James's *little tricks,* then? And the arrow through Frank Campbell's heart? Was that one of his little tricks, as well? She remembers the fingers on her wrist last night and the sound of children's voices in the grotto—more than three children. What if James had found in death more accomplices for his tricks? What if he had found a whole tribe of ghost siblings to do his bidding? Did she really want to summon that host forth in yet another séance?

As if in answer to her question, someone some-where starts to hum. Her skin, already chilled by her soakings, prickles, but then she realizes that the sound is coming from the pipes of the fountains. She remembers that the fountains at the Villa d'Este at Tivoli were designed to produce music—a music said to represent the voice of the Tiburtine Sibyl chanting her prophecies for great Rome. Of course Aurora, who had commissioned statues to cry, would want her fountains to sing. Maybe that's all this is. The *giochi d'acqua,* the singing fountains—all tricks to bring back her children, to make her believe they are still with her. *I'm afraid I wasn't always the best of mothers,* she said. From how she treats Alice, Corinth can believe it. Maybe this resurrection is supposed to somehow appease her guilt.

If so, Aurora will have to wrestle with her guilt on her own, as Corinth has done all these years since she laid her own child to rest under the tea-colored water of the bogs behind Milo Latham's cabin on the Sacandaga. She won't be the one to summon that horde of spirits, her little tea-colored one among them. She'll go to Tom Quinn now and tell him she's ready to leave Bosco, and Milo Latham, for good.

As she climbs the last steps to the last terrace, she feels strengthened in her resolution enough to hum along with the fountains, a simple tune that she soon remembers the words to:

> *Ring-a-ring o' roses*
> *A pocket full of posies.*

At the top of the fountain allée one last spray of water fans out in front of her, this one seeming to spring, not from the fountain, but out of thin air.

Ashes, ashes, the fountains sing as the water droplets form into the shape of a girl, her skirt billowing in a final curtsy as she drops to the ground.

We all fall down.

Violet Ramsdale, who has been sitting looking out her bedroom window since Dr. Murdoch left her a half hour earlier, watches Corinth climb up from the garden onto the terrace. The medium's hair and dress are soaked, and a halo of mist is falling around her like a moiré silk shawl. She is humming to herself. A few minutes later Tom Quinn emerges from between two cypresses on the west side of the fountain allée. Had they been together?

"Assisting Lantini with some engineering problems" is what he said last night when she asked him what he was doing in the garden yesterday. "It feels good to work with my hands again."

"Isn't that what you are in my employ to do?" she asked, laying her hand over his and feeling, as she always did, a shiver of pleasure at the smoothness of his skin, the tautness of his flesh. "To work with your hands?"

He'd turned his hand over and grasped hers, squeezing a little too hard and then letting go, his hand escaping from under hers so quickly she didn't even see it go, the long white fingers a blur, like the wings of a white dove released from its cage.

"I used to do more with my hands than take down someone else's words," he said.

"Of course," she cooed, trying to draw him back. "I remember your act. How could I forget how brilliant you were on the stage. I've always said that if you wished to go back—"

The color rose beneath his marble-white skin, and she knew she'd said the wrong thing. He was already up, buttoning his shirt, striding toward the door, saying he needed some air and would take a walk around the garden.

"But aren't you afraid," she called out to him, "after what happened to Mr. Campbell tonight?"

He turned and smiled at that. "Frank Campbell was an ass," he said. "He only got what he deserved." And then he was gone and he didn't come back all night. Punishing her for bringing up his act, no doubt. The Great Quintini! Of course he'd never go back after what happened.

It was a shame, because he was the most brilliant magician she'd ever seen . . . well, certainly the handsomest. What he had was promise. In time he could have surpassed even the great Robert-Houdin, whom she'd seen perform in Paris when she was a child.

She'd seen Tom Quinn perform for the first time in New York at the Odeon. She'd gone because she was gathering material for her next novel, in which the villain was a magician, but she'd gone back, again and again, because she'd become mesmerized by the handsome young magician. Tom had the quickest hands she'd ever seen. Plucking scarves and flowers out of thin air, conjuring orange trees and brightly colored birds from ether.

"He don't stay with the standard stock-in-trade," the Odeon's manager, Jimmy Priest, told her when she asked to be introduced. *All in the name of research,* she'd told herself. "He's ambitious, that one, always adding something new to the act to make a few extra dollars, but he don't spend it like the rest of the performers. He's got a girl somewhere, I think."

When she met him in his dressing room, he told her he was experimenting with escape acts. He'd gotten the idea from a medium's act he'd seen upstate. The girl had been bound to prove she was not producing her effects with her hands or feet, but he had noticed that because she had extraordinarily slim wrists and ankles she was able to slip out of the ropes when the lights went out.

"I think what the audience liked best of all," he told Violet, "was seeing her all tied up."

Yes, Violet could imagine that. In her books she always made sure that there was at least one scene in which the villain tied up the heroine, preferably in a high tower or a dark dungeon. There was something undeniably *titillating* about confinement. She had asked him to show her how he tied his knots—for research purposes of course—and, after feigning a blush or two, agreed to tie his wrists and ankles together so he could practice releasing himself.

"Aren't you afraid that one of the gentlemen in the audience will know how to tie a knot you can't free yourself from?" she asked. "Hadn't you better . . . um . . . enlist the aid of some colleague?"

"You mean use a plant?" he said, laughing at her euphemisms. "Not a bad idea."

She was in his dressing room when Jimmy Priest approached Tom with a proposal. The rope trick was getting old, he told Tom; there was a magician at the Regent who had himself tied up and sealed in a trunk, and one in England who had himself thrown in the river in leg irons. Couldn't Tom do something like that? They could stage the whole thing off the piers.

"But the river's frozen," Violet pointed out.

"Even better," Jimmy said, grinning around the stub

of cigar in his mouth. "A fellow went into a frozen river out in St. Louis. Makes for more drama. We'll drill a hole and toss him in, and he'll be out in three minutes at most. If he doesn't come out on his own, we'll fish him out. He's young." He slapped Tom on the back. "He'll survive."

She told Tom not to do it, but when Jimmy told him how much he thought he could get for the act with the right backing, she saw Tom's eyes widen and then draw inward, thinking, she guessed, of that girl he had tucked away somewhere.

The medium, Violet thinks, rising from her seat at the window and crossing her room to her Saratoga trunk. Hidden behind a loose corner of the lining are several posters that she had found in Tom's old valise and saved out of sentimentality. She loved the pictures of Tom in his magician's garb and the ones of him bound in ropes about to be sealed in a trunk or lowered into the river, but the one she's looking for now is from before they met, a program for July 9, 1882, at the Lyceum Theater, Gloversville, New York, advertising "The Great Quintini, Master of Disappearances." She reads through the other acts and finds her. The little medium. Corinth Blackwell. So it had been for her that Tom was willing to risk everything in that foolhardy exploit.

While Jimmy Priest papered the city with posters— THE GREAT QUINTINI DEFIES THE FROZEN DEEP! MOST SPECTACULAR WATER ESCAPE EVER DARED BY MORTAL MAN—Tom practiced holding his breath and she timed him. He was up to three minutes when the day came. New Year's Day. Tom had wanted to do it the week before Christmas, but Jimmy had insisted that New Year's Day would draw the bigger crowd. And besides, they had to make sure the river was frozen "because," Jimmy explained, "you've promised your public 'the frozen deep.' "

The ice on New Year's day stretched clear across to New Jersey, gleaming gold in the noonday sun. Only the hole ten feet off the pier where the ice had been sawed away was black, a dark eye surrounded by a corona of fire.

"You don't have to go through with this," she whispered to him as the throng of men and women on the pier parted to let them through. But when Tom turned toward her, his eyes were as dark as the black pit in the ice. It was as if he'd gone into some kind of trance to ready himself for his submersion and he was already far away from her, already in the black water under the ice. The crowd swept him away from her, pulling the fur cloak she had lent him from his bare shoulders, the men tying his arms behind his back.

"They're your men," she whispered to Jimmy, "the ones tying the ropes?"

"Of course, ma'am, do you think I want a dead magician on my hands?" Jimmy answered, exhaling rank cigar smoke into the cold, bright air.

She looked at the men and women in the crowd and saw that their eyes were all fixed on Tom as he was shackled. Tom had been right—the audience loved to see the ropes go on. It didn't have to be a girl captive; Tom's young flesh would do.

Closing her eyes against the glare of the sun off the frozen river, Violet felt herself transported to a little mountain village in Tuscany that she had passed through on her way to the baths at Saturnia (whose healing powers, an English friend had promised her, would put an end to all her pain). A boy, his hands and feet bound together, was tied to a statue in the town square's fountain. *To appease the nymph of the spring,* the tour guide had explained, pointing to the statue the boy was tied to, a half-naked girl whose arms reached up out of the fountain's spray to pull unsuspecting passersby under the veil of water. *So that the spring will never run dry. It's considered an honor for the boy.* The ladies of her party had insisted on offering him food and drink and begged the village men to let him go, but the men of the village had only laughed and the boy had refused all their offerings. Still, the women had hovered around the square, stealing glances at the boy where his flesh pressed against the cold, wet marble.

She heard a splash and opened her eyes to see the dark water lapping over the ice. She looked down at her watch and drew in her own breath. She swore to herself that she wouldn't draw breath until he did, but after two minutes she had to. She'd timed him before at three minutes. He had time.

When three minutes passed, she pushed through the crowds and grabbed Jimmy's arm. "Pull him up," she said. "It's been too long."

They hauled up the rope, but there was nothing at the end of it.

"He must have come untied from it while he was getting out of his bonds and the current took him downriver."

"Put the rope back down," Jimmy shouted at his men, "so he can see where the hole is."

Violet looked down at her watch. He'd been under the water for four minutes. He'd never held his breath this long. She scanned the river, looking for other breaks in the ice where he might have surfaced, but the ice was as smooth and unbroken as the lid of a marble tomb. She pictured the white marble limbs of that Italian spring nymph, waiting beneath the ice to pull Tom to his death . . .

Then she heard a shout and the men were hauling up the rope and pulling something out of the water. Later Tom would tell her that when he lost sight of the hole, he'd found that between the ice and the water there was a gap of several inches where he was able to draw breath, that he'd kept alive that way, but when they dragged him out of the water his limbs, free of the ropes, were as white and lifeless as a statue's. It was long months before he was well again, but she took care of him. Only for those few weeks when he went away that March was he away from her, and then he returned looking more frozen than he had when they fished him out of the river.

She looks at her watch—the same watch she held in her hand while Tom was under the river—and sees that it's after ten. Twenty minutes now since Dr. Murdoch left, saying as he did, "I'll leave you now to accustom yourself to the gravity of your condition." *The gravity of her condition!* As if the years she'd spent in all the best clinics and water-cures of Europe hadn't accustomed her to the shocks and indignities the human body had to offer. She didn't even have recourse to her green bottle after he left. The only thing she wonders is whether she should tell Tom about Dr. Murdoch's diagnosis now or later.

She opens the panel behind the bookcase and takes the secret passage up to the third floor. Aurora showed her the passage several summers ago. She always put Tom in the room on the third floor facing north, the one decorated in the rustic style that William West Durant was making so popular: bear rugs and furniture made from unpeeled birch logs, a massive headboard carved in the image of a great eagle. A room for a young Jupiter, Aurora said when she first showed it to Violet, but Violet thought instead of Ganymede, whom the god, in an eagle's guise, had snatched away, and it has always made her nervous that Tom sleeps there.

She knocks on the panel and Tom opens the door for her.

"I saw you in the garden," she says, holding up her skirt to fit between a chair and a dresser, both carved out of rough-hewn logs that, she well knows, will tear the good silk of her dress, "and wondered if you had heard anything more about Campbell's death. They've removed his body from the grotto, have they not?"

"Yes. They're saying he died of a heart attack." He sits down at the desk, where several blueprints are laid out beneath stone paperweights. The only place to sit, besides the unmade bed, is the rustic chair, which will surely tear her dress to bits, and so she sits on the edge of the bed.

"A heart attack?" She tilts her head and tries to coax Tom with a smile, but he looks away. "And the doctor is going along with that?"

"Apparently. No doubt the doctor is in Mr. Latham's copious pocket."

"All the same, perhaps we should cut our stay here at Bosco short. I can't afford to be mixed up in a scandal. My readers—"

"Your readers would like nothing better. But perhaps you're right. Should I make arrangements for us to leave tomorrow?"

"Why not leave today?"

"Today?" His full lips part as if to smile, but the corners of his mouth appear frozen.

"Yes, why not? There's nothing holding us here at Bosco."

"I thought you were collecting atmosphere for your next novel."

"I think I've collected all the atmosphere I need."

"But won't Mrs. Latham be disappointed? I believe she plans to go ahead with another séance tonight."

"Really? Who told you that? The medium?"

Tom looks down. She can see the shadow of his long dark eyelashes on the pale skin beneath his eyes, and the shadow of a blue vein at his temple. Its pulse, under his fair skin, reminds her of the river that day, rushing darkly under the smooth ice. *What are you up to, Tom?* she asks herself. *What trick are you working now?*

"I overheard Mrs. Latham talking to the medium in the garden. She wants her to try again to reach the children. She wants her to try again tonight."

"Poor Aurora. It is her *idée fixe*. Very well, then, we'll stay one more night, but then let us be ready to leave tomorrow." She stands up to emphasize her determination, but the effect is ruined by one of the pins in her skirt catching on the bedspread. She pulls at it impatiently, tearing the silk after all her precautions. "Unless, of course, you've made any other engagement?"

"Other engagement?" He looks up, the blood coursing through his face.

"I mean with Signore Lantini," she says, waving at the blueprints laid out on his desk. "I see you've been helping him with the fountains."

"Oh," Tom says. "I think we fixed the problem with the fountains."

"Good, you're free, then."

"Free?" he asks, smiling. This time the corners of his mouth curve, but his lips don't part. "I am always at your command."

Violet bows her head at the compliment, thinking, *Good.* She decides to leave her news until tomorrow and turns to leave, but at the entrance to the secret passage she turns back and takes the rolled paper out of the pocket of her skirt. "By the way," she says, "I found this piece of old memorabilia I thought you might like to have." She hands him the bill from the Lyceum Theater. "For remembrance's sake."

Not five minutes after Violet has left his room, Tom hears a knock at his door and, answering it, finds Corinth, damp and bedraggled, leaning against his door frame. He pulls her into the room before one of the servants can see her. Her skin, under her wet dress, is cold as ice.

"What's happened," he asks, dragging a fur throw from the bed and draping it over her shoulders.

"The children . . ." she begins, and then, taken by a fit of shivering, collapses onto his bed. He takes her hands and begins to chafe them to bring the blood back, but when he touches the scars on her wrists, she looks up at him, her black eyes so full of pain that it's like looking into cold water. Like looking into that hole in the ice the day he was thrown into the river.

"I have to leave here tonight," she says in a voice that seems to come from faraway, like her voice last night at the séance. Was it her real voice, or something she put on to convince her audience that she had entered a trance?

"Tonight? I don't see how we can get away without anyone seeing us before dark. Doesn't Mrs. Latham want you to conduct another séance?"

She nods, bowing her head, not asking him how he

knows about tonight's séance. She has the same resigned look she had when he asked her ten years ago to wait for him in Gloversville when he went back to New York City. How could he blame her for not waiting when he had taken so much longer to get back? Still, he has always felt that with all her medium's skill she should have known what kept him from returning to her. When he had been under the river, sinking into the cold water, he had felt her hand on his, leading him up to the narrow margin between ice and water where he was able to breathe. Then he had seen a long white shape swaying in the water and, when he swam toward it, had found the rope hanging through the hole in the ice. If he goes with her, he must know, once and for all, if she knew why he was delayed and still left him for Milo Latham. He has to know whether she's a real medium or if it's all an act.

"I say we leave after the séance," he tells her now. "I'll send you a note later to tell you where we should meet."

Chapter Seventeen

I stop at the office long enough to tell Daria to watch
Zalman, and then I rush down the hill toward the
children's cemetery, following the shortcut I learned
yesterday. When I enter the crypt, I think at first that it's
empty. I notice a pile of white rocks on the floor beside
the broken statue beneath the well, and when I kneel to
inspect them, I see that the floor is wet and covered with
a whitish slurry. I pick up a handful of the stuff and let
it sift between my fingers. Three blue beads fall to the
floor and dance there for a moment, vibrating; then I
hear the sound of someone humming and look up to
find Bethesda sitting on the steps.

"Where's David?" I ask.

She shrugs and keeps on humming. It's a children's
nursery rhyme, "Ring Around the Roses," a rhyming
game that my mother once forbade me to play because
she said it was about death. An odd restriction, I
thought at the time, for someone whose business was
contacting the dead. "Bethesda," I say, louder this time,
"do you know where David is?"

"He was in there clearing out the stones the children threw in the well, but I suppose he got tired of it. It's very hard to find someone to do proper work . . ." Her voice drifts off and she starts humming again. I notice that she's fingering one of the pearl-tipped pins, sliding it in and out of her sweater sleeve. And then I see it's not the sleeve she's piercing. It's the skin of her wrist.

"Bethesda!" I cry, standing up so quickly that the room spins. The white marble floor seems to ripple under my feet as I rush toward her. I grab the hand that holds the pin and wrench it away from her other wrist. She stares up at me and I'm startled once again by the color of her eyes. That pale blue I noticed this morning is actually a film that has crept over her irises. *Flow blue.* I hear the words inside my head, but I don't understand them. What I do understand is the look of hate that emanates from those eyes.

"Haven't you stolen enough from me!" she spits out. I feel her wrist twist in my grip and break free. She brings up her hand, the pin held out, and strikes for my eyes.

I lunge away from her, my feet slipping on the wet marble floor, and fall against the well. As she comes toward me, still holding out that long pin, I grab one of the white stones and, as she swoops down on me, bring up my arm and smash the rock into the side of her face. For a second the blow seems to make the whole room shake, and then I see something happen to Bethesda's eyes. The blue film slips away, like water gliding off a stone. Bethesda sits down hard on the floor, blinks, and raises her hand to her face to touch the rising welt on her cheekbone.

"Damn, Brooks, why'd ya—" Then she looks down and notices the pin in her hand and the scratches on her wrist.

Before I can answer—not that I have any good explanation for what happened to her—we both feel the floor beneath us shudder. This time, with my back against the well, I can feel it's coming from deep beneath the ground. I pull myself up and look over the edge of the cistern. Water is rushing into the well, churning over the white rocks, which have been pushed into a sloping pile blocking the pipe on the north side. Which is why, I suddenly realize, the water level is rising. It has no place else to go.

"We'd better get out of here," Bethesda says, leaning over the well next to me. "If the water floods the crypt, we could drown."

I nod, pulling myself away from the frothing water, which seems to have a mesmerizing effect on me. Just as I'm taking my hand away from the rim of the well, though, I feel something rough graze my hand. I look down and see that it's a rope on the edge of the cistern jerking back and forth. I grab it and tug, but it's held taut by something under the water. A bucket, I notice, is bobbing free on the surface. Bethesda is also staring at the rope as if trying to decipher a mysterious rune.

"Did David tie the rope to something in the well?" I ask.

She nods. "It was tied to the bucket," she says slowly, as if trying to remember something that happened days ago, "but then he said he was afraid the water might start rising quickly once he uncleared the pipe on the south side of the well. So he tied it to his waist." She looks up at me and then we both look down into the dark water.

"I'm going in," I say. "You stay up here. I may need you to help me get him up if he's unconscious."

I hoist myself onto the rim of the cistern and, grabbing the rope, swing my legs around. Bracing my feet against the wall, I lower myself down into the water, gasping at the cold. Above me I see Bethesda's face leaning over the well, framed by the oculus above her. Snow is swirling across the opening, spiraling in tight circles like the water that wraps itself around my legs. It feels as if the water is trying to suck me, and all of Bosco, down into its maw. I draw in a long breath and go under.

At first, looking down into the water, all I see is blackness, but then, lit by the light from the oculus, I can make out the faint glimmer of white stones on the bottom and, crouched above them, a dark shape. I use the rope to draw myself down through the water. As I reach out my hand to grab him, David turns and his face, stained white from the chalk dust, floats out of the dark, his eyes opened but unfocused. I nearly scream in the water, but then David's eyes fix on me and they widen with recognition. More than recognition. I can see a look of longing in them, as if he's been waiting for me all along, there at the bottom of the well. He reaches out his arms and I take his hand, pulling him up toward the surface. For a moment I feel myself being pulled down, but then, with my other hand on the rope, I manage to break us both free of the water's pull.

We surface, gasping in the cold air, and Bethesda reaches down to help first me and then David over the edge of the well.

"What the hell were you doing there?" Bethesda screams at David. "You could have drowned!"

"I was trying to read the inscription on the pipe," David says, surprised as I am, I think, at the hysteria in Bethesda's voice.

"You were willing to risk your life to read an inscription?" I ask.

"I know, I know. I don't know what came over me. When the water started pouring in, all I could think about was that it might be my last chance to read it. I know it sounds crazy."

I'm about to tell him that it *was* crazy, but Bethesda's nodding as if his explanation made perfect sense. "No, no, of course you had to read it. Were you able to?"

David gives her a smile full of gratitude for her understanding and begins to tell her, but I stop him before he can. "I'm sorry," I say, "but we just don't have time for this. Something's wrong with Zalman."

Diana and Daria Tate are with Zalman when we get to his room. Daria is scrubbing at the pink stripes on Zalman's cheeks with a washcloth; Diana is taking his pulse.

"I see you've cleared the rocks out," he says as Diana plucks the thermometer from his mouth, "and unblocked the spring."

"Zalman's told me all about the stones in the well, and the bones," Diana says, shaking down the thermometer. "As the rest of you should have yesterday."

"We were afraid that a police investigation might put an end to our residencies here," Bethesda says, stepping forward. I'm impressed that Bethesda is so quick to take the blame. I have a sudden vision of her as a girl at boarding school, facing the headmistress when something got broken or her hall was put on suspension.

"But clearly the police should be called," I say.

"Well, I don't know about *that*," Diana says. "Those bones have probably been there for a hundred years. I don't see what good the police will do now."

"But can't you see that something's really wrong here?" I say, pointing to David and Bethesda. I only mean to bring attention to David's wet clothes and Bethesda's scarred hand and bruised face, but I realize I was about to say something else—to accuse them of some more personal betrayal. When I look at the bruise on Bethesda's face, I can almost feel the weight of the rock in my hand when I struck her. The memory appalls me, but I notice that my fingers are clenching and unclenching—as if they missed the feel of the hard rock.

"I mean," I say, pronouncing each word carefully, as if I can't quite trust what will come out of my own mouth, "David nearly got killed in the well and someone decorated Zalman with war paint—"

"It was Aurora and the children," Zalman says patiently. "They don't really mean any harm, but they very much want to have their story told."

"Like those people who keep calling the office," Daria says, "looking for a writer to tell their stories. It's kind of sad, really."

Bethesda nods. "As if that's all it took: a story to tell."

"I've always felt," Diana says, "that there was some kind of force here at Bosco that speaks through the artists that come here. I've felt it more than ever this year."

"It's because of you," Zalman says, taking my hand. "You're a medium. They've been waiting for another one since Corinth Blackwell. They want to speak through you."

"I am not a medium," I say, the blood rushing to my cheeks, horrified at the thought of *anyone* speaking through me, forcing foreign words up through my throat and out of my mouth. I turn to David, the only one present who knows how I feel about my mother's profession, but instead of helping me he gives me away.

"But your mother is," he says.

"And you grew up in a town full of mediums," Diana adds.

"How . . . ?" But then I remember that of course Diana has read my application and knows I was born and raised in Lily Dale—a known center for spiritualists. I just hadn't thought that that part of my background would be of the slightest interest to anyone at Bosco. I've spent most of my life trying to evade the taint of mysticism that clings to me like the scent of Mira's patchouli incense. This is the last place where I thought it would catch up with me. Now everyone in the room is looking to me as if I were the answer to all their troubles. The one person whom I could count on to express a healthy dose of skepticism is absent.

"Where's Nat?" I ask, as much to deflect everyone's interest in me as to find out.

"He was in the kitchen with Mrs. Hervey when I came in from the office," Daria says, "but then he asked me if he could get some stationery out of my desk, and I told him to go ahead—"

"He's alone in the office?" Diana says, rising from Zalman's bed. "That's very irregular."

Daria rolls her eyes at her aunt. "I can't control what these people do," she says.

"I think we should all be here if we're going to decide what we're going to do about . . . about these incidents," I say. "I'll go get Nat—"

"That won't be necessary. I'm here," Nat says, coming into the room. He's carrying a stack of files, which he lays down on Zalman's night table. "How are you doing, Zal?"

"Oh, I'm fabulous, Nathaniel. I've always wanted to catch a glimpse of the visionary realm since my days studying Yeats."

"Yes, you mention that in one of the poems you included in your application to Bosco." Nat sorts through the folders, selects one, and pulls out a page of typescript. " 'Mysticism in the 1890s.' A good poem. I like it."

"Why, thank you—"

Diana glares at Nat, her face as pink as Zalman's had been when covered in war paint. "When the Board finds out that you've been going through the other guests' files—"

"The Board might be interested to know that you've been weighting the selection process in favor of artists who are pursuing projects of special interest to you," Nat counters. "Bethesda's biography of Aurora Latham; Zalman's series of sonnets inspired by the gardens of Bosco, coupled with his interest in nineteenth-century spiritualism, Ellis's novel on Corinth Blackwell and her family history of spiritualism; and David's research into Lantini's plans for the garden. Everyone here is doing work on something related to the events that transpired during the summer of 1893."

"You're not," Diana says coolly, the color in her cheeks subsiding. "As far as I can tell, you're not working on anything."

"No, you're right. But I think I'm here for another reason, and it has to do with my family." Nat takes out a folder from the bottom of the pile. "I was talking to Mrs. Hervey this morning about my family's old camp on the Great Sacandaga Lake and it turned out she knew it! Why, she even had a picture of it. It seems that it was originally owned by Milo Latham."

"That's quite a coincidence—" Diana begins.

"Not half as much a coincidence as the fact that you own it now."

Diana shrugs, but I can see that she's even more unnerved by Nat's unearthing this information than she was by his violating the privacy of the office's filing system. "Milo Latham promised that land to my great-grandmother and then reneged on his promise. When you mentioned your first year here that your father was selling it, I thought it was a good opportunity to get it back into the family. And yes, I've sometimes expressed my opinion to the Board that artists working on projects related to Bosco history should get preference. Why not? Bosco has a rich history; why shouldn't its story be told? It wasn't just the family and their guests who were affected by what happened here that summer."

"Your great-grandmother was the head housekeeper that summer," Nat says.

"Mrs. Norris?" I ask, unable to keep the excitement from my voice. "Your great-grandmother was Mrs. Norris?"

Diana nods. "You needn't act so surprised. She had ambitions for her children. Milo Latham promised to send her son—my grandfather—to college for some work she did for him. He also promised her the cabin on the Sacandaga, which was built on land originally held by her family's people, but then after he died Aurora Latham reneged on both promises. My grandfather worked his whole life here as a gardener and my mother worked here as head housekeeper, saving every penny so that my sister and I could go to college. My sister went to a fancy art school in New York City," she says, casting a spiteful glance at Daria, "and has squandered her talent in drink. When it came time for me to go, we could only afford a secretarial school in Albany and I couldn't even finish because Mother had a stroke and I came back to look after her. Evelyn White, the director, hired me as her administrative assistant and when she died, I was made director. No one knows as much about Bosco as I do, but the one thing I don't know is what happened to my great-grandmother that summer."

"What do you mean?" Bethesda asks.

Diana smiles. "For all your research into Aurora Latham's life and your research for your novel," she says, turning to me, "neither of you have noticed that there's no record of the housekeeper after that summer. Apparently a mere servant wasn't of interest to you."

"I guess I thought she was old and died," Bethesda says, looking uncharacteristically abashed.

"From what I read in the pamphlet I have, I thought she might have been let go," I explain, unhappy to be cast into the role of social snob. "It was suggested that Mrs. Norris might have been working with Corinth Blackwell to produce the effects of the séances, but I can't remember why—"

"Because she was Native American," Diana says, tilting her chin up defiantly. "She was born in an Abenaki settlement on the Sacandaga Vly."

" 'Vly'?" Bethesda asks.

"It means meadow," Nat answers. "It was the rich

meadowland and marshes in the Sacandaga River valley before the river was flooded and made into a reservoir. My grandfather told me stories about the Abenaki and Iroquois who lived there, how their burial grounds were underneath the reservoir."

"Are you saying that just because she was Native American, Aurora believed she had something to do with kidnapping Alice?" Bethesda asks. I can tell she's distressed at the thought that her biographical subject might have been prejudiced against Native Americans.

"Well, there was one other thing," Diana says. "On the night of the second séance, the night that Alice Latham disappeared, my great-grandmother also disappeared. She was suspected of aiding the kidnappers, which is why Aurora Latham refused to honor her husband's promises to my family. But I've always believed she died trying to protect little Alice Latham— she practically raised her—and that she never left Bosco at all. And now you all may have proven me right. I think the bones in the well belong to my great-grandmother, Wanda Norris."

"I think so, too," David says.

Everyone turns to him. He's hardly spoken since we've come into Zalman's room—except to identify my mother as a medium. I had imagined that he was still stunned from almost drowning in the well. Now, although everyone is looking at him, the only one he's looking at is me.

"How could you know that?" I ask.

"It's something I felt when I was reading the inscription."

"And what was the inscription?" Zalman asks. "I'd like to hear what's written at the source of the spring."

"Mnemosyne," David says, "the Greek word for memory and the mother of the Muses. The instant I read it I could hear someone saying the word aloud, but then the longer I heard it, the more it sounded like *Ne'Moss-i-Ne* and the surer I was that whoever had been buried in the well was calling on the Indian maiden whose statue is in the rose garden. Who else but another Native American would pray to an Indian maiden? I was so sure of it that when I saw you, Ellis, I thought for a moment that *you* were the statue come to life—that you were Ne'Moss-i-Ne."

David reaches out and gently touches my arm, that same look of longing he'd had in the well burning in his eyes. His hand slides down my arm to grasp my hand, but at just that moment Nat brushes by me, jarring my hand out of David's reach, and storms out of the room, muttering something about returning the files to the office.

"Excuse me a second," I say to David. "There's something I've got to ask Nat."

Ignoring the look of hurt in David's eyes, I follow Nat into the hallway, catching up to him just as he steps out of the east door under the porte cochere. He wheels around when I call his name and smiles, but it's not a friendly smile. I notice that his eyes have acquired the glittery green of that old glass bottle in his room.

"You read the recommendation letter Spencer Leland wrote," I say, "didn't you?"

Nat looks momentarily startled, but he quickly regains his poise and shrugs, feigning an indifference that comes off instead as coldness. "Yes," he says. "Apparently I had great promise but a fatal flaw. He said I lacked form and discipline, but that if I found those, I might one day become a very fine writer indeed."

"That doesn't sound so bad—" I begin.

"No? Do you want to hear what *your* mentor, Dick Scully, had to say about you?"

I hesitate and Nat tilts his head back and barks a single "Ha!"; his breath condenses in the cold air into a white puff that hangs between us like an evil genie summoned by malice.

"Or did he show it to you already?" Nat asks. "It certainly reads more like a love letter than a recommendation, but then, Dick Scully always was a charmer and he always managed to pick the prettiest girl in the workshop to seduce." Nat lifts one eyebrow and waits for me to contradict him, to deny that I was sleeping with my teacher, but of course I can't.

"It was a stupid thing to do," I say instead.

"Oh, I don't know," Nat says. "It got you in here, didn't it?" With that, Nat turns and walks off toward the office. The air stirs at his leaving, wafting the little white puff against my face. It feels like damp gauze and smells of drugs and decay. I turn back to the house and find David standing in the open doorway.

"I didn't mean to interrupt anything," he says. "I just

wanted to thank you again for saving me in the well." He holds out his hand and I take it. For a second I shudder, remembering something from the well. When I felt myself being sucked into the whirlpool, it wasn't the water that was pulling me down. It was David.

Chapter Eighteen

When she leaves Tom's room, Corinth feels less than reassured. Despite his promise to leave after tonight's séance, she saw the hesitation in his eyes. She also scented the sickly sweet odor of laudanum in the air and, while seated on his bed, noticed a pearl-tipped pin—the same kind she had noticed in Mrs. Ramsdale's dress—sticking out of the bedspread. Not wanting to confront him, she buried the pin deeper into the mattress. So his employer visits him in his bedroom. She should not, she knows, be shocked, nor is she in any position to reproach him. And what choice does she have? She needs him to get away. What money she's been able to save over the years she has sent to her sister (carefully keeping the girl's existence a secret from Milo Latham). If she can reach her, then they can make some kind of life together—with or without Tom.

She pauses on the landing and hears once again the tune she heard in the cemetery and then on the terraces. *Ashes, ashes . . . A pocket full of posies . . .*

Her skin turns cold under her damp clothes and she

begins to shake. The singing is coming from above her, from the children's nursery in the attic. She considers going back to Tom's room and begging him to leave now, but then she remembers his skepticism on these matters. He would tell her there is a logical explanation for the singing, and he might be right. The least she can do is find out for herself.

And so she heads up the stairs to the attic. She can hear along with the child's voice the creaking of floor-boards, as if the child were walking in a circle. Corinth is reassured that it sounds like one child's voice and one child's footsteps, and as she comes up into the attic, she sees only one child. Alice Latham, holding her hands out as if holding invisible hands, pirouettes inside a circle made up of two porcelain dolls with glass eyes, a carved wooden bear, a stuffed goose, and the rocking horse, draped in a red paisley shawl. On the last line of the rhyme she holds up her dress and plops down cross-legged on the dusty floor.

Corinth claps. "Very good," she says, laying a hand on the rocking horse's head. "Who taught you that?"

"Cynthia did." And then, as if to answer a tacit question, she adds, "Last year, before she and the boys got sick."

"You must miss her," Corinth says, moving the horse aside so she can sit on the floor across from Alice, who regards Corinth with the same glassy stare as the dolls that sit on either side of her. She picks up one—the one with yellow hair and blue eyes—and holds it in her lap. The doll has better color in its cheeks than she does. Does this girl get any outside exercise? Everything about her bespeaks neglect, from the way her clothes are a little too small for her to the tangles in her waist-length dark auburn hair and the dark rings under her eyes.

"She had blond hair like this," Alice says, fingering the doll's hair, as if this were an answer to the question of missing her sister. "So did James and Tam. They said I had dark hair because I wasn't really Mother and Father's child, that they'd found me in the woods. A little Indian baby left to die."

Corinth remembers Alice's remark about "stinking savages" and guesses that this story was not made up by her siblings as a compliment.

"I think your hair is pretty," Corinth says.

Alice sniffs, pretending, Corinth feels, not to be pleased. "You would," she says. "It's the same as yours." Alice untangles a lock of her hair and leans forward across the circle to show Corinth, who stares at the coil of hair as if it were a snake about to strike.

"Take down your hair so we can see," Alice orders in a peremptory voice that reminds Corinth of Aurora. "It's all wet and messy, anyway." Corinth reaches up and touches her hair, which is damper than she'd realized, and is beginning to take the pins out when she feels the air stir on the back of her neck.

"Alice, what are you doing on the dirty floor in your new dress? Your mother will be very angry."

Corinth turns and looks up at Mrs. Norris, who is scowling not at Alice but at her.

"What does it matter if I'm not allowed to attend the séance tonight anyway?" Alice replies, getting to her feet and slapping at her skirt in a way that smears the dirt deeper into it rather than shakes it off.

"Go straight to your room and I'll be down to give you a bath," Norris tells her. "And put that doll away," she adds, pointing to the doll that Alice is still holding. "It's not yours to play with."

Alice's face turns as bright pink as the doll's painted cheeks. "It's my fault," Corinth says. "I asked her to show me some of Cynthia's toys." Corinth takes the doll from Alice and combs her fingers through its blond hair. Real hair, she realizes with a shiver, remembering that the girl with the pink ribbon who led her to the cemetery had blond hair as well. But no, they wouldn't . . . As Alice slips out behind Mrs. Norris, she turns and gives Corinth a shy smile, and for an instant the sulky face is transformed into something almost pretty. Corinth risks a small smile, but it's quickly squashed by Norris's scowl.

"Leave the child alone," she says when Alice has gone down the stairs. "You were brought here for the others, not her."

"Someone ought to be brought here for her. Why doesn't the child have a governess?"

"I do for her," Norris says. "I nursed her through the diphtheria last year and she was the only one to survive it."

"You were always a powerful healer, Wanda White Cloud," Corinth says, pronouncing the housekeeper's

Abenaki name formally and bowing her head slightly to honor her. She would rather count Wanda as a friend than an enemy. She will need all the help she can get tonight. Wanda lifts her chin at the sound of her Abenaki name, and for a moment Corinth glimpses the strength in her jaw and her black eyes, the strength of the warriors she is descended from, but then the eyes narrow and the jaw trembles. "You still blame me for your lost one," she says. "You think I could have saved it."

Corinth shakes her head. It's not what she meant at all, but as Wanda stretches her hands out, she sees the two of them in the bog behind Latham's camp, Wanda's hands outstretched to take her lifeless child from her, and she has to admit that Wanda's right. She did blame her. At that moment on the bog she hated Wanda so much that she could not hand her dead child over to her.

This time, though, she hands the doll to the house-keeper, noticing as she does that the doll's porcelain cheeks are so pink because someone has drawn stripes of war paint onto the delicate bisque.

Corinth stays in her room through dinner, sending down word to her hosts that she must prepare herself for tonight's séance by meditating. She wouldn't call what she does *meditating*, though. She sits at her window and watches the garden grow dark and the fireflies emerge out of the deepening shadows. The moving lights remind her of a château she stayed at once in France. For a *fête,* her hostess had ordered candles affixed to the backs of turtles that were then released into the *bosquet* to roam at will to create the illusion of fairies flitting between the trees. It was a pretty effect, but near the end of that summer Corinth found one of the creatures sealed in its own shell by the dripping wax. It had suffocated under the wax carapace, a victim of its mistress's aesthetic whimsy. How long, Corinth wondered then, before she fell victim to a similar fate, before she was sealed within the role she played?

It had been an easy role to play at first: conjurer of voices, message bearer between two worlds. Her patrons were satisfied with so little. The men wanted to know their mothers had loved them, the women that their children forgave them their inability to save them. More and more over the years it had been the children whom she was asked to contact. It was her specialty. Corinth knew what the mothers wanted to hear. *I'm happy here, Mother. There is no pain. I'm with Grandmama (or Grandpapa or Aunt Harriet . . .). I want you to be happy. I am always with you.*

As if the beyond were an extended holiday and these were their children's *cartes postale!* She hadn't needed to summon any obstreperous ghosts (whose demands of the living were not so easily satisfied as the living's demands of them); she merely had to recall her own reluctance to pass her child over to Wanda to understand why these women clung to their lost children.

At first, though, she had been glad enough of Wanda's help. When she returned from the overlook to the brougham and found Wanda waiting for her, she remembered what her mother had said about her: *A good healer, no matter what anyone else says about her.* Corinth had shut out from her mind those other things when Wanda placed her firm, capable hands on her and half lifted her into the carriage.

"You shouldn't be wandering in the fog, especially in these woods. This is where that girl who was pregnant with a white man's child jumped to her death. She waits here, hungry for other women's babies. You didn't see her, did you?"

Corinth shook her head, but when she looked up, Wanda pinned her with her black eyes and Corinth nodded.

"Don't worry," Wanda said, "we'll burn an offering for her tonight to send her spirit on its way."

"Where are we going?" Corinth asked.

"To Mr. Latham's camp on the Vly. Land that belonged once to my people. It will be a good place to wait for the baby."

The camp on the Vly was not far from the overlook, but the carriage had to go slowly because of the fog that came off the river and filled the surrounding valley like a preview of the floodwaters that rose in the spring. Passing through it, Corinth imagined they were deep beneath a lake and the white mist was the clouds seen through the water. Where the Vly Creek flowed into the Sacandaga, they turned west away from the river, crossing flat meadowlands bordered by marsh and bog. Barktown, the settlement where Corinth's mother had grown up, was to the south. Corinth knew the bogs from the summers on the settlement when her mother would take her collecting for the plants that grew there. They collected spongy sphagnum moss to stuff mattresses and make diapers for babies, and bog rosemary and leatherleaf for making tea. Her mother taught her to burn sweet gale to ward off mosquitoes and how to make a wash from reindeer moss that would soothe a colicky baby. She showed her the white bog orchid that girls collected for a love charm and told her stories about the girls who came back to the bogs to drown themselves when that love went bad. Their bodies would sink in the bog, but their skin and hair would never dissolve, only turn the color of tea and float in that limbo between earth and water for all time. *That's what happens to spirits who take their own life; they can never be free of this earth.*

When the carriage left them at the camp on the edge of the bog, Corinth wondered if she had jumped off the overlook after all and this was her limbo. While Wanda carried to the house sacks of food (flour, potatoes, salted meat—enough for a month, although Wanda told her that the carriage would return once a week to bring them fresh food), Corinth made a fire, but its heat didn't stop her shivering. The fog wrapped around the cabin like a winding sheet. The sound of water dripping from the fancifully carved eaves (Corinth later saw something like them at a chalet in Switzerland) made her feel as if they were underwater, that the house had already sunk into the depths of the bog. That night she dreamed of women's faces, stained the color of tea, pressing against the windows.

In the morning the fog had lifted, and after a breakfast of Wanda's griddle cakes and bacon, she felt strong enough to take a walk. Wanda cautioned her to watch her footing in the snow, but under the trees nearly all the snow had melted. She found moss that had survived the winter and, in sheltered places, bog rosemary and leatherleaf that she gathered and stuffed into the pockets in her sleeves, in which she used to keep wires for levitating tables. As she walked over the damp earth, she could feel the water trapped beneath the ground and feel, too, the baby, slippery as a mink frog, stirring in its own pool of water beneath her skin. *Little bog baby,* she said to herself, lifting her face to the watery sunshine.

For the first time since Tom had left she allowed herself to feel hope. Although Wanda White Cloud might not be the best company, she was a good midwife and baby nurse. By the time the baby was born, it would be summer. She'd stay here until she had her strength back, nursing herself on the teas and plant remedies her mother had taught her about, and then she would travel down the Hudson River to New York City, where she'd find Tom. Opening her eyes, she saw, lifting its head up through a thin scrim of snow, a white bog orchid, its pale petals trembling in the sunlight. Her mother had another name for the love charm. Ghost orchid. Because of the girls who drowned themselves when their love went wrong. Corinth bent to inhale its spicy vanilla scent, but left it where it grew. It didn't matter, she told herself, if she found Tom. What mattered was the baby growing inside of her. As long as it was safe she'd take whatever else fate had in store for her.

And the baby seemed to thrive those last three months at Milo Latham's camp. Maybe it was Wanda's cooking or the teas she brewed from the plants they both gathered or the moisture that filled the air around the cabin. Corinth felt her skin soaking it up, drawing sustenance from the very air just as the sphagnum moss swelled in the spring rains. She was squatting in a patch of the emerald green moss when the first pain rose up as if out of the ground and toppled her off her heels. She felt the ground quake beneath her and a stream of water flood down her leg into the soft, absorbent moss. It was as if the bog were giving birth to her, she thought, sinking back into its clasp. Every spasm that rocked her was absorbed in the rocking of the matted ground, every gush of blood soaked up by the moss. She might have lain there until the baby came if Wanda, walking down to the road to meet the weekly arrival of supplies, hadn't heard her screams. Wanda managed to get her to her feet in between pains, but by the time they got to the cabin, the pains were coming so fast Corinth barely had time to put one foot in front of the other before the next one swept through her.

"It's coming too fast," Wanda said, getting her into bed. She made her drink a cup of bitter-tasting tea and threw a handful of sweet-smelling grass on the fire. "Breathe this," Wanda said, holding a switch of the burning grass close to Corinth's face. Looking up, Corinth saw that Wanda had tied a red shawl across her mouth and nose. Her eyes above the cloth were like two black stones at the bottom of a clear stream. Corinth tried to lock her eyes onto them as the pains rocked through her, but the water grew cloudy and she lost sight of them. She could hear the rush of water all around her, carrying her on a strong current. When she closed her eyes, she saw Tom as she'd last seen him in her dreams, trapped beneath the ice in the river, looking for her, but when she reached out for him, he grabbed hold of her and pulled her deeper into the water. Then she saw that it wasn't Tom at all, but the girl on the overlook, her black eyes dissolving into the water, her body shredding in the current just as Corinth felt her own skin ripping apart, her mouth opening to scream and filling up with black water. Just before the black water swept over her, she pried open her eyes and she was looking straight into Wanda's. Wanda was holding the baby, a slippery thing covered by a fine film of reddish brown stain. She had given birth to a bog baby after all, Corinth thought, and then Wanda waved another bundle of burning grass across her face and the black water rose up and swallowed her.

When she awoke, Wanda told her that the baby had breathed its last breath while she, Corinth, slept. When she heard the words, she closed her eyes and let the black water close over her again. It was broad daylight when she awoke the next time, but whether it was the same day or the next or the one after that, she had no idea. Every time she opened her eyes the light was too bright. Wanda gave her more tea and she would fall back to sleep until one time when she awoke and Wanda said to her, "It is time."

When she got to her feet, she could feel a current of blood flood out between her legs into the moss that Wanda had padded there. She could feel it leaking out of her with every step she took out of the cabin and into the bog as each step sunk deeper into the cushiony ground. She'd never walk out of here, she thought when they reached a place of open water. Corinth leaned against a tamarack tree to keep herself from falling. Wanda placed into her arms a swaddled bundle that was so weightless Corinth was sure her arms must be numb. "You must say good-bye to her," Wanda said, "or its spirit will never be at peace and it will follow you wherever you go."

Corinth looked up through the tight-bunched needles of the tamarack tree and said the words that Wanda told her to say. When she was done, Wanda held out her hands to take the baby back, but Corinth shook her head. She knelt by the side of the pond and, cradling the baby, bent over until the water reached her shoulders and her arms, and only then, when her skin and the child's were both stained the color of parchment and old lace, did she look into her child's face. But it was like looking at something that had happened a long time ago.

She felt how easy it would be to bend over just a little more and sink to the bottom of the bog, where her flesh and her child's would cling together for all time. She felt Wanda's eyes on her back. Not stopping her.

But then she remembered what her mother had said about the girls who took their own lives and how their spirits were never free. She imagined herself caught for all time in this place, her unhappy spirit dragging the child's down into the muck. Better to let it go free.

"Good-bye, little one," she said, realizing as she spoke that she hadn't given the child a name. But it was too late. The baby's face was already vanishing in the water, like a candle extinguished in the night.

The flickering lights of the fireflies have disappeared from the gardens at Bosco, replaced by the lights from the candles that the servants carry down the fountain allée to the grotto in preparation for the séance. Corinth checks that the wires are firmly tucked into her sleeve pockets and finds in one the hellebore root she dug up from the garden two days ago. The same root that she remembers removing from her sleeve and putting away in her toiletries case, but when she opens the case, she can't find it, and the handkerchief in which she wrapped it is also gone. She examines the twisted root and then sniffs it, which causes her to sneeze three times. Her mother had told her that, ground and mixed in a drink, the hellebore root could make a man's heart beat when it had stopped, but that too much of it would stop his heart for good. As she slips the root back into the toiletries case, she wonders why Aurora Latham would have planted it in her garden.

In the library Milo Latham opens the hidden shelf where he keeps his scotch and pours a glass for Tom Quinn. "Here," he says, handing him the heavy cut-glass tumbler with its two inches of amber-colored liquid. "My private stock imported from the island of Islay off the coast of Scotland. I have to keep it locked up or else Aurora's painters and gardeners would piss it all away."

While Latham turns back to the cabinet to pour his own glass, Tom takes a sip and winces at the taste. Like drinking peat. When Latham turns around, though, he takes a larger swig and nods appreciatively. "That's grand," he says.

"Drink up," Milo says, draining half a glassful in one swallow. "You'll need some fortification for tonight's show. Let's try not to get anyone killed this time."

"Like I told you, Mr. Latham, the arrow that killed Frank Campbell didn't come from the bow you gave me. I didn't even get a chance to use it; I was too busy putting frogs down Mrs. Ramsdale's dress."

"I bet you were," Latham says, draining the last of his drink and turning to pour himself another. "Listen, I don't care about Campbell; I'm glad to be rid of him and I squared everything with the doctor. But I don't want any mistakes tonight. I'm paying you good money to make these séances convincing so my wife will be satisfied that the spirits of our children are at rest and we can go on with our lives. I'm sick and tired of living in a goddamned crypt." He drains his glass and puts it down so forcibly that the crystal chimes against the ormolu tabletop. Then he crosses the alcove to a writing desk against the far wall, takes out a sheet of paper and a pen, and begins to write. Tom sees that his own glass is empty and, since Latham has left the bottle out, pours himself another.

"Pour me one, too, while you're at it," Latham calls from the desk. "I'm writing up a bill of sale for you, Mr. Quinn. I noticed that you admired my hunting cabin when we met there last month."

"That wasn't the deal," Tom says, the scotch bottle poised over Latham's glass. "The deal was cash." Cash he'll need, he thinks, if he's going to take Corinth away from here.

"Well, I haven't that much cash on me at the moment, Mr. Quinn. Real estate's becoming quite valuable in the Adirondacks, especially with the state buying up land for their precious park. I think you'll find that you can sell this parcel for more than the amount we agreed upon. Besides, I've been meaning to sell it for some time now—bad memories, you understand, from the trips I took there with the children." Latham blots the ink and folds the paper in half. Turning, he finds Tom Quinn right behind him holding two glasses of scotch. He takes the one offered him and gives Tom the paper. "Good hunting," he says, clicking his glass against Tom's and bolting down another two ounces of the Laphroaig. Tom nods at the toast, not sure if his host is talking about the cabin now or tonight's activities. Then he takes a sip of the scotch and finds that the taste has begun to grow on him.

Tonight there is no procession to the grotto. Corinth makes her way down the fountain allée accompanied only by the purl of the water and the rustle of the wind moving through the cypresses. Lonely sounds, certainly, but for now at least wholly natural. There's no singing in the fountains, no sighing in the wind. Wanda Norris, standing outside the grotto with a candelabra held aloft to light her way into the passage behind the river god, looks solid and substantial and very human. There's no mistaking her tonight for an animated statue. Corinth is determined that there be no magic, no stray whiff of spirit, in tonight's proceedings. Aurora Latham, like half a dozen of the women she's been employed by over the years, needs to say good-bye to her children just as Corinth said good-bye to hers. She has never in the ten years since she knelt by the water in the bog caught a glimpse of that tea-stained face, and she intends that after tonight Bosco will be as rid of its ghosts as she has been of hers.

The table has been set up just as last night, close enough to the stone bench so that one of the circle can sit there. They've left that seat for her. The men of the party rise as she enters, and Tom moves his chair so she can sit down on the stone bench, next to Milo Latham and directly across from Signore Lantini. Aurora sits next to her husband, Mrs. Ramsdale next to Tom. When she's seated, Corinth looks up and for a moment, instead of men and women, she sees the circle assembled earlier today in the attic by little Alice: the two dolls in the place of the women, the carved wooden bear and stuffed goose in Milo Latham's and Signore Lantini's places. Only Tom's eyes meet hers with human warmth instead of a glassy stare. She blinks her eyes and the members of the circle regain their human features.

"Let's begin," she says, taking Tom's hand first. When they've all joined hands, Corinth closes her eyes and tilts her head back far enough so that she can see through the narrow slits between her eyelashes. She counts in her head to a hundred and then, lowering her voice, she calls the names of the three children. "James. Cynthia. Tam." She pronounces each name separately as if reciting a recipe, while to herself she pronounces, over the name of each of the children, a word for something inanimate. *Stone. Water. Wood.* It takes a tremendous amount of concentration to say one word while thinking another; it takes up all the space inside her head, which is exactly what she wants. She doesn't intend to leave any space for the children to find their way in.

Checking through the slits of her eyes that no one is looking, she frees her right hand from Tom's and slides a wire beneath the table, gently guiding Tom's forefinger over the wire so that he can feel it, so he'll believe she's taking him into her confidence. She feels his hand startle for a moment, but then he grips her wrist to steady her hand as she rocks the table up and she feels a shiver of pleasure at the pressure of his skin against hers. "James," she says, thinking *stone* while picturing in her head a round white stone, "is that you?" The table rocks two times. "Are Cynthia and Tam with you?" *Water. Wood.*

Two knocks come from beneath the table. Through her slitted eyes she sees Aurora's face tighten, her brow furrowed and her jaw drawn back as if in pain. "My babies," Aurora says, "I want to see my babies."

"You mean the children," Milo Latham says, his head tilting toward his wife's voice. Even with his eyes closed Corinth can imagine the impatience that always flickers through his eyes when someone gets something wrong—a waiter brings a wine that's turned, or a bellhop the wrong valise. She's seen him at recitals striking phantom keys when the pianist makes a mistake. He is a man used to having his world ordered to his liking and will correct anything amiss. "James, Cynthia, and Tam," he says, and then, in a low hiss: "*You don't want the others.*"

"*No!*" Aurora spits in a deep, guttural croak that

raises the hairs on the back of Corinth's neck. "You can't replace one for the other. They're not dining room chairs that have been broken or figures in a ledger to be moved from one column to another. I want my babies back, my sweet babies, the way they were when I nursed them."

The table lurches beneath Corinth's hand and she's not sure if she moved it or if Tom did. "It's James," Aurora cries, her eyes flying open and looking straight at Corinth. "You must tell him to be quiet. He would never be quiet even when the others were sick, even when he became sick himself."

"James," Corinth says, thinking *stone,* only this time instead of a round white stone she pictures the marble of a statue. "Your mother will say good-bye now and then you can be free. The others can be free, too." She looks across the table at Aurora. "Tell him good-bye," she says.

"Go!" Aurora screams. "You must let the others rest."

Milo opens his eyes and, letting go of Corinth's hand, turns toward his wife. "That's quite enough. I've had enough of this foolishness. I had her brought here to give you some peace, but it isn't peace that you want."

By now Mrs. Ramsdale has opened her eyes and is watching the scene with evident interest. Only Signore Lantini keeps his eyes closed.

"You brought her here so you could bed her in our own house, in the house where our children died, because I wouldn't let you foist your dirty children on me anymore. She's my replacement, just as James and Cynthia and Tam were replacements for the ones who died. Look what you've brought into your home to replace your own—a stinking savage!"

At the word *savage* the grotto shakes and something cracks. Signore Lantini's eyes fly open. "*Dio mio*, it's an earthquake." He gets to his feet and runs out of the grotto.

Milo Latham throws back his head and laughs. "There, you see what you've done? You've scared your little gardener away. I, for one, have had enough spectacles for one night." He takes a cigar out of his pocket and lights it using the candle in the center of the candelabra. Then he gets up, bending stiffly at the waist for a moment as if he had a cramp. "I'm going to bed. Mrs. Ramsdale, perhaps you will attend to my wife?" He precedes the rest of the party out of the grotto, Tom directly behind him, then Mrs. Ramsdale, who's left Corinth to help Aurora to her feet. At the mouth of the grotto Milo bends over, draping his arm around the shoulder of the river god, as if he were doubled over in laughter and sharing the joke with the marble statue. Then he slides to the ground.

By the time Corinth is able to free herself of Aurora Latham's grip and squeeze herself out of the grotto's narrow entrance, Tom and Mrs. Norris are kneeling on either side of Milo's body. Wanda is keening a chant, while Tom leans over, pressing his head against Milo Latham's chest. He looks up at Corinth and shakes his head, and Aurora begins to scream. Corinth turns away from the sound and her eyes fall on the statue of the river god, the one that represents the Sacandaga. The marble has been cleaved in two, from the top of the shaven skull to the bottom of one moccasin-clad foot, and a quail-feathered arrow is sticking out of the crack in just the spot where the river god's heart would be.

PART THREE

Giardino Segreto

Chapter Nineteen

So much snow falls in the last weeks of November that I am forced to give up my plan of driving across the state to Lily Dale for Thanksgiving. I console myself by remembering that it's not a very important holiday for Mira, who, once Halloween is over, focuses all her attention on the approaching winter solstice or, as she calls it, *beating back the rising dark.* I would have liked a break from Bosco, though, and I considered asking David to make the drive with me, but then I couldn't quite make up my mind to do it. Since the incident in the well, I've felt uneasy in his presence. I've seen Bethesda watching me, noticing how tongue-tied I am around him, and I'm sure she thinks it's because I have a crush on him. She would be half right. I am drawn to him, but I'm also afraid of him—or maybe afraid of how he makes me feel. Truth be told, I have felt this same sense of unease before at the onset of a relationship. I felt it when I began seeing Richard Scully, and as the aftermath of that affair abundantly proved, I would have been wise to heed my instincts.

I'd meant it when I told Nat that having an affair with my writing teacher was a stupid thing to do. I didn't know how stupid until a month before graduation, when I realized my period was five days late. I made the mistake of telling Richard that I thought I might be pregnant. "Of course it's up to you," he'd said, "but I'd hate to see your promise as a writer swallowed up in the drudgery of child-rearing." I'd known in that instant how little our "affair" had meant to him. I could have the baby, but I'd be on my own. I'd go back to Lily Dale, the way my mother had gone back pregnant with me. I knew she'd take care of us both. I'd have a midwife-assisted childbirth in a birthing tank surrounded by a chanting spirit circle. And I'd grow old there—alone— just as my mother and grandmother and great-grand-mother before me. A line of women who seemed cursed to live without male companionship. By the time I realized I wasn't pregnant, I was finished with Richard. I wasn't even angry at him. I was only angry at myself for having chosen so poorly.

He was right about one thing: I would have hated giving up the opportunity to write this book at Bosco, especially now that it's going so well. I'd thought that after discovering the bones, and Zalman breaking his leg, and David almost drowning, and all the talk of ghosts, I wouldn't be able to work at all, but on the contrary, I awake each morning with the voice of Corinth Blackwell in my head practically dictating the next scene. I go straight to my desk and write through breakfast, scurrying downstairs after noon to collect my lunch box, which, I notice, seems to be the pattern that everyone else is now following. The lunch boxes, once collected soon after breakfast, sit in a row outside the dining room waiting for the guests to take a break from their work to claim them. Quiet hours, which used to end at five, have been extended by tacit agreement to six, when we all drift down to dinner in the dining room. There the silence lingers through the meal, as if we were each reluctant to leave the world of our own work. Or maybe we're afraid of acknowledging out loud what's going on. I would have thought that after everything that came out in Zalman's room, someone would have left, but I suspect that if my fellow guests have found the atmosphere as conducive to their writing as I have, then it will take more than a few "water tricks" to make them leave.

After dinner we all drift into the library, where we sit around the fire and drink Bosco's seemingly endless store of single malt. Diana has given up portioning out the scotch, since all the guests seem to have developed a taste for the eighteen-year-old Laphroaig (only Zalman, because of the painkillers he's taking, abstains). "It's a little bit like drinking potting soil," David says one night when he fills everyone's glasses (somehow he has become the default bartender).

When I take my first sip of the evening, I picture David's hands plunging into black soil and shiver as the warm liquid rolls down my throat. Nat talks about the bogs around his grandfather's cabin and how in the fall his grandfather would make a bonfire out in the bog and the smell of burning leaves would be mixed with the smell of peat. "He'd always make some joke about there being Indian bodies in that peat," he says. "He'd tell all these stories about pregnant Indian girls who'd thrown themselves off cliffs and drowned themselves in the bog . . ."

"Hm," Zalman says, "I've been thinking of writing a poem about one of those legends."

"Well, I'm sure you'd give the subject better treatment than my grandfather. He'd always end those stories by sniffing the peat smoke and saying, " 'Can't you smell 'um, son? Roasted Injun.' "

"What a lovely man, your grandfather," Bethesda says.

"Yeah, he was a real bastard," Nat replies.

Often we all conjecture on whether Corinth Blackwell ever went to the cabin and, if so, with whom? Did she meet Milo Latham there? Or did she and Tom Quinn flee there after the second séance? By my second glass, I'm not sure if we are talking about fiction or fact anymore. It seems as if we are each telling a part of a story that happened a very long time ago to all of us, only we all remember it a little differently. I fall asleep at night with all of their voices in my head, but when I awake, with the taste of peat still on my tongue, I hear only one voice: Corinth's.

Until one morning in early December, a morning of heavy snow and galelike winds, when I get to the scene of the second séance. I still hear Corinth's voice, but all she will say are three words: *stone, water, wood.* Repeated over and over again like one of Mira's mantras. It feels, maddeningly, as if my muse has had a stroke, and I wonder if my scotch consumption has finally eroded my own brain cells. I stare out the window at the steadily falling snow and feel as if my brain is muffled in the same thick white fleece that covers the garden. Finding the right words is suddenly as hard as making out shapes under the snow. What looks like a hedge might be a statue, and what looks like the shape of a body lying in the *giardino segreto* might only be a snowdrift sculpted by the wind. A moment later the body seems to take flight, and I see that what I had thought was a snowdrift was actually a flock of the pale gray mourning doves that winter in Bosco's hedges.

I will myself to see, in the shifting snow, Corinth Blackwell in the center of the séance circle with Tom Quinn on her right and Milo Latham on her left. Her old lover and her married lover: the two men fate had placed her between. But when Corinth opens her mouth, instead of "James, Cynthia, and Tam," the words "Stone, water, wood," come out.

I squeeze my eyes shut and concentrate until the image in my head says the words she's supposed to and then, just as the rest of the scene is coming clear, a noise outside my door makes me jump.

"Ridiculous," I say aloud, crossing the room. "I've scared myself with my own story."

When I open the door, I'm relieved by the homely sight of the old-fashioned tin lunch box. I look at my watch and see that it's almost three o'clock. Mrs. Hervey must have decided to bring it up when I didn't come down for it at noon. I look down the hall and see that Nat's and Bethesda's lunch boxes have been left outside their doors as well. Apparently I'm not the only one who's absorbed in his or her work today—although I may be the only one who's spent an entire day writing only three words.

I go back to my desk to work, but after some time— fifteen minutes? an hour? I have no idea—something slams into my window so hard that the blow reverberates in my chest as if I had been struck. When I look up, I see the spread of wings against the glass and realize that some large bird, lost in the storm, has flown into my window. As I watch the bird slide off the glass and drop to the terrace below, I feel a sickening lurch in my stomach, as if I were in a plane that had suddenly lost altitude. I run downstairs and out onto the terrace in my slippers and kneel down in the snow over an indentation in a drift marked by a single white feather. I lean over to scoop up the bird, my arms sinking into the snow up to my shoulders, but then the snow beneath my hands begins to stir. It feels as if the snow itself had come to life, and once again I hear the words Corinth spoke at the séance: *stone, water, wood.* This is water—frozen— come to life.

It must be my screams that rouse David from the library. He comes out brandishing a fire poker, but when he sees, as I see now between slits in my fingers that I have raised to protect my face, that the snow demon is only a large, angry snow goose, he drops the poker and grabs the bird with his bare hands. The wings beat against his face, strike his chest, and then it's gone in an upward spin of white down that merges with the falling snow.

He kneels down in front of me and tries to pull my hands away from my face, but his fingers on my wrists feel like burning brands searing into my flesh.

"Ellis," he says. "Ellis, it's okay, it's gone. Let me see your face."

I shake my head no, but he manages to peel away my hands from my face with the same gentle but firm motion I imagine he might use to peel a husk away from a seed. He cups handfuls of snow to wash my face and I see that the snow comes away red.

"Come on," he says, holding my hands in his. His are trembling, but then, I notice, so are mine. "Let's get you inside. I've got some bandages and antiseptic in my room." I must look suspicious, because he shows me his own hands, which are scratched and scarred. "Occupational hazard," he says, laughing. "I'm always getting scratched or nicked working outdoors. But I have to say, I've never gotten myself attacked by any of the waterfowl."

Instead of laughing with him, I lay my hand on David's chest. "You have now," I say. He looks down and sees that the left side of his shirt has been ripped open to the skin, revealing a two-inch scratch just above his heart.

When we get to David's room, I can still hear the beating of wings. I can hear them while he bandages my hands, and when I lay my hand over the scratch on his chest, I feel his heart beating to the same rhythm. The beating is loud enough to drown out the sound of my own heartbeat but not the sound of my fear.

"I can't . . ." I begin, but then he lays his hand over mine and, lifting it to his mouth, kisses the underside of my wrist. I shiver and the beating in my head becomes a drumbeat. When he pulls me down onto the bed, the papers beneath us crackle like fire. David sweeps the blueprints and maps off the bed in one stroke of his arm, and the papers spin in slow, lazy spirals to the floor.

My bandaged hands are too clumsy to unbutton my own shirt, so he does it for me, deliberately and gently, his own hands shaking. Not being able to use my hands makes me feel clumsy, but he anticipates every movement I want to make until I feel that someone else is inhabiting my body, moving my limbs, producing the moans that issue from my throat.

I stretch out beneath him, reaching to wrap my hands around the bedposts, but he catches my hands and, cradling them in one of his, holds them above my head. For an instant I feel trapped, but then I'm soaring, as if I've broken free of my body at last. I can feel myself rising above the bed, watching myself making love to this man I hardly know. Outside the snow howls and something cracks, and I hear someone cry out. Me.

"It's just the wind," David murmurs, soothing me, "a branch breaking in the wind."

But it wasn't the sound that made me cry out—it was something sharp stabbing into my wrist. I wrench my hand out of David's grasp and hold it up. Stuck half an inch into my flesh is a pearl-tipped pin. David pulls it out instantly.

"I have no idea how this got here . . ." he begins, but I'm already getting up, clutching my unbuttoned shirt over my breasts. I'm not listening. I'm looking over my shoulder at the headboard, where one of the eagle's wings has cracked in half.

David follows me out into the hall, pleading with me. "Ellis, what's wrong? Please tell me."

I keep going, my eyes blinded with tears, and so I don't see what trips me before I land on the floor. It's one of the white stones, lying in the middle of the hallway. I pick it up and notice that there's another one a few feet away . . . and another at the foot of the attic stairs. David reaches me there, and we both look up the stairs to see a stone on every step. He follows me up to the attic, where we find an entire circle of the stones in the middle of the room. Two glass-eyed dolls, a carved bear, and a stuffed goose are sitting inside the circle.

"It's some kind of joke," David says. "Nat and Bethesda probably set this up."

I don't say anything because I've noticed that there's another path of stones leading from the circle to a closet at the west end of the attic.

"Yeah," he says, following me to the closet, "they're probably hiding in there waiting to jump out and shout 'Boo!' Nat," he calls, "Bethesda, we know you're in there."

A thunk comes from inside the closet that sounds exactly like a stone dropping on wood. He rattles the door and calls their names, but there's no other sound. "I'm going to get something to pry this loose," he says, shaking the padlock that secures the door as if he were angry with the thing itself. "The metal is so corroded it won't be hard to break."

As David brushes past me, I look down at the ancient iron padlock. A thick crust of vermilion rust has grown over it, distorting the original shape and welding the case to the shackle. "It doesn't look like anyone's touched this in decades," I say, cupping the lock in my hand. The instant my flesh touches the iron I smell blood. I try to draw back my hand, but the lock sticks to my palm, the rust turning into a viscous paste that runs through my fingers and puddles on the floor by my feet until there's nothing left in my hand but a wet, sticky stain. And then, the lock melted, the door creaks slowly open, letting in the cold white attic light, which touches a ladder-back chair and, like liquid glass poured into a mold, fills the chair with the shape of a little girl who lifts the glassy shimmer of her head up and looks straight at me out of two black holes where her eyes should be.

"El—" David has come to stand behind me, but he's unable to finish even my name before the light drains out of the girl, leaving an empty husk that wavers for a second and then vanishes. I turn to David, afraid that he won't have seen it, but when I see the color drained from *his* face, I realize it's all the more horrifying that he has.

"Something horrible happened here," I say, scanning the four narrow beds against the wall, afraid that the children's bodies will swell into shape beneath the lumpy counterpanes. David doesn't answer. He's entered the storage room and knelt by the chair. He picks up a strand of rope that's tied to the rungs of the chair back and holds up its frayed end for me to see. The rope, hacked at with a knife, is stained with blood.

David unties the bloodstained rope from the chair and holds it out to me, but I find I'm unable to touch it. Even several feet away I can smell the blood again. A wave of nausea passes over me, and I lurch toward the windows to get some air, but when I push one open, the air that comes in is sharp with ice particles that feel like needles on my face. I close it and am just turning away when a motion down in the garden catches my attention. It's Bethesda making her way down the hill through the deep snow wearing only a cardigan, thermal leggings, and her green rubber boots. And then, some twenty feet behind her, is Nat, also underdressed in flannel shirt, jeans, and the moccasins he wears around the house as slippers.

"We have to go after them," I hear David say from behind me. "If they get disoriented out there, they could get hypothermia at these temperatures. Here"—David reaches into an open trunk and pulls out an old hunting jacket and a woolen cloak and two pairs of old hunting boots—"we don't have time to get our things." He heads down the steps, and I follow him, pausing only a moment to look over my shoulder at the door to the storage closet. It's closed again, but whether it was David who closed it or not, I'm not sure.

When we step out onto the terrace, we're assaulted by a fierce, icy wind. The snow is coming down heavier than before and the wind is sweeping it into drifts that come halfway up the balustrade.

"How are we ever going to find them?" I ask, looking at the deep snow from the terrace. "The wind has swept away their footprints."

"All Bethesda talks about these days is the children's cemetery," David says. "She's made diagrams of it and lists of the birth and death dates of all the children. I bet she found some discrepancy and decided to go down to check it out."

I can't help but wonder when David has seen these diagrams and lists, but I don't say anything. Instead I step off the terrace and sink to my knees in snow.

"We probably should have snowshoes," David says, "but there's no time. Can you still find that path you took us down that day? There might be less snow under the trees."

Although I haven't been on the path since the day Zalman broke his leg, I have no trouble finding it. Maybe because I follow it every night in my dreams. David is right—there is less snow under the ilexes. In fact, it almost seems as if a path has been shoveled through the snow. The thick hedges muffle the wind as well, letting in only playful gusts that stir the powdery snow, swirling it into patterns beneath my feet.

"I bet you can't wait to get to all of this with your

clippers," I say to David, who's walking so close behind me that I can hear his breath at my ear.

"I don't know," he says. "To tell you the truth, I really love how a garden looks when it's overgrown like this. Of course, don't tell the Garden Conservancy I said that."

I remember sensing back in the fall that David felt this way, but I had forgotten about it.

"This garden especially," he goes on. "I have this feeling like it *should* be overgrown—that nature should be allowed to claim it back. Maybe it's because of how it was hewn out of the woods and the money for it came from Latham's lumber business. I can't help but picture all the trees that were cut down to make it. I know that might sound sentimental—"

"No," I say, "I know exactly what you mean. It's something else, too. It's what Aurora built it for—as a shrine to the memory of her dead children—such an elaborate shrine, it's as if their spirits are trapped in it." I picture the girl tied to the chair in the attic room, her hollow eyes, and the girl I saw crouched beneath the hedge in the maze . . . and then I see, about ten feet ahead of us, a crumpled form under a light dusting of snow. David rushes forward and I follow him, arriving in time to see Nat's face as David turns him over. There's a gash on his forehead and a circle of blood spreading out beneath his head on the snow.

I hear someone muttering, "I don't understand, I don't understand," in a childish voice, over and over again. At first I think the words are in my head, but when David picks up his head and listens, I realize they're coming from farther up the path. There, sitting cross-legged in the middle of the path, is Bethesda. She's been sitting there long enough for snow to drift over her legs. "I was only playing. It was only a snowball I threw." She holds up a snowball to show us, but as I walk toward her, I see it's not a snowball but one of the white rocks.

"Explain again why you were going down to the children's cemetery," David asks that night in the library after dinner. He's standing in front of the fireplace, his elbow on the mantel, with a glass of scotch in one hand, still wearing the checked hunting jacket he found in the attic, which fits him as if it were made for him. Nat, his head copiously bandaged, watches enviously every time David lifts the glass to his lips. The doctor at the emergency room ("You writers are pretty accident-prone up there," he commented to us while stitching Nat's head) said absolutely no alcohol for forty-eight hours.

Bethesda, who is sitting on the footstool of Nat's chair, takes a deep breath and goes through her story once again. "I was working at my desk when a gust of wind struck my window so hard it broke the glass. Then the wind blew the drapes up and all my papers came unpinned. I was chasing them around the room when I noticed one was stuck to the glass, just above where it was broken. I was afraid it would fly out the window, so

I went over to get it . . ." Bethesda pauses, and I realize that she's paused every time she's gotten to this part of the story.

"You saw something at the window, didn't you?" I ask.

"It was nothing," she says. "It was just my reflection. But I thought . . ."

"You thought it was a face," I say.

Bethesda nods and takes a large gulp of her scotch, glancing at Nat guiltily as she does. "Yes, it looked like a face etched in frost. It scared the hell out of me. Then I took down the paper and looked at it—"

"Good old Bethesda," Nat says, "you wouldn't let a little ghost sighting get in the way of your research." There's a note of bitterness in Nat's voice that I haven't heard him use before toward Bethesda. Maybe it's from being given a concussion and a gash requiring five stitches.

"Well, it turned out to be important," Bethesda says, pulling a sheet of paper from her pocket. "See, it's a death certificate for Alice Latham dated April ninth, 1883."

"But isn't Alice the little girl who disappeared in 1893 and was never found?" David asks.

"This could be a different Alice," I say. "There were several duplicate names in the children's cemetery."

"But no 'Alice,' " Bethesda says. "I'm sure of it—or almost sure. That's why I wanted to go down to the cemetery and look. Then I got lost on the path and when I heard someone behind me I thought . . . I don't know

. . . I thought I heard someone laughing and a snowball hit my ear."

"I did *not* throw a snowball at you," Nat says, "and I wasn't laughing. I was half frozen because when I saw you from my window heading into the garden without a coat, I ran down to follow you without *my* coat."

"I'm just telling you what I thought was happening," Bethesda says. "I had this feeling . . . I know it was stupid . . . but I had this feeling it was the *snow* doing it."

"So David and Ellis were led up to the attic by a trail of stones, and Nat and Bethesda were led into the garden by a trail of ice," Zalman, who's sitting on the couch with his injured leg stretched out, says.

"What next?" David asks, looking down at the group. "Bread crumbs?"

"I heard wings today," I say. "And then . . ." I look up at David and blush.

"Uh . . . something happened in my room," he says. "The carved eagle on my bed split in two."

Nat looks at David and then at me, and then he leans forward and, before she can stop him, takes Bethesda's glass from her and swallows the last of her scotch.

"So we've got rocks, ice, and wings," Zalman says, ticking off each item on his fingers as if collecting supplies for a picnic.

"No," I say. "Stone, water, and wood." As I say the words, a log shifts in the fireplace and a spark jumps out onto the carpet, which David promptly grounds out under his boot. "I was writing the scene of the second séance today," I explain, "and what I wrote . . . I imagined what Corinth Blackwell might have done if she didn't really want to conjure the spirits of the Latham children."

"But why wouldn't she want to conjure the children?" Bethesda asks.

"Think of all those children in the cemetery," I say, "some who lived only a few hours. Would you want to come face-to-face with those?"

When no one answers, I go on. "So, what I had her do is think of something else while she said the children's names, and I picked inanimate things that seemed to have no personality."

"Stone, water, wood," Zalman says.

"Yes, that's what she said . . . or I mean, that's what I had her say. Only it doesn't work. The children come anyway, but they come . . ." I stop, too horrified to finish what I'd been about to say.

"They come," Zalman says, finishing for me, "as stone, water, and wood."

Chapter Twenty

Corinth knows as she walks through the garden on the way back to the house that something is wrong. At first it's just a sense that everything's more alive. The polished ilex leaves quiver in the moonlight like phosphorescence in a Mediterranean sea. The hedges rustle as she walks by, pulsing in and out with each step she takes. The statues, soaked in moonlight, are draped with leaf shadows that rise and fall across their breasts like patterned gauze stirred by their breath. It reminds Corinth of walking through the woods with her mother, how every plant and animal and stone and even the wind that stirred the leaves had a name. Only the spirits animating this garden do not seem benign to her. When she reaches the top terrace and turns to look back, she sees that the water in the fountain allée, whose murmur has accompanied her from the grotto, is flowing uphill.

She turns toward the house and crosses the terrace as quickly as she can, pushed by a wind that tugs at her skirts. The French doors to the library open easily, but she has to struggle against the wind to close them, the glass rattling in the wooden frames so hard that she thinks they will break. When she finally gets them closed she sees, on the glass pane below the knob, the imprint of a small hand. She turns away, relieved to see a fire in the fireplace and the calm solidity of the Morris chairs on the hearth, relieved to be inside and alone— but then she hears a rustle in the alcove and catches a scent that brings to mind the bog behind the cabin on the Sacandaga. *No*, Corinth thinks, closing her eyes, not *that*, but when she opens her eyes, she sees Mrs. Ramsdale step out of the shadows, a small sherry glass in one hand and a crystal decanter in the other. Mrs. Ramsdale pours a thimbleful of the amber-colored liquor and drinks it all down.

"Care for a drink?" she asks, pouring herself another one. "I couldn't find any sherry, but I don't think Milo would mind me drinking from his private stock of scotch. It's a little bitter at first, but you get used to the taste."

"Where have they taken his body?" Corinth asks.

"To the parlor, where he can keep Mr. Campbell company. Dr. Murdoch might have saved himself a visit. At least this time he won't have to lie on the death certificate. I believe this really was a heart attack. You knew, of course, that Milo had a weak heart?"

"No," Corinth says, crossing the room toward the door to the hallway, "I didn't know that." Mrs. Ramsdale steps in front of her, blocking her way out. Corinth can smell, beneath the bitter reek of the scotch, the sweeter smell of laudanum.

"Yes, we frequented many of the same spas and took the same water-cures, although my malady resides a bit lower in the body than his." She lays her hand over her stomach, pressing the cloth flat so that Corinth can see the swelling there. "I thought there was another tumor growing, but Dr. Murdoch examined me this morning and . . . well, I'm afraid my condition is a bit more *delicate* than that." She pauses, waiting for Corinth to absorb the import of her news. "Of course, I'm surprised. I'd thought I was too old and that the last surgery had removed any chance . . . but, as they say, life will find a way. Of course it will have to be a hurried wedding and some people will talk, but what does that matter? We'll go to Europe. I have a house in the south of France; I have enough money for the three of us . . ."

"I hope you'll be very happy," Corinth says, pushing past Mrs. Ramsdale. *A baby?* Could a baby really be born of that corruption? But as she presses by Mrs. Ramsdale, grazing the woman's shoulder with her own, she can feel the presence of the child and knows it is Tom's. It occurs to her, as she flees up the stairs to her room, that it might be the only life to break free of this sepulcher.

When she gets to her room, she finds a sheet of paper lying flat on the floor, just over the threshold. Picking it up, she sees that it's a theatrical poster, an old one from the Lyceum Theater in Gloversville on the night she and

Tom both appeared. She turns it over and sees on the back a handwritten message:

> Cory, I'm leaving Bosco tonight. If you want to go with me, meet me in the Rose Garden at midnight.—Q

And beneath that:

> We'll follow the rivers north.

Mrs. Ramsdale probably hasn't had a chance to tell him her news. When she does . . . well, it doesn't matter. He's no doubt arranged for a carriage to take them away. If he's not there, then she'll take it herself. She packs her trunk, but then realizes that she can't carry it herself down to the rose garden. And she's certainly not going to leave a forwarding address for Aurora Latham to send it on. She takes out her plainest dress and only what will fit in her small carpetbag, consigning the rest of her dresses, her toiletry case, and the unmatched glove to the trunk. She pauses over the case that contains her wires and picks, but then decides to leave it in the trunk—let whoever finds it unmask her as a fraud. What does it matter? She won't be performing any more séances after tonight.

Before she closes her trunk, though, she checks the toiletry case and finds the hellebore root that she put back earlier, relieved to see that it's still there. *A weak heart*, Mrs. Ramsdale had said. No, she'd never known that Milo had *any* weakness. When they met at the spas in Europe, he always said that they were taking the waters because of Aurora's neurasthenia, but now that she thinks of it, she remembers that he spent his days taking various water-cures and drinking from the springs. If he had a weak heart, it wouldn't have taken much of the hellebore root to kill him. But who would know that?

If her trunk is searched and the root found in it, she might be blamed for Milo's death. Or if she's stopped and it's found on her person . . . She looks around the room for a place to hide it, but decides she can't take the chance of it being found in her room, either. She has to hide it somewhere in the house. Opening her door and listening for voices, she hears Aurora's keening cry coming from the downstairs parlor. Now she really is Egeria mourning for her lost husband. It's almost as if she purchased the statue first and then rearranged her life to fit it.

At the back stairs she also hears voices—Mrs. Norris and one of the maids—coming from below, so she takes the stairs up to the third floor and then to the attic.

The long room is dark except for the light from the newly risen moon that cuts a swath from the window to the storage room on the west side of the attic, catching the glass eyes of the dolls and the rocking horse but leaving the beds along the north wall in shadow. She can't tell which bed Alice is in as she crosses to the storage room. She tries the door and finds that it's locked with a heavy iron padlock. She slips a wire out of her sleeve and within a minute she's picked the lock. As soon as she slides the padlock off the bolt, the door swings in and moonlight pours into the bare room. Corinth had expected a jumble of trunks and old furniture. Instead the only object in the room is a single straight-backed chair upon which sits a little girl in a white nightgown who stares up at Corinth with bottomless black eyes.

After he and Lantini have carried Milo's body into the parlor, Tom tries to get away so that he can find Corinth, but Aurora Latham pauses in her weeping long enough to ask him to go into town to summon Dr. Murdoch back to the house. Why the doctor is needed so urgently—or why he should be needed to accompany the driver into Saratoga—is beyond Tom's reasoning, but he can see that there's no point arguing with the grieving widow. Besides, he might need the driver's cooperation later and it won't hurt to scout out a likely hotel in Saratoga while he's fetching Dr. Murdoch.

He rides in on the box beside Latham's coachman, a taciturn young man in his midthirties with lank black hair and pitted skin, which he hides with a hat turned low over his forehead. Tom asks him if he'd be available later to drive him back into town, but he doesn't answer. Tom wonders if the man is deaf and dumb, but then he realizes that he's waiting to be offered money. He takes out a few bills and holds them out so that the driver can see them.

"Twice this if you wait for me at the bottom of the garden and don't tell anyone where you take us."

The driver takes the bills and stuffs them into his pocket, grunting assent.

Maybe the man is dumb, if not deaf, Tom concludes, which suits him just fine. Less chance he'll give them away. Maybe he could have gotten away with giving him less—as it is he'll barely have enough to pay for the hotel. He spends the rest of the drive into Saratoga calculating what he has left from the last time Violet paid him and how much he's likely to get by pawning the pocket watch and other trinkets she's given him over the years. By the time he's walking up the path to Dr. Murdoch's spacious Greek Revival mansion on North Broadway, he's come to the conclusion that he sorely needs more money if he expects to get any farther than Saratoga with Corinth.

The housekeeper tells Tom to wait in the library while she goes to wake the doctor. "He was up delivering a baby in Ballston Spa last night and turned in early tonight," she explains when Tom expresses surprise that the doctor is already asleep. "And this man's already dead, you say? Well, if it were anyone else but Milo Latham, I'd tell you to come back in the morning, but he and the doctor were good friends. He'll want to know."

It's hard to imagine anyone being good friends with Milo Latham, but when Tom enters the library he guesses that what the housekeeper means is that the doctor and Latham were good hunting buddies. The room is filled with trophies of the hunt: deer and moose heads mounted on the walls, bear rugs on the floor, and a stuffed loon hovering above the mantelpiece as if it were about to take flight. Below the loon Tom notices a photo—in a frame made of silver and carved antler—of Dr. Murdoch and Milo Latham standing in front of a cabin, rifles resting in the crooks of their arms and a pile of dead beaver lying at their feet.

"Best damn hunting in the Adirondacks over by Latham's cabin on the Vly," Tom hears the doctor say from behind him. "I'll sure miss it."

Tom turns, feeling in his pocket for the letter of sale Latham gave him earlier this evening. "You may not have to, Dr. Murdoch," he says.

⁂

"Have you come to let me out?" the girl asks.

Corinth puts her hand to her chest and wills her heart to stop pounding. It's only Alice Latham sitting in the chair, not her ghostly sister, but still, with her pale skin and black eyes glowing in the moonlight, she's a startling sight.

"What are you doing in here?" Corinth asks, thinking for a moment that the girl might be playing a game of hide-and-seek until she remembers that the door was locked from the outside.

"I'm being punished," Alice says, attempting a nonchalant shrug. The motion is awkward, though, because she keeps her hands behind her back. Corinth steps into the closet and, looking over the girl's shoulders, sees that her hands are tied behind her back.

"Who did this?" Corinth asks, her voice coming out

as a hoarse croak that she's sure must frighten the child. It certainly frightens her.

"Norris," Alice answers, "but only because mother told her I had to be punished for throwing rocks in the well, only I swear I didn't do it. So I'm being punished for lying as well."

Corinth kneels on the floor and begins to pick at the knots, but they are too intricate even for her. "I'll have to get a knife to cut the rope," she says.

"Tam's carving knife is in his night table," Alice says. "It's the second one from the closet."

Corinth retrieves the knife, marveling at the girl's calm. She's been sitting tied up in a dark closet and yet she's not even crying. Her calm is somehow more chilling than hysteria, as it suggests it's not the first time she's been punished in this barbaric fashion.

"Are you often punished like this?" Corinth asks as she saws at the thick ropes.

"Only when I've been particularly bad, not half as often as James and Cynthia, but"—she pauses, and from behind, Corinth can see the girl tilt her head as if she were considering a difficult arithmetic problem—"more often than Tam, I think. Tam was usually very good unless James *made* him be bad. At first, mother wouldn't punish him at all, but then she said one day"—again the girl tilts her head up to the ceiling, as if she were trying to remember a line of verse she's memorized—"that James's punishment would be to see Tam punished. It bothered James awfully, and for a while he tried very hard to be good— Ow! you've cut me!"

The knife has indeed slipped in Corinth's hand while she's been listening to Alice's account. It's only scratched the girl's wrist, though, and at least the ropes are free now. Corinth takes out her handkerchief and wraps it around Alice's wrist, holding both of the girl's hands in hers for a moment as she crouches in front of her. "Alice," she says, looking into the girl's black eyes, "your mother stopped punishing your brothers and sisters when they got sick last year, didn't she?"

"Of course," Alice says, looking surprised. "Mother nursed them all herself; she loved them all so very, very much." Alice yawns as if she were repeating a lesson she'd learned by rote. Corinth helps the girl up out of the chair and to the bed closest to the closet while Alice continues her account. "She made them all special teas and poultices so that they'd get well. Can I tell you a secret?"

Corinth nods while smoothing the covers over the girl and Alice whispers in her ear, "Norris gave my tea to the others and made me her own teas to keep me well and a charm to ward off the evil spirits that made James and Cynthia and Tam sick. An Indian charm! And that's why I didn't get sick, only"—she falls back down onto the pillow and crinkles up her forehead—"only I lost it. Now I'm frightened that I'll die like the others."

"Did the charm look like this?" Corinth asks, loosening the buttons of her dress and drawing from around her neck the leather pouch her mother gave her so many years ago.

"Yes! Only it didn't have this pretty beading on it. Oh, please, may I have it?"

Corinth slips the necklace off and hands it to Alice. Immediately the girl plucks at the drawstring holding closed the pouch. "Does it have special charms to keep me safe?"

"Yes," Corinth answers, "sweet gale to ward off snakes and rosemary to help you remember your way home—"

"And a feather!" Alice exclaims, drawing from the pouch a black, red-tipped feather.

"From the red-winged blackbird. My mother said that women of her tribe believed that the red-winged blackbird warned them of approaching danger, and see"—Corinth holds up a strand of Alice's hair in the moonlight—"you have hair just like the red-winged blackbird—black with tips of red—so it will work for you, too."

Alice smiles and snuggles deeper into the covers. "So I'll be safe," she says.

Corinth nods, unable to speak around the tightness in her chest that feels like ropes binding her. She leans down and presses her lips against the girl's forehead. What possible help will a handful of feathers and herbs be against a monster like Aurora Latham? But what can Corinth do? She's not the girl's mother.

When she raises her head, she sees that Alice is already sleeping. Corinth tucks the leather pouch under the girl's pillow and quietly steals out of the attic.

She takes the path on the west side of the hill down to the rose garden—both to avoid being seen on the fountain allée and to avoid seeing again that unnatural spectacle of water flowing uphill. She keeps her eyes to the narrow path, ignoring as best she can the rustle of leaves all around her. It sounds as if the woods are full of birds, and she finds herself thinking about the story her mother once told her about the red-winged blackbird that she'd mentioned to Alice.

> There was a girl of the Haudensosaunee people who, while gathering cranberries in a bog, came across a blackbird trapped in a thorny bush. The girl freed it, but still it could not fly away because its wing had been torn by the thorns, and so the girl bound up the bird's wing with moss and leatherleaf and carried the bird in her gathering basket for many days, always giving the bird water and letting it eat the berries she gathered. When the bird's wing was finally healed, the girl held it up to the sky to let it go, but before it flew away the blackbird spoke to the girl.
>
> "Since you have helped me, my kind will always warn you of approaching danger. Keep this feather in your hair so we will always recognize you." And when the bird flew away, a single black feather that was tipped in blood from where its wing had been torn fell into the girl's hair.
>
> Many years later the girl's tribe were at war with the Abenaki people. Among the prisoners they took was one of the black robes, a shaman who had come

from his land to teach the people about his gods. The girl took pity on him, though, and thinking about how she had rescued the blackbird, she untied his bonds and helped him to get away from the camp. Because he was much injured and weakened, she took him to a sacred spring by a cave and there she washed his wounds and gave him water to drink until he was healed. They spent three nights by the spring, sleeping in a cave nearby, until he was well enough to travel, and by then the girl had fallen in love with him. He told her that shamans of his people could not take a wife, and so, although he said he loved her, too, and lay with her as a husband for three nights, he told her that she could not live with him as his wife. At first she was very angry that he had not told her this earlier and she thought about betraying him to her people, but on the fourth day she let him go just as she had once let the blackbird fly away. This time, though, she felt as if something had been torn inside of her and when she plucked the blackbird's feather from her hair she saw that it was bleeding.

She became known among her people as Ne'Moss-i-Ne, She Who Remembers.

Corinth has reached the edge of the maze. She stops and listens to the rustle of leaves in the hedges and wonders if she had forgotten the name of the girl up until now or has she made it up and given the girl in her mother's story the name of the statue in the maze? She can't tell. Her head is full of the sound of wings beating all around her as she follows the downward sloping path to the center of the maze, remembering the rest of the story.

Once a year, on the longest day of the year, the girl's tribe camped at the spring by the cave to drink the water and so gain strength for the coming year. The woods around the spring were full of birds and animals come to drink at the spring, but it was not permitted to kill a bird or an animal at the spring, and so for the three days the tribe camped here the people and the animals lived side by side as friends. On the third day of her tribe's visit, Ne'Moss-i-Ne was sitting by the spring surrounded by her friends the blackbirds when suddenly the flock rose to the sky as if possessed of one spirit, the sound of their wings like a great wind. Ne'Moss-i-Ne looked up and saw the sun blackened by their flight, and a drift of feathers fell to the earth, each one stained with blood. She shouted out a warning to her people, but they did not listen to her. Soon the air was thick with the arrows of their enemies and the screams of their women and children. In the middle of this chaos Ne'Moss-i-Ne saw the black robe and knew that it was he who had betrayed the location of the spring to her people's enemy.

She was taken prisoner by the Abenaki, but later that night the black robe came to her and untied her hands and legs. He swore he hadn't known what would happen when he led the Abenaki to the spring, and he begged her to forgive him and come back and live with his people now that her own people were all dead or taken prisoner, but Ne'Moss-i-Ne only turned from him and ran into the woods. He followed her, but she ran faster, heading for the high cliff above the Sacandaga River. When she reached the edge of the cliff, she turned back to look at her lover one last time and he saw that her eyes had become two blackbird wings, spreading across the sky. When she jumped, he could hear the sound of wings all around him. Indeed he heard the sound of wings for the rest of his life.

Corinth has come to the center of the maze. She kneels beside the statue of Ne'Moss-i-Ne and, looking into her shadowed marble eyes, realizes just how cursed this place is. How can she leave that poor child here? She lifts her hand to wipe away a tear and feels something brush her face—something that she thinks are wings until she strikes out at them and they turn into hands clasping her own hands. Looking up, she sees a figure standing above her, and for a moment she's not sure if it's Ne'Moss-i-Ne's betraying priest or the ghost of Milo Latham, but then the man's arms slip around her and she recognizes Tom.

"It's okay," he says as he leads her out of the maze. "I'm taking you out of here." At the gate behind the rose garden, at the same spot where she told the driver to stop when she first arrived at Bosco, she sees the brougham with the cloaked coachman seated on the box. She catches a glimpse of the man's face in the moonlight as Tom helps her in and recognizes him. He's the same man who took her to Milo's cabin ten years ago and who came each week with supplies while she stayed there with Wanda—he is, Corinth realizes for the first time, Wanda's son. She tries to tell Tom as the brougham lurches out the gate, but he doesn't understand.

"It doesn't matter whose son he is," he says, stroking Corinth's hair and pulling her close to him to stop her shivering. "He's been well paid. I've got lots of money and by tomorrow we'll be far away." His eyes are glittering in the moonlight with a hardness that reminds Corinth of the glass eyes of the rocking horse in the attic. She starts to tell him about Alice, but then remembers also about the other child—his child with Mrs. Ramsdale—and then suddenly she feels overwhelmed by *all* of them. James and Cynthia and Tam who died in the cold attic and the children in the cemetery behind the rose garden and her own baby—Tom's and hers—dead beneath the bog mosses. She feels she has betrayed them all, but unlike Ne'Moss-i-

Ne she's escaping with her lover. She has no plans to throw herself from any cliff. She feels Tom lift her face to his, feels his lips sink into hers, feels his hands loosen her hair and his fingers combing through the length of it, shaking free a single black feather tipped with red.

In the hotel room they make love with the moonlight streaming in through the window, the white light lapping against them like water. The hardness is gone from Tom's eyes now, and Corinth realizes it was only the money-glitter that she's seen in men's eyes before. He'd sold something to get enough money for them to run away and he's exalted with it, a conquering hero, his smooth chest rising and falling above her like the white breast of an eagle.

Afterward she clings to him, fitting her knees into the bend of his knees and pressing her chest against his broad, strong back. Even when she falls asleep, she can feel herself holding him—only, as she sinks deeper into the blackness, he seems to shrink until she's lying at the bottom of a well holding only a white stone that glows in the moonlight. As she looks at the stone, though, it's eaten up by the darkness like the moon in eclipse and, looking up, she realizes that she's trapped beneath the earth. Buried alive.

She awakes gasping, alone in the tangled bedsheets. For a moment she thinks he's abandoned her, but then she sees Tom standing at the door listening to voices outside. Corinth slips out of bed, pulling a chemise over her head and wrapping herself in her shawl, and joins Tom at the door.

"You'll have to open it before she wakes up the whole hotel," she says.

He nods and opens the door. Wanda Norris is standing in the hallway, her hands held out stiffly at her sides like a statue of Justice, a leather pouch in one hand and a bloody handkerchief in the other. "What have you done with her?" she demands. "What have you done with Alice?"

Chapter Twenty-one

They come as stone, water, and wood.

That night, I'm unable to get the words out of my mind. I lie awake listening to the wooden frame of the old house creaking in the wind, the snow lashing against the windowpanes, and when I close my eyes, I imagine all the statues of the Muses, with their broken arms and damaged faces, stirring to life under the deep snow.

When I finally fall asleep, though, I dream not of the faceless stone woman but of the girl in the closet. In my dream I open the door (the padlock, unrusted, opens at a touch of my fingers) and free her hands, using a knife to cut the ropes. I lead her back to her bed and draw the white counterpane over her, tucking it beneath her thin shoulders. I can feel her trembling beneath the bedclothes. "Don't go," she whispers, "I'll be punished for leaving the closet. And you'll be punished for letting me out."

"It's all right—" I start to tell her, but then I see a shadow creeping over the white counterpane and the girl's eyes widen until they are as wide and black as the eyes of the ghost I saw yesterday. I turn to face what is behind us, but before I can make out the shape silhouetted against the moonlit windows, I startle awake.

Only I'm not in my room. I'm standing at the foot of the attic stairs and the dark shape from my dreams is standing above me. I can see now it's a woman who's pushing a girl in a white nightgown in front of her—pushing her so roughly that the girl stumbles on the last step and careens into me—or, rather, through me. I feel her move through me like a current of cold water, and then someone lays an icy hand on my back. I whirl around and find David standing right behind me in the hall.

"I'm sorry I startled you," he says, his lips curling in a smile that looks more amused than sorry. He's wearing the checked hunting jacket over his pajamas and holding a glass of scotch in his right hand. "I couldn't sleep, so I went downstairs to get a nightcap," he says, holding out the glass toward me.

The scotch—or maybe it's the jacket—smells so pungent, like leaves rotting in the fall, that I recoil. David tilts his head to one side and shrugs. "It's not poisoned. See?" He takes a generous swig of the stuff and steps toward me. I immediately take a step backward. "You know what your problem is, Ellis?"

"No," I say, making myself stand still. It's only that he's angry at me for running from his room today, I tell myself, and that he's had too much to drink. "What's my problem?"

"It's that you can't trust anyone."

I almost laugh at the banality of his assessment, but I manage not to laugh, because the last thing I want is for him to think I'm laughing at him. "Yes," I say, nodding seriously, "you're right, that's always been my problem."

"Well," he says, turning away from me and heading toward his own room. "You'll have to trust someone sometime."

I watch him retreat down the hallway, swaying slightly, and then I go back down to my room. I'm unable to go to sleep, though, for the rest of the night. Every time I close my eyes, I see the eyes of that girl in the attic and I wonder what she was so afraid of. Where was the woman taking her? My own eyes in the bathroom mirror the next morning have the same empty glaze. Still, I dress and struggle down to the dining room, because we all agreed to meet for breakfast.

We agreed to discuss the matter in the clear light of day when, we all believed, the events of the previous day might seem less ominous. The problem, I see as we gather around the dining table, is that the light of this particular day is anything but clear. The windows on the first floor are half covered in snowdrifts, so that the faint light coming in seems to be filtered by a thick screen of translucent marble. It's like being sealed inside a marble vault.

"Mrs. Hervey couldn't make it in," Diana Tate tells us as she wheels Zalman into the dining room and Daria lays out plates of runny eggs and burnt toast, "but the roads should be plowed by noon. The storm's eased up right now, but it's supposed to get bad again tonight. So if you need anything from town, best take care of it today. Anyone who wants to go in can take the Range Rover."

"I'll go, but I can't drive because it's a stick," Daria says, setting a cup of coffee down in front of Nat. "You can drive a stick, right, Nat?"

"That's right," Nat says, smiling at Daria. "I'd be happy to teach you . . ." Daria beams, but Diana hurries her back into the kitchen to get the rest of breakfast.

" 'You can drive a stick, right, Nat?' " Bethesda mimics, catching Daria's inflection to a tee.

"What?" Nat protests. "I can't help it if the girl's got a crush on me. The poor kid's got no one here to talk to but those crazy callers."

"Please," Zalman interrupts, "we're all tense after yesterday's events and tired from too little sleep—"

I notice how pale Zalman is. "Did you get any sleep last night?" I ask.

The poet looks up from his plate and his lip begins to tremble. "It's that *damned* dog," he says in a low voice that nonetheless causes everyone to look up. It's the first time that any of us has heard Zalman curse. "It comes every night and lies on my leg. At first I thought it was Madame Blavatsky's dog and it was healing my leg, but now—" He breaks off and pushes his untouched plate away from him. "Now I think it's sucking the lifeblood out of me. I haven't written a decent sonnet in days."

"Weren't you working on a sonnet about a Native American legend?" Nat asks.

"Oh *that*," Zalman says. "You gave me a good idea there, Nathaniel, only . . . well, here, let me read it to you." Zalman withdraws from his bathrobe pocket a page folded in quarters and, clearing his throat, announces the title of the poem: "Ne'Moss-i-Ne's Blackbird."

> *"The spirit of Ne'Moss-i-Ne survives,*
> *a red-winged blackbird swifter than starlight,*
> *revealing truth each time she soars or dives,*
> *a flash of wing by day, black ghost by night.*
>
> *"The Sacandaga hurts where she once fell,*
> *for once a year a crimson stain appears*
> *beneath that cliff. Her soul-bird casts a spell,*
> *and reddens near a mile with blood of tears.*
>
> *"Past nightfall, crimson shimmer vanishes,*
> *as soul-bird sprinkles starlight with her beak*
> *and sings of how sky spirit lavishes*
> *its love upon the gentle and the meek.*
>
> *"The tortured have not suffered all in vain:*
> *blood markings on her wings redeem their pain."*

When he's done, the room is quiet for a moment and then Nat says, "I see—you've connected the statue here in the garden to the girl who threw herself from Indian Overlook . . . Did I tell you about that?"

Zalman shrugs. "I'm not entirely sure anymore

where my ideas are coming from." He glances around the room nervously as if the source of his ideas might be hiding in the china cupboards among the blue-and-white teacups. "It's beginning to feel less like inspiration and more like an infection."

"I think Zalman is right," Bethesda says. "The spirits of the children have *infected* the place. We have to do something."

"But what?" Nat asks. "What do they want?"

"They want their stories told." The answer comes from the door to the kitchen, where Daria stands holding a pot of coffee and a basket of muffins. "Like the people who call here. God, don't you people read any ghost stories? They want their murderers unmasked, their bones found and buried, and their stories told." Daria puts down the coffee and the slightly burnt muffins, and sits down at the table, something her aunt would yell at her for if she were in the room. "We have to have a séance," she says, looking directly at me. "And you can do it. Mira said you were a natural medium, only you weren't ready to acknowledge your powers."

"Mira? You talked to my mother?"

"Uh, yeah. We ran into each other in the garden and shared . . . uh . . . some history of the place." Remembering the reek of marijuana in the garden on the day of my mother's visit, I'm pretty sure that's not all they shared. "And she told me about you. She's very proud of you, you know. She says you get your artistic ability from your grandmother who was a painter and your psychic ability from your great-grandmother—"

"The one time I attended a séance, I fainted," I say.

"Your mother thinks it was because you saw your great-grandmother's spirit," Daria says. "She said that she'd been trying to contact her for years, but you did it on your first try." Daria pauses, but I don't add anything to what she's said. I saw something at that séance, but it wasn't *anyone's* great-grandmother. "Only it scared you so much, your mother decided not to talk to you about it until you were ready," Daria goes on, "which she thought might be pretty soon. Come on," she says to the room at large. "We used to have séances at camp all the time. It will be fun."

"I can't," I say. "It's a horrible idea. Look what happened at the last séance . . . I mean, the last time a séance was held here. We don't know enough to start fooling around with that."

"I agree with that part," Bethesda says. "We need to know more. For one thing, I would like to know why there's a death certificate for a stillborn child named Alice Latham but no stone for her in the graveyard."

"Why is that so important?" I ask, amazed—and a little unnerved—that rational Bethesda has conceded so quickly to the idea that Bosco is haunted. Whatever she saw at her window must have been as real to her as the girl I saw in the attic.

"It's an idea I have that I can't explain yet. Maybe I just missed the gravestone. I'd like to go down to the cemetery today and look for it."

"The cemetery's under two feet of snow," David points out.

"Then maybe you can help me shovel it," Bethesda replies.

"Sure," Nat says. "We can all help. I need to get outside."

"No," Bethesda says. "I want you to go into town to City Hall and have a look at the birth and death certificates for 1883. Use your charm with the clerks to see if the same certificate of death for little Alice Latham was registered and if there's another birth certificate for an Alice who didn't die."

"You mean for the one who disappeared in 1893? You don't have a birth certificate for her?" I ask.

"No, I don't. Maybe you should go as well, Ellis. It's the kind of research you should get used to if you're going to write historical novels."

I feel a prickle of resentment at how Bethesda has managed to send me and Nat away and keep David to herself, but I don't want to give away my jealousy. After what I saw in the attic yesterday and my dream last night and the encounter with David in the hallway, I'm glad to be getting away from Bosco for the day. When I look around the table, though, I notice how tired everyone looks. David's eyes look as glassy and distant as the stuffed deer hanging over the mantel. In fact, looking around the table, I have an image of a circle composed of lifeless dolls and stuffed toys in place of the live guests, and I have a sudden misgiving about what Nat and I will find when we get back.

Chapter Twenty-two

"We don't have her," Corinth tells Wanda, stepping aside so that the narrow hotel room is open to her inspection.

Wanda rakes the room with her eyes, indicating to her son to look under the bed while she throws open the doors to the armoire.

"I found that poor girl in a dark attic closet, tied to a chair," Corinth says to Wanda. "She told me you put her there."

"So that her mother wouldn't do worse to her," Wanda says, rounding on Corinth. She holds up the bloody handkerchief. "You don't deny letting her out?"

"No, why should I? How could I do otherwise? Who could bear to leave a child alone like that? But I left her in her own bed. You mean to say she's disappeared?"

"Mrs. Latham found this handkerchief with your initials on it in her daughter's bed. Along with this pouch. And *this* was in the pouch." Wanda takes out the long thin hellebore root, and Corinth realizes that she must have put it down in the storage closet when she was untying Alice's hands. She opens her mouth to say that Aurora must have put the root in the pouch, but she realizes it won't make any difference.

"She asked me if I thought it belonged to you and I couldn't deny that it did, but I managed to take both things while she had the police sent for—"

"The police?" Tom asks, speaking for the first time since their room's been invaded. He's kept a wary eye on the coachman while buttoning his shirt and listening to the interchange between Corinth and Wanda. "She's accusing us of kidnapping her child?"

"Yes," Wanda says. "So you see, it's in your own interest to help me find her."

"But how would I know—" Corinth begins, but then she remembers her dream. She closes her eyes to picture it better. White stones, a shadow moving across them like an eclipsed moon . . . only now she can see that the shadow is red—a creeping tide of blood eclipsing one small life.

"I know where she is," Corinth says, opening her eyes. "But we have to hurry. She hasn't much time left."

Wanda rides on the box beside her son, urging him faster over the road to Bosco. Inside the coach Tom begs Corinth to reconsider, to turn back.

"I can't," she says, "I can't leave that child to die."

"But you said yourself that it might be too late, that

the child might be dead already. They'll blame us. Aurora's already told the police that we've taken her."

"Yes, when she found that I'd let Alice free, she must have decided she could blame us for her disappearance—" Corinth frowns. "Perhaps in her mind she thinks that Alice's death would be my fault. She hadn't meant to go that far until she saw I'd let her go, just as she didn't really mean to kill the others."

"What do you mean, 'kill the others'?"

"James and Cynthia and Tam." Corinth trembles as she says their names out loud, hearing, like an echo in a well, the words she'd superimposed on their names during the séance: *water, wood, and stone.* "She'd lost so many children already, I think she lost a little of her sanity with each one. She grew used to them sickening and dying, but if James and Cynthia and Tam could live, then it would be as if she'd saved the others."

"You mean she made her own children sick?" He whispers it, his voice thick with revulsion, and Corinth feels bile rising in her own throat, a nausea that reminds her of the first weeks of her own pregnancy.

"Yes," she says, her eyes shining in the darkness of the coach. "The hellebore given in small doses would just make them weak, but she meant to nurse them back to health, only . . ."

"What?"

Norris gave my tea to the others.

"Norris gave Alice's tea to the other children. She must have suspected that there was something bad in it." Corinth lowers her voice, gazing uneasily toward the roof of the coach, through which she can hear Wanda's voice urging her son to drive faster and faster. "But the extra dose of hellebore was enough to kill them—" Corinth clutches Tom's hand. "Wanda didn't mind letting the other children die for Alice's sake and she won't mind killing us. We'll be in danger from the moment we find Alice. Wanda will tell you to stay with the coach—"

"I won't let you go alone with her."

"I'll have to. Just watch yourself with the son, and if you can . . ." She stops because the coach has stopped. Beneath the hard breathing of the horses she can hear, as on the first day—was it really only three days ago?— the voice of the water from within the hedge maze. Only now she is beginning to make out its words—a triplet of murmured *m*'s that might be *remember me* or possibly *memento mori,* a little piece of Latin she's seen often enough on garden statuary to know that it means *Remember you must die.*

"When I've taken care of him," Tom whispers hurriedly with his hand on the coach door to keep it from being opened from the outside, "I'll come for you. I promise. This time I'll come back for you."

She nods and touches his face, unable to speak. She believes him but suspects that it will probably be too late.

When she gets out of the carriage, she finds Wanda

standing at the entrance to the maze and she knows from the frightened look in her eyes that she can hear the voice of the water, too, and that, although she may not hear the same words that Corinth hears, she's terrified. There isn't much that would scare Wanda White Cloud, but these are the spirits of the children she let die. Apparently, though, she is willing to brave them for Alice's sake. Corinth can't help wondering what claim the girl has on Wanda's affections.

"Let the men stay with the horses," Wanda says.

Corinth nods, catching Tom's eye and noticing the look that also passes between Wanda and her son. Then Wanda steps through the gap in the hedge into the maze and Corinth follows her. She hears a rustle of leaves behind her but doesn't turn to look, afraid that what she'll see is the gap closing in the hedge, cutting her off from the outside world—and Tom—forever. As they walk the rustling sound stays close behind them, and Corinth imagines the box hedge creeping across the path, growing higher and wider in their wake. The moon in the western sky pierces the thick foliage, creating patterns in the hedges that shift in the breeze, looking like overgrown rosebushes one moment and then, the next, like the figure of a woman fleeing.

"Do you remember," Corinth says as they come into the center of the maze, "that story about the Iroquois girl who loved the missionary captive and led him to a spring?"

"She betrayed her people," Wanda says.

"And then she was betrayed," Corinth answers. In

the rose garden the moonlight falls full on the white marble girl and the bloodred pool in which she kneels. Corinth catches her breath when she sees the color of the water, but when she gets closer she sees that the pool is covered with red rose petals. Looking around, she sees that all the rosebushes, which were at the height of their bloom only three days ago, are bare now. The ground, carpeted with their crimson petals, looks as if it were soaked in blood.

"It happened here," Corinth says. She bends to pick up one of the petals, but what she finds in her hand instead is a black feather tipped with red.

"Yes, it's a bad place, but we don't have time for this. You said you knew where the girl was."

Corinth walks behind the pool, feeling a prickling on her scalp as she passes under Jacynta's raised sword and between the cypresses into the children's cemetery. Here instead of a carpet of red she finds a draping of white like fresh-fallen snow. White flowers that weren't there yesterday are growing up around the gravestones in thick profusion. She recognizes them: black helle-bore, which blooms only in winter.

She walks between the gravestones, being careful not to step on any, but when she reaches the top of the steps leading down into the crypt, she finds a white gravestone that she could swear wasn't there yesterday. Kneeling, she sees that it's not a stone at all. The hellebore has grown into a lacy *parterre de broderie* spelling a name and a date.

ALICE

APRIL 9, 1883

Corinth turns and rises so suddenly to her feet that Wanda, usually so surefooted, stumbles. "Aurora was pregnant that year," Corinth says. "The baby was delivered"—she sees Wanda's eyes widen at the sight of the name spelled out in the deadly white flowers—"and died."

Wanda looks up and, looking straight into Corinth's eyes, nods. "Yes. Mrs. Latham nearly lost her mind—Mr. Latham thought she really would this time. And so, when he heard that your child was born healthy, he sent the dead child to the cabin and told me to give over your child. I've watched over her ever since, but now she will die, too, if we don't hurry."

Corinth turns away from her and hurries down the steps to the well, which has been covered by the heavy marble cover. She pushes at the lid, but it's too heavy. Even when Wanda joins her they can't move it.

"We'll need to get the men," Wanda says.

"There isn't time," Corinth says. When she closes her eyes, she's inside the well, looking up into a blackness that presses down on her chest.

She looks frantically around the crypt and spots a coil of rope left behind by Lantini. She grabs it and wraps it tightly around the circumference of the lid, pulling so hard on it that the rope burns her hands, and then wraps it around the waist of the statue of Egeria. "If we push the statue over, the weight of its fall will drag the lid off," Corinth tells Wanda, leaning her shoulder against the statue. "You get on the other side."

On the count of three, both women throw their weight against the cold, unyielding marble. Corinth hears a groan, which for a moment she imagines is the voice of the grieving nymph complaining of this rude treatment, but then realizes it is the statue's base grating against the marble pedestal. The statue trembles, then tilts, and then slowly falls, dragging the lid of the well with it until it smashes onto the floor in an explosion of dust and flying marble splinters—one of which strikes Corinth just below her right eye. She barely notices, though, as she scrambles to the side of the well that has been uncovered.

"Alice!" she calls into the darkness. She hears the name repeated, echoing up through the oculus, but there is no answering word from the well. Then, as the moon moves above the oculus, the white rocks at the bottom of the well come into view and, nestled among them, a curled fist, which loosens as they watch, like the petals of a dying flower falling from the stem.

"I'm going down." Corinth pulls the rope from around the lid and wraps it around her waist. "Tie the other end to the pedestal. It should hold."

Corinth doesn't wait for an answer before swinging her legs over the edge of the well and, tugging against the now taut rope, lowering herself down through the column of moonlight, which feels, to Corinth, like a cold spill of water carrying her into a deep pool. The girl doesn't stir when she touches her, but her skin is still warm. Corinth presses her cheek against her thin, bony chest, but all she can hear is the water below the stones.

Remember me, remember me.

Corinth lets herself see, for the first time in ten years, the face of the child drifting down into the tea-colored water of the bog. The child she thought was hers. And all this time her own child had been here, waiting for her at the bottom of this moonlit well . . . only she's found her too late. She lays her head back down on Alice's chest and lets herself weep for the first time in ten years for her lost child. She weeps so hard she feels herself breaking—like the statue of Egeria smashed on the floor above—and then, just when she thinks she really will crack apart, she feels a stir of breath in the girl's chest.

She pulls the rope off her own waist and ties it around Alice, deftly shaping a sling out of the rope. When she looks up, she sees Wanda's face at the edge of the well.

"She's still breathing," Corinth calls up, "but she's unconscious. You'll have to pull her up."

Corinth holds on to the girl until she's carried above the reach of her fingertips, and then she holds her breath until Wanda has her over the edge. For a moment the circle is empty except for the moon, which she can see shining through the oculus, and then she sees Wanda's head appear back at the edge of the well, silhouetted against the full moon. Wanda tilts her head, and something about the gesture strikes Corinth as wrong— as if Wanda had become a lifeless automaton controlled by an outside force. But when Wanda speaks, Corinth understands what's wrong. It's not Wanda standing at the edge of the well.

"I knew you would be able to find her," Aurora Latham says. "It proves you're her real mother, doesn't it?"

"You didn't know?" Corinth asks, rising to her feet. The top of the well is still ten feet above her head. The walls are smooth marble, with no cracks to use as handholds.

"Do you think I would have willingly harbored your bastard all these years if I had known?"

"Then we were both deceived," Corinth says, trying to keep the anger out of her voice. She thinks of how badly Aurora treated her own children and thanks God that Alice survived.

"Do you really expect me to believe that? That you didn't conspire with my husband to set up your own spawn here and then, when my own children had been murdered, to take my place? Why else did he bring you here?"

"You don't really believe that Milo would murder his own children—" She stops as a shadow moving across the well tells her that Wanda is still in the crypt. If she tells Aurora that it was Wanda who was responsible for the children dying, Aurora will turn on her—and then Alice will have no one to protect her if Corinth doesn't get out of this well alive.

"I thought you asked for me," she says instead, "for the séances—"

"He pretended it was my idea, but I knew he was only trying to establish you here as my replacement. I went along with it because I thought a séance would be an opportune place to die—especially for a man with a weak heart."

"So you planned to give him the hellebore all along? How did you disguise the taste?"

"In that damned scotch he's so proud of," Aurora says with a touch of pride in her voice.

"But what about Frank Campbell? Was he part of your plan as well?"

"Not originally, but then he figured out what was happening and threatened to unmask me. I had to stop him. Fortunately, Norris here is a good shot with a bow—or with a gun." Corinth sees Wanda's head appear beside Aurora's. The moonlight catches on something metal in her hands. Corinth crouches down in the darkest part of the well, away from the swatch of moonlight. "I was in favor of having you die slowly in the well," Aurora says, "but Norris has some heathenish notion that you might curse Bosco that way. So I'll leave you to her."

Before Corinth can think of anything else to say, Aurora is gone. Not that there's anything she could have said, she realizes. How could anyone reason with a woman who'd sickened her own children and then, when they actually died, blamed her husband for their deaths and planned his murder. She hears an echo of laughter in her head and feels the scars around her wrists tighten, as if the ropes that had made them were still there. Yes, that was what had fueled Mr. Oswald's murderous rage, she realizes now, many years later, his need to blame someone for what he had done to his wife. She waits for the sound of Aurora's footsteps to recede and then tries to reason with Wanda.

"She'll never let you have Alice," she says. "Even if she's not hers, she bears the Latham name. She'll destroy her."

"I'll take care of Alice, better than you could, at least."

"I can take her out of here," Corinth says, "with Tom—"

"Tom Quinn?" Wanda laughs, the sound echoing off the marble walls and reverberating in Corinth's chest, which feels as tight as it did that night Oswald had bound the ropes around her. "Don't you know he was working for Latham all along? He was hired to make sure your séances were impressive enough to satisfy Mrs. Latham. He betrayed you, just as you betrayed him. Why should I trust Alice to either of you?"

Corinth sees moonlight catch the gun in Wanda's hand, and then there's a flash and a shower of sparks, as if the moon had exploded. It feels as though a chip of the moon has broken off and flown into her heart, an icy splinter that turns to fire in her flesh as she falls back onto the rocks.

Above her she can see the moon, brilliant and white, so large it seems to fill up the entire oculus, so large that she can feel its pull on the water of the spring, feel the water yearning upward to it. She wills her own spirit up toward the moon, anything to keep from being trapped down here, but then she hears the sound of stone moving against stone and the moon is eclipsed, leaving her alone in the darkness with nothing but the muttering of the spring for company.

Chapter Twenty-three

Just before we are set to leave for town, Daria decides that she ought to stay behind with Zalman. "Aunt Diana gets busy in the office sometimes and loses track of time," she tells us.

I'm surprised that the girl would give up a trip to town to sit with a middle-aged poet, but when I say so, Daria shakes her head very seriously. "Zalman's such a sweetie, and besides, I feel kind of responsible for his accident. If I'd given him the right message from his grandmother in the first place, maybe he wouldn't have fallen down the stairs."

"Do you think Daria's right?" I ask Nat as he steers the Range Rover down the curving icy road to the front gate. Nat, his eyes glued to the road, laughs. "About what? That Zalman's a sweetie?"

"No, we all know *that*," I say, stealing a glance at Nat's profile to see that he's smiling. In all the publicity photos I've ever seen of him his face is turned to the right, casting the right side of his face in shadow. I notice now that there's a small scar on his right cheekbone—a quarter-inch indentation that looks as if it might have come from either a bad case of adolescent acne or childhood chicken pox. It makes me realize how hard he works to keep some parts of himself hidden. "Do you think she's right about the message she got on the phone—that it really was Zalman's grandmother trying to warn him?"

"Considering everything else that's happened here, I don't see why it matters," Nat says.

"Yeah, but everything else has to do with Bosco and with what happened here in 1893. Last night I felt like the house and the gardens had come alive, that the place itself is taking all of us over. What I wonder is if it matters who this is happening to."

Nat takes his eyes off the road for a moment to look at me. I'm afraid that I've said it all wrong, that he'll think I'm trying to make myself sound important, that I agree with Zalman that my being the first medium to return to Bosco is the reason the spirits of the children have awoken, but when Nat speaks, his voice is kind and hoarse with feeling. "It always matters who it's happening to," he says. "In the end that's all that really does matter."

At City Hall I see why Bethesda sent Nat. Although the young female clerk starts out by explaining that genealogy searches always take at least a week to process, as soon as Nat explains that he's engaged in very important research for his next novel, she concedes that since it's not too busy today, she could go have a look at the records for 1883 herself.

"That would be great, Katy," Nat says, plucking her name from the gold ID necklace at her neck. "I promise I'll mention you in the acknowledgments. Should we check back in half an hour?"

Leaving the blushing clerk, we wander down the echoing hallway. "People love that 'researching a novel' line," Nat tells me. "They all want to be part of the process."

"Yeah, well, it helps if you're a famous novelist," I say. *And good-looking,* I almost add.

"Why?" Nat asks. "Do you think she recognized me?" He looks hopeful for a moment, but then he shakes his head. "Unless you've been on *Oprah,* no one in the real world—I mean the world outside of MFA programs and writers' retreats—is going to recognize who you are." He looks downcast for a moment, but then, passing a glass door etched with the words *Conference Room,* his face brightens. "Hey, I think I attended a hearing here once—one of my grandfather's many frivolous lawsuits *trying to reclaim the family's inheritance.* If it's the same room, there's a cool mural."

Nat opens the door an inch and when he's sure the room is empty, he motions for me to follow him in. The light from the frost-covered windows is so faint that I can hardly make out the painting on the wall, but then, as if emerging from an early morning fog, the figures take shape as a tribe of Native Americans gathered around something that looks like a miniature volcano.

" 'His grateful Iroquois followers lead Sir William Johnson to High Rock Spring,' " Nat quotes—not, apparently, from any plaque or inscription, but from memory. "This painting really pissed my grandfather off."

"Why?"

"Oh, everything pissed him off. He was a mean old bastard. My mother said it was because his own father disowned him when he refused to follow in his footsteps and go to medical school. He was always in court trying to reclaim his legacy: a house here in Saratoga and a bunch of properties in the Adirondacks. The cabin he managed to get back or, as he put it, *wrest back from the hands of some dirty half-breed Indians.* " Nat laughs bitterly. "I guess it really galled him to have his case heard under the watchful eyes of the Iroquois Nation." He turns away from the mural and looks at me as if surprised that I'm there. "Sorry," he says. "White Protestant guilt is so lame. I'd better get back and see what Katy's dug up. Want to wait here?"

Guessing that Nat might want to conduct the rest of his flirtation in private, I nod and sit down in a chair in front of the mural. What has struck me, listening to Nat talk about his grandfather, is that even though our families couldn't be more different, we're both suffering from a similar malaise. An inherited dysfunction. In my own case a family history of bad luck with men that, according to Mira, goes back to my great-grandmother, and in Nat's case it's a sort of inherited meanness that he reverts to almost reflexively and yet that I sense is not his true nature. There's this more-generous person trying to get out.

After waiting for another thirty minutes in the cold courtroom with only the solemn glare of the Iroquois for company, my view of Nat's generous nature begins to fray around the edges. It seems as if he's completely forgotten me. When he comes back, though, he looks so stunned that I don't have the heart to complain. He's holding several slips of paper in his hand as he drops heavily into the chair next to mine.

"Did you find the death certificate for the first Alice?"

He shakes his head. "There's no record of an Alice Latham who was born and died on April ninth, 1883," he says, "but there is a record of a birth for an Alice Latham on April fifteenth of that year." He passes the photocopied birth certificate to me.

"So the certificate that Bethesda found at Bosco was never registered," I say. "Do you think there was a child born on April ninth at all?"

Nat nods. "I think so, but it died like Aurora's babies before that. Can you imagine losing so many children?"

"No," I say, "I can't. Aurora must have been half-mad with grief. So Milo . . . he found a child for them to adopt and they registered that child's birth in Town Hall, but where—?"

"Bethesda is sure that Milo Latham's affair with Corinth Blackwell started years before he brought her to

Bosco. They would have known each other at his lumber mill in Corinth—"

"And in Gloversville," I add, "where Corinth appeared at the Lyceum and Milo Latham owned a glove factory. Do you think the child could have been Corinth's?"

"Yes. Milo would have wanted his own bloodline," Nat says.

"But why would Aurora go along with another woman's child being substituted for her own? And why would Corinth give up her own baby?"

"Aurora might have been so delirious she didn't know what was going on, and Corinth wouldn't have had much choice if she was dependent on Latham for financial support. Who knows, maybe the child was taken from her without her knowing—her own baby switched with the dead Latham baby."

"But that's awful."

"Who knows what these men were capable of," Nat says in a curiously dead voice.

"*These* men?"

Nat nods and points to a line on Alice Latham's birth certificate. "The doctor who signed the birth certificate was Dr. Nathaniel Murdoch of Saratoga Springs."

"So?"

"*Murdoch* was my mother's maiden name. Nathaniel Murdoch is my great-grandfather. I looked up my mother's and my grandfather's birth certificates just to make sure. That's probably how the Sacandaga camp came into the family. Payment for favors rendered. God, I knew I was descended from a long line of bastards, but I didn't think we actually had baby-stealers to boast of in the family tree." Nat starts to laugh—a slow, mirthless chuckle that raises the hairs on the back of my neck.

"What's so funny?" I ask.

"I never knew my great-grandmother's maiden name," he says. "She died soon after she married my great-grandfather, and there was something in her background my grandfather was ashamed to talk about. Now I know what. I saw it on my grandfather's birth certificate." He passes the photocopied birth certificate over to me. Under MOTHER'S MAIDEN NAME I read "Violet Ramsdale."

"So," Nat says, turning to me, his lips contorted in a death mask's grin, "I guess we know now where I get my writing talent."

Nat continues to look downcast as we make our way through the deep snow to the Range Rover, which is parked on a side street beside City Hall.

"You're not seriously upset that your great-grandmother was a novelist?" I ask.

"Violet Ramsdale wrote sensation novels. It's not exactly a prestigious literary heritage. If it ever got out—" He rounds on me so abruptly that I nearly slip in the snow. "Listen, you can't tell anyone about this."

"Nathaniel Loomis," I say, invoking his full name to

get his attention, "listen to yourself. We just found out that your great-grandfather might have aided in the kidnapping of a woman's child and what you're worried about is being related to a popular writer?"

Nat looks away, seemingly to a road sign for County Route 9N. "I'm upset about that, too—and it's probably all true. My grandfather said something about it once— that his father wasn't above helping unmarried girls out of a jam by securing *'their bastards'* good homes. And that if he hadn't, a lot of those babies would have ended up drowned in the bogs . . ." Nat's voice trails off and he stares into the distance—down Route 9N, where storm clouds are massing over the foothills of the Adirondacks.

"What?" I ask.

"He showed me a grave once—well, not actually a grave, just a sort of marker carved into the trunk of a tamarack tree out in the bog. He said it was some Indian girl's *'dead brat.'* But what I remember thinking was that it wasn't an Indian name."

"Was it Alice?"

Nat closes his eyes. "It could have been. I can't remember."

"That cabin belonged to Milo Latham in 1883. Corinth could have had the baby there—"

"And Latham could have switched it with his own dead child." Nat points down the road. "It's only an hour's drive from here—more by horseback then, of course, but you could have made it in a day, for sure."

Nat opens the Range Rover, and before I can get my

seat belt on, he's pulled out and is headed north on 9N, heading in the opposite direction from Bosco.

"Nat, we can't go there *now*. There's a storm coming. They won't know what happened to us back at Bosco." I remember, too, that last image I had of the circle of guests in the breakfast room replaced by lifeless dolls, and I realize I'm afraid of what might be happening there while we're gone.

Nat stops at the next stop sign, puts the car in park, and turns to face me. "Don't you want to know?" he asks, his eyes gleaming feverishly in the white light of the approaching storm. "Don't you want to know the story?"

I look away from Nat to the northern sky, where storm clouds are pleating the sky like tracks in the snow. Yes, I do want to know the story, and something—some instinct that I have spent my life denying—tells me that the answer is at the camp on the Sacandaga. When I look at the gathering storm clouds, though, I'm seized with a sense of dread, the same dread that came over me last night when I was with David, that sickening sense that the ground beneath my feet was giving way and that *something* was pulling me under. And then this morning I realized why the feeling was familiar. I remembered that it's what I had felt during the spirit circle my mother conducted when I was twelve and what I've felt every time I've dared to get close to anyone since then. It suddenly angers me—the way Nat's squeamishness at being related to Mrs. Ramsdale angered me a moment ago. What kind of way was that to live? Mired in the past. David said I'd have to trust someone someday, but what he should have said was that sooner or later I'd have to learn to trust myself.

"Okay," I say, turning to Nat, "let's go."

We drive north on Route 9N and then turn west toward the Great Sacandaga Lake, the reservoir created by the damming of the Sacandaga River in the thirties. As we follow the reservoir road around the lake, the terrain becomes increasingly dreary. We pass white farmhouses that look in disrepair, their paint peeling, black shutters hanging crooked, and their barns collapsing into themselves in fields where unmowed stubble sticks out of the deep snow. We pass aluminum-sided trailers listing windward in sunken hollows beside the road. We pass through deep patches of fog, so thick that I can't make out the lake just beyond the road. The fog is so deep that I can barely see the sign for the "Indian Point Overlook" that Nat points out.

"I always begged my grandfather to stop there," Nat says as we drive by the sign, "but he never would. I told him that I'd heard it was a battle site from the French and Indian Wars, because I knew he loved stuff like that, but he said it was just some local legend about an Indian girl throwing herself over the cliff because her boyfriend left her. He called me 'squaw boy' for the rest of the summer and I stopped asking to go there."

I feel chilled by the story. The dead girl. The

shamed little boy. I also remember Zalman's poem linking the statue of Ne'Moss-i-Ne at Bosco to a girl who threw herself off a cliff and wonder if the sign might name the Indian girl. "Let's go back and look at it," I say.

Nat looks at me with a flash of gratitude that heats the air between us, and then swerves the Range Rover into a U-turn, its back end fishtailing on the fog-slick road. He drives us back to the overlook and pulls into a semicircular drive underneath a pine tree and next to a garbage can. A sign pointing to a gap between the pines reads, "Scenic Overlook .5 mile."

"We're not going to get much of a view today," Nat says.

"That's okay," I say. "We're not here for the view."

Nat nods and gets out of the car and starts up the path. By the time I zip up my parka and follow him, I can barely make out his back five feet in front of me through the vaporous fog that rises from the deep snow. It's easier to follow in his deep footsteps in the snow than to keep an eye on him. Easier, too, to stay in his tracks than to make my own. I'm concentrating so hard on fitting my feet into his tracks that I run into him at the end of the trail, nearly knocking him off his feet. He clenches my arm hard with one hand and grabs a metal sign pole with the other to keep us both from toppling into the abyss. Inches from our feet stretches a white void.

" 'On this spot,' " Nat reads in a deep, sonorous voice, " 'an Iroquois maiden running from invading French and Algonquin forces to warn the British army fell to her death. She died a heroine of the French and Indian Wars.' I knew it had something to do with the French and Indian Wars. My grandfather said it was *bullshit*. That it was just another pregnant Indian girl doing away with herself."

There's a note of vindication in Nat's voice, but when I look at him I see that there's no triumph in his expression. Instead there's a look of immeasurable sadness—as if he'd been personally acquainted with the "Indian maiden." I look away from him and over the cliff, into the swirling fog, into a space where the thick white cloud thins and then tears like a run in a stocking. I'm staring over the edge of the cliff at the lake. I can feel myself getting dizzy, but I'm unable to pull away.

"Hey," Nat says, pulling me back from the edge. "You don't want to end up like one of those Indian girls dashed on the rocks below. I mean, things aren't that bad with *the gardener*, are they?"

I look up, startled by the nastiness in his voice. Five minutes ago he'd seemed like a wounded boy, and now . . . Well, I guess I shouldn't be surprised that a wounded boy might strike out at the nearest target. What does surprise me is the undercurrent of jealousy in his voice. "He's a landscape architect, not a gardener." I'm trying to keep my voice neutral, but it comes out icy instead. "And there's really nothing going on between us at all."

"Oh," Nat says. He turns away quickly, but not before I've seen him smile.

As I follow, both of us sticking to the tracks Nat

made on the way in, I wonder what in the world all that was about. I know that Nat's been irritated by David since we all arrived at Bosco, but I always thought it was an almost reflexive rivalry between the two men. Now I wonder if it's developed into something more—and if it has something to do with me. I also wonder why I was so quick to deny that anything was going on between me and David.

I'm so engrossed in these thoughts that when I look up, I realize I've lost sight of Nat in the fog. He must be back at the car, because I can see a light in front of me that I assume is one of the Range Rover's headlights, though it's not exactly where I thought the parking lot should be. I head toward it, struggling through the snow, each step sinking deeper as if something were pulling my feet down into the earth. When I've gone another ten feet or so, I realize I've strayed out of Nat's footsteps. I stop and listen for the sound of the Range Rover's engine, but instead I hear a roaring sound—like a river in spring swollen with snowmelt. The light in front of me thins and wavers like a candle flame, and then I see her: a slim girl in a white buckskin dress, made out of fog, her eyes two holes torn out of the fog, black as raven wings. As she looks at me, I can feel the weight of betrayal in those eyes—the betrayal she suffered, the betrayal she caused. She holds out her hand to me and I step forward. The roaring sound becomes louder, and I see that I've come full circle to the cliff again. When I look down over the cliff now, though, instead of the placid lake I see a rushing river.

Above the sound of the water I can hear the girl's voice at my ear, murmuring seductively . . .

"Ellis, what are you doing back here?" It's Nat, his voice breaking into the fog-girl's seductive whisper. I turn to him and look right through her, her shape shredding into ribbons of fog.

"I—I remembered something," I say, kneeling in the snow. I sweep an armful of snow off the edge of the cliff, which falls soundlessly into the void. Words have been carved into the rock below the snow.

" 'Ne'Moss-i-Ne's Rock,' " Nat reads. "Damn, how did you know—"

I shake my head and get up, brushing the snow from my jeans. "I don't know," I say as we turn back to the car. I stay close to Nat this time, but still I can hear with every step I take the fog-girl's whisper. "Remember me," she'd said, "remember me."

Chapter Twenty-four

Deep below the earth Corinth listens to her blood seeping through the rocks to join the water of the spring, which is still muttering its sad refrain, *Remember me, remember me.* She purses her lips and expels a current of precious breath into the airless well. "Shhhh . . ." The sound a mother makes to soothe a fretful child.

She shifts herself on the rocks to take the weight off the shoulder the bullet pierced. At least she got to hold her child once. Alice would be all right now. Wanda must plan to take her away—else why would she have shot Corinth and left her down in here? Maybe it was Wanda's plan all along—to make it look as if Corinth took the child once Aurora was through with her. Aurora wouldn't follow and expose Wanda because Wanda would then reveal that Aurora killed Milo. Perhaps Aurora even promised Wanda the child in exchange for helping her wreak her vengeance on Milo and Corinth. What, Corinth wonders now, was Tom's price for betraying her?

Tom. Perhaps he'd been working for Aurora as well

as for Milo. Where was he now? Had he taken his fee and fled Bosco, or had Wanda's son killed him for the part he played in aiding Milo Latham? Was he lying someplace in the garden, his own lifeblood draining into the ground? She tries to find him in the darkness. She lets her spirit flow out of her body as freely as her blood is flowing out onto the rocks. She pictures the blue bird on one of Aurora's teacups, the blue of its wings bleeding into the surrounding white, and imagines her spirit as that bird, a blue whiff of smoke with wings, rising into a white sky. But just when she feels her spirit rising to the top of the well, she's held back by the cold marble and she can feel it trembling there like the wings of a trapped bird beating the stagnant air. She can feel the panic rising in her as her spirit slams back into her torn flesh. Quickly she pushes the spirit out of her again, but this time she sends it downward, through the cracks between the rocks and into the pipes, where it snakes below the rose garden and the grotto and into the hillside through a hundred copper pipes, pushing the water aside to surface for one last gasp.

Standing in the center of the rose garden in a sea of fallen crimson petals, Tom pauses and listens. All he hears, though, is silence. *Damn it, Cory,* he says to himself, *I've done what you told me to.* She was right, of course. Not ten minutes after she and Wanda left, he saw the driver get ready to make his move, but Tom was too quick for him. He hit him hard enough to kill him, but Tom was pretty sure he was still alive. He bound him with a rope that he found coiled in the man's overcoat pocket—no doubt meant for Tom—and left him in the hedges. They could decide what to do with him later—but where is Corinth? Did she let herself be overpowered by Mrs. Norris?

He turns in a slow circle, even his footsteps queerly silent on the soft red carpet, but the rose garden is empty except for the marble Indian girl, who holds her bound hands out to him as if imploring him to release her.

For a moment he is back in the Lyceum Theater in Gloversville, watching helplessly as Corinth is bound tighter and tighter until something breaks his spell of inertia: a voice, as if speaking inside his own head, calling his own name.

He stares at the statue of the Indian girl and realizes why it's so quiet. The water from the fountain has stopped flowing. Instead, where jets of water leapt around the statue, a faint breeze stirs the water, swirling the rose petals on its surface into loops and eddies that form, as he watches, three letters.

TOM.

He blinks and his name is gone. A sudden gust of wind whips the petals on the ground into a red ribbon that leads from the fountain to the back of the garden, where the statue of the warrior with his upright sword seems to rebuke Tom for his tardiness. *Get moving,* he hears the voice inside him say—only he knows that this is his own voice.

He follows the red path beneath the statue and pauses between two cypresses to look into a round clearing where the rose-strewn path continues like a stream of blood between the white stones and bitter-smelling white flowers. At the other side of the circle he sees the housekeeper emerging from the underground crypt to look around the circle. Tom stands still in the shadow of the cypress trees, willing himself as still as the statue standing above him. He watches as Wanda Norris kneels and picks up a handful of rose petals, which she crushes in her hand and then sifts between her fingers. Then she turns and goes back down into the crypt, muttering something under her breath that sounds like a curse.

She's waiting for her son, Tom figures. Does that mean she's already killed Corinth?

The rose petals stir at his feet and a scent rises—Corinth's scent—or maybe only the smell of her still on his skin, but it's enough to convince him she's alive. He walks out of the cypress shadows and crosses the clearing, the rose petals muffling the sound of his footsteps. They spray themselves across the marble steps so that as he creeps down into the crypt even Wanda's keen hearing misses his approach. She's kneeling by the side of the little Latham girl, waving some herb under her nose and chanting. Tom kneels and picks up a piece of broken rubble from the floor and raises it over Wanda's head. He steps forward onto bare floor and at last she hears him, but it's too late. When she turns the last thing she sees is a marble arm, one of her mistress's statues come to life at last, descending from the sky to strike her.

In the well, Corinth breathes slowly, constricting her throat to make each breath last longer. Each breath sounds as if it's moving through a rusty pipe. This is what she pictures herself becoming as the years pass: another pipe in the great fountain, her bones channeling the water, her flesh resurgent in the sprays and jets that flash in the sunshine. It's not an entirely bad way to spend eternity. Even the voices of the children have ceased to bother her. They don't blame *her*, even though it was her child they were sacrificed for. She can feel them gathered around her, as if waiting for a bedtime story, which she would be happy to oblige them with if only she could find the breath. She draws in one more breath, which feels as if it will be the last breath in all the world. As she lets it out she purses her lips to make a shushing sound. If she's going to be trapped here for all eternity with these children, she had better at least calm them. The shushing noise, though, turns into a long, low moan—a grating cry that sounds as if the whole garden were keening for its lost children.

When Tom lowers himself down into the well, he's

relieved at first to see that Corinth's eyes are open, but when he speaks to her she doesn't seem to hear him. He runs his hands over her, feeling for broken bones, and feels the stickiness covering the left side of her chest and arm. He finds where the bullet went through her shoulder and where it came out.

"You've lost a lot of blood," he tells her, taking his own shirt off and tearing it into strips to bind her wound, "but I don't think the bullet hit your heart. We've got to get you out of here, though. Can you put your arms around my neck?"

Corinth watches her own arms circle Tom's neck as if watching an automaton performing tricks in one of his magic acts. She wills her body to do what he tells her to, wrapping her legs around his waist as he pulls them both up out of the well. He leans her against the wall while he drags Wanda's body across the floor.

"She's still breathing," Corinth comments, surprised more at her own survival than Wanda's.

"Well, she won't bother us in there," Tom says, hauling the heavy woman up to the rim of the well.

"You can't leave her in there to die," Corinth says, her voice still hoarse as old pipes.

"It's what she planned for you," Tom says, looking down at Corinth.

Corinth looks across the room to where the girl lies on the marble floor, her frail chest rising and falling under her white nightgown in the moonlight. Alice. Her child and Tom's. But it's Wanda who's cared for her—killed for her—all these years. Wanda who will follow them to the ends of the earth to find Alice if they leave her alive.

"All right," she says, closing her eyes. But when Tom pushes the marble lid over the top of the well, she opens them again because for a moment she was back in the well, down in the dark with Wanda and the children.

Tom carries Alice back to the coach and Corinth walks by his side. She has to stop every few feet to rest. Through her bandages, she can still feel her blood seeping out of her, leaving a trail from the center of the maze to the hedge wall, like the ball of thread Ariadne gave to Theseus to find his way out of the labyrinth, only Corinth can feel this scarlet thread attaching her to the center of the maze, pulling her back.

Tom shows her where he's left the driver—bound and unconscious, but still breathing. "It would be better to kill him," he says, but Corinth shakes her head. "Leave him be," she says. "He won't come after us."

Tom lays Alice on the cushioned bench inside the brougham and then helps Corinth in beside her. The carpetbag she brought with her from the hotel in Saratoga is still there and, tucked beneath the seat, a small trunk with the initials *A.L.* stamped into the leather. *So Wanda had planned to take the girl away.* As Tom whips the horses into motion, Corinth sees that Alice is staring up at her. She braces herself for a reproach—or at least for the girl to ask what's become of her caretaker—but instead Alice pushes herself forward on the seat until her head rests in Corinth's lap, and with a deep sigh that Corinth feels reverberate through her entire body, she falls back asleep.

The movement of the carriage soon lulls Corinth to sleep, as well. She is instantly drawn by the scarlet thread back through the maze and down into the well, where Wanda is breathing her last breaths. The children who had gathered around Corinth have come closer now, but instead of waiting for a story, they are telling one—one only Wanda can hear. All Corinth can hear is the rattling of their bones, which sounds like china teacups shivering in their saucers.

Corinth startles awake to find that the carriage has stopped. Pale light filters through fogged-over windows. Alice is crouched on the floor below her, sorting through the clothes and toys packed in her trunk. Corinth wipes at the window with her handkerchief, but the fog is too thick to see through. She slides open the little window to the driver's box and asks Tom why they've stopped.

"I'm just waiting for the fog to clear," he says. "There's a steep drop off the road up ahead that I don't want to risk going over. Are you all right in there?"

"Yes," Corinth tells him, looking down at Alice, who has pulled out of the trunk a doll with yellow hair and blue eyes. With a pang of remorse for Wanda, Corinth sees that it's the same one that she had taken from Alice in the attic yesterday. The one Wanda had told her wasn't for her. But it's not the doll that Alice is interested in. She's unwrapping something from a nest of white tissue paper. Corinth hears what it is before she sees it.

The dry rattle of bone against bone.

"Look, Wanda packed my teacup," Alice says, holding up the cup and saucer. "See, you can tell it's mine." She tips the cup over so Corinth can see inside. Corinth leans forward. She feels as if she's looking down into the white marble well again. At the bottom of the cup, in flowing blue script that bleeds into the white background, is written the name *Alice*.

"See, that's how I always knew which one was mine," Alice says.

Corinth doesn't say anything, picturing the row of flow-blue tea-cups in Aurora Latham's china cabinet that she ordered specially from England *for the children*. Each with one of the children's names on the inside.

"And Wanda told you to be careful always to drink only from your own cup."

"Of course," Alice says, laying the teacup down in its nest of tissue paper. "It would be dirty to share with the others. How long are we going to stay here?" she asks, climbing back up onto the seat. She kneels under the window and rubs it with the sleeve of her dress to see outside. The fog is burning off in the morning sun, dissolving into shreds. "I *know* where we are—the overlook on the way to the camp. Are we going to the camp, then?"

Corinth hesitates. Yes, this is the road to the camp, but how would Tom know the location of Latham's hunting cabin? Had Latham taken him there? And why would Tom take them someplace that belonged to the Latham family? Is it possible he's still acting for Milo— or for Aurora?

Alice is still staring at her, waiting for an answer. "Yes," Corinth says, thinking it simpler to reassure the girl that they're going someplace familiar.

Alice turns away from the window and smiles. "Oh, good, you'll like it there," she says. "I'll show you the secret Indian grave in the bog."

Corinth smiles back at the girl even though her flesh has gone cold. Alice can't mean the desolate spot beneath the tamarack tree where she consigned that poor dead infant (Aurora's child, not hers, she reminds herself) to the tea-colored water. She must have overheard one of Wanda's stories about the Indian girls, abandoned by their lovers or repudiated by their tribes, who drowned themselves in the bog. The carriage jolts into motion and the wisps of fog stream away from the window. For a moment the two spots that Alice rubbed clean on the window darken into two black eyes and Corinth feels, rather than sees, someone watching from the side of the road.

Chapter Twenty-five

By the time we arrive at the turnoff to the camp, it has started to snow again. We drive through a stand of black spruce so dense it's as if we are driving through a tunnel. Nat makes another right at an unmarked turnoff and then a left onto a drive whose only marking is the weathered blade of a canoe paddle nailed to the peeling bark of a birch tree.

"I'm guessing your family didn't invite a lot of overnight guests to the camp," I say, bracing myself as the car lurches on the unplowed road.

"Yeah, they saw remoteness as a virtue in location as well as emotional tone. It would have been even more remote before the valley was flooded in the thirties. Nothing but marshland and bog for a hundred miles in any direction. My grandfather said that back at the turn of the century an escaped convict hid out here all winter long. In the spring they found footsteps leading into the bog, but they never found his body. It was my grandfather's belief that he'd been swallowed up by the bog and preserved in the peat."

I wonder if this was another boogeyman Nat's grandfather invented to scare him, but I don't suggest it. Since Nat's outburst on the cliff, we've both tried to stick to emotionally neutral content.

The narrow drive climbs up a small rise and then descends abruptly to the edge of a small pond. If you didn't know the pond was there, you'd be in danger of driving straight into the water. Nat puts the car in park and turns off the engine. Instantly we are enveloped in a silence that feels as deep as the woods that surround us. Across the pond is the house—a low chalet built of rough-hewn logs, its roof and eaves sheathed in bark. It blends in so well with the surrounding woods I have the feeling that if I blinked, it would waver and be gone.

Nat sits looking at the house for a few minutes, as if more than a stretch of black water divided him from it—as if he were looking at the back of the last ferry as it pulls out of the dock. Then with one sharp expulsion of breath he gets out of the car and I follow him. Outside, the only sound is the soft whisper of snow falling through acres of black spruce.

"There's a path that goes into the bog behind the house," Nat says. "The grave site—or whatever it is—is about half a mile in. Stay close behind me, because there are sinkholes on either side of the path and we won't be able to see them under the snow."

I nod, feeling curiously unwilling to disturb the silence of these woods. As I follow Nat I can feel even through the layers of snow that the ground is buoyant and unstable. A *floating world,* my mother called it when she took me to visit a bog near our house in Lily Dale.

We had gone because my mother was looking for a love charm for one of her clients. Mira had described the orchid to me ("small white flowers growing on a tall spike with a scent like vanilla and cloves") so that I could help find it. Usually I was reluctant to go on one of my mother's foraging trips, but when I heard what she was looking for, I volunteered. I was just twelve, but I had begun to think about boys and to wonder what I might do to get them to think about me. The other girls in my school seemed equipped with an arsenal of attractions—lip glosses that made their lips shiny (unlike the waxy bee's balm Mira gave me for chapped lips), and close-fitting jeans and T-shirts that disclosed their bodies instead of hiding them the way the shapeless linen shifts Mira made for me did. I suspected, as well, that these girls were getting advice from their mothers about boys that I would never get from Mira. Mira wouldn't even talk about my father except to say that he was a boy she'd met at the agricultural college in Cobbleskill, where Mira had gone for one year, and who, when Mira got pregnant, hadn't been interested in coming back to Lily Dale and starting a family. She'd moved back in with my grandmother, from whom she inherited the yellow Victorian house on the edge of town, her clientele of tourists who flocked each summer to Lily Dale to contact their dead relatives, and her bees, who were duly informed of Grandma Elly's death so that they wouldn't swarm. Sometimes I think it's funny that Mira, whose calling is to recover lost loved ones or procure through charms and potions new loves, is so little interested in finding love herself. I picture a hollow place inside my mother where other people keep a place for a lover or husband that allows her to bring other women's loved ones back from the dead. Like an empty seat at a table. Or the hollowness beneath a bog.

"In ancient times," Mira told me while we looked for the white orchid, "bogs were recognized as sacred places consecrated to Mother Earth. Sacrifices were made to ensure fertility for the coming year. The bodies of sacrificial victims, along with fertility statues, are found today perfectly preserved."

"That's because of the tannic acid in the water," I replied, repeating something I had recently learned in science class to still the quaking feeling in my stomach. I'd gotten my period for the first time the day before, but I hadn't told Mira because I knew she'd make a huge fuss and probably burn some nauseating incense over my head and dance naked around me, or perform some equally embarrassing spectacle, when all I wanted was a box of Kotex and some Midol to stop the cramps. They weren't so bad by the time we were walking in the bog, but I could feel a churning that made me queasily aware of my insides, and my stomach had the same spongy texture as the peat mat we walked over. Picturing preserved dead people beneath the sphagnum moss wasn't helping.

Now, walking behind Nat on top of the snow-covered bog, I catch myself scanning the snowdrifts for the elusive white orchid my mother and I had gone looking for that day. What an odd juxtaposition, I realize now, that I went into the bog with my mother to gain some insight into love and instead heard about sacrificial victims preserved for all time in the peat. What I wanted to hear from my mother was that there was a possibility of finding a love that lasted, but instead I came away that day with an image of everlasting death seared into my brain.

"What's so funny?" Nat asks, suddenly turning to face me. I didn't even realize that I had laughed out loud.

"Oh, I was just remembering something I learned about bogs when I was young. My mother was interested in the bog people—"

"You mean *The Bog People* by Peter Glob? I love that book! My favorite bog person was the Tollund Man, the one with the little skullcap and the peaceful expression on his face, like an old guy sipping soup at Ratner's Deli. But my favorite bog reference has to be Emily's."

"Emily's?"

"Yes," he says, placing his hand over his heart and striking the pose of an orator. "How dreary—to be— Somebody! / How public—like a Frog— / To tell one's name—the livelong June— / To an admiring Bog!"

The heavy, leaden sky sends back an echo of the last word of the poem, a mocking reminder of the futility of shouting out one's name in this place where the shadows of the black spruce trees seem to eat what little light remains of the day and the spongy ground swallows whatever falls into its maw. Nat runs his hand through his hair, dislodging a flurry of snowflakes, and laughs.

"You know," he says, "when I first read that poem in college, I thought it was pretty disingenuous—the whole recluse-in-a-white-dress-shunning-publication thing. Who wouldn't want to be published, after all? But the older I get, the more futile seems the idea that you can leave anything worthwhile of yourself behind, that it makes any difference. Sometimes I feel like Emily's frog and that every word I write is just croaking in the graveyard."

"The graveyard?" I repeat, suddenly feeling the same queasiness I had on that day I'd come to the bog with my mother.

"I'm sorry," Nat says, noticing the stricken look on my face. "I guess that's not the kind of thing an aspiring writer wants to hear. Remind me not to sign up for the Bosco mentoring program." Nat stamps his feet against the ground. "And remind me not to give long lectures in the freezing cold. Come on, let's find that tree."

He turns around and continues into the woods and I follow, unable to explain that my reaction has nothing to do with my writing aspirations or hopes of publication. Instead, I'm remembering how I became increasingly nauseated that day in the bog, how every step seemed to be dragging me deeper into the bog's maw. I was haunted by the idea that I was walking over the bones of those sacrificial victims my mother had told me about. No, not bones but whole bodies, tanned in the peat like leather purses.

As we descend into the sloping bowl at the center of the bog, I feel the same sinking feeling that I've felt since I lost my way in the snow at the overlook. Nat, though, lopes ahead, sure-footed, his gaze on the overhanging spruce boughs, his hands reaching out to graze the rough fringe of blue-green needles as if he were greeting old friends. I can imagine him tromping through these woods as a boy, playing Indian scout, looking for old Indian graves.

He stops at a tamarack that has fallen across the path, its yellow needles staining the new-fallen snow. It must have fallen in the last storm. Nat kneels to inspect the dark red bark, which is flaking off in patches.

"Could that be the tree?" I ask, disappointed to think that the tree we are looking for might have so recently succumbed to age. Looking around, I notice that many of the trees here slant at precarious angles, their roots straining for purchase in the soft soil. Dead trees litter the forest floor, half sunken into patches of frozen water. We've come to the heart of the bog, where the soil is thick enough to nurture tamarack and spruce saplings but too unstable to support the grown tree, which falls back into the ground to nurture more seedlings—a cycle of growth, premature birth, and decay that strikes me as cannibalistic—as if the bog were a devouring mother eating its own young. I only hope that *our tree* hasn't been eaten by the bog.

"I think that's it down there," Nat says, pointing down the slope to a gnarled tamarack leaning precariously over the frozen water. I follow him down the steep incline, struggling to keep my footing in the snow. At the bottom I find Nat running his hands up and down the rough bark with the same intent look that Mira would get on her face when she did a palm reading.

"What are you looking for?" I ask.

"Shhhh," Nat hisses, as if he were listening for a heartbeat in the tree. "I think the bark has grown over the name," he says a moment later.

It seems quite possible. The tamarack's bark is gnarled and twisted, as if it had chosen to grow inward rather than upward and so escape the fate of its brethren that litter the mossy floor of the bog. Even so, it's pitched over the frozen water at an angle that suggests it might at any moment dive into the pond. Nat's hands come to rest over a swollen node, and he begins to pick away at the flaky bark. Peering over his shoulder, I see appear beneath the reddish bark a patch of white that is as hard and shiny as bone. I gasp, as alarmed as if he'd really cut through living flesh to the bone. An image of a body trapped beneath the reddish bark, *buried alive* within the tree, flits through my mind, but when I reach past Nat to touch the white surface, I recognize that it's only *bone china*. A tiny thread of blue flows along the edge of the bark like a vein. We've found the petrified heart of the tree.

Nat takes a penknife out of his back pocket and uses it to scrape away more bark. The blue vein reveals itself to be the curling loop at the end of a cursive letter. As I watch Nat's blade uncover the letters, I have the odd sensation that he's carving them as they appear. But of course that's not the case. This name has lain here, buried beneath the tamarack bark, for a long, long time.

" 'To tell one's name the livelong June,' " I say aloud.

Nat looks over his shoulder at me, his eyes shining. "Not to be forgotten," he says. "They left this here so she wouldn't be forgotten."

He turns back and brushes away the shredded bark from the porcelain plaque. It's round and slightly concave. Written in a flowing blue script is a single name. *Alice.*

"I think it's the bottom of a teacup," I say, running my fingers over the smooth white porcelain surface. "If we could get it out, we might be able to see the manufacturer's mark on the other side."

I pry my fingers around the edges of the porcelain circle—it appears to have been wedged into a knothole that then grew over—but Nat lays his hand over mine.

"I don't think we should remove it," he says.

"Why not? I thought you wanted to know what happened."

"Yes . . ." Nat falters, looking uncharacteristically unsure of himself. ". . . but it seems that someone went to a lot of trouble to leave this name here. I remember finding it when I was a kid and thinking it had been left here just for me. I used it in a story once—an amateurish thing that I wrote in college—about a boy finding a name carved on a tree in the woods behind his house, only it's his own name and he thinks it means he'll die under that tree." Nat smiles sheepishly. "I called it 'The Namesake.' Eventually when the boy's an old man he hikes into the woods and finds that the tree's been struck by lightning and his name is rent in two. He has a heart attack and dies." Nat grimaces. "My writing teacher, Spencer Leland, said it reminded him of one of Edith Wharton's ghost stories . . ."

"I love Edith Wharton," I say.

"Yeah, but Leland didn't. It wasn't meant as a compliment." Nat strokes the porcelain. "I think I forgot that the real name on it was Alice because I changed it in my story. It's like I wiped out her name to write my own, which, when you come to think of it, is all writing is."

"I thought it was croaking in the graveyard," I say. "Jeez, Nat, you've got more reasons not to write than any writer I've ever known." As soon as the words are out I regret them. Who am I, after all, to criticize Nat Loomis's ideas on writing? But Nat is laughing, big booming laughs that echo in the bowl of the bog. I can feel the reverberations in the spongy ground and see them in the tamarack's shivering bark. Then I hear a loud groan and realize that the tree is careening forward—straight toward Nat. I grab his arm and pull him out of the way just before the tree hits the pond, shattering the thin scum of ice on its surface. We watch as the tree slowly sinks into the dark water.

"Damn. If I'd written *that* in a story, Leland *really* would have lambasted it."

I don't say anything. In the patch of reddish brown

soil that's been upturned by the tamarack's roots lie a handful of white shards. Like tiny bones. I remember then what I saw that day in the bog with my mother. At the edge of a pond I had bent to pick a white flower that I thought might be the orchid my mother was looking for and saw, staring up at me from the water, a baby's face. Its skin tanned like old leather. By the time Mira found me retching into the reeds, the face was gone, but I believed I had seen the face of a child sacrificed to the bog.

Nat kneels and picks up one of the white fragments and turns it over. I see half a wing of a blue bird merging into the white background.

"It's the rest of the teacup," I say with relief. "It's just like the ones that are at Bosco."

We don't talk much on our way back to the car. I sense that Nat is immersed in his memories of the childhood summers he spent here with his grandfather—perhaps reevaluating those memories in light of what he's learned about his family history—just as I am drawn back to that day in the bog with my mother.

I remember Mira finding me by the edge of the pond, sick and frightened by the baby's face I had seen in the bog water. She cradled me against her soft breasts and belly—it was like being hugged by a Bronze Age fertility goddess come to life—and told me that it was because I was a woman now (apparently Mira had known all along I'd gotten my period) and that this happened to the women in our family. They saw things. They saw people who were dead and sometimes they saw people who hadn't been born yet. The thing I had to do was *gain control* of it before it gained control of me. We'd have a séance that night to confront the spirit that had frightened me in the bog. But the séance Mira held that night hadn't helped at all. All it had done was teach me how to close my eyes to the things I saw, to never let myself relax, to never trust myself entirely or allow myself to fall in love—a strategy that had worked fairly well until I came to Bosco.

"I may have some trouble getting the car turned around and up this hill in the snow," Nat says when we get back to the Range Rover. "I'll concentrate better alone. Why don't you hike up the drive and wait for me at the top of the hill."

I do what he says, but when I've reached the top of the hill, the sound of the Rover's engine racing makes me turn around. The car is slipping backward, sliding toward the black maw of the pond, as if it were a mouth waiting to swallow Nat up into the bog. I realize that this is why Nat didn't want me in the car: he knew it might be dangerous. I open my mouth to scream, but then the car comes to a halt and, in a burst of grinding gears and spraying snow, gains purchase and hurtles past me, skidding to a stop a few yards away. I stand for a moment looking back at the pond and the bog beyond the cabin, as if making sure that nothing is coming after us, but the only movement is the falling snow and the gentle swaying of the spruce trees.

I trudge toward the Range Rover, my eyes on the lowering sky that hovers over the black spruce trees that line the drive. It's like looking down a dark tunnel spanned by a marble arch. As I stare into it I sense that something is coming down the drive. I squint into the swirling snow and see, at the end of the drive, a dark shape detaching itself from the spruce trees. I feel the boggy ground beneath my feet pulsing in a steady pattern that could only be horse hooves striking the ground. And then I see it. The black carriage driven by a man cloaked in black, a glimpse of the red interior— like a beating heart—a woman's head craning out the window to look at . . . what? She seems to be looking straight at me.

Then it's gone. The shadows resolve into trees and one large, raucous blackbird that takes flight into the overhanging sky and passes low over my head. I see something drop and bend to pick up what I think will be a feather, but instead when I open my hand I find that I'm holding a white flower. A bog orchid, crushed but still retaining the faint spicy scent of vanilla. The charm my mother and I had looked for in vain years ago. I slip it into my coat pocket, along with the pieces of the broken teacup, and get into the car.

Chapter Twenty-six

The fog is so thick that the only way Corinth knows they've reached the camp is the smell of peat in the air. Alice must sense it, too, because when the coach pauses she opens the door and jumps down.

"I'll race you to the cabin," she calls over her shoulder. "I know a shortcut."

Corinth calls after her to tell her not to go, that she'll get lost in the fog, but she's already vanished and Corinth has no strength to follow her. She barely has the strength to prop her elbows on the coach's window-sill and stick her head out to look for Alice. The fog lies thick on the spruce boughs overhead, like a mirage of winter. At the end of the long colonnade of trees she sees a shape emerging from the fog that must be Alice, only then Alice herself leaps out from the woods just beneath the coach window. She's holding a flower up, which Corinth just manages to grasp before Alice runs back to the woods. She looks back up the drive to where she saw the figure coalescing in the fog, but what looked like a woman a moment before now grows wings and takes flight. It's only a large blackbird whose plaintive caw as it flies overhead so startles Corinth that the flower Alice had given her—a white orchid—slips from her fingers and falls beneath the wheels of the carriage, leaving behind only a fleeting scent of vanilla.

Tom carries her into the cabin, Alice close at his heels chattering happily about the cabin's peculiarities and special features. She knows how the woodstove works and where the tea and sugar are kept in special sealed tins to keep the mice out. Does Corinth want her to make her a cup of tea to revive her from the journey? (She recites the offer like something she must have overheard.) Corinth nods weakly, more to give the girl something to do than from any great longing for tea. So far the child seems unperturbed to be here with two nearly total strangers, but surely she'll start asking questions soon. What, Corinth wonders as she leans back on the bed, will they tell her? Should she tell her that Aurora Latham, who never treated her as a mother should, was not, in fact, her real mother? And what should she tell her about Wanda—the one person who treated her with any kindness?

Corinth closes her eyes and once again she is back in the well. At first she thinks Wanda must be dead, because it is so silent, but then she hears a harsh hiss, like air being slowly let out of a pneumatic tire, and she realizes that Wanda is conserving her breath as Corinth had toward the end, and as Corinth had, she is turning each exhalation into a shushing noise to silence the children. Only it's not just the restless stirring of the dead children she silences but the muttering of the spring itself. The water is moving more slowly, drying up; soon it will cease to flow altogether. Wanda is cursing all of Bosco with her dying breath.

"Here's your tea."

Corinth opens her eyes, more grateful for the sound of Alice's voice than the proffered cup. She's poured the tea into her own cup—the flow-blue cup with her name at the bottom. Corinth reaches for it, but her hand is shaking too hard to hold it.

"I'd better help you," Alice says, bringing the thin china rim to Corinth's lips. She tips the cup and Corinth sees the letters at the bottom of the teacup—only now instead of Alice's name she sees the name she gave to her own child.

The tea must have some kind of calmative herb in it because, while Tom is tucking Alice into a bed on the other side of the woodstove, Corinth falls asleep watching the light fade from the little window above her bed. When she wakes up, much later, the window is dark and the only light in the cabin comes from the dying embers in the woodstove. Tom is lying next to her in the narrow bed, asleep, but the moment she stirs he's awake. He gets up and stokes the fire and boils water to wash her wound and then rebandage her shoulder.

"You've lost a lot of blood," he says. "I think I should get a doctor for you."

"It's too risky," Corinth says. "They'll find us and take Alice. I'll be fine." She's far from sure that she'll be all right, though. Along with the loss of blood, she feels she's left some part of herself back in the well at Bosco—a part that Wanda is holding on to as she dies. That she is being silenced by Wanda's dying breaths just as the children and the spring are being silenced.

"It's too risky to keep her with us," Tom says. "We could leave her someplace safe where she could be returned to her mother—"

"*No!*" Corinth says, surprising herself with the strength she's able to summon. "Whatever happens, you must promise never to let Aurora get her hands on her. If something happens to me—" Tom starts to interrupt, but Corinth places her hand over his mouth and goes on. "If anything happens to me, take her to my sister in Buffalo. The address of the family she's with is in my diary. I've been sending money for years—enough for them to take care of Alice, too. Please, Tom, promise me."

She sees something cloud in his eyes. "You haven't had much reason to trust my promises in the past," he says, "and there's something I think I should tell you before I make any more." She tries to lift her hand to silence him, but he clasps her hand and brings it to his lips. "I wasn't at Bosco only as Violet Ramsdale's employee," he says. "I was working for Milo Latham as well. He approached me in New York and said he had need of my 'skills as a conjurer.' That's how he put it. He said he was bringing a medium to his home at his wife's request to contact their dead children, but that he wanted to make sure his wife was satisfied with the results of the séance. So I agreed to . . . *augment* the effects of the séance . . ."

"Tom, I know . . ."

"No, you don't know everything. I knew you were to be the medium. I knew you were Latham's mistress. I agreed because I wanted to get back at you for not waiting for me in Gloversville. I was going to plant the tools I used in the false séance in your room and then unveil you as a fraud—Violet would have been only too happy to help."

"But you didn't," she says. "You didn't go through with it."

"The minute I saw you again I knew I couldn't. But still, I faked the séance—"

Corinth begins to laugh, but the motion hurts her shoulder too much. "If only Milo knew! There was no need to fake anything. His children's spirits are only too real. He found that out too late . . ." Corinth's voice trails off.

"You mean he died of fright?"

"No," Corinth says, shaking her head, "or at least, not fright alone. Aurora put hellebore in his scotch. It can kill a man if his heart is weak."

"Then I'm lucky my heart's not weak: I had two glasses of Latham's scotch last night."

Corinth looks out the window by her bed and sees the great shaggy shadows of spruce trees emerging out of the darkness and hears the call of a red-winged blackbird. It's almost dawn. She looks up at Tom, his face bathed in the pale light, and then looks toward the bed where Alice is sleeping, the girl's dark eyelashes fringing her pale cheek, which is pillowed on her long, slender fingers.

She lays her hand on Tom's chest. "No," she says, "you have a strong heart."

She'll have to tell him that Alice is his daughter, she realizes, but tell him in a way that will leave no doubt, so that he'll protect her no matter what happens. She takes her hand from his chest and reaches for his hand, wrapping her fingers around his wrist, and pulls herself up to a seated position. The blood swims from her head, but she bites the inside of her cheek to keep from fainting.

"There's something I have to show you," she says, "before Alice wakes up. It's only a short walk and I'm feeling much stronger."

When she hears the cabin door close behind them, Alice opens her eyes. She counts to a hundred (the number James insisted upon when they played hide-and-seek) and then jumps out of bed and runs to the window. She can see them, Miss Blackwell leaning heavily on Mr. Quinn's arm, entering the path that leads into the bog.

Whatever can she mean to show him in *there*? Not that there aren't many wonderful things in the bog—emerald green pitcher plants that hold water like a vase, tiny frogs that look like Mother's best enamel brooches, white flowers that smell like fresh-baked cookies, and twisted pieces of wood that the bog water polished and hardened to look like the carved ebony in Papa's walking stick. James said that the bog water preserved everything. That if you slipped and fell into the water and drowned here (which could happen very easily because there was quicksand everywhere and traps set by Indians), your body would never rot, but be preserved like the Egyptian mummies that Papa took them to see in the big museum in the city. There were bodies of Indians, James said, perfectly preserved at the bottom of the bog and waiting to reach up and drag you down to keep them company. His stories scared Cynthia so much that she would never step a foot off the cabin's porch, but Alice wasn't afraid. Wanda had taught her spells to say and plants to pick to keep as charms to protect her. She knew where the sinkholes and the quicksand traps were better than anyone. And so she decides to follow Miss Blackwell and Mr. Quinn into the bog to see what it is Miss Blackwell wants to show him.

⤝

Walking is harder than Corinth thought it would be. She finds she hasn't breath enough to talk at the same time, so she's quiet until they come to the tamarack tree that leans over the pond at the center of the bog. Fog still covers the opposite bank, but the sun has burnt through the mist here. The sphagnum moss below the tree is emerald green and brightly colored dragonflies flit over the surface of the water. At first she's afraid that the name she carved was gone, but then she finds it.

"My mother named me for the place I was born so that my spirit would always know where to come back to, but I didn't know what this place was called," she told Tom, "so I named her for my sister." She smiles when she sees Tom make a face at the name. "My sister was named for the place where she was born. The family that took her moved to Buffalo a little later."

"You were pregnant, then, when you left Gloversville."

She nods, unable to speak. How can she explain that day when she met Latham on the post office steps? How she doubted that Tom would ever come back? Corinth digs her fingers into the rim around the knothole where she carved the baby's name.

"I can see you in her, Tom," she says.

"See? You can see her now?" He looks around the bog as if afraid that the tiny spirit of the child is floating above the water in the thick banks of fog. Out of the corner of her eye, Corinth catches something moving across the water, something in the sedges concealed by a shred of morning fog, but then she sees that it's only a red-winged blackbird, which rises up out of the fog and alights in the branches of the tamarack tree.

She tries to tell him that the baby she buried here wasn't theirs, that it was Aurora and Milo's child. She must tell him that Alice is his so that he will watch over her and so he'll know . . . know what? That she let another man think the baby was his because she didn't trust that he'd come back? How can she tell him that? There isn't time or words enough to explain. Already she can feel the strength rushing out of her. She can feel the ache in her shoulder as her wound opens and begins to bleed again. She can feel the unsteady ground beneath her shudder and the pull of the water beneath it, as if the bog were connected by underground tunnels to the well at Bosco and when it opens up she'll be sucked under. She can feel the hiss of Wanda's last dying breath cursing her as she begins to fall, can hear herself calling his name, but she doesn't feel Tom's arms catching her.

Chapter Twenty-seven

It's after ten by the time we get back to Bosco. The storm made the roads nearly impassable. For a moment on the reservoir road the Range Rover went into a long, slow, sickening skid that nearly took us over the guardrail, but Nat managed to straighten the car out at the last minute. I realized later that I'd been gripping the shards of broken china in my pocket so hard that I'd drawn blood.

The worst part of the trip, though, proves to be the drive up to the house. No one has plowed the private road that snakes up through the gardens to the mansion. Nat tries to power through with the Range Rover, but the drive is too steep. "We'll have to hike up," he says after his third or fourth attempt.

It's a long walk to the top, miss.

I hear the words carried on the wind that whips around me as I step out into the deep, soft snow. We're at the bottom of the garden, just outside the hedge maze. For a moment I hear another sound, a sound like running water, only it's water with a voice. *Remember me,* it's saying, *remember me.* The same thing the fog-girl had whispered in my ear. A plaintive refrain, I think, nothing to be afraid of, but then I realize that the voice is coming from below my feet and it's saying, no longer *"Remember me,"* but *"Memento mori." Remember, you must die.* I look down and see that the snow is lapping over my legs like the ocean's surf, and when it retreats, I can feel the snow beneath my feet pulling away and my body sinking into the ground. I stumble, but Nat catches my arm and the undercurrent of snow withdraws back into the hedge maze, where, I sense, it's gathering strength for the next wave.

"We have to get back to the house," I say. "The garden—" I'm about to say, *The garden has come alive,* but then I see that Nat's staring in the direction of the house. The storm is clearing and the moon appears from behind the clouds, illuminating the black hulking mass of the mansion.

"That's funny," he says.

"What?"

"There are no lights on in the mansion."

"The storm must have knocked out the electricity," I say.

"Bosco has its own generator," Nat says, shaking his head. "I can't imagine that David couldn't have gotten it started."

I don't answer, because I know, too, that David would have no problem accomplishing that feat. That he hasn't suggests that something has happened to him—and to the others. An image flashes through my mind—

the same image I had just before I left—of David, Bethesda, Zalman, and Daria transformed into lifeless dolls and stuffed toys sitting in a circle.

"We have to get up there as quickly as possible," I tell Nat, taking a step up the drive.

He holds on to me as I lurch headlong into the snow. "The snow in the drive is too deep," he says. "We'd be better off following the paths through the garden. Look"—he points toward a gap in the hedge— "there's hardly any snow in there."

He's right. The path beyond the hedge looks as if it had been freshly swept of snow. "I don't know—" I begin to object, but Nat's already propelling me through the gap.

"Don't worry," he says, "I followed Bethesda down here yesterday. I'm pretty sure I can find the path again." Nat looks down and seems embarrassed to notice he's still holding on to my arm. He starts to pull away, but I hang on.

"I think we'd better stay close together," I say. "This maze is . . . kind of tricky."

"Sure," he says, giving me a crooked smile. "Whatever you say."

I realize he thinks I'm making up the danger to stay close to him, but what surprises me is how pleased he seems by it. He tucks my arm more firmly under his and we set off. Like Hansel and Gretel into the woods. When I sneak a look back over my shoulder, though, I realize how futile it would be to leave a trail of bread crumbs behind us. The snow is sweeping the path behind us, erasing even our footprints. It's as if it wanted all trace of our passing scoured from the land.

I look ahead and follow Nat's lead, turning with him even though I suspect we're not getting any closer to the house. He's following the path that's cleanest of snow, I realize, which is also going steadily downhill.

"Damn," Nat says when we emerge into the center of the maze, "this isn't where I thought we were going. We need to go up the hill."

But this is where, I am sure, the maze wanted us to go. The statue of Ne'Moss-i-Ne is holding up her hands to us as if pleading with us to set her free. I kneel down in front of her and look into her hands, where water has frozen into a transparent bowl. Suspended in its center is a drop of frozen blood. As I look closer I see it's a red rose petal.

"Where would a rose petal come from in the middle of a snowstorm?" I ask.

"I don't know," Nat says, "but it's not the only one. Look." I follow Nat's gaze and see a trail of rose petals leading behind the fountain and toward the statue of Jacynta. Some of the petals have even frozen to the warrior's sword, so that it looks as if he had just drawn fresh blood.

"That's the way to the children's cemetery," I tell Nat.

"Yeah, well, too bad—we're going to the house." I can hear the fear in Nat's voice and beneath it a disdainful whisper. *Squaw boy.* His grandfather's ugly sneer. Poor Nat, I realize, it's always with him. "You said we needed to get back to the house right away," he says.

"I was wrong," I say, making my voice firm. "David and Bethesda were going to the cemetery today, remember? To look for Alice's grave."

"Yeah, but that was hours ago. They can't still be there; they'd be frozen—"

I stand up and start following the trail of rose petals. "Let's hope we're not too late," I say to Nat, who's following close behind me. We squeeze through the hedge behind Jacynta and enter the circle of the children's cemetery. At first I think the snow is deeper here, but then I realize that the three or four feet of white froth gleaming in the moonlight isn't snow. It's flowers—white flowers that have crept over the graves of Aurora's children and swelled into a deep pool. I pluck one of the blooms, hold it to my nose, and immediately sneeze.

"It's hellebore," a voice says from behind me. I turn, expecting to see Nat, but Nat is wading through the waist-deep flowers toward the crypt. This man behind me appears to be the statue of Jacynta come to life. He's holding a long curved sword and his hair and clothes are covered in white. Even his eyes, coated with a whitish film, seem to be carved out of marble. It takes me another second to realize it's David.

"Black hellebore," he says, "although its flowers are white." He brushes at his shoulders, and I realize the white dusting isn't snow—it's a coating of white blossoms. "A medicinal plant, my wife called it. A little can strengthen the heart, but too much—" He shakes his head, dislodging a flurry of petals. "She gave it to the children and then she gave it to me." He pulls the sword—no, not a sword, but a scythe—back behind his shoulder and swings it forward in a low arc. I leap back to avoid the blade and stumble backward into the hellebore. The thick black stems fall before the scythe. There should be a swath cleared, but there isn't. The black stems grow back as soon as David's blade passes through them and new white flowers blossom before my eyes. He curses and I hear the scythe whistling through the air above my head and I scuttle backward. I have to get to the crypt, which must be where Bethesda is. Or at least I hope that's where she is. If David has been possessed by the spirit of Milo Latham, then I'm pretty sure Bethesda must have taken the role of Aurora. I can only hope she hasn't been mowed down by the scythe already.

As I creep backward I shudder as my hands come in contact with the fleshy hellebore stems, thinking each time I've touched a severed limb. And I do feel as if *someone* is in the hellebore with me—Aurora or Bethesda, I'm not sure—some presence rustling the white blossoms and pushing up through the earth. My hands sink into the stalks and I can feel *them*—tiny fingers scratching at the earth, trying to break through. I squeeze my eyes shut lest I see them: the hands of Aurora's children reaching up through the ground, the black hellebore smothering them. That's why I feel as if I'm surrounded by Aurora. She's *in* the hellebore, her spirit residing in the poisoned flowers that her dead husband mows down again and again, only to have them spring to life again, the two locked in a never-ending battle.

I stop to wipe tears from my face and the scythe slices into my ankle. I plunge my hands back into the tangled stems and a hand encircles my wrist and pulls me back just before the scythe comes down again. Another hand is on my arm and another snakes around my waist. I can feel them pulling me down. Instead of the earth beneath me I feel the cold marble of the crypt and darkness. And all the time I hear that whisper. *Memento mori.* Remember, you must die. As if anyone could forget that *here* of all places.

"All right," I scream into the darkness. "I'm here. I'm here."

One of the hands moves over my mouth and a match flares in the darkness, lighting up a ghostly white face. A woman with pale blue eyes. "Shut up," Bethesda says. "We know you're here already. Do you want to get us all killed?"

"Thank God," I say as soon as Nat takes his hand away from my mouth. "You're alive. And you're not Aurora."

Bethesda shakes her head. "That's who *he* thought I was," she says, tilting her head up toward the cemetery. "He damn near killed me. We came down here to find Alice's grave and found these flowers growing. At first he was the picture of botanical interest. *'Oh, black hellebore'* "—Bethesda mimics David's Texas accent to a tee—" *'sometimes called Christmas hellebore because it blooms in winter.'* He went back up the hill to get the scythe so he could clear it to find the grave, only when he came back he was acting odd. He'd found a bottle of scotch somewhere and drank half of it before getting back here. Then he started going at those bushes like he had a personal vendetta against them—"

"He does," I say. "I think Milo Latham, whose spirit has taken hold of David, was murdered by Aurora, and Aurora—" I pause, finding it more difficult to explain that Aurora's spirit has found its way into the hellebore—as though it were easier to believe that a spirit could lodge itself in someone else's flesh than come as stone or water or a flower—but Nat and Bethesda are no longer paying attention to me. They're staring up at the entrance to the crypt, where a shadow has fallen across a swath of moonlight. David is standing at the top of the stairs, the scythe hanging from his right hand.

"Maybe he's snapped out of it," Nat says.

"I wouldn't count on it," Bethesda says. The shadow moves at the sound of her voice and grows down the steps. "Shit," Bethesda says, "he still thinks I'm Aurora."

"Quick," I say, "stand over there by the well with your hand on the edge looking down. Stay very still. In the moonlight he might think you're the statue that used to stand there."

"*Might*?" Bethesda hisses.

"We'll only need a minute," I say, grabbing Nat and pulling him into the shadowy corner of the crypt. I pick up a piece of the old statue—an arm, as it turns out—and hand it to Nat. "You have to hit him hard enough to knock him out," I whisper in his ear, "but not hard enough to kill him."

"Sure," Nat says, "I'll try my best."

I can't see his face in the dark, but I could swear he's smiling. I'm thinking that maybe I should do it myself, but David is already in the crypt. He stops for a moment at the foot of the stairs and looks at the figure by the well. In the moonlight, with her back turned and her head bent over the well, Bethesda *could* be a statue. In fact, for a moment I'm afraid she has been conjured into stone, but then a breeze blows through the crypt and stirs her hair.

"Aha!" The sound comes from David's throat, but no one would mistake that bloodcurdling cry for David's gentle Texan drawl. He raises the scythe high above his head and takes two giant strides toward Bethesda. Nat is instantly behind him, holding the marble arm up over his head like a club. He starts to bring it down and I can see that the force will kill David. I open my mouth to call out his name, but instead of *Nat* the name I call is *Tom*.

Chapter Twenty-eight

"Tom!"

From her hiding place in the reeds Alice hears Miss Blackwell call Mr. Quinn's name and sees her fall back to the ground. Just before, though, she looked over here in her direction. Had she seen her? Would she be mad she was spying? Alice decides to run back to the cabin.

Alice beats them back to the cabin because Mr. Quinn is slowed down carrying Miss Blackwell. Or maybe they were still talking about the baby buried in the bog. Of course Alice knows all about the dead baby. She found the name on the tree ages ago. James and Cynthia and Tam laughed at it. What a silly name for an Indian girl! But Alice liked the name and secretly named one of Cynthia's dolls (the doll that Norris had packed in her suitcase) for it.

Alice makes the fire and boils water. Miss Blackwell will need tea. She looked so weak when she fell. Alice fixes the pot and rinses the cup out with hot water, staring at her own name on the bottom.

Her hands are shaking as she pours the boiling water

from the heavy iron kettle into the teapot and then pours the tea into the blue and white cup. She picks up the cup and saucer just as the cabin door opens. Mr. Quinn is holding Miss Blackwell in his arms and she sees from the look on Mr. Quinn's face that it's too late—that the tea won't help at all—and so she lets the cup and saucer drop from her hands. Lets them shatter on the hard wood floor along with her name. She feels like a piece of herself breaks when the cup breaks. But when she looks down, she sees that the only part of the broken cup that has remained is the bottom circle with her name on it.

Tom lays Corinth's body down on the bed and covers her with a blanket. Then he kneels on the floor and picks up the bottom of the broken teacup and holds it out to the girl. "You can save this part with your name," he says. He almost says, "so you'll remember it," but that might scare the girl. Of course they'll have to change her name so no one will recognize her as the Latham child. It would be a million times easier just to drop her in the nearest town with instructions to take her back to Bosco. He could take her to Gloversville—to one of Latham's factories—and leave her with the factory fore-man. She'd get back safely enough. It made a lot more sense than taking her to Corinth's sister in Buffalo. Corinth must have been losing her senses already when she asked that of him.

"Where will we take her?"

For a moment Tom thinks the question comes from his own head, but then he looks up and sees that the girl is looking at Corinth's lifeless body.

"We'll have to bury her," he tells the girl, wondering if she understands about death. But then he remembers who she is—how many sisters and brothers she's lost—and figures she, of all people, should understand about death.

Alice nods, her eyes shining with tears, but she bites her lip and juts out her chin, and in the end she doesn't cry. "Of course," she says, "we'll bury her with the dead baby."

⟨⟨⟨

Tom would have picked someplace other than where "the dead baby" is buried. It's the last place he wants to go, not just because it's where Corinth died, but because it's occurred to him by now that the baby might have been his. Of course she would have made Latham think it was his own child. He can't really blame her. When he didn't come back at Christmas, she must have felt she didn't have any other option. Still, it means she must have given Latham good reason to think it could be his—and way before Christmastime.

Tom carries Corinth in his arms. He wrapped her in a blanket and tied the blanket with rope, but at the last minute he couldn't bear to think of her spending all eternity bound like that.

Alice said it wasn't necessary. "She'll be like

Ophelia floating in the water," she said. She picked flowers to braid in Corinth's hair. Bog rosemary and laurel and the little white orchid that smelled like vanilla. She made a bouquet of all the flowers and wrapped them in a green pitcher plant, and carries it as solemnly as a flower girl in a wedding procession behind Tom as he carries Corinth into the bog.

When they reach the tree where the name is carved, Tom lays Corinth down at the edge of the water and stands while Alice takes out the broken teacup from her pocket. She kneels at the foot of the tree and digs a little hole with her bare hands. He knows he should help her, but he feels frozen, his feet leaden. He's afraid that if he kneels down in the peaty soil, he might never get up again. He keeps his eyes on the trees, looking away from Corinth and the water, afraid of what he might see in its tea-stained depths. Even his own reflection would be a horror to him right now.

"There," Alice says, getting to her feet and brushing the dirt from her hands onto her dress. The girl doesn't even have good manners. Why on earth didn't the Lathams take better care of her? "I'll need your help for the next part, Mr. Quinn."

"We really should be going," he says.

"It won't take long," Alice says, biting her lip. He hopes the girl isn't going to cry. She holds out the bottom piece of the teacup with her name on it. "I want you to put this over the other name on the tree," she says. "If you carve a little hole for it, you can wedge it in. You do have a pocketknife, don't you?"

Yes, he has a pocketknife. He takes the teacup bottom and measures it against the tree. "I could put it beside the name," he says, "then they'll both be here."

"No," Alice says, stamping her foot on the ground. "It has to go *over* it."

Tom shakes his head and begins scooping out a circle from the soft bark of the tamarack tree. Who knows what the girl has in mind, but it feels curiously right to erase the name of this baby—perhaps *his* baby— and rechristen it with Alice's teacup. It feels as if he were erasing his past as the name shreds under his knife. When this is all over, when he's gotten rid of the girl, he'll change his own name. To satisfy Corinth's last wish he'll take the girl to the sister in Buffalo, but that will be it. From Buffalo he'll take a train west—maybe as far as California—and start over. He'll forget Corinth's name and his own name. He'll certainly forget this baby's name.

As he wedges the china disk into the tree, he feels he's already forgotten it. He kneels down beside Alice and together they ease Corinth's body into the bog. He doesn't watch as the water closes over her face, and yet he can almost hear, beneath the sighing of the sedges and the reeds, her voice. One last time, he hears her calling his name.

Chapter Twenty-nine

When I call Tom's name, Nat hesitates for just a moment, but he still brings down the marble arm into David's skull with a crash that reverberates through the crypt. David staggers and begins to fall, but Bethesda catches him and keeps his head from hitting the marble floor.

"You didn't have to hit him so hard," Bethesda scolds.

"You're welcome," Nat says sarcastically. "Next time I'll let him slice you open with this thing." Nat picks up the scythe, but I take it from him and drop it down the well, where it clatters against the stones at the bottom. Then I kneel down next to Bethesda, who has her ear pressed to David's chest. "Is he—?"

Bethesda shakes her head. "He's breathing," she says, "but shallowly. We have to get him back up to the house."

"Well, I'm not carrying him," Nat says petulantly.

Bethesda and I both look up at him and someone sighs as if exasperated, but then I realize the sound is coming from David. I look down and see his eyes flicker open. They settle on Bethesda, and I'm afraid for a moment that he'll attack her again, but the white film is gone.

"I'll go get that scythe now," he says. "I left it in a storage shed up the hill—" Then he sees me and Nat and, I imagine, notices that it's dark. "What—?"

"We'll explain later," I say. "We've got to get back to the house. Can you walk?"

David nods and struggles to his feet, leaning on Bethesda's and my arms. Nat stands a few feet away, his arms crossed over his chest. "How's your head feel?" Nat asks.

"Like I was rammed by a truck."

"Sorry about that," Nat says with a smile that looks anything but apologetic. Before David can register what's happened, Bethesda and I steer him up the steps. In the cemetery the white flowers have withered and shriveled up. They crackle under our feet as we walk across them. When we enter the narrow path back to the house, we have to walk two by two. I motion for Bethesda to go with David to keep an eye on him, and I fall back to have a word with Nat.

"It's not his fault," I tell Nat. "It's not David who was trying to hurt Bethesda—or me—it's this place."

"Yeah, I get it, Ellis. He was possessed. So, maybe I was possessed, too."

"The only one you're possessed by right now is your grandfather. All the ugly things he ever said to you are all right in here"—I tap my finger on Nat's forehead—

"and you're going to keep spewing out the bad stuff until you turn around and face it."

"Oh, please," Nat says, dodging away from my finger, "spare me the psychobabble. I thought you were a psychic, not a psychiatrist."

I stop in my tracks, and Nat goes on a few more feet, his head ducked and his shoulders hunched. When he sees that I'm not following him, he stops and turns back toward me. "Oh, for Christ's sake, don't be so sensitive. I'm *sorry*. It's just that right now I think we probably need your skills as a psychic more than as a psychoanalyst. Okay?"

It's the closest I'm likely to get to an apology, so I continue walking. He's right, I realize: whatever is happening here at Bosco requires the skills of a medium and, unfortunately, I'm the closest thing we have to one.

When we emerge onto the terrace, the snow is a deep wave that sweeps up over the hill and crests the marble balustrade. Although the snow has stopped falling, a steady wind blows a cloud of fine icy particles across the frozen expanse. A tsunami of snow that might at any moment break over the house and carry it away.

Or has it already carried everyone away?

Turning to the house, I see a wall of darkened windows that have been sealed by a milky coat of ice. Like blind eyes, I think, shivering as a gust of icy wind hits my back with so much force it almost knocks me off my feet. It's like standing in the ocean and getting hit by an unexpected wave. I can feel the pent-up pressure of Bosco's dead springs gathering to unleash their rage on the house.

David and Bethesda come back from the east side of the house to report that the door on that side, the one under the porte cochere, is locked.

"That's funny," Nat says. "In all the years I've been coming to Bosco the porte cochere door has never been locked."

"Well, the porte co-SHARE door is locked now," David says, drawling out the French word. "So much for tradition."

Nat takes a step toward David, but Bethesda gets in between them. "Let's check the library doors," she suggests. "It's got the best working fireplace. I bet Diana and Daria would take Zalman there if there wasn't any heat."

"The library doors would be the first ones they'd lock in a storm," Nat says as we trudge through the deep snow to the double French doors.

A drift has risen halfway up the doors. Even if they aren't locked, we won't be able to open them without digging them out. As I stare at them, though, I see a flicker of light coming from beneath the waxy layer of ice that covers the glass. "Look," I tell the others, "I think someone is in there. If you start clearing some of this snow away, I'll try to get their attention inside."

I press my face to the frosted glass to look in, but all I can see are amorphous globes of light hovering in the room like huge fireflies. I breathe on the window until a crack appears in the ice and I'm able to get my fingernails underneath to pry it away. I've cleared a small circle when one of the lights suddenly flares right in my eyes, blinding me. I take a step back and fall into the pile of snow that Nat and David have pushed away from the door.

"Who's there?" a tremulous voice calls as the door opens a crack.

"Diana?" Nat calls. "It's Nat Loomis." David and Bethesda add their names, but the door still doesn't open. I struggle to get up, but the wind pushes me down, as if I'm being dragged under by a riptide. My ears are filled with a sound like rushing water and I'm blinded by a gust of snow. Then I can feel someone pulling me up and through the narrowly opened doors. I'm still blinded by the powdery ice in my eyes and my tangled hair and the flaring candlelight in the dark room. Then my vision clears and I see it's Nat who's helped me through the door. He pushes away my hair, which is hanging in icy strands as if he'd fished me out of a frozen sea.

"Shut those doors," Diana yells at us.

I'm surprised at the note of hysteria in Diana's voice, but then I look back at the glass doors to the terrace and understand. Even now snow is lapping across the lintel, drawing wave patterns in a drift that reaches to the wainscoting, like surf marks of an encroaching tide. David and Bethesda have to struggle against the wind and drifted snow to close them.

"Maybe we should make for higher ground," I say, only half joking.

"We can't leave Zalman," Diana says, waving toward the alcove. We all follow her into the alcove, where Zalman is seated in his wheelchair beside the library table. At the center of the table is a large branching candelabra—a hideous kitschy thing made out of the antlers of a moose. Daria's sitting to Zalman's right, scribbling away on a steno pad as Zalman dictates. It takes me a moment to realize, though, that Zalman's words are barely audible and that his eyes look as blind and unfocused as Bosco's frozen windows.

"I've gotten a few more words filled in," Daria says, holding up the spiral-bound notebook. "You were right, Aunt Diana, if you break it into lines of ten syllables each, there are fourteen lines that he's repeating over and over again."

"Fourteen lines?" Nat asks.

"You mean he's reciting a sonnet?" Bethesda asks, sitting down next to Daria and looking over her shoulder at the lines.

"Yes," Diana says, walking over to the sideboard. "He lost consciousness earlier this evening and then when he came to, he started reciting. He's been repeating the same sonnet for three hours now, but so softly we couldn't tell at first that's what it was. I asked Daria to write it down. I told you that steno class would come in handy." Diana turns from the sideboard with a glass of scotch in her hand and David takes it from her without asking and sits down next to Bethesda. Glaring at him, Diana pours herself another glass and sits down next to David. I notice as she passes me that she reeks of the peaty scotch.

"Well, I have gotten pretty good, what with all the phone messages I've been taking. Here, do you want to hear it?"

"Absolutely," Nat says, sitting down next to Diana. There's only one chair left, the one between Zalman and Nat, which I take.

"Okay, but let me wait until he comes around to the beginning again. It would seem kind of rude to read out of step with him."

No one questions Daria's sense of decorum. Instead, we all do what she does, follow Zalman's lips until he pauses, and then with a sharp intake of breath that sounds painfully hoarse (*three hours repeating the same sonnet!*), Daria's voice chimes in with Zalman's barely audible one.

> *Elusive, evanescent as twilight,*
> *this velvet snow obscures the murky bog.*
> *A spirit, barely in your mortal sight,*
> *moves shadowy and sudden through a fog*
> *that slithers across a pond's slick mossy skin*
> *and merges with the weave of silent snow.*
> *The spirit is an infant lost at birth,*
> *forever roaming here; the blackbirds know*
> *her loss, mark it in red, just as the earth*
> *is mourning her with clouds, with snow, with rain.*
> *Her tiny silhouette chills to your bone,*

especially the shadow of her eyes,
so innocent and lost, so all alone,
for no one ever hears her ghostly cries."

When they finish, we can all hear the moan of the wind outside, and then the hiss of Zalman drawing another painful breath as he begins again. I reach out and touch Zalman's hand. "It's all right," I say, "we found her." Then I take out of my pocket the broken china and spill the blue-and-white shards onto the table along with the crumpled white orchid. Instantly the room is filled with the scent of vanilla.

Bethesda reaches across the table and touches the china pieces. "Where did you find these?" she asks.

"What do you mean that you 'found her'?" Diana asks at the same time. "Who did you find?"

"Alice," Nat answers. "The first Alice, the one who was born and died on April ninth, 1883. Bethesda was right—that death certificate was never filed, but there was a birth certificate filed for an Alice Latham on April fifteenth—"

"So it was just a mistake—" Diana Tate begins.

"That a child was born on April ninth, died, and was suddenly reborn on the fifteenth?" Nat asks. "I don't think so."

"They must have replaced the dead baby with another," Bethesda says. "But where . . . ?"

"With Corinth's child," I answer. "Nat remembered a grave site in the bog behind his family's camp, and we went to look there. We found the name *Alice* written on a piece of china that had been wedged into the tree, and then we found these pieces beneath the tree—"

"But that can't be right," Bethesda says, "Aurora bought these teacups for the children in 1892, so that name couldn't have been put on the tree when that baby died in 1883."

"No, I think it was put over another name," I say, "when Alice Latham came to the cabin in 1893 with Corinth Blackwell and Tom Quinn."

"Well, at least that proves that they *did* kidnap Alice Latham," Diana Tate says, taking a sip from her drink and putting the glass down so hard on the table that some scotch sloshes over the side. I turn to her, surprised at the emotion in her voice.

"Alice was her own child," I say. "If the babies were switched without Corinth knowing, she wouldn't have known that until she came to Bosco in 1893. By then all the other Latham children had died. Corinth would have been afraid for Alice's life. I think that's what *they* want us to know—what happened to them. What happened to Alice."

"That's why all the teacups have been breaking," Daria says, taking out of her pocket a handful of broken china pieces and spilling them across the table so that they join the shards that I brought back from the bog. "This was Cynthia's cup," she says, picking out a *C*, *Y*, *N*, and *A* on the pieces of white china. "I was giving Zalman his tea around four o'clock today, and suddenly the cup just shuddered itself off the table."

Nat and I exchange a look. Four o'clock was around

the time the tamarack tree fell in the bog and I found the pieces of Alice's cup buried beneath it.

"That's when Zalman started babbling," Daria says. "I went to find Aunt Diana and I heard a noise from one of the rooms upstairs, so I went up there and found Miss Graham's door open."

"My room?" Bethesda asks, turning an outraged glance at Daria. "I'm quite sure I left my door closed and locked."

"Well, it was open and the noise had come from there," Daria says, blinking back tears. The stress of having been here alone all day with a drunken aunt and a semicomatose poet has obviously gotten to her.

"And what did you find?" I ask more gently.

"There were pins all over the floor and pieces of broken china," she says. "I picked them up." She takes a few pieces of broken china from a different pocket and places them on the table. I spy a *T* and an *A*.

"Tam's cup," I say.

"And where were you when your niece was invading my room?" Bethesda asks Diana.

"I was having a cup of tea in the kitchen," she says, "when the cup I was drinking from exploded in my hand. It cut my finger. See?" Diana holds up her bandaged hand.

"Do you have the pieces of that cup?" I ask.

Diana looks at me as if I'm crazy. "Why in the world would I save—" But before she can finish, I've noticed that a sliver of china, shaped something like an arrowhead, is clinging to Diana's cardigan. I reach across Nat and pluck it from her sweater. Turning it over, I see the letter *J* written in loopy blue script. When I put it down on the table, the other shards begin to tremble.

"Shit," Nat says. "Who's doing that?"

"Shh," Bethesda hisses. "Be quiet!"

The shards begin to move until they've formed a circle around the base of the candelabra and then stop. The letters have arranged themselves to spell a word. *Jacynta.*

"It's all the children," Bethesda says, her voice hushed with awe, "turned into one spirit."

"Great," Nat says, his eyes wide. "So what are we supposed to do now?"

"I think we're supposed to have a séance," Daria says. "I think that's what the children want."

Everyone looks to me and I shake my head. "I can't—" I begin, but then I hear Zalman draw another painful breath and I realize that I have to do something to break the spell he's under.

Nat turns to me. "It's like you were saying to me on the way up the hill. You're going to keep spewing out the bad stuff until you turn around and face it. You have to do this as much for yourself as for Zalman."

I could remind Nat that he called what I said on the hill psychobabble, but I don't. "I'm not even sure what to do first."

"Well, duh," Daria says, rolling her eyes. "We start by joining hands."

Nat reaches out his hand to take mine, and I feel as

if he's reaching across a void. But when I put my hand in his hand, it's warm and I feel the distance between us contract.

When I take Zalman's hand, though, it's alarmingly cold. "Poor Zalman," I say. "It doesn't seem fair that he's had to bear the brunt of this."

"He's the *genius loci*," Daria says, causing everyone at the table to stare at her. "I looked it up," she says defensively. "It means the pervasive spirit of the place. So of course he feels everything that's happened here more than the rest of us."

"She's right," David says, taking Bethesda's hand. "Remember what he said that night in the library about how he felt as though there was a voice speaking through him?" He reaches out to take Diana Tate's hand, but the director stands up abruptly, pushing back her chair. "I don't think I should be part of this," she says. "I'm not a guest here."

"It's your grandmother's bones lying in the crypt below the garden," David says, still holding out his hand to her. "You're as much, or more, a part of this than any of us."

"That's right, Aunt Diana," Daria says. "Haven't you ever wondered why our whole family is so screwed up? It's like there's a family curse. Maybe this will set things straight."

Diana lets out an exasperated sigh, but sits back down and takes David's and Bethesda's hands. "There's no family curse," she mutters under her breath. "Your mother's an alcoholic and I've always been the one to keep things together. To clean up after her messes."

I see that Daria's blinking back tears again. "That's enough," I say, surprised at how forceful I sound. "Everyone be quiet. We have to focus."

A gratifying hush follows, but my confidence quickly seeps away. What the hell am I supposed to do now? I wish more than anything that Mira were here. I close my eyes, trying to remember the séance Mira held the evening of the day we'd gone to the bog looking for the white orchid. Mira had said that I was ready, that we had to confront the spirit of the child I'd seen in the bog, but instead the spirit confronted me. Will I see it again? I take a deep breath to calm my steadily rising panic, constricting my throat muscles to slow the breath the way Mira taught me. When I inhale I smell the vanilla scent of the orchid and think maybe that's what was missing the first time. If we'd found the orchid in the bog, maybe things would have been different.

"We've made a circle to welcome you," I say, not sure where the words have come from. "No one need be left out. We're ready to listen to your story."

A cold current moves through the air, carrying with it particles of ice, the peaty smell of Diana's scotch, and the fragrance of vanilla. I open my eyes and see that the air is sparkling with ice crystals borne upward in a spiral eddy, like moths circling the candles. Then the air suddenly goes dead and the crystals float down over our heads, catching on hair and eyelashes, settling over our hands, and dimming the candlelight.

"It's so cold," someone says.

I look around to see where the voice—a girl's voice, but not one that matches those of the women at the table—came from. In the diminished light of the candles I think that I see Bethesda's lips moving, but I'm not sure.

"It's so cold in the well," another voice says. It seems to be coming from David, but the voice is much too young to be his.

"And too quiet."

This time I know for sure that it's Nat who's spoken, but when I turn to him, I see that a film has settled over his eyes, like a glaze of ice, and the voice is not his. It's a boy's voice, older than the first one and more clipped and confident, but still nothing like Nat's.

"James," I say, "is that you?"

"Who wants to know?" comes the voice, sarcastic and brusque but with a little waver at the end that gives away the falseness of his bravado. I can almost see him—a pixie face, brown from running outdoors, long, gawky legs and arms. He was thirteen when he died.

"El—" I start to give the name I've gone by since I published my first story, but then I change my mind and give the name I was born with. "Elmira," I say.

There's a flurry of voices around the table, hurried whispers that I can't quite make out or identify the source of. I think I see Nat's lips moving, and Bethesda's and David's. Diana's lips are pursed, but the only sound coming from her is a long, low hiss.

"James," I say, turning to Nat. "You can speak for the others. Tell us what happened."

"I *would*," he says, his boy's voice petulant, "but *she* won't let us." He cuts his eyes—no longer Nat's eyes—over toward Diana Tate. "*She* makes us be quiet. When we were sick," he says, lowering his voice to a conspiratorial whisper, "she only took care of *Alice*." He nearly spits the name.

" 'Drink the tea your mother's made for you', she said," the girl's voice says, and then the younger boy's, echoing, " 'Drink your tea. Drink your tea.' " More voices join in, merging and overlapping, a dozen voices, more voices than there are mouths to speak at the table, building to a crescendo that shakes the table, rattling the broken china. Like dry bones rattling. What am I supposed to do now that I've summoned these unruly spirits? Everyone else at the table has slipped beneath the same glassy film—except, I suddenly notice, Daria.

"One at a time," Daria says, with the authority of a veteran camp counselor. "We can only understand you if you speak one at a time. And you," Daria says, turning to her aunt, "let them speak. You're not in charge here anymore."

Diana hisses and spits out a few words in a language I can't identify, but then she's quiet. The only words spoken in the room are Zalman's half-audible sonnet lines, fragments of which I catch in between the sounds of the wind flinging snow at the windows. ". . . the eloquence of water . . . while strolling past a sigh . . . a soothing blood for ancient bones . . ."

I realize that Zalman is now reciting all the sonnets he's written here at Bosco. This disconcerts me more than the broken teacups and disembodied voices and Diana speaking in tongues—that Zalman's beautifully ordered poems have gotten scrambled together in a chaotic maelstrom. But then, in a lull of the wind, I'm able to catch two of the lines together, then three, then four, and I realize that Zalman is somehow composing a new sonnet, made up of lines or parts of lines from all the sonnets he's written at Bosco, which he recites now in a hoarse whisper.

> *"And yet one hears, while strolling past, the sighs*
> *of red-winged blackbirds swifter than starlight;*
> *no one has ever heard such ghostly cries;*
> *among them from a soul that never dies,*
> *a flash of wing by day, black ghost by night;*
> *a spirit, barely in your mortal sight,*
> *the spirit of an infant lost at birth*
> *in tragedy as old as heat and light.*
> *Her loss is marked in red, just as the earth,*
> *so silently its pulse beats without sound,*
> *in honor of Egeria's sad day,*
> *will redden rivers with the blood of birth,*
> *its source forever hidden underground.*
> *Such mysteries the earth secretes away!"*

" 'Such mysteries the earth secretes away,' " I repeat. "Something in the well? But all we found were Wanda's bones. What else is there?"

"She's trapped there with us," Bethesda says in Cynthia's voice.

"Like a bird trapped in a net," Tam's voice comes from David, just slightly out of sync with the movement of his lips.

"We can't be free until she is," James concludes, turning Nat's blank eyes toward me. Under the milky film I see a remnant of Nat looking out at me, and I realize that his freedom is also at stake.

"Who?" I ask.

The three faces, David, Nat, and Bethesda, instantly turn their ice-glazed eyes on me.

I feel a wave of cold pass over me as if a mantle of ice had settled over my shoulders. I feel it wrapping around me, tight as a winding sheet. I can see from Daria's frightened expression that something's happening to me. I'm changing: the film that had settled over the others is falling over me . . . and then the icy cloak falls over my eyes.

It's just like at my first séance. I can feel myself being pulled down, the ground beneath me giving way. The bog, hungry for another sacrifice, is swallowing me up whole. And as I rush downward what rises to greet me is the face of the baby, its lips pursed to suck, its blue eyes open.

I open my eyes to banish the image and see that I'm surrounded by green. I'm standing under the tamarack tree in the bog, only it's summer, the ground at my feet carpeted by the emerald green sphagnum moss, the air full of darting dragonflies, like jewels that have come to life. Brighter than the dragonflies, though, are the eyes of the man standing next to me. A man with dark hair and blue-green eyes that I know I've seen before. He's looking at me as if he were trying to hold me upright with the force of his gaze—a look so full of love that it has the opposite effect and makes me feel weak.

"I can see you in her, Tom," I hear myself say. Tom. The man in front of me—the man who loves me this much—is Tom Quinn. No, it's not me he loves, it's Corinth Blackwell.

"See?" he asks. "You can see her now?" His gaze travels over the surface of the pond as if looking for someone. I follow his gaze and see something move on the other side of the water, but whatever it is is hidden by a patch of fog. A bird is startled from its hiding place among the sedges, and I see Tom watch it fly across the water; I feel Corinth watch it, too, but I keep my eyes on the opposite bank and see, when the fog burns off in the morning sun, a dark-eyed girl crouched behind the sedges. Alice.

As I turn back to Tom I feel something pulling at my feet from beneath the quaking ground. Like quicksand. I hear the sound of wings over my head as the blackbird alights in the tamarack tree, but I can also hear the sibilant hiss that came from Diana at the séance, pulling me back to Bosco, back to the well beneath the garden. That's what the children meant. Corinth's spirit was pulled back into the well at Bosco before she could tell Tom . . .

I reach out as I fall and grasp Tom's hand. I can see, just over his shoulder, the tamarack tree, where Alice's name was wedged into the knothole, but instead of the blue and white china plaque, I see a name carved in the bark.

Elmira.

Just as in Nat's story, I've found my own name. And as if I were hearing my name called, I feel it pulling me back to the library at Bosco, just as Corinth is being pulled down into the well with Wanda and the children and, most frightening of all, that small, dead infant that was left here in the bog. I'm out of time . . .

"She's yours," I say as I sink to the ground, squeezing Tom's hand to keep myself inside Corinth's body for one last moment. I feel an answering squeeze that for one moment is both Tom's hand and Nat's back in the library at Bosco. "Alice is your child, Tom." I look across the water and I see Alice. She's listening, too. I'm telling all this to her as well. "Take her to my sister, Elmira," I say, not sure who's talking now, me or Corinth. Then I look up at Tom. "And stay with them," I tell him. "You're all she has now."

There's so much more to say, but I feel myself rushing out of Corinth's body, not down into the ground, but up. The last thing I hear before the darkness falls is the sound of wings beating the air around me.

When I open my eyes, I'm alone at the table. Everyone, even Zalman, is gone. For an instant I'm afraid that I'm still back in 1893, but then I hear their voices coming from the terrace. I get up, still unsteady on my feet, and walk over to the doorway, where Zalman's chair is blocking the way out. I put my hands on his shoulders and lean over to see if he's all right. He smiles back at me, the color returned to his cheeks and reason returned to his eyes—or at least I think so until he speaks.

"You set them free," he says. "Look."

I look out on the terrace where Nat, Bethesda, David, Daria, and Diana are all standing at the balustrade. Zalman angles his chair so I can get by him, and I walk across the terrace. The snow has been blown away, revealing deep cracks in the marble that I don't remember being there before. When I join the group at the balustrade, Nat turns toward me and smiles—a smile so wide and open I'm startled. His eyes, I notice, are the same blue-green as Tom Quinn's.

"David's afraid it's going to crack the pipes, but I don't care if it brings the whole place down. I've never seen anything like it."

I join him at the balustrade and look down on the garden. From beneath the snow a thousand jets of water shoot up into the night sky, the droplets turning to ice before they fall back to earth, glittering in the moonlight. All the fountains of Bosco have come to life at once.

"But how?"

David shakes his head. "It's completely impossible," he says, "and it can't last. The pipes will burst—"

As he speaks I hear something explode like a

firecracker and then another and another. All up and down the hill we hear the sound of old copper pipes bursting under the snow. And then the hill begins to crumble. At first I think it's an illusion—another one of Bosco's water tricks—but then I realize I dreamed this once a long time ago. The gardens are caving in, sinking before our eyes, and still the water leaps into the sky. I hear again the sound I'd heard in the bog just before I lost consciousness. The beating of wings. A thousand birds rising to the sky as one. I look up, and for just a moment I see them—a flock of red-winged blackbirds silhouetted against the moon—and then they turn into crystal drops that evaporate in the night air.

Chapter Thirty

Alice beats them back to the cabin because Mr. Quinn is slowed down carrying Miss—

Not Miss Blackwell. She said that she was her mother. That Alice didn't belong to the Lathams. Well, she's never felt that she belonged to them. But then who was the baby buried in the bog? Elmira? The name on the tree that her brothers and sister had laughed at?

Alice makes the fire and boils water. She'll need tea. She looked so weak when she fell. Alice fixes the pot and rinses the cup out with hot water, but as she's washing it she stares at the name on the bottom. Alice. If she's Miss Blackwell's daughter, then she's not Alice Latham. And if she's not Alice Latham, then Alice Latham must be the baby at the bottom of the bog. Then what's her name? Who is she?

Her hands are shaking as she pours the boiling water from the heavy iron kettle into the teapot and then pours the tea into the blue and white cup. She picks up the cup and saucer just as the cabin door opens and she sees from the look on Mr. Quinn's face that it's too *late—that the tea won't help at all—and so she lets the cup and saucer drop from her hands. Lets them shatter on the hard wood floor. Why not? She's not Alice anymore. She doesn't need Alice's cup.*

But when she looks down, she sees that the only part of the broken cup that has remained is the bottom circle with her name on it.

I pause, my hands hovering over my laptop keys like those dragonflies hovered over the bog in my vision. I look down and see an actual dragonfly land on the pond just below the dock where I'm sitting. I watch it flit across the sparkling green water like a sentient emerald. When Nat and I came here this past winter, I couldn't have imagined that the black water could turn this color green. Or that the bog could be transformed from a place of darkness and shadow into this gorgeous floating world. Of course, I hadn't imagined that I'd come back here with Nat. That it was Nat whom I wanted—and who wanted me—and not David. Still, when Nat asked me if I wanted to spend the summer here finishing my novel, I wasn't sure if I should say yes. I knew he still wasn't writing and I was afraid that seeing me work all day might make him . . . well, jealous. The old Nat would have been jealous. But the new Nat, the one who's emerged since the séance, merely smiled at my worries and asked me, "Where else are you going to finish this story? It's where it ends, right?"

But it's the ending that's been giving me the most trouble. I can't seem to get past the moment when Corinth dies. The irony that it's the one moment of the past that I've actually experienced that's not lost on me.

I sigh and lower my eyes back to my screen and, because it's gone black, tap the mouse pad like a lab technician palpating flesh to raise a vein, and then stare at the words that rise up out of the black screen. Yes, Alice breaks the teacup and then asks Tom to wedge the part with her name on it into the tamarack tree. It's her way of leaving the name behind and leaving something for the lost baby, whom she thinks of as a sort of sister. She gives the baby in the bog her name and takes the name Elmira—or a variant of it that resembles her original name. Which would explain why in 1893, a few months after Alice Latham disappeared from Bosco, a ten-year-old girl named Ellis Brooks, with her seventeen-year-old sister, Elmira, moved to Lily Dale, New York.

"My mother," Mira told me over tea in Mrs. London's Teashop in Saratoga last week when she came to visit, "always said that Elmira was a family name. She was adamant that I take it, and when I had you, she made such a fuss about giving it to you that I figured I'd better do it. She was right about most things. But I always wondered about *Elmira* and *Ellis*. Of course it wasn't uncommon for girls to have different versions of their mothers' names, so maybe your great-grandmother was really 'Elmira.' I can't find a birth certificate for her, so we'll probably never know."

The reason there wasn't a birth certificate, I'm fairly sure now, is that ten-year-old Ellis Brooks, my great-grandmother, was Alice Latham. She was the right age when the sisters moved to Lily Dale and she appeared out of nowhere. Mira brought with her to the tea shop a copy of the 1890 census for Erie County listing only one daughter, age fourteen, living with the Brooks family on Forest Avenue in Buffalo. Where else would a ten-year-old daughter come from just three years later?

"Of course she was Corinth's daughter," Mira said, taking a delicate sip of the house blend, a lavender-scented Earl Grey that I could have sworn my mother picked to match her outfit: a lavender linen shift with a deeper lilac sweater tied across her shoulders and amethyst crystal drops hanging from her ears. The color suited her and what was more, while the outfit was not radically different from her usual garb, it looked somehow better cut and more expensive. When Mira retied the sweater, I noticed an Eileen Fisher label on the neckline. "My grandmother always said that her mother was a famous medium," Mira continued, "and that they'd had to leave Buffalo because the neighbors complained about 'strange noises' coming from the house at night. Well, I had a look through the archives of the Buffalo newspaper and found that there was, indeed, an article about neighbors complaining about rapping noises coming from the Brooks house on Forest Avenue. The reporter compared the incident to the Fox sisters back in the 1840s, but what's interesting is that the rapping at the Brookses began in the fall of 1893."

"When Alice would have arrived."

"Yes, the article mentions two young sisters and says that they had decided to seek out a 'more sympathetic' community in Lily Dale, where an aunt and uncle of theirs lived—"

"An aunt and uncle? You never mentioned that your grandmother was brought up by an aunt and uncle."

"Didn't I?" Mira asked, tilting her head to one side. "Of course, they were both very old when I was born and died soon after."

"They were still alive when you were born? Do you remember them? Are there any pictures?"

Mira looked up to the ceiling as if trying to discern a likeness to her ancestors in its stamped-tin pattern of vine and flower. "I do remember she had very beautiful hands," she said, a vague, dreamy expression stealing over her face, "but she always wore gloves when she went out except . . . Oh, my, you know, I haven't thought of this in years . . ."

"What?" I said, leaning forward so impatiently that I knocked my teacup out of its saucer and onto the floor, where the delicate china shattered. The teenaged girl behind the counter hurried over with a whisk and dustpan, and I knelt on the floor to help her collect the broken pieces. When I took my seat again, I saw that Mira's attention had drifted toward the front of the shop.

"There's an adorable man looking this way and waving with a handkerchief," she said. "Do you know him?"

An adorable man? When in the world had my mother ever referred to a man as *adorable?* I looked behind me and saw Zalman Bronsky, in a very handsome white linen suit, leaning on the silver-tipped cane he'd used since his cast came off, saluting us with his handkerchief as if he were signaling from the deck of a yacht. He looked, indeed, as if he could have just sailed in a regatta at Newport. He looked, I had to agree, adorable.

"That's Zalman Bronsky, the poet; he's one of the guests at Bosco. You know, the one who broke his leg last winter? Diana Tate extended his stay while his leg is still healing."

"Oh, the man who writes such lovely poems about Madame Blavatsky. Don't you think we should ask him over? There are no other free tables and he oughtn't to stand too long on his injured leg."

Put that way, I could hardly object. Nor could I help but offer to get Zalman his tea and pastry. When I came back to the table, I found that my mother and Zalman had discovered that in addition to Madame Blavatsky they shared a passion for Pythagoras and were happily discussing the Greek philosopher's vegetarianism and ability to talk to animals. I stayed for a while, but when Zalman offered to show Mira the springs in Congress Park, I realized that I'd become a bit of a third wheel. I pleaded work as an excuse for heading back to the cabin. When I kissed my mother good-bye, I noticed that Mira had also changed her perfume. Instead of patchouli she was wearing a light floral scent that smelled like roses and vanilla. I left Zalman and Mira on Broadway and drove back to the cabin in Nat's beat-up old Saab. Only later did I realize that I never found out what Mira remembered about her great-great-aunt's hands.

Now, on the dock, I flex my own hands over the laptop. When I brought up the anecdote on the phone with my mother later, Mira said that her memory must have been playing tricks on her. The image of the glove-wearing great-great-aunt had slipped away. If she remembered anything else, though, she'd tell me when she came to town in August, when, she told me with an uncharacteristically girlish lilt in her voice, Zalman and she were going to the races. I haven't heard from my mother since and I'm not counting on any more revelations. Clearly my mother is busy thinking about other things and I would be the last one to begrudge her—or Zalman—some happiness. The glove-wearing great-great-aunt was probably nothing more than what Mira called it: a trick of memory.

When I look down I see that my laptop's screen has gone black again, but instead of resuscitating it, I snap the lid shut and slide it into my backpack. I look back toward the house and see that Nat's on the front porch, where he's set up his typewriter on an old card table. As usual he's got his feet up on the card table and he's staring out into the distance. Clearly he's not writing, but still I don't want to disturb him in case inspiration is about to alight. I decide to take a walk into the bog instead. Maybe if I go back to the spot by the tamarack tree and sit there long enough, I'll finally be able to write the scene of Corinth's death and its aftermath.

I take the path into the bog, stopping to pick some bog laurel and peppermint, which I use when I make iced tea. Nat swears it has the same smoky undertone of a good Laphroaig, which is as close as he gets to the scotch these days. Although Diana Tate offered him a bottle to celebrate selling the cabin to him when he left Bosco, Nat turned it down. "I'm sure David will make good use of it," he said with only a hint of his old sarcasm in his voice.

Even though the destruction of the garden had discouraged the Garden Conservancy from funding the restoration ("They don't like it when a garden is in *worse* shape after the conservator has a go at it," David had told me on my last visit to Bosco), David and Bethesda decided to stay at Bosco to write a history of the gardens together. I've gone back a few times to visit them and Zalman and to see if the ruined garden would inspire me to write this last scene, but the last time I was there I felt sure that the end of the story wasn't there. I'm beginning to wonder, though, if it's here.

I find the toppled tamarack tree, which has already turned a reddish brown in the water since it fell last winter. If I lean over the water, I can just catch a glimpse of the china plaque with Alice's name on it. Soon, though, it will be covered with moss and hidden from sight, swallowed by the bog just as baby Alice was.

I sit down on a bed of sphagnum moss by the water's edge. I'm not afraid of seeing her anymore. Since the séance I've felt she's at peace. But what about Corinth? I unleashed her spirit from Wanda's spell and let her tell Tom that Alice—or Elmira—was their child. Was it enough? Had it satisfied her spirit? I close my eyes and listen to the birdsong in the trees and the croaking of mink frogs and the whir of insects in the bog. I can even hear water dripping into pitcher plants and soaking into the emerald carpet of moss beneath me and draining into the mat that floats over the bog's deep underground pool. I feel as if I'm floating, but I can't feel Corinth here. And yet, wouldn't they have buried her here—with the baby?

I open my eyes and see something white beside my foot. Even before I pick it up I know by its scent that it's a ghost orchid, not growing, but loose, as if someone picked it and left it here. I pick it up to take back to Nat, but when I arrive at the cabin, I hear a tapping that I think, at first, is a woodpecker, but then realize is the sound of Nat's typewriter. So I slip inside and put the orchid into a glass bowl of water.

Only much later, when the typing has long stopped, do I go out to the porch with two glasses of iced tea. I hand one to Nat, who's sitting in one of the old Adirondack chairs. In addition to the tea I've brought out the bowl with the orchid in it, which I place on the porch railing, where it catches the late afternoon light. Then I sit in the other Adirondack chair and take a sip of the iced tea—which does, indeed, have the smoky taste of good scotch. I'm dying to ask Nat what he was writing today, but I'm afraid to focus too bright a light on whatever wisp of inspiration he's gotten ahold of. So instead I ask him if he's remembered anything new today. Like Mira, Nat's memory has been playing tricks on him this summer, inventing incidents that seem entirely new to Nat. And although one might expect such *recovered memories* to be of traumatic events, they're usually of something kind of nice. A memory of his grandfather taking him fishing on the reservoir and even taking him to the overlook to see the sign about Ne'Moss-i-Ne.

"Well, there is something," he says. "Here, let me show you something."

Nat leans forward in his chair and holds out his hands, turning them first palms up, then palms down. Then he reaches toward me and pulls a flower out from behind my ear. Even before I see it I can smell it: sweet, spicy vanilla. Nat displays the white orchid with a flourish and hands it to me.

"How did you do that?" I ask, dipping my head to inhale the orchid's creamy scent.

"Well, I suddenly *remember* that my grandfather taught me how. On my fifth birthday—an event I could have sworn was *not* attended by him at all since it was in Darien, Connecticut, and he *hated* Darien. But now I've got this picture"—Nat holds up his thumbs and forefingers to make a frame—"of him in the backyard pulling coins out of my ear to the amusement of all my friends. And he tells me that on *his* fifth birthday the carnival came to town and a tall, dark-haired magician taught him that trick."

I open my mouth to say something but then think better of it.

Nat takes a sip of his iced tea and lets his eyes drift over the pond. The late afternoon sun has turned the water copper and gold. In the distance I hear the long eerie cry of a loon and then, a moment later, the answering call of its mate.

"It's crazy," Nat says, "but I swear I never knew how to do that magic trick before." I look over to the glass where the orchid I found today still floats. What I'd like to ask is where he found the orchid in my hands. Instead I ask him if he'd like to take a drive.

"Sure," he says. "Where to?"

"The overlook," I say.

On the way to the overlook we stop in the little post office in town and pick up our mail. Most of it is for Nat—copies of *Bomb* and the *New Yorker,* fan mail forwarded from his publisher, and a letter from his agent—all of which he tosses in the backseat of the car. The only thing for me is a small parcel from my mother, which I open as Nat drives. I'm distracted from its contents by Nat suddenly saying, as if continuing our conversation of half an hour ago on the porch, "You think the past has changed because of what happened during the séance, don't you? And you know who the magician was."

I turn to him, but he's looking straight ahead at the road. Even on a clear day the reservoir road can have unexpected patches of fog. "Yes," I say, "I think it was Tom Quinn and that he became a different person because of what Corinth told him before she died. He didn't go out west, he stayed with Alice in Lily Dale, and maybe he came back to see his and Violet's son."

"*His* and Violet's son? You think my grandfather was Tom Quinn's son?"

"Well," I say, "that's how I wrote it." I finished the scene a few days ago, describing Violet Ramsdale's last days in Dr. Murdoch's household, when she knew that the baby she'd borne was not the only thing growing in her womb all those months. I had been surprised at how painful it had been to write it because Mrs. Ramsdale wasn't a particularly sympathetic character, but who wouldn't pity a woman looking at her child's face and knowing she wouldn't live to see its first birthday? So I'd given Violet one last redemptive act: writing the pamphlet that exonerated Corinth Blackwell and then sending it to the Spiritualists' Society in Lily Dale in the hope that if Corinth Blackwell and Tom Quinn had survived it would find its way into their, or their descendants', hands someday.

"It would explain why Murdoch was so awful to the child," I say, "if he knew it wasn't his. And it might explain why your grandfather was such a miserable man."

"You realize that means we're related," Nat says, sliding his eyes toward me.

"Distantly. We're like half cousins twice removed or something. Would that bother you?"

"Not at all. I'm just thinking about our kids . . ."

"*Kids?*" I repeat, but we've reached the overlook and Nat is already out of the car and heading toward the cliff. The path that was knee-high in snow last winter is now carpeted in gold pine needles. The view was obscured by fog then, but now I can see the Great Sacandaga Lake, swollen wider and deeper than the original river, covering the old valley. The sun is sinking behind a line of mountains to the west, painting a wavy gold path that springs from a cleft in the mountains and snakes across the lake like the ghost of the old river. For an instant I see the valley as it was before it was flooded and hear the river rushing over the rocks below me. I reach into my pocket and pull out the white kid glove that was in my mother's package. *I found this in one of your great-grandmother's old trunks,* Mira had written. *Take a look at the initials sewn on the hem.*

I brush my fingers along the delicate stitching. *CB.* Of course it could be anyone, but when I look down over the cliff I see, instead of the dark water of the reservoir, a beach of smooth white stones. A girl is kneeling on the beach making a pyramid out of the stones; a tall man is standing with his back to the cliff. A woman kneels by the girl as together they place a round white stone on top of the pile. The woman's hair falls forward and merges with the girl's hair, both flashing red in the last rays of the setting sun. I blink against the glare, and when I open my eyes the white rocks have disappeared under the dark water and the only flash of red comes from a red-winged blackbird skimming the smooth surface, flying west.

ALSO AVAILABLE IN ARROW

The Lake of Dead Languages
Carol Goodman

Jane Hudson never thought she would return to Heart Lake. Her years there as a scholarship girl ended in a double tragedy: the drowning of her two roommates. Now she is back, struggling to adjust to her new life teaching Latin and as a single mother. But the events that haunted her memories for so many years begin to recur in front of her eyes. It seems she alone can see what is happening, and only she will be able to prevent a second catastrophe.

Surrounded by the lake that gives the school its name, steeped in history and overflowing with the emotions of teenage girls, Heart Lake guards its past . . . but cannot keep it hidden.

arrow books

The Seduction of Water

Carol Goodman

Many years ago, Iris Greenfeder's mother disappeared. They were living at Hotel Equinox where Iris's father was the manager, and where Iris's mother wrote delicate, powerful fantasies. Then she took a train and never returned, dying in a hotel fire in Brooklyn where she was registered as another man's wife.

Returning to Hotel Equinox, now an established English professor, Iris needs to find the truth about her mother; some keys are held in those fantastical writings and others in the memories of those who knew her. Kay Greenfeder, it seems, was a woman without a past.

But as Iris begins to untangle the secrets of years before, she realises that the past was very different to what she had believed, and much more dangerous . . .

arrow books

ALSO AVAILABLE IN ARROW

The Drowning Tree

Carol Goodman

At Penrose College, Christine, Juno and Neil were inseparable.
But life tore them apart: Juno dropped out, pregnant with Neil's
child, Neil was admitted to a mental hospital having tried to
drown his young wife and daughter, and Christine succumbed
to drink and depression.

Now, years later, Christine returns to her alma mater with shocking revelations which bring with them shadows of madness,
deception and betrayal. Then she disappears, and Juno realises
that Christine discovered a secret worth killing for. A secret
so damning it ripples through the past into the present . . .

arrow books